THE MANDARIN
OF MAYFAIR

THE MANDARIN
OF MAYFAIR

Patricia Veryan

ST. MARTIN'S PRESS ✹ NEW YORK

Design by Judith A. Stagnitto

Library of Congress Cataloging-in-Publication Data

Veryan, Patricia
     The mandarin of Mayfair / Patricia Veryan.
         p. cm.
     ISBN 0-312-13562-9
     I. Title.
     PS3572.E766M28 1995
     813' .54--dc20   95-34745
                                                                  CIP

First Edition: November 1995
10 9 8 7 6 5 4 3 2 1

The   Adversaries

THE LEAGUE OF JEWELLED MEN

A secret society of aristocrats, deeply resentful of the fact that Britain's throne was awarded to a German prince, the Elector of Hanover, whose son, King George II, now rules. Despising the "Hanoverian Succession," the League of Jewelled Men plans to overthrow the monarchy and institute a republic, with themselves as rulers. Because of the hideous penalty for high treason their identities are concealed even from each other, and they are known only by the jewels in the antique figurines carried by the members as identification. The ruling council consists of:

The "Squire," who is the leader of the society. A tall man of vaunting ambition, he is utterly ruthless. His symbol is of amethyst set with four large diamonds.

"Emerald," his lieutenant. A powerfully built individual, whose miniature is of pale green jade set with three emeralds.

"Sapphire," big, bumptious, and a grumbler. His figurine is of lapis-lazuli inset with six sapphires.

"Opal." Very large, aggressive, and opinionated. His token is of quartz set with two fire opals.

"Topaz." Short, with a husky voice and a slight build, identified by a figurine of golden crystal set with three topazes.

"Ruby." Tall and slim. Less violent than the others and more inclined to caution. His icon is pink jade set with five rubies.

A group of young men, each of whom has been victimized by the League, and who have banded together in opposition. They are led by:

Captain Gideon Rossiter, invalided out of the army in 1747 after having been critically wounded during the War of the Austrian Succession. His father, Sir Mark Rossiter, was the head of a great financial and shipbuilding empire. Determined to acquire his great estates, which were entailed and could not legally be purchased, the League deliberately ruined Sir Mark so that his properties would be seized and sold for debt. After a successful battle to thwart the plot, Gideon and his friends formed their opposition group called "Rossiter's Preservers."

Lieutenant James Morris. Was in hospital with Gideon in the Low Countries. Returning home on the same ship, Morris' friendship with Gideon drew him into the struggle and he joined the fight, unaware that his father's cousin, the head of his house, is an influential member of the League.

August N. K. Falcon. A dashing and extremely wealthy young man about Town, despised because of his mixed blood, but feared because of a well-earned reputation as a dangerous duellist; fiery-tempered, proud, and very much a "loner." His sister's close friendship with Gideon Rossiter's bride originally drew him into the struggle against the League.

Horatio "Tio" Viscount Glendenning. Heir to the powerful and wealthy Earl of Bowers-Malden, and a former Jacobite. In an attempt to acquire Glendenning Abbey, the League plotted to destroy his family by proving that he had fought for Bonnie Prince Charlie in the Jacobite Uprising. After a desperate struggle, Horatio was able to elude the League's trap.

Gordon Chandler. Son and heir to Sir Brian Chandler of Lac Brillant, near Dover. Barely escaped the League's scheme to accuse his family of wrecking ships off the coast near their great Dover estate, and of conspiring with his younger brother, Quentin, a Jacobite, who fled to France after the Jacobite defeat at the Battle of Culloden.

Jonathan Armitage. Was a captain for the East India Company. After he unknowingly witnessed a meeting that could incriminate three members of the League, he was targetted for destruction. His ship was wrecked, he was blamed, and for two years was believed to have drowned. Although he recovered his health he is still struggling to prove his innocence.

Sir Owen Furlong. He joined the Preservers when his close friend, Horatio Glendenning, was endangered. The beautiful "Italian" lady Furlong loves is actually the sister of a famous Frenchman who has, without the sanction of his government, negotiated a treasonable personal Agreement with the League. Furlong was able to seize a copy of the Agreement, but to protect her brother, his beloved Maria very reluctantly shot and wounded Furlong and took the Agreement.

Peregrine Cranford. A former artillery officer who lost a foot at the Battle of Prestonpans. He was used by the League as bait to trap a friend who carried a copy of the Agreement that could destroy them. With the help of Falcon and Morris he rescued his friend, but the vital agreement was stolen by the lady Sir Owen Furlong loved.

The Mandarin
of Mayfair

P R O L O G U E

ENGLAND, 1748

---

he November day had been chill and darkly depressing, but just before sunset pale fingers of sunlight slipped through the low-hanging clouds to brighten the land, if only briefly.

Many centuries had passed since any gleam of sunlight had penetrated to a certain large chamber situated in an area that had once housed the dungeons of a feudal lord. The air in here was dank and musty and much colder than that which towards midnight still rustled the trees above ground. The floor had been swept clean but there were few furnishings: an old and worm-eaten credenza that loomed dimly beside the ponderous iron-bound door, and an oak table surrounded by six chairs. The candle in the middle of the table did little to alleviate the pitchy darkness, its solitary flame creating a small oasis of light but failing to penetrate to the corners of the room and providing only a hint of massive stone walls mouldering with age.

The candle fluttered as men arrived and took their places. They were clad in dark cloaks, with hoods drawn close to throw a deeper shadow over masked faces. As though they were awed by their gloomy surroundings, or by thoughts of the unfortunates who had suffered here not so very long ago, there was no conversation while they gathered, the silence so intense that it seemed to beat against the eardrums.

A large individual stamped in, and muttered testily, "Zounds, but how glad I shall be when we can dispense with these trumpery dramatics! 'Tis like being buried alive to lurk about in this wretched hole! Hoods and masks, and secret meetings at dead of night and miles from anywhere! Children's games! Tchah!"

"But very necessary, Sapphire," drawled a man seated at the far end of the table. "I for one—" He checked, glancing around as the candle's flame danced.

The last man to enter had swung the heavy door shut and moved forward. "And this is ground we have gone over before, I believe," he said in a thin high-pitched voice sharpened by irritation. Coming to the position at the head of the table he rested a flat leather case on the vacant chair. The other men started to their feet, but with an imperative gesture that they remain seated, he himself continued to stand. "As a member of the League of Jewelled Men, you *are*, one trusts, aware of our aims, Sapphire?"

"If I am not, then you may curse me for a fool, Squire," grunted the large individual. "We are sworn to create a mightier England by putting an end to the monarchy for all time."

The man he had addressed as the "Squire" said with more than a touch of condescension, "And by what means do we accomplish this ambition?"

"What *means*? By damned clever means to my way of thinking!" He held up his fat hand and counted off the points on his fingers. "We enrich our war chest by—ah, appropriating cargoes of great ships, *before* they sail, sending them off with dummy cargoes and arranging that they be, "lost at sea." We disgrace and discredit powerful men in government so as to undermine public morale. We place our own people in responsible positions at the Horse Guards, the Navy Board, and in government, and at military posts throughout the nation. We unleash our army of mercenaries to create riots and stir up discontent. We purchase the chain of estates we need for our bases, and if we can't purchase 'em from the owners legally"—he snorted with amusement—"then, by God, we remove the owners and acquire 'em anyway!"

There were some chuckles at this, and the Squire said silkily,

"And when we have filled those properties with our troops and weapons—how then, Sapphire?"

"Why, we attack the vital installations close to our bases, of course! Seize power, and set up a republic ruled by the six of us, which—"

"Which constitutes High Treason!" The Squire leaned forward, his eyes glittering behind the mask and his voice scornful. "Have you the remotest notion of what happens to anyone so accused? Do you know the punishment for High Treason?"

Sapphire said resentfully, "Devil take it, I do! The prisoner is publicly hanged till near death, then cut down and revived, whereupon his limbs are hacked off, one at a time, after which he is disembowelled and beheaded, and his head stuck up on Temple Bar for—"

"Just so. A charming end. But before those horrors, the traitor is put to the question. You will recall the exploits of Guy Fawkes, a century ago?"

"Aye." Sapphire gave a bark of derisive laughter. "Tried to blow up the House of Lords. The Gunpowder Plot. And betrayed his friends when he was taken, like—"

The man he had addressed as the Squire interrupted in a near snarl, "He was a fine soldier, a gallant and courageous gentleman, and when arrested bore himself with honour and dignity, refusing to name his fellow conspirators. By the time he was forced to confess, he was so feeble from the torture that he could scarce stand or sign his name. They *broke* that valiant spirit, but he yet spoke bravely as he faced his frightful death! Whatever you may think of his politics, could you better him for courage?"

"Er—hah!" blustered Sapphire, "I'll wager I'd give 'em as long a run for their money! If not longer!"

The individual sitting next to him, who appeared small and slight by comparison with his bulk, said in a husky voice, "Would that I might be as sure. I doubt I'd make so gallant a showing."

The Squire nodded. "I know damned well I would not! Topaz is in the right of it. When the rack and the boot and white hot irons are brought to bear, the bravest of the brave can only withstand for a time. What *we* plan, would earn us just such unkind treatment. And was only *one* of us taken, 'twould be but a matter of time"—his lip curled—"a short time with some, before we were all betrayed! If we use desperate means to keep our identities secret, 'tis so that no one here, whomever he may *suspect,* can truthfully swear he has ever actually *seen* a fellow conspirator at this table! And I venture to guess that the identities of one or two of us would be a surprise to you, dear Sapphire." He straightened. "However, we are very close, my friends, to dispensing with the ah, 'trumpery dramatics.' To which end, let us get to our meeting."

Chairs were pushed back. The candlestick was taken up, and the small group of plotters followed the Squire to the rear of the room. The shift would have puzzled an unlooker, because it appeared to lead nowhere. The wall was of solid stone blocks, marked by lichen and mould but unbroken by door or windows. The Squire halted beside a slightly recessed alcove framing a waist-high marble bowl that in some far distant time had presumably been used to hold water. Save for the pervasive damp, the bowl was empty. It was a surprisingly beautiful object, clean and well maintained, the rim edged by a wide stone band of exquisitely carven flowers and intertwined leaves.

The Squire drew a long-barreled pistol and held it at the ready. "Proceed, gentlemen."

Each of the five held up a small figurine. The pieces resembled miniature gravestones and at first glance appeared identical. They were roughly three inches in height, an inch thick, the tops rounded, and on each figure a crudely carven primitive face, with a suggestion of squat legs below.

The Squire nodded. A tall, broad-shouldered individual stepped forward and leaning over the bowl set his miniature in the centre of a carven flower. As he moved back another took his place and repeated the procedure. The flame of the candle awoke brilliant sparkles from the little figures and it could be seen now that each was subtly different. The first to be put in place was of pale green jade, having three fine emeralds inset about the face. The second was of lapis-lazuli, enhanced by six sapphires. Next came a figure of quartz, with two fire opals forming the eyes; the fourth was a golden crystal in which three topazes were arranged in a sort of necklace; and, lastly, a pink jade figure with five rubies spaced about the face. Each figurine was positioned carefully, two in the flowers, one amid the leaves of the carvings, one amongst the stems, and one fitting exactly into a shallow slot in the very centre of the bowl. The Squire, who had trained his pistol on each man as the figures were set in place, handed the weapon to the individual who had held the emerald miniature. The pistol was then levelled at the Squire, who held up the sixth figurine, this being of amethyst set with four superb diamonds. He positioned it carefully in an acorn. There came at once a muted rattling and a soft thud, and the marble bowl jolted slightly, as though touched by an invisible hand.

Emerald lowered the pistol and returned it to the Squire.

Sapphire and Opal placed their hands at the right side of the alcove, and pushed. With a whisper of sound, the entire alcove swung back upon a Stygian gloom. The Ruling Council of the League of Jewelled Men retrieved their figurines from the bowl, and the man with the ruby figurine lifted the candle higher. He was tall, and although not as brawny as some of the others, moved with assured grace, but it was with obvious unease that he stepped into the inner room. The light revealed a credenza against one wall, and a chest opposite, both holding fine silver candelabra. In the centre, a table on which there was a third candelabrum was surrounded by comfortable chairs. The table held also two uninvited guests that darted away with a scamper of claws and the whipping of long tails. The hand of the man holding the candle shook, and he drew back with a shudder of revulsion.

The Squire, who had followed close behind him, fired, the pistol shot deafening in the enclosed space. "One less," he said coolly. "They're gone, Ruby."

The tall man grunted and went about lighting candles.

As the features of the room sprang into view the other members came in, most glancing about cautiously.

"No more livestock," mocked the Squire. "You may be à l'aise, my timorous heroes."

Topaz gave a snort of disgust. "Faugh! It stinks in here!"

Ruby muttered, "I think I am not easily cowed, but those hellish rodents freeze my blood! Why a God's name do you not get rid of 'em, Squire?"

"Why bother? We'll not need this room for very much longer, and they won't come out whilst we're all in here with the light."

"God help any one of us who chanced to be left in here alone," grunted the man called Emerald.

Topaz shivered. "They're ravenous by the look of 'em."

"An excellent reason to move briskly," purred the Squire.

His hint was taken. The secret door was swung back into place revealing a bowl identical to the one on the outside. The large and bulky member who was called Opal produced a kerchief and dusted off table and chairs. The Squire sat down, opened the case he carried, and retrieved a folded sheet of paper. As the others took their places, Ruby murmured, "I've wondered, Squire, if any of the icons was improperly placed, would the lock still open?"

Spreading his sheet of paper, the Squire answered absently, "No. Nor would the one who erred have time to correct his error."

Sapphire gave a rather hollow laugh, "Come now, Squire! You'd not really shoot down one of the Ruling Council? Couldn't afford to replace us, m'dear fellow!"

"You would be surprised to know how this council has changed since 'twas formed." The Squire added coldly, "Nor have we experienced great difficulty in finding—ah, replacements. Now—to business, gentlemen! Your report, Emerald, if you please."

Tall and powerfully built, Emerald stood. "We have acquired all but one of the properties which had been selected. In three instances these were secondary choices thanks to the damnable interference of Gideon Rossiter and his cronies. But all the estates now in our hands are fully manned, training is completed, and we are ready."

After a short burst of applause, Opal hoisted his bulk erect. "As you know, gentlemen, our first site in Cornwall had to be abandoned. That curst Rossiter has much to answer for! However, we found an even more advantageous site in north Devon. Our cargoes are being shipped there daily. It has proven an excellent reception and training point for new recruits. 'Tis an equally excellent dispersal point for those men ready to move to their assigned stations. All proceeds as scheduled."

The next report was offered by Ruby. He advised that thanks to their members at the Horse Guards, the Navy Board, and the East India Company, the authorities appeared to have no suspicion that the recent heavy shipping losses were not purely accidental. Communiques from the League's district commanders in the midlands, the west country, East Anglia, and the north, were all most satisfactory and there had been remarkably little opposition in those areas.

Topaz rose to his feet. His quiet voice hardened, and he was clearly angry when he said that there had been major opposition in London. "Our negotiations for arms and supplies from a—er, foreign source were seriously disrupted," he declared. "Suspicion was thrown onto two of our most staunch supporters, and a document that could well have destroyed us almost fell into enemy hands!"

At this there was consternation. Chairs scraped on the stone floor as the members jumped up. There were shouts of "What kind of document?" "Why were we not warned?" "What a' God's name happened?"

The Squire pounded on the table with the butt of his pistol and roared a demand for quiet. When order was restored, he said with an irked glare at Topaz, "There is no cause for alarm. The document was an Agreement we entered into for the supply of arms and mercenaries, and—"

Opal bellowed, "And *that* fell into military hands? My God! If our names were appended, our lives would not be worth—"

"Dammit!" snarled the Squire, "Nobody said it fell into military hands, nor that your names were listed! Our—er, supplier allowed his copy to be stolen by an Intelligence agent, but— *Will* you be quiet? I fancy that only those directly involved could identify the signatures. They were inscribed in haste and are fortunately not very clear except to those familiar with the writing. At all events, comparison is no longer possible since we were able to retrieve the document."

Ruby said shrewdly, "I don't see that. If others have read it, they will surely report the contents to—"

"Three men may very well have read it," said the Squire. "Of those, two have been dealt with. The third is ill, and in the absence of any proof to support his statement would likely be laughed at in Whitehall rather than believed. Certainly, even if he were heeded, the result would be a cautious and lengthy investigation. And I do assure you, my friends, the authorities have no time for such procedures." There were murmurs of relief, and he went on: "I will tell you, however, that something good came out of the business. One of Rossiter's irksome crew has been put out of commission. Sir Owen Furlong was shot down by"—he chuckled—"the lady of his dreams, who filched the Agreement from him."

Sapphire asked eagerly, "He is killed, I hope?"

"Not quite," said Emerald. "But I hear the—er, poor fellow is not doing very well."

"Bravo!" exclaimed Opal. "Would that the rest of the bastards were in like case!"

"To the furtherance of which," said the Squire, "have a look here, my friends."

They gathered about the map he had spread on the table. It was an odd sort of map, consisting of a rough outline of the three kingdoms, but having no topographical detail. Scattered about were squares outlined in red, most of which were lightly shaded in. Each square had a neatly printed name, and lines connected them to adjacent blue circles, marked by initials.

"We have made great strides," the Squire asserted. "The cargoes we have—um, diverted"—there was laughter at this—"have enriched our war chest. The London riots have far exceeded our expectations, and still the authorities dither and delay—to their cost, poor fools! The army is undermanned, the troops undisciplined, ill-equipped and poorly commanded. By contrast, our people are well organized and well armed. Our strategy is clear and comprehensive, our commanders efficient and dedicated. We are ready at these locations." He pointed to each of the squares in succession, pausing at the only one that was outlined in red but not shaded in. "Here alone are we weak. And this is a key area."

Ruby argued thoughtfully, "But we do have a base, see—here."

"True. But Larchwoods is a small base. We need a large one.

And here, my faithful patriots, we achieve our greatest triumph! A chain, as they say, is only as strong as its weakest link. Gideon Rossiter and his damnable busybodies have disrupted our plans, and caused the deaths of some of our finest. But they have a weak link, my friends, who has played right into our hands! Fate has smiled on us, for in my wildest dreams I'd not have envisioned a more delightful state of affairs nor sweeter timing. We are enabled at one blow to not only acquire our final prize, but also to see Rossiter and his wretched followers utterly and completely annihilated!" He smiled at the clamour for details, then went on: "Everyone here has good cause to rejoice in this, our fourth and final chastisement of those who have so ruthlessly opposed us, but one of you has a particular score to settle." He turned and handed his jewelled figurine to Topaz. "To you, my friend, go the honours."

Topaz held the figurine for a moment, gazing down at the map as though savouring the moment. Then he cried harshly, *"Châtiment quatre!"* and amid an outburst of cheers, set the figurine squarely upon the red outline that was marked "Ashleigh."

CHAPTER I

The atmosphere in the Rose and Crown had changed from congenial to anticipatory, noting which the proprietor, a small, bright-eyed individual eyed his argumentative customers warily and reached for the belaying pin under the bar. He had risen, by rather dubious stratagems, from a lowly position in a solicitor's office to proprietor of this modest but well patronised tavern near Gray's Inn. He liked being a proprietor and had no intention of seeing his tavern reduced to rubble.

"Now then, gents," he cautioned. "Now then!"

His high-nosed, thin features flushed from a generous consumption of ale, Mr. Belew waved a hand aloft. "I said it before, and I'll say it again," he declared. "As one what has been a gentleman's gentleman these twelve year and more. You was lucky, Mr. Tummet, when Captain Gideon Rossiter took you on. You don't have the *air* for it, sir! Not that I means no offense. You should've thanked your stars and stayed with the gentleman. To leave his service and take on one what is"—he smirked—"the joke of London-Town, was ill advised, Mr. Tummet. Exceeding ill advised."

There were several nods and grins and a few muttered "Aye's" to endorse his sentiments.

Enoch Tummet's jaw became more prominent. A squarely built man who reckoned his age at "about forty," he had powerful shoulders and big scarred hands. His features had been charitably described as "rough hewn" and included a square head on a short muscular neck, a "cauliflower ear," a nose that had clearly been broken several times, and small brown eyes that just now glittered a warning. He was clad in the neat dark habit of a superior servant. The material was of excellent quality, the tailoring left nothing to be desired, yet it could not be denied that the garments seemed somehow incongruous and at odds with the personality of their owner.

"Number one, Mr. Bellows," he growled, "It's true that I don't put on no airs. Not like some as I could name. Number two, I didn't leave Cap'n Rossiter's service. Not exzack. 'E got married and took 'is bride orf on a ship, and I don't 'old with ships, so I give Mr. August Falcon a 'and when 'is reg'lar valet was called away, which is what Cap'n Rossiter wanted. And if it suits Enoch Tummet to stay on with Mr. August Falcon, that is none o' your affair. Number three, Mr. Bellows, me present guv'nor, Mr. A. Falcon by name, besides being the best-looking and best-dressed young gent in the City, 'appens to be one of the richest, and cries friends wiv viscounts and earls and honourables and nobs of all kinds. There ain't a gent in all the southland can match 'im wiv swords or pops. And if 'e is the joke of London, I don't 'ear no one laughing. But"—he set down his tankard and thrust his crooked nose under Mr. Belew's supercilious nostrils—"but if I *did* chance to 'ear some cove making a joke about such a swell as me guv'nor—"

"*Swell!*" Mr. Belew glanced around the interested gathering and sniggered. "August Falcon's wealth buys him a place in the *haut ton*, in spite of the fact that his great grandmother was—"

"Was a Russian princess," snarled Tummet, moving closer to that elevated and so smug nose.

"Who went and married a Chinaman," sniggered Mr. Belew. "Which makes your—er, guv'nor no more'n a—"

"Careful, Bellows," growled Tummet, his shoulders hunching up.

"Now, now, gents," cautioned the proprietor, bringing the belaying pin into plain sight.

"I'm jest *telling* 'im," said Tummet reasonably, while putting a little more distance between himself and the belaying pin, "so 'e'll understand. Mr. Falcon's great grandpa wasn't no ordinary Chinaman, Bellows. A *Mandarin* 'e were, and wiv a mighty fortune. Me guv's got royal blood in 'is veins, and 'e's a proud man, and rightly so!" He turned to a slim young footman standing nearby, "And wot be you grinning at, my cove? You got some disparry-gin remarks to offer?"

"Oh, I ain't, Mr. Tummet," declared the footman hurriedly. "Your gentleman's got something to be proud of, like you said. I know that some folk make fun and call him the Mandarin—" He leapt back as Tummet leaned forward, and gabbled, "But I ain't one, sir! No, not me! Everything you said is—er, quite right. And—and his sister, Miss Katrina Falcon—well, no one couldn't deny as she is exceptional beautiful, and the Toast of London!"

"And if he's so royal," said Mr. Belew, who had resorted to his tankard with the result that his nose was a deeper hue than ever, "why does he spend so much time fighting duels?"

"*Winning* doo-ells," corrected Tummet. "Mr. August Falcon is partic'ler 'bout the gents wot tries to fix their interest wiv Miss Katrina, and the gents don't like it when they is sent abaht their business."

"*Particular* is it?" Mr. Belew brayed a laugh. "Beautiful she may be I won't argue that. But your gent runs off every man what offers. And considering she's just as much of a half-breed as he is—"

"And that's done *you*, swivel-nose!" Tummet hurled the contents of his tankard into Mr. Belew's face, followed with an upper-cut that sent the superior gentleman's gentleman heels over head to join the proprietor on the other side of the bar, and ducked the belaying pin that flailed at him. The belaying pin found a home on the ear of a large dragoon who'd been attending to the discussion with interest. The dragoon staggered back, knocking over a table and the several full tankards that had rested on it. The owners of the tankards took exception.

Having managed without too much difficulty to make his way outside, Mr. Tummet walked sedately up the street congratulating himself on a job well done, and nodding beneficently to the watchmen who raced to the scene of the riot.

He was less complacent the following morning when he

slipped into the kitchen of palatial Falcon House on Great Ormond Street. He had gone to some pains to avoid the housekeeper, a majestic middle-aged lady who might easily pass for a dowager duchess, but she emerged from the pantry to confront him and surveyed his split lip with disapproval.

"Brawling again," she observed, folding her arms across her splendid bosom. "Did you chance to meet some unfortunate acquaintance who questioned your position in this household?"

He tried a grin and said confidingly, "Er—not exzack, Mrs. Vanechurch. Jest a littel—er, difference of 'pinion, as y'might say."

"I had wondered why you did not appear in the Hall for breakfast," she said, blocking his attempt to escape. "It came to my ears that there was a riot in the Rose and Crown last evening. But I feel sure you would not have been involved, since you know Mr. August disapproves of that common ale house."

"It ain't common," he protested indignantly. "A very respectable tavern, and—"

"So you *were* involved!" She sniffed. "Another vulgar brawl. Whatever poor Mr. August will say when he sees you, I dread to think."

"Well 'e did see me. And he didn't flay-a-bird, neither!"

In point of fact August Falcon had looked at him steadily when he'd carried in his breakfast tray. One flaring black brow had lifted, managing to convey considerably more than a word, but he had made no audible comment.

The housekeeper shuddered. "One might think, Mr. Tummet, that you would try to remember that you are now on the staff of a member of the Quality, and try not to let your master down by brawling and using cant terms." She spoiled this fine scold by adding, " 'Flay-a-bird'—that means 'say a word,' right?"

"S'right, ducks." He saw her look of outrage and went on desperately, "I do me best, Mrs. V. But y' can't make a silk purse out of a sow's ear, as they say. Not in a few months, anyways. And when that high-nosed cove what works for Lord Sommers starts—"

"Mr. Belew? Hmm." Her lips pursed. "I know his wife. If he's cut from the same cloth, he likely had nothing good to say of Mr. August."

"Right, mate. But 'e 'ad plenty bad to say. I didn't mind s'much about the guv's doo-ells, 'cause I don't like 'em neither. Gents wanta fight they'd oughta do it wiv their fists, not stick swords in each other's gizzards, it—"

"If ever I heard of such a thing," she exclaimed, scandalized. "A gentleman defends his name as demanded by the Code of Honour! Fists, indeed! If that was all Mr. Belew had to say—"

"Well, it wasn't, marm. But I took it like a lamb till 'e comes the ugly abaht the Guv and Miss Katrina being 'alf-breeds. And that I couldn't let go by."

"Most certainly not!" She drew herself up to her full height, her eyes flashing wrath. "Be so kind as to advise me what steps you took. I trust you levelled the bounder!"

When Tummet was able to restore his sagging jaw to its normal position, he advised her in some detail. She beamed upon him, offered him a currant bun, and they parted with mutual expressions of admiration.

London's hopes that there would be a break in the gloomy weather had been doomed to disappointment, and today the skies were leaden once more. There was no rain, but a bitter wind sent the temperature plummeting and Mr. Tummet took his chilblains in search of warmth. There was a splendid fire burning in the book room, and having settled himself into a comfortable chair and stretched his large feet to the blaze, he sighed contentedly. Just a few minutes of peace and quiet wouldn't hurt no one. This was the life! During the course of a chequered career he had followed the callings of pick-pocket, ostler, free-trader, pugilist, lackey, bailiff, and valet. He had originally been elevated to the latter and most unlikely position by Captain Gideon Rossiter upon that young soldier's return from the War of the Austrian Succession. To have been "loaned" to the dashing August Falcon while Captain Rossiter sailed off on his honeymoon had not at first been a welcome development, for Tummet was fond of his Cap'n. He'd known that those who served Mr. Falcon were well paid, but the gent was not an easy man to work for. His temperament was mercurial, he was demanding and impatient, and possessed of a wickedly sardonic tongue. Yet although Captain Rossiter had now returned to England, Tummet had developed a paternal interest in and affection for August Falcon, and he stayed on at the mansion on Great Ormond Street.

He was discussing his employer now. "Trouble with the guv'nor," he explained, eating his currant bun and watching sparks fly up the chimney, "is Ancestors. Now *you* don't know who yer ancestors was, and I don't *care* who mine was. But me temp'ry guv, being a swell, 'e *do* care. Leastways, the rest of the nobs, *they* care. They're all afraid of 'im, but they do what they can to rub 'is nose in it."

Receiving only a grunt in reply, he was silent for a few minutes, picking currants from the bun and consuming them daintily. Then he enquired, "D'you know 'ow many times 'e's been out, 'Pollo? That means fought a doo-ell, mate. Well, I dunno neither. But it's a lot. And wot worries me, is that 'e's too reckless. A man—even a grand fighting man, which 'e is—a man's gotta stop and think as luck can turn on yer. It don't go on forever, mate. Cor, don't I know it! But the guv don't know it. 'E can't 'ardly wait to fight poor Lieutenant Morris. And now there's all these nasty doings with that there League o' Jewelled Men!"

His black and extremely large companion yawned noisily, rolled over on his back and stuck his legs in the air.

Tummet watched this process critically and advised Apollo that he lacked proper conduct. "Without Mr. August, who'd put up wiv you? You ain't no better looking than wot I am, and yer pedigree's even worse. So you'd oughta worry 'cause 'e takes too many chances. When we was in Cornwall . . ." his voice lowered, and he shook his head. "A proper ugly mess that were. Lucky any of us got out of it breathing. And then wot must 'e do but pick up that there nasty bag o' feathers! I tellya straight, if I'm not there to watch 'im every minute—"

"Bag of—what?"

The feminine voice drew a shocked yelp from Tummet, and he leapt from the chair like a snapped spring. "M-Miss Gwen," he gasped, whipping the de-curranted bun behind his back.

Unseen by him Gwendolyn Rossiter had come in to select a book, and, amused by his one-sided discussion, had not interrupted it. Since she and Katrina had become fast friends she'd been a frequent visitor at Falcon House. She was tiny and fine-boned, with a high forehead and delicate but unremarkable features. If she could not be described a beauty, she had something more lasting, for a smile was never very far from the generous mouth, nor a twinkle absent from the blue eyes. A knee damaged at birth had left her with a limp which surgery had failed to correct, and at four and twenty she was resigned to the life of a spinster, but if this caused her grief she had never been known to complain. Now, book in hand, she watched the big man curiously.

"I—thought as you was wiv Miss Katrina," he stammered.

"I seem to have mislaid her. So I came to find something to read."

"I 'spect as she's waiting up in the morning room," lied Tummet, who knew perfectly well where Katrina Falcon was, but had an axe to grind.

Apollo wagged his tail and hove himself up. He loved Gwendolyn slavishly, but instead of launching into his usual noisy and exuberant search for a ball for her to throw, he gave his attention to something behind the valet.

Tummet surrendered the remains of the bun before his thumb went with it, and said persuasively, "There's a lovely fire up there, Miss. Proper cozy fer you and Miss Katrina to 'ave a littel gab till the gents is done wiv their meeting. I were just—er, making sure everything's ready for 'em in 'ere."

"Yes," said Gwendolyn with a smile. "I heard you. Did you say something about Mr. August having picked up a bag of—feathers?"

"Right." Tummet's agile brain raced. "At me rhyming cant I were, Miss Gwen. Mr. August don't like it, but old 'abits ain't easy to break, y'know." He saw the girl's speculative look and said in desperation, "Bag of feathers—meaning . . . er, nag from Weathers. Mr. August bought this 'ere chestnut mare, y'see. From a farmer name of Weathers. In—er—"

"Cornwall," supplied Gwendolyn obligingly. "Nasty, was it?"

Bewildered, Tummet stared at her while Apollo scoured the hearth for crumbs.

"You said Mr. August picked up a *nasty* bag of feathers," she reminded.

"Ooh—ar. Yus. Well, it were, mate. I mean Miss. Terrible

broke down nag. Proper took in, was the guv'nor."

She wrinkled her brow. "How very unlike him. He is such a fine judge of horseflesh."

Tummet's inventive mind failed at this point, and taking pity on him, Gwendolyn walked to the door.

Breathing a sigh of relief he moved away from hearth and hound, wiping his fingers on a red handkerchief.

Gwendolyn turned back. "What became of it?"

He blinked at her.

"The nag," she said demurely. "Was he able to sell the poor beast? Or was it too—nasty?"

"Couldn't give it away," he answered, rallying. "Had to turn it loose on the moors. I'd be obliged if you didn't say nought to me guv abaht it, Miss Gwen. Awful embarrassed, 'e were."

Gwendolyn chuckled. "Well done," she said, and left him.

In the upper corridor a tantalizing aroma led her to the morning room. She knew Katrina would not be in there, but she was surprised to find August sitting cross-legged before the fire holding a long-handled pan over the flames. It was an unlikely and unfamiliar occupation for that haughty individual, and he swore and drew back as a cloud of smoke billowed from the chimney to envelop him.

"Chestnuts! Lovely!" Gwendolyn peered over his shoulder, then retreated to occupy a fireside chair and open her book.

"Pray join me," he spluttered sarcastically.

" 'Tis as well I have," she said. "They'll never cook through if you hold them so far back. You should have let Chef—"

"I am perfectly capable—" He coughed and waved smoke away, blinking tearfully.

"And I am a heartless wretch! Truly, I never meant to bring you to tears, August. Do pray keep on as you were doing. We shall enjoy our roasted chestnuts just as well tomorrow."

"*Our* roasted chestnuts?" Indignant, he turned to her. She looked quite pretty, he thought, in a gown of cream silk with a design of tiny pale blue nosegays, the waist fitted above a panier skirt. As he had expected, despite the contrite words, her little face was alight with mischief. She was the sister of one of the few men he admired, and her friendship was highly prized by his own sister. Because of this, he had come to accept the fact that Gwendolyn Rossiter appeared to consider Falcon House her home away from home. He was even willing to admit that her nature was kind and affectionate, and that she was unfailingly cheerful. Unfortunately, her affliction freed her from some of the restraints exercised by maidens hopeful of making a good match. She had a lively curiosity, discussed topics which propriety decreed should not be mentioned by gently bred up young ladies, and was outspoken to a fault. As a result, she was ignored by most of London's *haut ton*.

For various reasons, the most telling of which was his wealth, Falcon was not ignored. He made no attempt to conceal his contempt for Polite Society, and his caustic tongue and aloof manner repulsed most men, even those who admired his sporting prowess. He was well aware that he was despised because of his mixed blood, and both knew and loathed the nickname given him. It was a name never spoken to his face, because his reputation was well earned, and few men would dare meet him on the field of honour. He was known to be dangerous in other matters also. Matchmaking mamas shudderingly warned their daughters against him, but privately joined the countless London ladies who found the handsome pariah irresistible, and flirted with him at every opportunity. And bored him to distraction. His *chères amies* adored him, endured his sharp tongue and stormy disposition, were delighted by his generosity, waxed ecstatic over his charm in *affaires de coeur*, and unfailingly left his protection with genuine regret. And bored him to distraction. Gwendolyn Rossiter was unmoved by his fiery temperament and indifferent to his hauteur. She entered into sharp debates with him, scolded him for his arrogance, was all too willing to enumerate his faults, and had the unspeakable effrontery to speak of the forbidden: his lineage. Far from adoring him, if she was even mildly fond of him, which he doubted, she concealed it admirably. She had no least knowledge of his prowess in the field of *l'amour*. And although the only passion she inspired in him was quite frequently that of near apoplectic rage, she did not bore him.

"What a pity," he said, "that I am preparing the chestnuts for your brother and his friends. Had I known you were starving, ma'am, I should have offered you sustenance. May I require Chef to prepare you a snack? A baron of beef, for instance?"

"Oh, lovely," she trilled, clapping her hands.

His lips tightened, and he set the pan aside.

He was, she knew, perfectly capable of calling her bluff. She said, "But let us wait till the others arrive. In the meanwhile, you can surely spare one or two roasted chestnuts, *dear* August . . . ?"

He grunted and pulled out his watch. The other members of Rossiter's Preservers should have arrived by now. There was probably no cause for alarm. As yet. But with all the street rioting and the ever-present threat to their lives—

Gwendolyn gave a sudden shriek.

Falcon's reaction was instinctive and lightning fast. He sprang up and whipped around, crouched for action, a small pistol in his hand.

Apollo had arrived and was investigating the contents of the pan.

"Don't shoot him!" implored Gwendolyn. "Oh, pray do not!"

"Get away, you hound of infamy!" snarled Falcon, levelling an open-handed swipe at the dog's massive shoulder.

The hound seized his wrist and shook it playfully.

Falcon howled.

"Apollo! Put that down!" commanded Gwendolyn.

Released, Falcon aimed his pistol between the dog's eyes.

"Horrid creature!" said Gwendolyn.

"For once I agree with you! 'Tis past time that I put an end to my ex-dog! You saw the brute savage me!"

"In the first place, I referred to yourself, sir. Not poor Apollo. In the second place, he is not your ex-dog, and—"

"He was a dashed good watchdog till you ruined him!"

"—And in the third place, he thought you were playing, merely. *Must* you be forever panting to slaughter someone?"

"I never pant! Furthermore, he is not a 'someone,' he's an 'it.' " Pushing the affectionate "ex-dog" away Falcon exchanged the pistol for a handkerchief and wiped his chin. "Damn you, Apollo, I don't want my face washed! You see what's happened since you taught him to play, madam? He's always ready for a game. I vow were the Squire and all his murderous lieutenants to march in here this instant thirsting for my blood, this idiot brute would roll over and grin at 'em!"

She put the book aside. "I suppose," she said, with a martyred sigh, "I shall have to roast the chestnuts myself."

"Oh, get on with your reading." He sat down and took up the pan once more. "I cannot shoot him now, at all events. His yard of tongue has likely wet the powder and I'll have to reload."

Gwendolyn sat back and opened her book. Instead of reading, however, she watched the man half-turned from her. Even engaged in so plebeian a task, he was all lithe grace. A superbly tailored coat of dove grey embellished with quantities of silver braid hugged his broad shoulders. Small silver birds were embroidered on his pale blue waistcoat, and dove grey satin breeches revealed long muscular legs. His jet black hair was worn powdered today, which seemed but to emphasize the classic perfection of his features; the strong, straight nose and high-cut cheekbones, the heavy flaring brows, rather thin but well-shaped lips, the firm chin. Only his slightly sallow complexion and the hint of the Orient in the shape of his eyes betrayed his mixed blood. But they were magnificent eyes, she thought; wide and deep-set, fringed with long curling lashes, and so dark a blue as to appear almost black. What a pity that although he was not yet thirty, he must be so rigidly immovable in the matter of his lovely sister and poor Jamie—

"Well?" he said, without turning.

She looked down at once. "I am reading."

"No you're not. You're staring at me. I can feel your eyes— like spears in my back! What have I done now?"

"Lud, what conceit! You suppose that every lady in London must gaze at you!"

"Why should they not? I don't begrudge them a sight of manly perfection."

"Hah!" snorted Gwendolyn. "Rather than dignify such blatant conceit, I will read you something that—"

"Oh, no you don't! I'm unhappily aware of how you delight to irritate me by flaunting books about China under my nose!"

"It should be a point of interest rather than an irritant. I am in fact astonished by what I have learned. For instance, did you know that during the T'ang Dynasty—that was in the eighth century A.D. . . ." She glanced up when he made no comment and saw that he had put the pan down and held both hands over his ears. She chuckled, and went on, "While we in the British Isles were largely unlettered and primitive and forever waging war 'gainst each other, in China they already had poets, and skilled painters and beautiful porcelains. They had discovered printing, also—is that not incredible? And thousands of books were published and sold to students—*students!*—at low prices so that they might qualify for civil service examinations! And they had invented raincoats and had found a breed of horses said to have danced to music. And then, in the Sung Dynasty—that would be about the year A.D. 1005—the emperor had a one-thousand-volume encyclopaedia printed and there is a bee on your neck."

At this warning, spoken with no change in tone, Falcon started and instinctively jerked a hand to his throat.

Gwendolyn laughed merrily. "I knew you were listening, though why you should pretend not to I cannot fathom. How can you be ashamed of ancestors who seem to have gone on a good deal better than the rest of the—"

"Madam," he said through his teeth, "when I require to be educated I shall return to University! Meanwhile, I would *politely* request that you confine your extremely dull lectures to my sister. And possibly Tummet. And—leave—me—in—peace!" Still glaring at her, he snatched up the pan so violently that several chestnuts escaped and he had to scramble to retrieve them. From the corner of his eye he saw the swift flash of dimples beside Gwendolyn's generous mouth, but she said nothing, bowing her head over her book in a chastened attitude he thought extremely suspicious.

Briefly, the room was quiet save for the pleasant sounds of the fire and the occasional rushes of wind in the chimneys.

Gwendolyn frowned, and asked suddenly, "Pray, what is meant by 'li'?"

'*Confound* that book!' thought Falcon. He grunted, "I should think that by now even you would realize that I have not the slightest interest in—"

"Oh, don't be stuffy, August. It says here that Confucius believed in the principle of 'li.' I am sure you must have learned something of his teachings, even if only at school."

"You are mistaken, ma'am."

"I think not. Though *you* are mistaken on one point. Or the tale has come down to you in a scrambled way, perchance." She paused, her brow wrinkling thoughtfully as she gazed at the printed page.

"You waste your time with such silly tricks," sneered Falcon. "I've not the least intent to ask what you're jabbering at."

"No, because you're afraid I may be right. But I am too generous to deny sharing what I have learned. 'Tis my understanding that your maternal great-grandmama was a Russian princess, who married a Chinese Mandarin of great wealth. Correct?"

He stiffened. "I believe I have never been so gauche as to enquire about *your* ancestors, madam. Who were doubtless," he added savagely, "a lot of murderous wolfs-heads."

"Oh, very likely," she agreed with maddening amiability. "Only the *reason* you do not ask is that you are such a care-for-nobody and have not a shred of interest in other people." She pursed her lips and added, "Still, I'm bound to admit our family history is really quite dull. Yours is not. But—"

"Since you find it so interesting, you are doubtless aware of the Falcon motto and should pay heed to it."

"*Dieu et Mon Droit?*" she said innocently.

He had to fight a grin, "No. I believe that one was taken by some commoners."

"Oh, ho," she said, laughing at him. "To insult the Crown is treason, sir! Have a care! No, do not scowl so, August, or your eyebrows will get knotted together and you'll never be able to smile again. Your family motto is 'We Avenge.' " Taking advantage of his astonishment, she went on quickly, "But the thing is, it makes no sense, do you see? From all I have been able to discover of China—which sadly is very little—they allow no 'Ocean People,' as they call Westerners, into the country, and no Chinese are permitted to leave. How, then, could your great-grandfather possibly have married a Russian princess?"

The amusement had faded from Falcon's eyes. For a moment he was rigidly still, then he said harshly, "Ah, but you have found us out, Miss Snoop, and may wallow in the scandalous truth. Great-grandpapa never did wed the princess. In fact, I wonder you've not noticed that my mama's maiden name was the same as that of her spouse. It shames me to own it, but Katrina and I are, alas, bastards!" From under his lashes he slanted a glare at her shocked face. "Are you satisfied at last, madam?"

"If ever I heard such stuff! Your family is large, with branches spread over half the globe, so Katrina told me. Your Grandmama Natasha married Sir Geoffrey Falcon, who was an Ambassador or some such, then living in Paris. Their daughter, Miss Francine Falcon, married Mr. Neville Falcon. In fact, that is how your parents first met—they discovered they were distant cousins, and—"

He said irritably, "Oh, have done, for heaven's sake!"

"Yes, well I will. But—were you not so abominably proud—"

"I am an abominable man. And since I have finished my cookery, I will withdraw and allow you to ponder the mystery of me to your heart's content. I should warn you, however, 'gainst getting your hopes too high. Many other ladies have—dropped the handkerchief in my direction."

He bowed and left her, and went along the corridor grinning and triumphant because his outrageous declaration had, for once, rendered her speechless. She would recover her wits at any second, of course, and hasten to hurl some set-down at him. That it would be a splendid set-down, he had no doubt. *'Dieu et Mon Droit'* . . . He chuckled. She'd scored with that sally, the wretch. He slowed, listening. But there came no hurried and uneven footsteps; no furious assessment of his conceit. Beginning to be a touch uneasy, he halted. Had he perhaps been too sharp with her? He'd become so accustomed to their verbal duels that he did not always treat her with the deference a gentleman should show a lady. Which was her own fault for teasing him so unmercifully that his temper was apt to get the better of him. She wasn't coming, that was evident. Oddly, Apollo had not followed, either.

Frowning, he retraced his steps and walked very softly back into the morning room.

Gwendolyn was still seated in the chair. Apollo sat in front of her with his unlovely head on her knee, and she was pulling his ear absently as she gazed into the fire. She looked, thought Falcon, almost like a child; small and vulnerable. He took a chestnut from the pan and tossed it into her lap.

In the nick of time she snatched it from Apollo's attention and turned, smiling sunnily. "Thank you, kind sir. Did you come to rescue me from starvation?"

He threw one leg over the arm of the sofa and perched there, watching her. "I was curious to know why—having given you a perfect opportunity to deal me a fine set-down—you let it slide past."

She concentrated on peeling the nut. "I am preparing my counter-attack. Beware."

"No you're not. You're worrying. Why waste your time in such a senseless pursuit? Your brother is perfectly able to take care of himself. You should be glad that he came home safe from the war."

"Can you think I am not glad? Heaven knows how often we nigh lost Gideon during the terrible year he spent in hospital."

"Yet despite all your miserizing, he survived and is now wed, poor fellow, and appears to be alive again. A prime cause for rejoicing, instead of which, woman-like, you must continue to wallow in maudlin moping!"

She flushed and said heatedly, "There is no such word as 'miserizing,' as you know very well! And can you really expect me to rejoice because my dear brother is out of the frying pan and into the fire? Am I to dance with joy because he dares stand in opposition to an evil secret society which is now sworn to destroy him?"

Falcon's heavy brows twitched into a black bar across his nose. "Be damned if I ever expected to see you turn into a professional mourner! Should you rather we stood aside and let that band of aristocratic maniacs create their murder and mayhem and seize control of the government unopposed?"

"No, of course not, but . . ." Troubled, she watched the flames and said slowly, "The League is so *powerful*, August! 'Tis dreadful to think of the families they have wiped out, only so as to seize their estates! The honourable gentlemen they have entrapped and slandered and dragged to prison or brought to despair and self-destruction! All the lives lost at sea when they've deliberately destroyed great ships so as to steal the cargoes!" Apollo edged closer and nudged her hand, and she pulled his ear again and murmured almost to herself, "I know there was more to that horrible business in Cornwall than you have told us."

Falcon started and fixed her with a keen stare.

"If only someone in power would *listen* to Gideon's warnings!" she went on. "For him to try to stand 'gainst them all alone is—"

At this, his eyes opened very wide and he interposed with considerable resentment, "*Alone*, is it! 'Faith, but you dismiss the rest of us lightly, Madam Glummery!" He ignored her attempted apology, and added a thoughtful, "But in all honesty I must admit that you're justified to some extent. Jamie Morris, for instance, don't count for much, and Perry Cranford's of little use, since he hops about on a peg-leg. As for—"

Gwendolyn had just popped the chestnut into her mouth and was unable to do more than splutter an incensed, "Ooh!"

"As for Furlong," he continued blandly, "You're correct in believing him *utterly* worthless. Any man who—"

"Odious! Unkind . . . *creature!*" panted Gwendolyn, choking down the nut and springing up, her eyes sparkling with wrath. "I meant nothing of the sort, as you know perfectly well! You will *never* find a good word for Jamie Morris, will you? Though he is the best and kindest of—"

"The best and kindest of nincompoops, who thinks nothing of firing off his pistol at any fellow who chances to ride up when—"

"That was months ago! And it was night, and he mistook you for a highwayman, as well you know! But although he explained and begged your pardon—"

"While I lay bleeding at his feet!"

"—you mean to force him to a duel—which will be as good as murder! Much you care if—"

"Tit for tat, my child. Besides which, Gideon won't let Ja— Morris give me satisfaction till this League business is done with."

"And you cannot wait to slay him, even though 'twill break

your sister's heart! You know poor Jamie worships Katrina! And—"

"So do half the men in London, but that don't make 'em worthy of her hand. Do you really fancy I'd let her throw her lovely self away on *that* dimwit? Never!"

"And how *dare* you think I do not value Peregrine Cranford?" she swept on, temporarily abandoning that bone of contention. "Only because he lost a foot while serving his country? He is a splendid young man and a wondrous fighter, foot or no!"

"Faith, but you should have been a lawyer, ma'am! I am agog to hear how you will defend Owen Furlong, whose infatuation with a pretty face lost us the one piece of evidence that could have destroyed the League!"

"If you had one *speck* of kindness or understanding in that draughty void where should rest your heart, you'd not sneer at poor Owen! He adored Maria Barthélemy, and she was not merely pretty! She was—is—very beautiful, and Owen gave her his heart never dreaming she was a scheming spy! Oh, how *can* you be so harsh and unforgiving?"

He shrugged. "Any man who becomes so besotted over a woman—*any* woman—that he not only allows her to shoot him down—"

"He didn't *allow* her! How should he dream she would do so ghastly a thing?"

"—but comes nigh to grieving himself into an early grave over the wench, is a sorry fool in my book!"

"Then you write a horrid book, August Falcon," she declared, baring a set of white and even teeth at him. "Which is logical enough, since you are a horrid man!"

His dark eyes twinkled. "Very true," he admitted. "But you love me just the same."

"I would love you more—" she began stormily, then stopped. "Oh! You said all that deliberately, just to vex me!"

He said with a smile, "Had to do something, Miss Gwendolyn. If Gideon saw you sitting about like a wilting dandelion, he'd surely blame me and I go in terror of his wrath!"

Her response was drowned as Apollo sprang up and began to bark shatteringly.

"Quiet, ex-dog!" commanded Falcon. "I think the rest of our—er, little club have arrived. Adieu, sweet raincloud." He bowed low, dodged the nut she snatched from the pan and threw at him, and went, laughing, from the room.

He walked toward the stairs head down, lost in thought. The Smallest Rossiter was worrying. Heaven knows with some cause, for there was no doubt but that each one of them had been marked for vengeance by the loathsome League. Even so, Gwendolyn was such a courageous and sunny-natured creature. It was not like her to be cast into the dismals like this. And she'd spoken of Cornwall . . .

"Damn!" he muttered.

"Ar," said a gruff voice beside him.

He jerked his head up, his frowning gaze causing Tummet to eye him uneasily. "They're here, I take it?" he said, thrusting the pan of chestnuts at his "temporary" valet.

"Two is. And there's bin—"

Falcon caught his arm and pulled him to a halt. "Try if you can cast your mind back two months or so," he growled, "to Cornwall, and our little encounter with the Squire's merry men."

"That weren't no 'littel encounter,' Guv," argued Tummet. "A good-sized war is what it was! But we brung Cap'n Armitage outta that bog he'd got hisself into and—"

"Very good," purred Falcon. "Your brain is more or less active, I see. Then you'll doubtless recall the matter of a certain bag of feathers . . . ?"

The picture of innocence, Tummet said, "If you mean that there bag wot was throwed atcher, and wot you shouldn't never 'ave took up, even if you didn't believe in spells and curses and—"

"Of course I did not believe in such superstitious balderdash!"

Tummet winked and said with a knowing leer, "Changed yer mind, is that it, Guv?"

"No that is *not* it! Did you tell Miss Rossiter about the stupid nonsense?"

"Cor! Wotcher take me fer? As if I'd tell the lady you've been 'ill-wished,' as them Cornishers call it! 'Sides, in another few weeks the spell's wore out."

"Which does not signify, since there is no such thing as a

spell!" Falcon stamped along the wide corridor, but nodded to a lackey who stiffened to attention as he passed. "What d'ye mean, 'another few weeks'?" he demanded suddenly. "I wasn't aware there's a time element attached to the silly twaddle."

Tummet stifled a grin. "When that there Cornish witch come to London last week, she told me—"

"And there's no such thing as—"

"That there *charming* lady wot everyone *thought* were a witch," Tummet amended hurriedly. "She told me the curse of the bag of feathers falls on the one as it's sent to. It was throwed at *you*, and *you* picked it up, which you never should of—"

"Tum-met . . . !"

"Orl right, orl right! No need to get into a garden-gate—er, state! She said the curse must be fulfilled 'fore the—um, valley day Noll, or—"

"Hold up! The—what? Oh! *La vieille de Noël!*"

Tummet sniffed and said with an injured air, "No need to make fun."

"No, indeed. You said it very well." Falcon's rare and blinding smile accompanied the words and he clapped his unorthodox valet on the back. "For a rascally hedgebird,"

Tummet felt warmed and said in a rather gruff voice, "Yus. Well, that means Christmas Eve, don't it, and the spell's broke then, so all you gotta do is make sure we don't 'ave no not-so-nices 'twixt then and now."

"I suppose that piece of your confounded rhyming cant translates to 'crises.' "

"Yus, Guv. Ex-zack. And a fat lotta good it'll do fer me to tellyer to stay away from 'em. Miss Gwen'd 'ave to be a proper widgeon not to see wot's boiling up, even if she don't know about spells and—"

Pausing with one hand on the carven end-post of the grand staircase, Falcon said with grim emphasis, "Miss Gwendolyn is a high-couraged lady with always a bright and cheerful spirit, no matter how dark things look. This is the first time I've known her to be blue-devilled. If I thought you'd filled up her ears with a lot of superstitious rubbish . . ."

"Didn't I say as I never done no such thing?" Tummet lifted

one gnarled hand and declared piously, "See this wet, see this dry!"

"Very well. You may straighten your halo." Falcon started down the stairs.

Tummet called, "The gents is in the kitchen, Guv."

"The *kitchen?*" Swinging around, Falcon asked, "Why the deuce—"

"Bin a spot of 'ubble-bubble. Tried to tellyer, but you was too busy grousing."

'Hubble-bubble—trouble,' translated Falcon mentally. He swore and ran downstairs at speed.

Following, Tummet looked glum. "You shouldn't never of picked up that there littel bag o' feathers, mate," he muttered. "Curl me crumpet but you shouldn't!"

CHAPTER 11

alcon's precipitate arrival in an area he'd not visited since his school days startled an already nervous kitchenmaid into uttering a piercing shriek and dropping a pan of hot water.

The housekeeper was busily engaged in winding a bandage around the wrist of a dark-haired young man seated at the table. She swung her ample form aside in a not altogether successful attempt to avoid the deluge. "Stupid girl," she scolded. "Mop it up at once! Oh, I am so sorry, Captain Rossiter! Did I hurt you again?"

Gideon Rossiter assured her that he was not further damaged, and raised a pair of fine grey eyes to meet Falcon's concerned gaze. "A short detour for repairs, August," he said ruefully.

"So I see." Falcon was surprised to find his sister among those present, and his expression hardened.

In spite of her unfortunate heritage, Katrina Falcon, enchantingly beautiful and of a far sweeter disposition than her brother, was known as the unacknowledged Toast of London. Admired and well liked, but seldom included on the guest lists of leaders of the *haut ton*, she had received many offers of marriage. Without exception, her brother had rejected them, scornfully naming her suitors "silly fribbles," "military rattles," or "gazetted fortune hunters." Several gentlemen of birth, breeding, and fortune, who had defied their families and offered for the beauty, had taken exception to this high-handed attitude, with resultant dawn meetings in Hyde Park or at some other secluded duelling ground. None of the suitors had been seriously wounded. Nor had they felt inclined to continue to court the lady in the face of such ferocious opposition, and at three and twenty, the fair Katrina remained unwed.

Charmingly attired in a *robe volante* of light pink velvet, with a pretty lace-edged cap atop her luxuriant black curls, she looked up from bathing a cut on the forehead of the second casualty, and said in her gentle voice, "Jamie and Gideon were set upon in the street, dear. Only see this nasty lump."

Lieutenant James Morris was all too aware of the "nasty lump." Sitting hunched over the table, he opened one green eye, took in Falcon's scowl, and closed it again. He was pale, the freckles on his boyish face more marked than usual, but he said with the suggestion of a grin, "Never look so anxious, old boy. Your sweet sister's tender care makes a broken head quite desirable."

"So I see." Falcon reached for the cloth in Katrina's hand. "I'll do that. Another street riot, Gideon?"

"More or less," answered Rossiter with an enigmatic look.

Katrina swung the cloth away. "Thank you, but I can manage," she said. "Turn your head to me, Jamie."

There was a deep bond of affection between brother and sister. For the most part Katrina either bore with August's domineering ways or tactfully outmanoeuvred him. It was extremely rare for her to openly defy him, and this small evidence of insubordination caused his eyes to flash with surprise and annoyance.

It awoke a very different emotion in the breast of Lieutenant Morris, who murmured blissfully, "With the greatest pleasure in the world, my angel of mercy."

In company with the rest of Mr. Neville Falcon's large staff, the housekeeper knew that poor Lieutenant Morris was head over heels in love with Miss Katrina, and that Mr. August was bitterly opposed to the match. She also knew about the unfortunate episode earlier in the year when the lieutenant had come upon an attempted hold-up and shot down Mr. August, mistaking him for a highwayman. A dreadful mistake, certainly, but the wound had been comparatively slight, and the lieutenant was such a nice gentleman. She liked his shy eyes and innate courtesy, and suspected that Miss Katrina had become fond of him. In an effort to ease this taut moment, she tied her bandage and said with a shake of the head, "Whatever has come over our poor London? The streets are not safe any more. Not for anybody! Should we send for the Watch, sir?"

"Much good they would do. A nice bandage, Mrs. V. I thank you. Katrina, a piece of sticking plaster should suffice now."

The door opened and a footman announced sonorously that Mr. Peregrine Cranford had arrived and been shown into the book room.

"Very good." Falcon helped Morris to his feet and enquired low-voiced, "Can you manage the journey, my crafty clod?"

Morris clung to his arm and smiled up at him. "With your kind aid, Lord Haughty-Snort," he said just as softly, adding in a normal tone, " 'A friend in need is a friend indeed!' "

"How true," exclaimed Mrs. Vanechurch with a fond smile. "How very true!"

Falcon, who loathed maxims, gritted his teeth and guided the walking wounded along the corridor, across the wide hall, and into the book room.

Peregrine Cranford had settled his lean frame into a fireside chair, propping his left foot and the short peg-leg that served in lieu of his right foot on the gleaming brass fender. He was an energetic, good-natured young man, showing few signs now of the fact that he had almost died when his foot had been crushed by a gun carriage at the Battle of Prestonpans and had been amputated under extremely harrowing conditions. The most recent addition to their little band, he waved a chestnut and turned a laughing, fine-boned face framed by brown curling hair that was today powdered and tied back.

"Advance and join the chestnut brigade," he called, "before I devour—" The light words faded into a gasp and the twinkle in the blue eyes was banished by alarm. "Jupiter!" he exclaimed, springing up. "You've been in an engagement, I see! Sit here, Ross!"

Falcon seated Morris in an adjacent chair and crossed to the reference table and the decanters and glasses the butler had left there. "Those nuts are our entire supply," he scolded. "If you've wolfed the lot down, Perry . . . !"

"No, no, I promise you," declared Cranford, peering anxiously at Morris' rather wilting form. "What happened? The Squire's fine hand?"

"Directly, or indirectly," said Rossiter. "A small street disturbance some way from us, but when we came up all the activity suddenly shifted and we were surrounded. Had not some troopers arrived on the scene it might have gone hard with us. As it is, I took no worse than a cut. How are you, Jamie?"

Morris lifted his throbbing head and declared he was "right as a trivet. Though," he went on, looking mournfully at Cranford, "I would be more likely to survive if sustained by a chestnut. Or several."

Cranford rushed to pass the bowl of nuts to the casualties, and Falcon handed out glasses of sherry. Morris set his glass aside, noting which Falcon said, "I think Jamie has taken a hard rap on the brain box. The unfortunate woodworms must be rattling around inside. Shall I call up my coachman to waft you home, dear dolt?"

"You are all heart," said Morris. "Whereas I am all nobility, and will stay."

Despite his grin he was extremely pale, and Falcon hesitated, scanning him narrowly before sitting on the leather sofa beside Cranford. With characteristic impatience he then demanded, "Well? Are we expecting any of the others, Gideon? Or can we get on with this?"

Rossiter glanced at the tall case clock. "I'd hoped Tio might be here."

"I thought you'd sent him off on some sort of reconnaissance," said Cranford.

"Yes, I did. I fancied he'd have returned to Town last night, but—" Rossiter paused, slightly frowning.

Cranford, who'd known Viscount Horatio Glendenning most of his life, said, "Never worry for Tio. He knows what 'tis like to be hunted, and will be on his guard."

"As we all have to be nowadays," said Morris, stifling a sigh.

Falcon shrugged lazily. "We all are watched, certainly. As we watch them. I've no quarrel with that. But when they turn their venom on our families . . ."

"Speaking of which," said Rossiter, "How did you find your sire, August? That was a nasty toss he took last month."

"The old fellow appears fully recovered, fortunately. In fact, I'd expected he would insist on accompanying me to Town yesterday. I was floored to find that he has no plans to return as yet. You know how he detests country life."

Morris looked dubious. "Perhaps he's not as well as he pretended."

"Oh, I think he's well enough." Falcon's lips quirked. "He was quite eager to see me leave."

A trace of sympathy was in their laughter. They all knew that the antics of Mr. Neville Falcon were a source of constant anxiety to his heir, and on more than one occasion they had marvelled among themselves that a man of August's volatile temperament should somehow manage to be patient with his exasperating sire.

Falcon could guess their thoughts. They didn't understand. How could they? It was very true that there were times when his father would try the patience of a saint. Neville Falcon's marriage had been a disaster into which he'd been pushed by avaricious parents, but never—*never* by the slightest hint had he shown a trace of resentment or the disappointment that would have been natural enough in a proud man saddled with a son whose appearance must be a constant embarrassment to him. To the contrary, August's earliest memory of his father was of being held up as a very small boy and gazed upon with pride. He was as sure as he was sure of anything in this world that his parent still looked at him with pride and with an unshakeable devotion. And if he now and then yearned to strangle the old gentleman, he knew that however profligate his spending, however foolish his behaviour with the ladies, however infuriating the predicaments in which he constantly embroiled himself, the bond between them never had, and never would waver.

Amused, Rossiter said, "That rascal! Which one this time?"

"Heaven knows, and I did not stay to find out. I'd a lot sooner he kept in the country with one of his birds of paradise than be cavorting about Town without a thought for all the mayhem on the streets." He heard Apollo barking somewhere, and glanced to the door expectantly. "I've warned our steward to be on the look-out for intruders and to keep a guard on the house day and night, just in case the Squire again decides to level his guns at Ashleigh. Hello, Chandler. You're late."

Gordon Chandler joined the group. Two and thirty, clean cut, with the bronzed face of the man who spends most of his time out-doors, he was strong-willed and inclined to be stern, but Rossiter had found him loyal and reliable and valued his shrewd common-sense. The power of the League of Jewelled Men had been demon-strated to him painfully when the League had launched a murderous and almost successful assault on Lac Brillant, the Chandlers' great estate near Dover. Now a dedicated member of Rossiter's Preservers, he took the chair Falcon pulled up for him, smiled his thanks for a glass of wine, and listened gravely to a brief account of the attack on Morris and Rossiter. "I suppose we may be thankful it was no worse," he said. "Did I hear you say the Squire might *again* level his guns at your sire, August? You're sure then? It wasn't simply an accident?"

"I'm damned sure. My father is a disastrous rider, I admit, but the saddle girth was cut. The League was responsible, all right. As they were responsible for the accident to the coach of Morris' sis-ter, and the destruction of Gideon's Emerald Farm."

"Luckily, m'sister was only bruised, and the children weren't hurt," said Morris. "But I'd give something to get my hands on the bounders!"

Cranford nodded. "Yes, by Jove! What about your farmhouse, Ross? Shall you rebuild?"

"Perhaps. After we've dealt with the League." The cut in Rossiter's arm was troublesome, and he eased his position in the chair, thinking sadly of the beautiful sprawling old house in the Weald that was his legacy from his grandmother. He and his bride had intended to spend much of the year there. Now, it was a charred and pathetic ruin.

Watching him, Morris said sympathetically, "Those filthy bas-tards have much to answer for."

"Aye," agreed Chandler. "There's not a one of us but has suffered at their hands!"

"And we're only a few of their victims," said Cranford.

"Very true. So we must see to it that they're brought to book!" Rossiter straightened his shoulders. "Let's get to work." He took a paper from his pocket and unfolded it, revealing a rough sketch of England having several circles and X's scattered about. The X's, he explained, indicated properties the League now owned, while the circles represented estates they'd tried, unsuccessfully, to steal. He passed the map to Gordon Chandler. "God alone knows how many more they have that we don't know about."

Chandler glanced at Cranford. "Perry, you were pitchforked into this mess in a rather scrambling way, I believe. If you've questions as we go along, pray shout, and we'll explain."

"The devil!" exclaimed Falcon indignantly. "We did explain! Clearly. Only a blockhead would not have understood. Acquit us, Perry!"

Cranford said with a grin, "If I have it correctly, when first you encountered those scoundrels, you thought they were out to discredit and ruin gentlemen of wealth, power, and influence, and to undermine public trust in government. But you later discovered there was more to the plot and that the League was also after the country estates owned by those same gentlemen."

Chandler nodded. "Their purpose being to use the estates as training or storage facilities."

"Yes, I got that much through my head. I don't quite know how long it took you to realize that the properties were close to strategic military or naval sites."

"Oh, a great time," drawled Falcon ironically. "But our feeble minds at long last contrived to put two and two together. The League was killing two birds with one stone: destroying famous men, and at the same time acquiring sites from which attacks will be launched on vital installations."

"Not if we can prevent it!" Rossiter stood and went to prop his shoulders against the mantel from where he could watch them all. "As you know, we've been successful in stopping three of their attempted estate snatchings. Notably, Glendenning Abbey, near

Windsor; Lac Brillant, near Dover; and the Blue Rose Mine at Castle Triad, on the northern coast of Cornwall."

Cranford said hotly, "I think it damnable that the authorities refuse to believe there is anything to connect those events, or that they have anything to do with the League!"

"Why should they?" drawled Falcon, "when they do not believe in the existence of our wretched Squire and his cronies?"

"Well, it occurred to me," Rossiter went on, "that if the League really did mean to use those estates as bases from which they'll launch their attacks, they're not likely to change their plans only because we beat them at their ugly game."

"Burn it!" exclaimed Morris. "D'you think they'll make another try for 'em? We'd best warn old Tio. He nigh lost his head when the League went after Glendenning Abbey!"

Chandler said, "I'd think it more likely for the Squire to set about acquiring other large properties in the same general area."

"I agree!" Falcon's eyes glittered with excitement. "And if we could prove that to be a fact, the dunderheads in Whitehall might at last sit up and take notice, eh?"

Rossiter said, "We can but hope. Now, if you will, give us your report, Perry."

"Ross sent me to Dover," said Cranford, "to sniff about and see what I could learn."

Chandler interposed frowningly, "Why not send me, Gideon? I know the Dover area better than Perry."

"Yes, and would be recognized at once," said Rossiter. "Perry was able to wander about and make his enquiries without attracting attention."

"A notable achievement for a man with a peg-leg," murmured Falcon.

"Had you any interest in your fellow man," snapped Cranford, who had a temper, "you might have noticed there are very many ex-soldiers and sailors who lost limbs during the war."

Falcon stood and offered a deep and flourishing bow. "I stand corrected. And apologize for my error. 'Twas not a notable achievement."

They all laughed, and Gordon Chandler threw a handful

of nutshells at him. "Addleplot! Have done!"

"But with the best will in the world." Falcon sat down. "Are the results of Perry's wanderings a secret, or are we at some time in the future to learn them?"

Rousing himself, Morris said, " 'He that hath patience, hath fat thrushes for a farthing.' "

The amused gleam vanished from Falcon's eyes. "Why in the name of creation would I want *thrushes*, be they skeletal or obese, you silly block?"

"You may not want 'em, but I'll wager you've got some," argued Morris reasonably. "Down at Ashleigh, at all events, and I'd not wonder—"

Falcon clutched at his thick hair and swore in exasperation.

The other men exchanged grins, and Cranford said, "Well, I found something that sounds extreme suspicious. A fine estate a short distance inland from Folkestone changed hands a couple of months back. The owner was a man in his prime who had no least intention of selling his lands and was in fact annoyed by several offers, all of which he refused."

"Whereupon," murmured Gordon Chandler, poring over Rossiter's map, "I'll wager he suffered a fatal accident of some kind."

Cranford nodded. "Right you are. His widow was so grieved by her loss that she retired from the world and has entered a nunnery, poor lady. The heir appears to be a wild young Buck. He fell into bad company, took to drink and gaming, and within a month lost the property."

His kind heart touched, Morris shook his head, then held it painfully. "Jove, what a tragedy. So now the League has it?"

"I was unable to get near enough to find out, I'm afraid." Cranford said wryly, "The house itself is remote, and guarded by grim-looking fellows. Each time I tried to gain admission, I was denied. Politely, at first, when I claimed to be a friend of the former owner. Less politely, when I persisted."

Falcon said, " 'Twould certainly seem to confirm your theory, Gideon."

"Yes, but we'll need more than one instance."

Chandler asked, "Is that what Tio's about, Ross?"

"More or less. I sent him down to Bosham on a rather different search, but—"

"But, behold! I am safely come back again!" Viscount Horatio Glendenning had flung open the door and paused on the threshold, a smile on his lips, but a touch of defiance in his green eyes. "And only see who I've brought along."

Sir Owen Furlong was a shadow of the dashing ex-army officer they'd known, with dark shadows under his blue eyes, and a sunken look to the fine features that were marked by the pallor of illness. He leaned heavily on the viscount's strong arm, watching the silenced group apprehensively. "Hold up, Tio," he said. "I shall quite understand if you don't want me, gentlemen. If I hadn't been so—er—"

"Besotted?" supplied Falcon dryly.

Sir Owen's gaunt cheek flushed, but he admitted, "And gullible. I held in my hand the Agreement between the League and their new French allies, and I let Miss . . . Barthélemy . . . take it from me. Thanks to my stupidity we lost our chance to not only prove the existence of the League of Jewelled Men, but—but to destroy the murderous traitors."

"And the Frenchman. Your lady's famous brother," said Falcon, relentless.

Sir Owen winced, and his voice was not quite steady when he acknowledged, "And Marshal Barthélemy."

Despite his aching head, Morris had been annoyed by this exchange. He had a deep sympathy for the grief Sir Owen had suffered when the lady he loved had shot him down. "Have done, August!" he exclaimed. " 'Milk the cow, but don't pull off the udder!' "

Shouts of laughter broke the tension in the room, and Gideon Rossiter crossed to shake Sir Owen's eagerly extended hand. "Did you really suppose we'd hold you to blame for getting yourself shot trying to take back the Agreement? Lord, but you're a dunce, Owen!"

The other men crowded around, full of reassurances and anxiety that the tall soldier had defied his doctors in going out so soon after being wounded, and in such bitter weather. He was settled into the most comfortable chair, Chandler sketched the attack on Rossiter and Morris, and Falcon came over to offer a glass. "Sherry," he said unsmilingly. "Is that allowed?"

Taking it in an unsteady hand, Sir Owen met those cold blue eyes and said humbly, "I quite agree with you, you know. For your opinion of me."

Falcon shrugged. "I'll not deny I don't admire you." He ignored some irritated murmurs, and carried another glass to the viscount, adding, "Still, I respect courage, and it took plenty of that to bring you here today."

Chandler asked curiously, "Now may we know why you were sent to Bosham, Tio? The League already has Larchwoods, which is close by."

"Aye," answered Lord Glendenning. "But 'tis a comparatively small estate. If the League arms it with a view to attacking Portsmouth, Gideon thinks they must have a much larger base in the area. Which," he added, "They don't, so far as I was able to ascertain."

The map had reached Morris. Peering at it, he muttered, "I can see your reasoning on most of these, Ross. But be dashed if I can understand why the League went to all the trouble to ruin poor Admiral Albertson."

Owen Furlong said quietly, "Peasant Poplars was Albertson's country seat. A large and beautiful estate. The League wanted it, and took it."

Morris said, "And destroyed him, the merciless bastards. But 'tis near Welwyn. Ain't nothing vital or strategic up there."

Falcon looked at his tired face and said gently, "Your brains have fallen asleep, Jamie. Think what runs through Welwyn."

Morris blinked up at him. "Let's see now . . . Is it the—um, the River Ash?"

"Right," said Gideon. "But more important is the Great North Road. A key artery from London to the north, and would create chaos were it blocked."

Horatio Glendenning took the map. "I see your own country seat is still on here, Gideon. No luck reclaiming it whilst I was away?"

Rossiter's lips tightened. "No, unfortunately." Promontory

Point was one of the showplaces of the southland. The League had spun its webs well and Sir Mark Rossiter had been ruined, discredited, and disgraced, his bankruptcy creating a major disaster for hundreds of investors. Gideon and his friends had helped Sir Mark establish his innocence and his financial empire was now well on the way to recovery, but Gideon said bitterly, "Rudi Bracksby, who so *generously* bought the Point to hold it for us till we could afford to buy it back, continues to find legal stumbling blocks to prevent us doing that very thing."

"What would you expect?" drawled Falcon. "Bracksby is one of the Squire's merry men, past doubting. And the League would be stupid to give up a great house and an enormous property located close to the Thames Estuary, and near the Downs, where the fleets gather offshore; to say nought of the naval station at Chatham!"

As if this inventory had brought home to them the chilling scope and menace of the League's connivings, there was a moment of quiet.

Gordon Chandler said broodingly, "They really must be insane, you know. To think they can succeed at such an undertaking."

"They have amassed enormous wealth," Rossiter pointed out. "They've been planning this for three years that we know of, and they now have hundreds of well-trained and well-equipped mercenaries concentrated at key points through the southland."

"Which is more than you could say for our own defenses." Glendenning looked grim. "England never learns the lesson that she *must* keep an effective standing army. From what I've seen of our military lately, we'd be in sorry condition to withstand a series of determined and well-planned assaults."

Falcon nodded. "Worse, were they all launched simultaneously! One of Bonnie Prince Charlie's main problems was his inability to get his troops to England. The Squire's troops have been drifting in through Cornwall for months! They're here! And I think half *our* military men aren't even fully armed. In September, when a troop of dragoons was after us near Plymouth, I'd swear many of the poor sapskulls carried carven wooden muskets! D'you recall, Morris? Jamie . . . ?"

Morris had dropped off to sleep in his chair. Cranford reached out to shake him.

"Do not!" said Falcon sharply. "He's worn to a shade." Several surprised looks came his way, and he flushed and grunted, "It's as I said."

Cheered by this betrayal of concern, Rossiter said, "In that case, we must pray that we can present our evidence to Whitehall before the League makes its move."

"What about all this damnable wrecking?" asked Glendenning. "Have we learned anything new on that front? Another East Indiaman was sunk last week."

Falcon said disgustedly, "And I fancy they're already claiming the insurance on her cargo, which they stole before she sailed!"

Shaking his head, Cranford muttered, "What a curst devil's trick that is! And never a thought for the innocent lives sacrificed to their greed!"

"We can thank Johnny Armitage that we learned what they're about," said Rossiter. "What we need to know is how and where the thefts take place. Johnny's gathered some sailormen about him and they're haunting the docks here and in Bristol, hoping to uncover some of that skullduggery. Meanwhile, we will investigate each of the areas where we've defeated the League, and determine if they've managed to get their claws on another nearby estate. And we must guard our loved ones lest they be targetted."

Chandler said, "Tall orders, and we're spread dashed thin now, Ross, keeping an eye on the movements of the rogues we know are League members."

Cranford suggested eagerly, "Why not hire more men to follow them? Tummet's rascals seem to have done well thus far."

Rossiter pursed his lips dubiously. "Not in all instances, Perry. Some of the reports brought back by our makeshift spies have turned out to be no more than Canterbury tales invented to account for hours they'd actually spent in the nearest tavern."

"Besides, they cannot always follow where our aristocratic League members go," said Chandler. "They know we're watching, and they're extreme adept at vanishing while attending some crowded social event."

Falcon said thoughtfully, "If we could but discover where they rendezvous."

"We've tried, Lord knows," said Glendenning. "Almost certainly they meet at one of their homes, or country seats."

Rossiter nodded. "They probably begin the evening at some party, as Gordie said, then slip away to their meetings. The pity is that we've never caught 'em at it."

"I seem to recall that there is to be a winter fete at Overlake Park," murmured Falcon. "On the sixteenth, I believe. When is that?"

"Saturday, you caper-wit," said Rossiter. "What of it?"

"I believe I shall attend."

Except for Morris, who was snoring softly, they all stared at him.

Sir Owen broke the stunned silence to ask incredulously, "You've never been invited?"

Falcon's chin tossed upward. He said with quelling hauteur, "Astounding as it may seem to you, Furlong, I am considered socially acceptable by many *ton* hostesses."

Sir Owen flushed. "I—I never meant—"

"He knows what you meant," said Rossiter. "Are you forgetting, August, that Rudi Bracksby owns Overlake Park?"

"Oh, no," said Falcon.

Awed, Cranford observed, "You're mad!"

"Use some sense, man," urged Rossiter. "We know Bracksby is a member of the League. He may very well be one of the six founders."

"And since he's damned sure you're one of us," said Gordon Chandler, "I share Owen's astonishment that you were invited."

Falcon confessed, "Well, I wasn't. Not specifically that is. Actually, I have a sort of—standing invitation." His lips quirked. "Though that is perhaps an—ah, inappropriate adjective." Over the hoots and laughter he went on, "Dear Rudi's widowed sister, Lady Dunscroft, has a *tendre* for me." He grinned in response to another derisive chorus, and added, "And I am very sure her ladyship has no remotest knowledge of the League of Jewelled Men."

"Perhaps not, but Pamela Dunscroft is a tigress!" said Glendenning, half amused, half dismayed.

Not in the least amused, Rossiter said, "No! You'd be walking into the lion's den, you fool."

"Life in the jungle . . ." Falcon's eyes glittered with anticipation. "It should be interesting."

"The male sex is ridiculous!" declared Gwendolyn unequivocally, closing the morning-room door behind her. "Absolutely! I do not know why we—" She checked, then stepped over Apollo and hurried to her friend. "Dearest! Why are you weeping?"

Katrina Falcon stood at the window. She had jerked her head away when Gwendolyn came in, and was dabbing a handkerchief at her eyes. "I—am not." Managing a tremulous smile, she sniffed and added, "Well, not very much."

"One weeps, or one does not weep." Gwendolyn took her hand, led her to the sofa, and sat beside her. "Are you anxious for your Papa? August said Mr. Falcon is quite recovered of his fall."

"Yes. But—oh, who knows what may happen next? This horrid League, and—and all the violence in the streets, and—" The rush of words ceased. Katrina faltered, "How glad I am that your papa allows you to stay with me, Gwen. Of late, I am always . . . so afraid."

"I know." Gwendolyn pressed the cold hand she held. "But your fear is not of the League, I think. We have known about their wickedness for months, and I have never before seen you give way to tears."

Katrina withdrew her hand, and blew her nose daintily. "No. But—but they have never before deliberately attacked my own father."

"Whom you love deeply. I can understand how you must have worried. But I think your fear now is for—someone else you love."

Avoiding her eyes, Katrina mumbled, "Well—well, you know how I adore August."

"And knowing how much he loves you I confess I have often wondered why you so fear him."

"I do not!"

"Then why are you afraid to tell him that you care for Jamie?"

The magnificent eyes that were so like her brother's widened, and Katrina said threadily, "What a thing to say."

"I say it because you are my dear friend. I believe Jamie gave you his heart the first time he saw you. 'Tis an honest and very faithful heart, Trina. If I were so fortunate as to be offered such a wondrous gift, I think—I *know* I would fight tooth and nail 'gainst anyone who tried to make me throw it away."

At this, Katrina burst into tears. Gwendolyn hugged her close and patted her shoulder comfortingly. "You have come to love him," she said gently. "I've seen it this month and more, and I could not be more pleased. Jamie is such a fine man. He may not be as wealthy as some of your other suitors, but—"

"Much I . . . care for that!" sobbed Katrina. "He is the kindest . . . most gentle . . . most br-brave and honourable of . . . of men!"

Gwendolyn drew back, smiling into the woebegone face and marvelling that even with teardrops gemming the long thick lashes, and a pinkish tint to the delicate nose, Katrina was still exquisitely lovely. "Then tell that tyrannical brother of yours that you are of age; that you will no longer allow him to bully you; that your papa likes Jamie; and that Mr. August Falcon is not the head of his house and has no right—"

With a muffled wail, Katrina bowed her head into her hands.

Troubled, Gwendolyn watched in silence until her friend recovered herself, dried her tears, and sat straight again to say in a steadier voice, "August does not bully me and—and he may be a little . . . managing, but he is not a tyrant. 'Tis just . . . Oh, you do not understand!"

"Perchance I might, if you would tell me, but—if I am too pushing—"

"As if you could be such a thing—my sweet Gwen! I know you are only concerned for my happiness. But—'tis hopeless. Quite hopeless. I will not marry to disoblige August. I shall . . . never be able to wed Jamie."

"Oh, pish and posh! If you are afraid of their silly duel, I'd not give it another thought."

"You have never seen my brother fight." Katrina sighed. "I did once. I chanced to overhear the arrangements for a meeting. I was thirteen years old then, and didn't understand what kind of meeting the men were talking about. I was full of curiosity, so I stayed up half the night, took my pony, and followed them."

Gwendolyn loved Katrina dearly, but sometimes thought her rather too conformable and lacking in spirit. Astonished by this glimpse of real intrepidity, she gasped, "You never did! What was it like?"

"It was horrible." Katrina stared into the fire for a moment, saying nothing. Then she went on, "August was only nineteen, but he seemed to delight in taking the most dreadful chances. I was sure he would be killed. I heard the seconds say that the other man was a good fencer and should never have called out a boy who was not yet of age. I suppose he never dreamt he would face a brilliant swordsman. It was so fast, Gwen! So fierce and terrible. Then—" She shuddered. "None of them could believe August had survived. I was so thankful, but . . . I crept away and was sick."

"August told me of it. He didn't mean to kill the poor man, Trina. And you certainly cannot think he would hurt Jamie? However he frets and fumes, I think he has become fond of him."

"But—that makes it worse, do you see? And Jamie teases him so."

Gwendolyn exclaimed angrily, "You wrong August! He dotes on you, and if they ever do fight, which I doubt, he would die sooner than harm a hair of Jamie's head if he thought—" She realized that Katrina was staring at her wonderingly. Her face burned. She said rather feebly, "But—but there is not the need for it to come to that. 'Tis very clear that Jamie would walk through fire for you, so all you've to do is forbid him to fight. Tell August that you *are* going to marry Jamie, and that if he ever threatens him again, you will never talk to him for as long as—"

Katrina swooped to kiss her. "How good you are. And how glad I am that you came back upstairs. I wondered what had become of you. Why were you so angry when you came in? Is Gideon's hurt very painful? They should neither of them have stayed for the meeting."

A door had been closed. There was sadness but resignation in

Katrina's eyes. With an inner sigh, Gwendolyn thought, 'I really had no right to say as much as I did. Well, I tried.' She said simply, "I was listening to their meeting."

"Gwen! How could you?"

Deliberately misinterpreting that shocked exclamation, Gwendolyn explained, "Well, there is that little cupboard in the red parlour, you know, and I was rummaging about in there one day, looking for a slipper Apollo had taken from your aunt. I could hear Mrs. Vanechurch talking to Pearsall, and I was most surprised when I realized they were not in the corridor as I'd supposed, but in the book room. So today I—"

"Went into the parlour cupboard to eavesdrop?"

"Yes, I did. And I know 'twas naughty. But I will tell you, Trina, that if we are not very careful those silly creatures are going to run themselves into a proper bog with this wretched League." She paused, and murmured, "I wonder why it is that little girls grow up, but that men—nice men especially—are always little boys?" She shook her head. "Oh, well, so 'tis, and we must do all that we can to help the poor dears."

Fascinated, Katrina asked, "How? We are ladies. What can we do?"

"Queen Maud was a lady! And so was Boadicea, and—and the Queen of Sheba! *They* managed to get things done, and—"

"But were not Queen Maud and Boadicea put to death?"

"Oh, dear! Were they?" Gwendolyn wrinkled her brow. "You may be in the right of it. But, after all, in those days everybody who was anybody seems to have been put to death, so perhaps 'tis all of a piece. The thing is—we must do *something*, Trina! Before August—"

"And your dear brother and the rest of them," Katrina put in softly.

"What? Oh. Well, of course. You know what I mean."

Katrina nodded, and thought, 'Yes, my dear. I know exactly what you mean.'

Chapter III

og settled down over the City the following day, making of it a hushed, spectral place, slowing traffic, and causing shopkeepers to look glum as business lagged. By evening the vapours were less dense, but it was penetratingly chill, and the fire in the small dining room at Falcon House was banked high.

Gwendolyn was the only guest to join the family for dinner. Mrs. Dudley Falcon was in her usual merry humour and invited both girls to join the card party she was giving later that evening. She was a kind and gregarious lady, and had been the wife of Neville Falcon's younger brother. When she was widowed suddenly by a hunting accident, Neville had installed her in his great house, happy in the belief that he'd provided his daughter with a proper chaperone. He had not. Mrs. Dudley, as she was known, was on the light side of fifty and on the heavy side of plump. She was pretty, amiable, lazy, and dedicated to comfort. Her own. She doted on her niece—and was perfectly willing to play chaperone, so long as it did not interrupt her daily ritual. This consisted of keeping to her bed until noon while enjoying breakfast and her voluminous correspondence; spending an hour or so on her toilette and another on luncheon; sallying forth in mid-afternoon for a drive or shopping, or to visit friends; and returning to rest and change clothes before going out to dine or attend the opera or the play, or some social function. The arrangement suited three of the parties concerned, and although August thought it deplorable and was constantly threatening to engage "a conscientious chaperone" for his sister, he had as yet failed to do so, and the arrangement continued.

This evening Katrina declined her aunt's invitation, on the grounds that she felt as if she might be sickening for a cold, and meant to go early to bed. Mrs. Dudley said indulgently that it was an excellent notion although Katrina never took colds; indeed the entire family was remarkably cold free. She then embarked on a detailed listing of the symptoms of ailments suffered by her wide circle of acquaintances but which had never afflicted herself or her late husband. August listened to this recital with increasing irritation until she paused for breath, whereupon he asked rather brusquely how Miss Gwendolyn meant to pass the evening.

"There are several parties you might enjoy to attend," he said, "and I will gladly escort you, if you wish it. Or—the theatre, perhaps?"

His sister looked at him in dismay, but Gwendolyn thanked him politely and said she had promised to read to Katrina.

"Not precisely scintillating entertainment to offer a guest," he drawled, frowning slightly.

"Ah, but dearest Gwendolyn is not just a guest," said Katrina with a fond smile at her friend. "She seems almost part of the family."

"Yes, indeed," trilled Mrs. Falcon. " 'Faith, but I've become so accustomed to seeing her about the house, I vow I don't know how we should go on without her!"

August slanted a grim look at Gwendolyn but was undone by the laughter in her eyes, and made a smiling gesture of capitulation. Serenely unaware of this by-play his aunt launched into another monologue deploring the fact that they entertained so seldom, and saying she could scarce wait till the repairs to the ballroom were completed so that they could give some lovely parties as they had been used to do. Her guests arrived shortly after dinner, and as soon as manners allowed, Katrina and Gwendolyn said their goodnights and went upstairs.

Falcon had his own plans for the evening, but over Tummet's

protestations, he chose not to summon his carriage and sent a lackey out to call up a chair.

"I wonder you don't 'ave fur nightdresses made fer them nags o'yourn," grumbled Tummet, settling a black cloak lined with scarlet satin onto Falcon's shoulders. "They won't fall down in a swoond if they breathe a bitta fog, mate."

"*You'll* fall in a swoon if you persist in calling me 'mate'! And I see no reason to keep my horses standing about in the damp. A chair will do just as well."

"Yus, it won't! You'd be safer in yer own coach, and you knows it! And if you will persist in going out in this muck, you should oughta wear a proper sword. Not that there overgrowed darning needle!"

"If your man's information is reliable," said Falcon, surveying his tall figure critically in the cheval-glass, "I'll find Lord Hibbard Green polluting The Madrigal. Do you seriously expect me to walk into a gentleman's club sporting a Colichemarde? I wonder you don't advise that I carry my great-grandfather's Andrea Ferrara!"

"Ar, well that were a sword, that were! I'd a sight sooner see you wiv something to defend yerself, Guv. You know the League's arter you. And a perishing flea-troop like this is just what suits 'em!"

"I wonder what I have done," said Falcon bitterly, "that Providence so punishes me. What with the disgusting maxims constantly hurled at my head by Lieutenant Morris, and the rhyming cant I endure from the rascally hedgebird who masquerades as my valet, my life is dismal indeed!"

Dismal? Tummet shot a critical glance at his employer. Falcon did not look in the least dismal. In fact, he thought resentfully, he'd done very nice with his valetting tonight. The Guv looked a bitta orl right. You couldn't ask fer a better fit than that black velvet coat with silver frogging down the front openings and on the great cuffs of the sleeves. Mechlin lace fell gracefully over his long slender hands, and at the throat was enriched by a fiery ruby. The red silk waistcoat was quilted with silver thread. And unlike some valets, he hadn't had to add padded "muscles" to the white satin unmentionables and silver hose; the guv's long legs had an ample supply of the real thing. It had been a joy to shake powder into Falcon's thick black hair, and to arrange it so the ladies woulda bin dropping like flies. He mighta knowed the guv would curl his lip up, and make some unkind remarks about wearing breeches not skirts, so that E. Tummet had been made ('gainst his valetting judgment) to undo the black riband and tie the hair back severe, what had ruined it and and made the guv look even more haughty (which he'd said straight out, and been ignored). They'd also disagreed about the silver patch. Mr. E. Tummet, perfessional valet, had give it as his opinion that the patch should be set below the lips. Needed a bit of softening, did that mouth (as he'd also said). But—no, again! The guv had give him one of them looks what turned folk to chopped giblets, and set the patch in place hisself. High on the right cheekbone he'd stuck it, drawing attention to them foreign eyes, deliberate like.

There was a glint in those eyes now, noting which, Tummet grunted and said, "Sorry ma— er, yer Guv-ship. 'Flea-troop' meaning—"

Falcon raised a silencing hand. " 'Pea soup' or not, I'm off, and— *Now* what're you doing? I *have* a pistol in my pocket! Will you stop fussing? Gad, but you're turning into an old woman! What's that?"

"Letter fer you. Sir," said Tummet, offended. "Lad brung it round."

Falcon broke the seal and stepped closer to the candelabra. The writing was the product of an educated hand, the message brief:

Words of advice to the unwise Mandarin *of Mayfair:*

> *Never sleep, guard your back, and,*
> *like a craven fool—hide.*
> *Few will weep, alas, alack, but*
> *you'll not see this Yule-tide.*

S.

Watching him, Tummet asked, "Bad news, Guv?"
"Just nonsense." Falcon shrugged, folded the letter and thrust

it into his coat pocket. And with an impatient swirl of his cloak and a brisk, "No need to wait up!" he was out of the room and walking along the corridor with his quick, firm tread, leaving his faithful retainer to voice some bitter predictions on the life expectancy of Mr. August N. K. Falcon.

"The N. K.," Tummet advised the bedpost, "stands fer No Kommon-sense! And if common ain't spelled with a 'K,' mate, it should oughta be!"

Despite his airy dismissal of the note, Falcon was alert as he entered the sedan chair and was borne along the chilly streets. The warning was from the Squire, of course. He uttered a terse command that his bearers not sing tonight, as was their practice. His keen eyes searched the shrouded darkness constantly, and twice his hand flashed to the deep pocket of his coat when passers-by loomed uncomfortably close.

They reached the top of the quiet lane off Bond Street without incident, and he paid off his bearers and wandered along on foot, his stride lazily unhurried, but his every nerve tensed for immediate action. It would be interesting to know whether he was the only recipient of the League's threat—and that it was a very real threat, he had no doubt. 'If so, I am honoured,' he thought with a sardonic smile, and, for the moment, relegated the matter to the back of his mind.

If Tummet's spy had not erred, Lord Hibbard Green was at this moment in The Madrigal. A gross and bestial creature was his lordship, last encountered in Cornwall three months since. Green had been up to his fat neck in some very murderous business for the League. He'd come damnably close to destroying Johnny Armitage, and for a while it had seemed they all would—

"Buy a pretty posy fer yer lidy, sir. Only a groat, yer lor'ship. I'll make it thruppence, since ye got such a kind smile, sir."

The pleading whine came from a diminutive flower-girl, who hobbled along beside him, clutching an open box in which a shallow pan of water sustained small bunches of blooms tied with gay ribbons.

Falcon, who was not smiling, said, "What the deuce are you about, woman? You should be up in the theatre district. You'll get poor pickings here!"

"But, if y'please, y'r worship, there's so many flower-sellers over that way. An' I thought some o' you gents might wanta tyke a little present fer yer lidy-loves. Only thruppence. *Please*, sir."

"Good Lord," muttered Falcon, taking out his purse. "Here—here's your groat. Now get along with—"

He checked. The hand that held out the posy was pitifully small; the fingers protruding from the ends of the dirty mittens, blue, and shaking with cold. She seemed very young, and she limped. He was reminded of the Smallest Rossiter, and felt a pang of sympathy. The Smallest Rossiter was by now cuddled under a warm eiderdown in a soft feather-bed, whereas this poor creature . . . He looked at her curiously. Her face was half hidden in the folds of a forest green shawl pulled close about her head. He said, "Let's have a look at you," and reached out to tilt up her chin.

By the hazed light of the flambeaux outside The Madrigal, he viewed a very dirty little face, disfigured by sadly crossed eyes and many spots. Greasy wisps of dark hair hung down over her brow, and her hopeful grin revealed three missing teeth.

'Oh, Gad!' he thought. He took the flowers hurriedly, and walked on. But in spite of her unlovely countenance the poor creature had managed a smile. He turned back.

She was watching, and hobbled to him eagerly. "You want another'n, melor'?"

He asked in a voice that would have astounded his acquaintances, "How old are you, child?"

"Seventeen. I think. If y'please, y'r honour."

"Well, seventeen is too young for a female to be out and alone after dark."

She said staunchly, "Don't you never worry 'bout me, sir. Me fyce ain't never gonna be me fortune, as they say. But—I thanks ye kindly, yer lor'ship."

Falcon's jaw set. So she hadn't yet learned that there were some predatory animals dressing like gentlemen, who'd not give a tinker's damn whether she had a face at all. "Here." He dropped a gold crown into her tray. "Now get along home. And next time you sell your flowers, do it where there are plenty of other people about."

He walked away, leaving the girl staring down at that small

fortune as if frozen with shock. Then, she called, "Oooh . . . sir . . . ! Oooh . . . *thankee*! An' Gawd bless yer lor'ship!"

Not looking back, Falcon waved his posy in farewell. 'Poor little chit,' he thought. 'I wonder what kind of "home" she goes to. Or if she sleeps under some wretched barrow.'

He trod up the steps of the club, and the little flower-girl slipped from his mind as the porter swung open the front door. It was going to be worth something, he thought, to see old Hibbard Green's expression when he confronted the bastard.

The lounge of The Madrigal was a warm and cheery place on this foggy evening. Falcon paused on the threshold and took a quick inventory of those present. A splendid fire blazed on the hearth, and among the members who had succeeded in securing fireside chairs were Mr. Ramsey Talbot and Richard Tyree. Talbot, of ample girth and a rather tired face, was the scion of a noble house and a former Member of Parliament. He was now making a name for himself as a political writer, and despite a reputation for outspokenness he was highly regarded and generally well liked. His favourite niece had married Tyree, an extremely fat young man of middle-class parentage whose quick brain had enabled him to build a comfortable fortune in the maritime world. Talbot's pale and near-sighted eyes peered at Falcon, and he smiled and raised his glass. Bowing in response, Falcon was quite aware that Talbot was inclined to like him, and that Tyree was not. One plus and one minus, he thought carelessly.

In a corner of the room Gilbert Fowles and his cronies were smirking behind their hands. The dandified Fowles was a probably minor member of the League of Jewelled Men, and both hated and feared him. And there, by a potted palm were Colonel Welles, his square face flushed and belligerent as always, and Lord Eckington. The bumptious colonel was a hopeless snob who despised Falcon for his birth. Eckington, however, had a more substantial reason to dislike him.

Falcon chuckled softly, and sauntered across the large room, nosegay in hand, amused by the buzz of excitement that greeted his arrival. As he had expected, the new patch created consternation and several gentlemen sprang up and surrounded him, demanding to inspect his latest contribution to fashion. He answered their questions with cool courtesy and moved on, aware of the less tolerant stares, and of the stifled titters when Sir Delbert Vardy and Mr. Neilsen deliberately turned their aristocratic backs as he approached.

It still stung. Faith, but he wondered sometimes if he was mad to endure it. He'd be much wiser to retire to Ashleigh and live peacefully among his country acres, where he would less often have to face scorn and repudiation. It would be a retreat, of course; a bow to those who would gloat that they had forced him out as they'd forced out his grandfather before him. Be damned if he'd give 'em that satisfaction! And besides, though he loved Ashleigh, he also loved this great city with its theatres and clubs, its teeming thousands, its endless excitements and challenges, even though he knew he would never win the greatest challenge—respect. He thought defiantly, 'I *am* respected, burn it! They respect my fortune, and they fear my sword!' And not even to himself would he admit that his deepest yearning was not to inspire that kind of respect or fear, but to win the same smile that came into mens' eyes when they saw Jamie Morris.

As he progressed towards the stairs Lord Cyril Eckington watched him steadily, his hard brown eyes glittering. A luscious wife had dear Cyril. Falcon met the man's baleful and frustrated glare with the amused lift of one eyebrow. Zounds, but the fool hated him. He'd no one to blame but himself, for had he shown his lovely young spouse a scrap of the attention she deserved, she might not have looked elsewhere for affection. He was said to be a good swordsman. Pity he had not the gumption to declare himself.

Eckington glanced from patch to posy, and temptation was strong. When Falcon was safely past, he said to his friend, "How sweet of the Mandarin to deck himself with flowers for our delectation."

There were some chuckles, but Eckington had underestimated his enemy's sense of hearing.

Turning at once, Falcon looked pleased and wandered to face the now uneasy peer. "So here you are, my lord," he drawled. "And I so lost in thought I almost failed to give you my humble gift." His hand flashed out. Eckington recoiled instinctively, but Falcon only tucked the posy into a thick curl of his lordship's wig and said soothingly, "Do not be frightened. I merely offer a token of my appreciation for . . ." He paused, rubbing his quizzing glass on the bridge of his nose.

The room had become tense and hushed.

Ramsey Talbot wrenched a pencil and pad from his pocket gleefully.

Lord Eckington uttered an inaudible snarl and flushed scarlet. He tore the posy from his wig and clutched it as though nerving himself to throw it in that hated handsome face.

Falcon murmured to no one in particular, "Now whatever have I had from you that rouses me to such appreciation? Be dashed if I can recollect. But—doubtless you will know, my dear fellow."

The peer's hand tightened convulsively on the posy, and his lips writhed back from gritted teeth, but he had once witnessed Falcon's swordplay, and the most he could bring himself to do was to splutter, "One . . . of these days, you'll— I'll—"

"Dear me, such indecision. Until you make up your mind, do pray take care of my gift." Falcon leaned over his lordship's chair and said with a gentle smile, " 'Tis folly to crush tender blossoms, dear Cyril. I wonder your mama never taught you such a simple lesson."

He could all but hear Eckington's teeth grinding as he wandered on amid a flurry of chatter and subdued laughter. He was hailed by a slim young Corinthian named Bertram Crisp, who, besides chancing to be an extremely wealthy marquis, liked to row with the Thames watermen. Falcon knew that Crisp admired him, and he had a grudging liking for the marquis who had once faced him on the field of honour and put up a surprisingly strong defence before being disarmed. Crisp had heard about Andante and was eager to see the stallion, but their conversation was drowned by a slurred roar from behind a group of standing gentlemen who were covertly inspecting Falcon's daring new patch.

"I toldya . . . need ya chair, you stu-stupid block. Get 'way!"

"Green," said the marquis with distaste. "They say he lost heavily upstairs and has been drinking like a sot ever since."

'Aha!' thought Falcon. He stepped aside so as to see the offender, only to utter a snort of exasperation. Tummet's spy had followed *Rafe* Green, instead of his repulsive sire! "Confound it!" he muttered. "I could have gone to the Lancer's rout!"

Lord Hibbard Green's son and heir was sprawled in a chair, his coarse features brooding and flushed, his eyes glassy. Clearly, he was in an ugly temper and by the looks of things had decided to turn it on some hapless fellow seated near him. Who was it? Ah—Reginald Smythe. Poor game, but Green took after his sire and delighted to bully weaklings.

Smythe's voice, thin and trembling, was raised. "Really, s-sir. You already have a chair. I am w-willing to oblige, but I do not see why—"

"Wanta put m'feet up," bellowed Green. And before Smythe could move, he swung up his chunky legs, planted his feet deliberately in the lap of the tall Dandy, and uttered a wheezing snort of laughter. "Y'too slow, by half!"

Smythe seemed to have stopped breathing. The insult was not one any gentleman could overlook, and once again necks were craned and there was a hum of interested comment.

Falcon swung his quizzing glass and watched the little drama thoughtfully. They were two excessively unlikeable men, but despising one, he had a deep and unalterable loathing for the other.

During the first of his unhappy years at Eton, Reginald Smythe had been the ringleader of a group of young bullies who had mocked and derided him mercilessly. Oliver Green, or Rafe as he preferred to be named, had been as vicious but lacked the subtlety of the others, his heavy fist less painful than the sly taunts and name-calling of Smythe and his cronies. It was Smythe who had dealt him the deepest wound he had ever sustained, and who had taken advantage of his own stunned immobility to make good his escape before retribution could be exacted. During the weeks that followed Falcon had tried often to even the score, but always Smythe had either been surrounded by his cronies, or had, as was his habit, spread his poison and run. At last, he'd cornered the toadying sneak, and had attacked, having warned with a boy's implacable hatred, "to the death, you unspeakable cur!" It had come perilously near to being so. Smythe, a year his senior, had proved the adage that even a worm will turn, and had fought with desperate ferocity. He had not, of course, fought fair, resorting to every possible unsportsmanlike kick and gouge, while screaming for help. It had taken two masters to pry Falcon's hands from his throat. Both boys had wound up in the infirmary, and Falcon had been expelled, although when the facts were conveyed to the headmaster by his outraged sire, the expulsion had been revoked. He'd never forgiven Smythe, and in later years had attempted several times to manoeuvre him into a duel, but without success. As slippery as ever, Smythe knew the enormity of his offence, and being sure that Falcon's boyhood challenge still held good, had chosen to be branded a coward sooner than risk almost certain death.

Falcon's thoughts drifted. It was at Eton that he'd first met Gideon Rossiter, who had collected a broken nose and a black eye in coming to his aid when he'd been waging a solitary battle against four "sporting" young aristocrats. He had rejected Gideon's offer of friendship that day, as he'd rejected all such overtures. Who'd have guessed that almost twenty years later they would stand side by side in this far more deadly struggle 'gainst—

"I say, Oliver! Poor fellow. Fell over, did you? Here, I'll help you up." James Morris, looking somewhat battered, but wearing a well-tailored habit of dark gold, and with his sandy hair neatly powdered, was tugging at Green's arm.

Falcon scowled. What the devil was the birdwit about? Morris disliked Green just as much as he did. He excused himself to Crisp and strolled nearer to the trio.

Reginald Smythe was a pallid man with pinched features and large grey eyes that managed always to avoid meeting the gaze of another. They were now fixed however, and Smythe watched Morris as a drowning man might watch the lifeline thrown his way.

Irritated by the use of his abhorred Christian name, Green

hiccuped and uttered a glowering recommendation that Morris keep his damned silly nose in his pocket.

Morris glanced up.

Meeting an angelic smile, Falcon grinned and entered the farce. "Trying to unearth poor Reginald, are you Jamie?" he enquired. "Going about it the wrong way, dear boy. I'll help."

"If you would just . . . get him off me, Morris," muttered Smythe, slanting an uneasy glance at the other half of the rescue party.

"But of course we will, Reggie," drawled Falcon, standing close beside the chair and levelling his glass at Green's large shoes.

"Devil you w-will!" snorted Green, heaving himself upward.

Morris caught his elbow and tugged, throwing him off balance. Simultaneously, Falcon grasped one of the legs Green was lowering from Smythe's lap. It was a large and muscular limb, but Falcon jerked it upward without apparent effort, drawing an alarmed oath from Green as he was sent lurching back. "Here you go, Reggie," said Falcon kindly.

Smythe's efforts to escape, which had redoubled, were thwarted by the weight of Green's other leg across his lap, and the fact that Falcon stood close by. "I cannot unless you move out of the way, damn you!" he hissed.

"Is that gratitude?" asked Falcon, aggrievedly.

Necks were craning, heads turning in their direction. Morris was popular here, and judged to be a gallant soldier and an honourable man. Falcon, whatever else, was acknowledged to be a gentleman. Green had been expelled from Eton for cheating—a stigma he would carry to his grave—and he shared his sire's reputation for shady dealings and unbridled brutality to man and beast. He had been blackballed at White's and several of the leading clubs, and was believed to have bribed his way into The Madrigal.

It was with delight, therefore, that spectators were gathering, while others drawn by the laughter, hurried down from the gaming rooms. More pressed in, and even the most conservative among them, while frowning at such "schoolboy horseplay," stretched their ears so as not to miss anything.

Morris said in a judicial manner, "I don't think we are going about this the right way, August." He tightened his grip on

Green's arm, was sent reeling by a wild swipe, but at once returned to the fray. "I—er, cannot seem to get a purchase," he said, watching that flailing arm in bewilderment.

Laughter rang out unrestrainedly.

"Get a . . . purchase . . ." gasped Bertie Crisp, convulsed. "Oh, begad! Oh, stap me, I can't bear it!"

"I'll . . . *purchase* you . . . !" howled Green, adding a lurid description of Morris' forbears.

Morris blinked. "I say, Falcon," he called. "He wants to purchase me. Whatever for?"

"To teach him manners, probably." Falcon maintained his steely grip on the elevated limb. "Better not haggle over price now, Jamie. We've to get poor Smythe out from under all this—pork."

Green's virulent curses were cut off when Morris stood behind his chair, seized him by the throat, and pulled. Equally obliging, Falcon hoist the captive limb higher.

Rendered helpless, Green looked like nothing so much as a gross and overturned beetle as he flailed his arms about, and the room rocked with hilarity.

Alternately white and livid, Smythe snarled, "Having a jolly time, ain't you Falcon?"

"Wouldn't have missed it for the world, Reggie. Now just be à *l'aise*, dear friend of my youth, and we'll get you out of this yet."

All but sobbing with fury, Green wrenched free of Morris' hold. "Get away, you miserable Chink lover!"

The laughter faded into gasps.

Morris' hand clenched, then was lowered slowly.

"D'ye think we've not all noticed," panted Green, "how you—"

The words were drowned as Falcon took a full tankard from a nearby table and poured the contents deliberately over Green's wig. "You are too heated, by far, my poor insect."

Coughing and spluttering, and unable to free his right leg from Falcon's grip, Green panted, "May you rot in hell, Falcon! You'll meet me for that!"

Morris said, "You never plan to fight this rubbishy person, August?"

"He is not worthy of my steel, I grant you," said Falcon. "However," he looked down at the enraged Smythe, "whatever else, he is at least man enough to challenge."

At this there was a flurry of excitement and Lord Eckington was heard calling for the betting book.

Morris saw a steward trying to push through the titillated throng. "We really must help poor Olly," he murmured, and stepped out from behind Green's chair.

Falcon released the captive limb. Green roared, and kicked out with such force that his chair shot over backwards, spilling the infuriated man heels over head to the floor where he lay sprawled, gulping like a fish out of water.

"Bravo," murmured Falcon. "Clever trick, that."

Smythe seized his opportunity and fled.

The steward reached them and said in agitation, "Really, gentlemen! This sort of conduct is most inappropriate. Mr. Green, allow me to help you up."

Green put a chubby hand under his cheek, curled up, and snored raucously.

Morris tapped the steward on the shoulder. " 'Let sleeping dogs lie,' " he advised solemnly.

Over the laughter, the steward said indignantly, "But we cannot leave him lying in the middle of the floor!"

"Move him to the side, then," advised Falcon. "But you must look for volunteers elsewhere. I am not in the business of rubbish hauling. Besides, I now have another matter to attend to."

Morris volunteered, "Be glad to second you, August."

"Thank you, but it won't serve. You're going to meet me next."

"So I am. Forgot. Well, you'll find someone else."

Bertie Crisp waved, and hurried over to the betting book, calling, "I'll act for you, Falcon."

"And I." That noted sportsman Hector Kadenworthy was pushing through the crowd on the stairs, his rather saturnine features wreathed in a rare grin.

"Thank you, your lordship," said Falcon, with a magnificent bow. "I stand in your debt."

"You do." Kadenworthy nodded. "That'll make the third—and *last* time."

" 'Faith, but your generosity is positively dizzying. The ground shakes 'neath my feet. Or is that Green snoring?"

Laughing, Kadenworthy took him by the arm. "Come upstairs, you rascal. I'll give you a chance to beat me at hazard." He glanced at Morris. "That's a damned ugly bruise on your noggin, Jamie. Are you up to joining us at the tables?"

Morris refused the offer, explaining that he wanted to see them get "dear Olly" on his feet.

"When he's sufficiently sober," said Kadenworthy, "tell him to send his seconds to call on me."

Morris nodded, and the two men left him and went upstairs, a renewed outbreak of comment and laughter following them.

Falcon liked very few men, but he was drawn to this laconic peer, whose tongue was almost as sharp as his own. If ever he should decide to gather a few friends about him, Bertie Crisp and Hector Kadenworthy, he thought, might just qualify to enter that select circle.

You are freezing!" Katrina wrapped a blanket about Gwendolyn's shoulders and set a steaming mug of chocolate on the dressing table in her bedchamber. Sitting on the bench beside her friend she watched her convulsive shivering, and moaned, "I thought you would never get back! I have been beside myself with anxiety! I should not have allowed you to take such risks!"

Gwendolyn scanned her reflection in the mirror. "I'm sorry you worried so." She crossed her eyes, smiled broadly, and added, "But—oh, I do look deliciously dreadful, you must admit."

Katrina's laugh was a trifle shrill. "You look a sight, you mean! That horrid wig! And—you'd best take that hideous stuff from your teeth before you drink your chocolate!"

"Yes, indeed!" Gwendolyn peeled the dark wax away, revealing her "missing" teeth, then sipped the chocolate gratefully. "But 'twas my idea, not yours, Trina. Besides, I think there was really little risk. Most of the establishments in the area have flambeaux lighted."

"Yes, but 'twas night. And foggy!"

"Not sufficiently so to conceal my ravishing complexion."

· 63 ·

Gwendolyn removed the black wig with care and handed it to Katrina, then began to spread cucumber cream over her unfortunate face. "My very ugliness was my protection, do you see? Even my brother was repulsed when he 'finished' me."

"So I should think!" Arranging the wig on a stand, Katrina said, "Though had Newby guessed you meant to take such risks instead of going to a masquerade party—"

"He'd likely have thought it great fun, and insisted upon accompanying me!"

Katrina did not admire Newby Rossiter, and she said dryly, "I think Gideon would not have shared that view."

"Heavens, no! He'd have straitly forbidden it. They are alike in face and form, my twin brothers, but they are very different men. And though I fibbed, Trina, 'twas a fib committed in a good cause. Newby was pleased to give me what I would need, and show me how to do it all. He is very good at theatricals, you know. When he was at school he was marvellous as Othello."

"Perhaps so, but if Gideon should find out what you are about, I think he would do more than 'mourn a mischief that is past and gone'!"

Gwendolyn chuckled. "Clever one! That is a quote from the Bard, I collect. Though I do not count my spying as having been a mischief."

"No. Far worse! A horribly dangerous risk for a lady to run. And—for what? We learned nothing!"

Gwendolyn put down the rag she had used to remove her "spots," and turned to her friend. The dark blue eyes were wide and strained, and the cheeks pale. "Poor dear," she said, patting Katrina's hand comfortingly. " 'Twas worse for you, having to wait here. But this was only the first time. We cannot expect to be lucky right away."

"I know, I know. I suppose I would feel better could I take my turn at watching. But my foolish eyes would betray me at once," Katrina said wistfully. "Which is just as well, for I am not brave, like you, and would be much too afraid to be out alone at night, much less daring to address strange gentlemen, and beg them to buy the nosegays."

"You must not name such a great gift 'foolish,' for God has

given you very lovely eyes. And how could I manage without you arranging for the chair and helping me to slip out by the back stairs, and pretend I was gone to bed?" Gwendolyn squeezed her hand and said thoughtfully, "Besides, I did learn something. Though whether 'tis important or not, I don't know."

Katrina asked eagerly, "Tell me! No—do not. Begin at the beginning. Did you sell any posies? Did the gentlemen question your speech?"

"I spoke just as we rehearsed, and I think no one suspected. And I did sell some posies, though I was like to swooning when August came and—"

Katrina gave a hurriedly smothered shriek. "*August?* Oh, my heavens! Did he see you?"

"Oh, yes." Gwendolyn was warmer now, and she removed the blanket from her shoulders. "He tugged my chin up and looked at me." She giggled at the memory. "You should only have seen how quickly he drew back."

Awed, Katrina half-whispered, "You must have been terrified!"

"Well, I was rather frightened for a minute. But as you said, it was dark and foggy, and how should he suspect the poor little flower-girl was me?" She smiled faintly. "He bought one of my nosegays."

"He never did! You're teasing!"

"No. I swear it. In fact, he gave me that guinea."

Katrina frowned at the coin that lay on the dressing table. "The wicked rogue!"

"No. That was not his thought."

"It wasn't?" Katrina scanned the rather pensive smile curiously. "Then—whatever did he say?"

For a moment Gwendolyn did not answer. Then she said, "He was rather amazingly kind. He told me to go home." She took up the coin. " 'Twas a side of Mr. August Falcon I've not seen before."

"You'll see another side if ever he learns of this! And so will I. Lud, but I dare not think of it! Did anyone else buy posies?"

"Yes. An older gentleman I did not know. And one other." She frowned. "He was drunk I think, and rather horrid. But luckily, my chairmen came around the corner just then, and I ran and he went reeling off."

"Oh! *What* an adventure! Did you see any rioters?"

Gwendolyn shook her head, and drew a little silver-chased pistol from the pocket of her ragged skirt. "But I was prepared."

Staring at the weapon, Katrina shivered. "Do you really think you would be able to use it? I am very sure I could not pull the trigger."

"I think if I just brandished it about, I'd not have to shoot. Gentlemen are always terrified to see a pistol in the hand of a female."

"Yes, but you might not be faced by a gentleman. Some of the rioters I've seen look more like savages."

"Well . . . in that event, I suppose I might really have to use the horrid thing."

Awed by such resolution, Katrina said, "Tell me what it is that you learned."

"Well, you know that they suspect Gilbert Fowles of being a member of the League?"

"Yes. Such a silly creature, too. Was he there?"

"He left soon after your brother arrived. And do you know, Trina, I thought it rather odd. No one seemed to be following August. But when Mr. Fowles left, I distinctly saw a man come out of the fog and slink after *him*."

They looked at each other uncertainly.

Katrina said, "It might have been one of Tummet's spies, I suppose. Or perhaps a pick-pocket. Or even some ruffian Mr. Fowles had hired as a guard, with the streets so unsafe as they are."

"Hmm. Somehow, he didn't look like a pick-pocket. And if he was a guard I cannot think he would have ducked into a doorway when Mr. Fowles glanced back, as he did once."

"That does sound odd. Do you think he was supposed to follow my brother and made a mistake?"

"Good gracious, no! Anyone who could mistake that scrawny Gilbert Fowles for August would have to be half blind! He has no grace when he walks, and the set of his shoulders is a far cry from—" Gwendolyn checked abruptly, then said, "I think I must tell Tummet about it."

Katrina's eyes opened wide. "How ever can you do that? He would be as horrified as my brother to know what you are about, and would tell him at once!"

"Oh dear, I suppose that is true. But if we ever *do* learn anything important, we shall have to pass the information along somehow. Gracious! I had not stopped to think of that. How very tiresome it is that the gentlemen are so selfish and always want to keep their adventures to themselves!"

CHAPTER IV

t was peaceful in the book room on this unseasonably bright morning, and Gwendolyn hummed to herself as she perched on the ladder, riffling through the pages of a slim volume. She heard a familiar and loved voice, and glanced up, disquieted by the brusque tone.

"Yes, indeed, Pearsall. A relief to be rid of rain and fog for a change. I must see Mr. August at once . . . No, do not announce me, I'll go straight up."

There came the polite murmur of the butler's voice, then a shadow crossed the open door. "Gideon!" called Gwendolyn, setting her book atop the other volumes on the shelf.

Her brother's tall figure was briefly silhouetted against the pale sunlight that flooded through the dining room windows across the corridor, then he came striding in, smiling, and reaching up to lift her down.

"Cheerful sparrow!" he exclaimed, swinging her around and giving her a smacking kiss. "You're early abroad, and in search of knowledge, I see."

She clung to his arm, looking up lovingly into the face of this brother who was closest to her heart. "I wanted a book. And if August sees me in here he takes it for granted I am preparing to tease him about China again."

His laugh was a trifle forced. "And are you, scamp? You really should not, you know. 'Tis not as if he was family, and he has enough to bear on that suit."

"Most of which he brings on himself by being so impossibly proud and— Oh, never mind." She sat on the sofa. "Will you reach down the book for me, please, love? 'Tis so good to see you. Did Papa send you to fetch me home?"

"No. He's off to the shipyards." He retrieved her book and glanced at it curiously as he wandered over to sit beside her. "Cornwall? Has Falcon been telling you of his exploits out there? Or has Mrs. Armitage piqued your interest in her birthplace?"

"I've only met Jennifer Armitage twice. She is the sweetest creature. Jonathan must be very happy to have won her. As for August, he is close-mouthed as any oyster, and says only that the wind blew most of the hair from his head, and that Johnny almost got him killed, and that 'twas a great bore, except for when Johnny sailed an ark down the face of a sheer cliff!" She asked an amused, "Is there any least vestige of truth in it, Gideon?"

"Oh, yes. Though not quite in the way Falcon would tell it. 'Tis a long story, Gwen, but from what I hear, he did jolly well— for such a confirmed cynic. In fact "—he glanced to the open door and lowered his voice—"don't tell him I told you, but he saved Jamie's life."

Her voice squeaked with pleased surprise. "*August* did?"

Rossiter nodded. "Morris told me that he'd have been knifed in the back had not Falcon pushed him aside and dashed near taken the blade himself." His lips tightened. "As you may guess, Falcon says the only reason he did it was to make sure Jamie keeps alive long enough for their much delayed duel."

"You never believe that?"

He said thoughtfully, "Is hard to guess what goes on in his head. He's a law unto himself, in many ways. Each time I think I know him a little better, he does or says something outrageous, and I am all at sea again."

"Yes, I know. But one cannot judge by what he says. Only by what he does. And—you do like him a little, Gideon?"

She was looking at him anxiously. He felt a stirring of unease. Falcon was such a damnably handsome fellow, but none of the ladies who had been so unwise as to give their hearts to him had for very long held his affection, and two were said to have gone into a most serious decline. He gave himself a mental shake. Falcon's conquests were without fail poised and dashing beauties, either married or widowed. The single maidens of Quality who had fallen under his spell had done so with small encouragement from him, and he likely viewed dear little Gwen only as his sister's rather irritating friend. Besides, Gwen herself had often said she'd no least interest in a romantical attachment. Poor mite.

Reassured, he smiled and answered, "Cautiously—yes, I have come to like him. Mayhap his loyalty to us has lasted only because he loves the excitement and danger of the game. At times his arrogance and cynicism make me yearn to strangle him. But he is high couraged and loyal, and has served us well, and I cannot but be grateful for that. Here." He passed the book to her. "I fancy this will tell you about the weather and some of the history of Cornwall. 'Tis a wild coast, I've heard."

"Yes." She looked at the book rather blankly, then said, "I was more interested in the people. They say many of the old superstitions still flourish down there. Do you know aught of them, Gideon?"

"Very little. Tio does, though. He has quite an interest in that sort of mumbo-jumbo. If you really want to know about it, you should probably talk to Jennifer Armitage when Johnny next brings her to Town. Now tell me about yourself." He touched her cheek. "You look a trifle wan. Too many late nights, naughty girl? Perhaps I *should* take you home!"

"Foolish boy. You know I seldom go to *ton* parties. Must I come home? Mrs. Dudley chaperones us, you know." He grunted and looked dubious, and she went on quickly, "Katrina is very kind and presses me to stay here. She misses Naomi, I think, since you bewitched her into marrying you. And how thoughtless I am! How is my new sister?"

His grey eyes brightened. "Much better, thank goodness, and able to eat breakfast! I'd hoped to move her to Emerald Farm, but—Well, the fire put an end to that, for now, at least. Still, I mean to get her out of London after you become an aunt, m'dear."

She said with real enthusiasm, "I can hardly wait!"

They both stood, and, hugging her, he said fondly, "Don't stay away too long, little Gwen. We miss you."

"And I you, dearest. Why are you cross?"

He was seething, but said blandly, "I had thought I was at my charming best. Alas, there is no pleasing—"

"There is no hoaxing me where you are concerned. You are properly into the boughs. Pray do not call him out for whatever he has done!"

He looked searchingly into her sweet face. "Would it distress you if I did, Gwen?"

"You know it would," she said pertly, but with an odd twist of the heart. "I value my brother."

"Oho! So you fancy me no match for him, do you? A fine family loyalty!"

Abruptly grave, she said, "You are more than a match for August Falcon on every suit but one, Gideon. If rumour speaks truly, he is one of the finest swordsmen in England. And you, my dearest, have a beautiful lady and a new little life to live for."

"And one or two other people I chance to care about," he said, laughingly. "But never fret, I've no intention to challenge the mighty warrior."

"Good," said Gwendolyn, walking to the door with him. "Then be so kind as to detain him for as long as you can."

He turned back, eyebrows raised. "Why? Gwen? I know that pixie look! What—" And with sudden suspicion, "Where is Katrina?"

"At the moment? I have no notion." She added with a twinkle, "Save that she is out riding. With Jamie."

"Lord save us all," muttered Gideon, and went up the stairs.

Tummet was gathering up newspapers in Falcon's private parlour, and when he saw Rossiter walk in, he said with a grin, " 'Morning, yer Guv-ship! I was just—er . . ." He knew that set to the firm jaw, and left the sentence unfinished.

Rossiter smiled, but jerked his head to the door, and Tummet said under his breath, "What a fright! Goodnight!" and took himself off.

Still wearing a dressing gown of quilted purple satin, Falcon sat at the mahogany desk in his great bedchamber, busily engaged in cleaning a fine holster pistol. He set the gun down and stood, smiling a welcome. "Just the man I need."

"What the devil d'you think you're doing?" demanded Rossiter, his voice clipped and angry.

Falcon's chin lifted and his eyes became bleak. He leaned back against the desk and folded his arms. "Is your eyesight failing? My occupation, I would think perfectly obvious."

"And your memory abominably short." Rossiter stamped to a chair and straddled it, glaring at Falcon over the back. "You gave me your word, August!"

"Ah," said Falcon softly. "So you heard."

"I heard you went to The Madrigal last evening in search of a quarrel—"

"As is my wont? I feel sure that was added to the recital of my sins."

"—And that having failed to provoke Eckington into fighting you—"

"Well, but he is a dreadfully cautious fellow, you know."

"—you made such a fool of Rafe Green, although you must have seen he was well over the oar, that he had no choice but to call you out!"

"There is no justice," sighed Falcon. "You say nought of how gallantly I rescued poor dear Reggie Smythe."

"I know damned well you'd not lift a finger to rescue him! You loathe the reptile."

"An apt description." Laughing, Falcon threw up one hand, "No, Gideon. Do not rant. I gave you my word not to fight *Morris*; at least, till our struggle with the League is won."

"I'd not realized," said Rossiter bitterly, "that gave you *carte blanche* to annihilate the rest of the human race."

"But my dear fellow, Rafe Green is not of the human race."

"Damn you, August! You know how much we need you! This is no time to be calling out everyone who annoys you."

Inspecting his fingernails, Falcon murmured, "I presume your informant was Morris. Did he also tell you what Green said?"

"I've not seen Morris today. Kadenworthy told me that Green insulted your sister, but—"

Falcon's dark head jerked up. He snapped, "Had he done so, I'd have had his heart out there and then! Green uttered a crude remark about—" His eyes widened. He said in a half-whisper, "*Sacrebleu!* I never thought—"

Watching him uneasily, Rossiter saw one long hand clench hard. "My apologies an I misunderstood."

"You did." Falcon took a steadying breath, but he had paled. "And I shall have a talk with Kadenworthy. He should know better than to bandy Katrina's name about!"

"Oh, burn it! Kade meant no harm. He was trying to explain your crazy antics at The Madrigal. Nothing more, I promise you!" Falcon turned his head and looked straight at him and Rossiter was shocked by the glare in those deep eyes. "Good God, August! Green is a boor but—he was drunk, man! If you kill him you'll have to leave the country for six months, and—"

"But I have your permission to kill him at a more—ah, opportune time. Is that it?"

"No, blast you!"

"And I suppose had some great filthy oaf made a disparaging remark about Miss Gwendolyn in a gentlemans' club, you'd smile and kiss his foot? Hah! I wish I may see it!"

Rossiter frowned. "In that event, of course— But perchance Kade misinterpreted—"

"No. I think I am the one to have done so. Which will be dealt with." Falcon laughed suddenly. "Now, do stop behaving as if I were a lowly private and you a major-general! I'll honour my word about that blockhead, Morris. More I'll not—and never have—promised." He reached back and took up a grubby and wrinkled sheet of paper. "I'm glad you came, even though so dictatorially. See what you make of this."

Struggling with the crude printing, Rossiter read slowly: "*Sum one follered Mr. Fowls lars nite. No one follered Mr. Falkon. Jos. L. (reporting As paid fer.)*" Puzzled, he asked, "This Jos. L. is one of Tummet's people?"

"No." Falcon went back to his chair and the business of cleaning his pistol. "It seems that a shabby fellow gave it to the gardener's boy and claimed to have been hired by Bowers-Malden to keep an eye on 'Some Gents,' and report anything interesting. Sounds a bit havey-cavey, don't you think? Why not report to you?"

"Perhaps he was given several names and simply came to whomever chanced to be nearest. Certainly, my father and the earl have their spies out. Though they are concentrating on the shipping end of this ugly business."

"I doubt this report is of any significance." Falcon tilted the graceful pistol to the light and inspected the barrel. "Gil Fowles is a nasty insect and a member of the League, certainly. But I'd be surprised if he's one of the six leaders."

Rossiter muttered, "So should I, but I wonder . . ."

After a brief pause, Falcon glanced at him and prompted, "Well? Well? Wonder—what?"

"Cast your mind back a few weeks," said Rossiter, "to when you and Cranford and Morris were in Yerville Hall and had spoiled the scheme of Lady Julia Yerville and—"

"And that dragon of Society, my erstwhile devoted admirer, Lady Clara Buttershaw."

"Erstwhile!" enquired Rossiter.

Falcon grinned. "Considerably erstwhile. As you said, we spoiled their traitorous scheme. But I think we stray from the point."

"Not far. We know that the League has formed an alliance with some powerful French interests. During your—er, retreat from the Yerville house—"

"Retreat be damned! We had to blasted well fight our way out!"

"During which scuffle, Fowles learned of the French alliance. I think you said he was not enthusiastic."

"I said nothing so milky! What I said was that Fowles practically turned inside out!"

"From which one gathers he had no previous knowledge of the French involvement."

Falcon shrugged and looked bored. "I see nothing odd in that. He's scarcely the type to have risen to eminence in their ugly club. Perchance he's a relatively new member and they've not seen fit to familiarize him with their schemes."

"Yes, but what if they've familiarized *none* of the rank and file with this particular scheme? What if most of the men they've recruited joined believing the League meant to follow a certain course of action, and—"

"And now their trusted leaders have gone off at a tangent, and entered into a secret agreement with France?" Falcon whistled softly. "They'd be on very tricky ground indeed! You may be sure Fowles has been ordered to keep his mouth shut. Jupiter! I'd not care to be in his shoes!"

"Nor I. If we've guessed rightly and Fowles suspects that he's into something more than he'd bargained for, he may be very frightened, and with good cause. The League takes no chances. If they decide he knows too much and cannot be relied on to hold his tongue . . ." Rossiter drew a finger across his throat.

Falcon grinned. "One less, eh? Jupiter! I wish we could spread the word!" His eyes glinted, "We should, Gideon! Be dashed if I don't go to the *Spectator* this afternoon and take out an advertisement! That'll have the Squire chewing his teeth!"

Rossiter liked Falcon in this schoolboy mood. "I wish you well," he said smilingly. "Thus far, every time we try for a mention in the newspapers they say we are 'revolutionaries' or trying to embarrass the Horse Guards, or some such rubbish." He took the pistol and examined it. "This is a jolly fine piece. Do you carry it in your coach?"

"Carry a pair. Matter of fact, I mean to try some targets. Care to join me?"

"Where? I'm a trifle short on time."

"Here. We'll have Tummet load and—"

"*Here?* You mean—in the garden?"

Falcon put up his brows. "Did you fancy I'd meant to practice in the ballroom?"

"But—you madman! You cannot fire off pistols in the heart of London!"

"Why not? 'Tis my own house and—"

"And you'd have the Watch here in two shakes of a lamb's tail!"

"Do not, Gideon!" Falcon shuddered. "You sound like Morris!"

Although London basked under pale sunshine, and the air lacked the penetrating chill of the past several days, there were few riders in Hyde Park at this early hour, and Lieutenant James Morris dared to guide his fiery chestnut thoroughbred closer to Katrina Falcon's dainty black mare. "Go—*away?*" he echoed, peering in horror at the lady he worshipped. "But—but—where? I—I mean . . . *why?*"

A vision in a pearl grey riding habit and a grey hat with a scarlet feather flaming against her black hair, Katrina stretched out a gloved hand to him. "Anywhere." She sighed unhappily. "So long as 'tis far from me."

To his chagrin, the handsome and flighty Windsong decided to be frightened by Katrina's glove and danced back the way they had come.

Morris applied a firmer hand than usual, and upon hearing a few facts about his probable future, Windsong pretended to be meek and did as he was told.

The sadness in his love's eyes had not diminished during this brief diversion, and, troubled, Morris led the way to a secluded area behind a clump of silver birches, and reached over to draw her mare to a halt.

"You may believe I know I'm not worthy of you, dearest girl," he said, trying to see her hurriedly averted face. "If you—I mean, I'll not be surprised if you've found—er, someone more—er, up to the mark, as 'twere. Is—er, is that what you're trying to tell me?"

He waited, scarcely daring to breathe, through the longest pause in the world.

"Yes," said Katrina at last, but her voice shook betrayingly.

Encouraged, Morris made a cavalryman's easy dismount and went around to lift her down. He did not at once release her, but gazing lovingly at the feather of her hat, said, "I think you are fibbing. Just a ladylike fib, you know." Receiving only a smothered sob by way of response, he turned her cheek and, greatly daring, planted a kiss on that smooth warmth. "There!" he said flushed and triumphant. "Now we're betrothed! 'Tis of no use to try to send me away, beloved. You're too much of a lady to have let me do that unless you—er, cared for me." Still she turned her head from him, and, doubt returning, he said humbly, "Just a—er, tiny bit would be enough for me to be going on with, Katrina."

"Oh . . . Jamie . . . !" she wailed, melting into his arms. "You are so very dear!"

"God be thanked!" he whispered, holding her close to his thundering heart. "When may I approach your father? When may I tell my parents?" It didn't seem possible that he had the right to ask this, and he stammered nervously, "When—when will you m-marry me, most beautiful lady in all the world?"

"Oh . . . *Jamie* . . . !"

"Yes." He smiled fondly. "You said that already, love. And if you're worried about that silly duel, pray do not refine on it. When I tell August you've agreed to become Mrs. James Morris—"

She pushed him away and said almost fiercely, "No! Don't you see? You cannot!"

"But—but if you are so kind as to have become a little fond of me—"

Before he could stop her she had seized his gauntletted hand and kissed it. "I am not 'a little fond' of you, my dear, gentle, kind soldier," she said over his horrified protests at such a waste. "I love you! I always will love you! And—I shall never marry you, Jamie. Never!"

"But—but, my love, he will—"

"He will not. Ever. And—"

"That is stupid!" He took her hands and held them strongly, and said with rare eloquence, "Oh, I know there are very many gentlemen who adore you, and who could offer you so much more than I. I know I have no title, nor a great fortune to lay before you, but—"

"Do you think that would stop me? Oh, my dear, if only that were all!"

Some riders were approaching. He restored her to the saddle and, after a short tussle with Windsong, mounted up again.

His heart, that had been so exultant a few minutes ago, was thrown into despair when he noted the resolute tilt to Katrina's chin. He said, "I know what it is. You think August will say I'm a gazetted fortune hunter. But I'm not, my dear! I will gladly sign a statement relinquishing any claim on—"

" 'Twould make no difference. He knows you're no fortune hunter."

Grasping at straws, he asked, "Dearest, did you care for—for any of the gentlemen who fought him when he rejected their offers?"

She shook her head.

"Then I don't understand. Unless—if 'tis because my father's cousin—I mean, Lord Kenneth Morris *is* the head of my family, and to our shame seems to be involved with this wretched League, but—"

"It is," she interrupted sadly, "that I have been unforgiveably selfish and unkind. I am so sorry. I knew 'twas hopeless. I should have sent you away long ago, only . . . only—" Her voice broke. She turned from him, one hand brushing at her tears. "I am weak and . . . I could not . . . bear to."

"I think I'd not mind it so much," he said miserably, "if you found me repulsive."

"Oh . . . Jamie! As if I could!"

He frowned. "Then you do love me. And you would be my wife, if it weren't for that pepper-pot brother of yours!"

Startled by the unaccustomedly harsh tone, she said nervously, "Y-yes, but—"

"Then I will *not* go away, ma'am," he declared. "I'm not a clever one, but I can tell that you bid me go with your lips, while your eyes say 'please stay.' I will tell Lord Haughty-Snort that I mean to pay my addresses, and—"

"No! Oh, you must—"

"Exactly! I must! And I will go down to Ashleigh and ask your father for your hand. Whether August likes it or not! And—and be dashed to the silly fellow!"

Agitated, she seized his arm. "No! Jamie, no! Even if Papa should give us his blessing—and I am sure he would, for he likes you—I will never marry 'gainst August's wishes! He loves me, and I love him! I could not marry to disoblige him, and—and be cut off from him for the rest of my life! I just . . . *couldn't!*"

"But—he don't approve of *anyone*, dearest!"

"Well," she gulped, "perhaps . . . someday . . . If only . . . Oh—Jamie!"

He took her outstretched hand and, holding it, muttered helplessly, "Deuce take me, what a pickle!"

They rode at a walk, hand in hand, silent, seeing nothing of the sparkle of sunlight on wet leaves and grasses, hearing nothing of the exuberance of the busy sparrows, both lost in contemplation of their apparently insurmountable problems. But it was impossible for Morris to be downcast for long, and after a few minutes he said, brightening, "Well, now at last I know you care for me, my dearest! Which is of itself a great miracle. And I know I shall never love another lady. So I shall just have to try and force August to like me." He paused, then added, "I wish he did like me, you know. Just a little, perhaps."

She blinked, and asked, "Why?"

"Oh, I don't know." He said shyly, "I suppose—I mean—Well, the silly fellow has enough pride for a hundred, and he's as hot at hand as a Tartar with the toothache. But—I think he's . . . rather splendid."

The tears brimmed over. She said, "Oh, Jamie! I do love you so!"

Gwendolyn had not seen Gideon leave, but when she encountered Tummet in the morning room he told her "Cap'n Rossiter" had gone, but that his "temp'ry guv" was still at home.

"Oh, dear," she said.

"Right, mate. I mean—miss!" With one of his horrendous winks the valet said, "Best if they come back fly-an'-spoon, if you was to ask me," and hurried off in response to a distant shout.

Gwendolyn went down the stairs and peered out of the breakfast room windows. A greengrocer's cart came rattling around the corner, and two youthful gentlemen astride horses that appeared no more than half broken to the bridle made their erratic way as often along the flagway as on the road, but there was no sign of the pair she hoped to see. She thought absently, ' "Fly-and-spoon . . ."? I suppose it means something and soon, but—'

The blast of a shot drove every vestige of colour from her cheeks and set her heart leaping frantically. She hurried into the corridor. A shriek from above-stairs undoubtedly emanated from Mrs. Dudley's bedchamber; a pale-faced lackey was hurrying down the stairs, and there came a babble of alarmed cries from the direction of the kitchen. All this Gwendolyn noted as she limped to the dining room, her heart in her mouth and the small pistol in her hand.

Another shot blasted at her ears as she crossed the terrace and went down the steps towards the summer-house. Trembling with the terror that she would at any second come upon August's lifeless body, she rushed inside and stopped abruptly.

He had discarded coat and waistcoat, and stood on the far side of the little house. He held a long pistol steady, and was taking aim at a row of bottles balanced on a plank between two upturned barrels. Tummet sat on the steps, loading another pistol.

Gwendolyn's almost overwhelming relief at once became fury. "Ooh!" she cried.

Falcon, who had not heard her impetuous approach, fired and wiped out the centre of Mrs. Dudley's favourite rose bush. "Oh, hell and damnation!" he howled, throwing down the pistol and clutching at his hair.

"Are you gone *quite* demented?" demanded Gwendolyn, confronting him.

"Very likely," he snarled. "Why the *deuce* must you come creeping—"

"Never mind about that! Do you know that you frightened me—everyone—to death? You cannot fire off that horrid thing in the middle of London Town!"

"Indeed?" His lips curled back in a savage grin. "Watch!" He stretched out an imperious hand. "Tummet!"

"Ain't no use waving yer famble at me, Guv. It takes more'n two seconds to load this 'ere deadly wepping. 'Sides, Miss Gwen's right. You'll 'ave the Watch dahn on us, 'fore you can shrink-and-cry—"

"Blink an eye!" translated Gwendolyn, lapsing.

Tummet leered at her.

"I know what it means," said Falcon. "And when I want your opinion, Tummet— Hey! What're you doing with that?"

Gwendolyn glanced down. She'd quite forgotten she held her little pistol. "It's mine. Now do you see how you scared me?"

A smile awoke little blue gleams in his eyes. "Rushing to my rescue, were you?"

"No, I was not!" she lied, feeling her cheeks burn. "I—I thought Katrina was being kidnapped!" Up went his horrid eyebrow in that beastly way that conveyed so much mockery, and she said hotly, "Had I thought you were out here playing—"

"Playing! I'll show you— Here, give me that little pop!"

"I will do no such thing!" she cried, whipping the pistol behind her.

"Why not? You don't know how to fire the foolish article, and even if you did, the ball wouldn't come within a mile of what you aimed at!"

"Is that a fact?" She flung up her arm so swiftly that Falcon gave a shout and jumped clear in the nick of time. Her shot went straight and true and a bottle exploded in fragments.

"Gwendolyn . . . *Rossiter!*" shrieked Mrs. Dudley Falcon, her voluminous Passionata Blush silk negligee billowing as she panted her agitated way through the summer-house.

"Has everyone in this house gone stark raving daft?" trumpeted the Dowager Lady Mount-Durward, marching in from the side gate followed by her footman, a gardener, a groom, and two interested urchins.

"Oh, my *heavens!*" moaned Gwendolyn, red-faced and red-handed.

August Falcon leaned on Tummet and laughed hilariously, without—as he was later informed—a shred of conscience.

Y ou did nothing!" accused Gwendolyn, reining her polite dapple grey to a walk as they approached the gardens of Bloomsbury Square.

Mounted on his fiery black, Andante, Falcon said blandly, "Absolute truth. *You* on the other hand, were fairly caught in the act." He chuckled. "Gad, if ever I saw poor Lady Mount-Durward so shocked!"

"I was the one to be shocked! She snorted at me like—like a bull!"

"How harsh! And to speak so of an elderly lady . . . !" He clicked his tongue.

"Oh dear. You are quite right, of course. That was very bad." Her eyes kindled. "But—she did!"

"Yes," he agreed, laughing. "She's a terror. Which is why I walked home with the lady before submitting to your demand that I carry you out of retribution's way."

Turning to him eagerly, Gwendolyn said, "Were you able to redeem me in her eyes? Gideon will surely take me home if he learns of my shocking behaviour."

"No he won't. I used my considerable charm to calm the outraged dowager, and you are forgiven. Come, let me lift you down." He hailed a hovering boy and sent him off to walk the horses for ten minutes or so and they went into the gardens.

In spite of the early hour the unexpected sunshine had lured several people here. A nursemaid was walking with a pretty rosy-cheeked small girl who pushed a little cart, and two elderly gentlemen strolled side by side, embroiled in a heated discussion.

Taking the arm Falcon offered, Gwendolyn limped along the footpath amid flowerbeds empty of bloom now, save for some chrysanthemums that were beginning to look scrawny.

"Were you really able to placate Lady Mount-Durward?" she persisted doubtfully.

"But, of course. Did you think me incapable of bringing such as her ladyship around my thumb?"

She frowned. "I should have remembered how you charmed poor Lady Clara Buttershaw."

"That female dragon? *Poor?* Good God!"

"Yes, I know she is very dreadful, and that she and her sister are involved with the League. But—I believe she really cared for you, and you just laughed at her."

"I did no such thing!" He grinned unrepentantly. "Not openly, at least."

"No, but behind her back—"

His eyes narrowed, and his voice was ice when he snapped, "I do not make fun of people behind their backs, Miss Rossiter! London is already overburdened with mean-souled sneer artists! I neither like nor admire Lady Clara Buttershaw. She is a selfish bullying harridan, but—"

"Well, if that is not mocking someone behind her back, I'd like to—"

"I state facts, which are well known. And I speak to you privately and in confidence. I hope I am not so lacking in gallantry as to shout such remarks in clubs and coffee houses."

"Well I hope you are not, either." His head jerked around, anger blazing in his eyes. Gwendolyn smiled and patted his arm. "No, do not fly into a pelter. Tell me, pray, how you managed to bring your fearsome neighbour around your thumb. I suppose you flattered her so that she quite forgot how angry she was."

He shrugged. "All women are susceptible to flattery."

"At which you, of course, are a past master, beside being quite without scruples. Oh dear. Your eyebrows are knitting again. Now, admit it, August. I'd not be in trouble had you not done so outrageous a thing as to practice your aim in the heart of Town."

"You are becoming tiresome. I shall take you home."

"I am not being tiresome. I am trying to come at why you have no vestige of consideration for anyone but yourself."

He put a hand across his eyes and moaned, "Oh, Lud! Must I endure all this preaching only because I fired a few shots in my own garden?"

"No, do be serious. Did—"

"If we are to be serious, I must sit down, for the strain will be terrible. Here—this bench will do."

He dusted it with his handkerchief, and when she was seated, sat beside her. "Very well," he said with a deep sigh. "Have at me."

She said anxiously, "Am I being a nag? I expect Gideon would say I am."

"I have the greatest respect for your brother's opinions."

"Yes, so do I. But we must help our friends, you know, whether—"

"I have told you before. I neither need nor want friends."

"And there you go again. *You* neither need nor want. Does it not occur to you that *I* might need you for a friend?" His lips tightened, and he stared at a bent chrysanthemum in silence. "Did it not even dawn on you this morning," she went on, "that your target practice might have really frightened your aunt? She is—well, not so young as she used to be, and she was very upset."

A frown came into his eyes. He guided a confused ladybird from his hand onto a shrub beside the bench, and said, "I suppose next you will be telling me there was a lady in the Mount-Durward house who fainted and lost the child she was expecting! Or that the old duffer who dwells in the house behind us and is in a drunken stupor nine-tenths of the time suffered a heart seizure! If it pleases you to concoct such nonsensical dramas, by all means indulge your morbid imagination, and believe me to be, as you have so often said, a hard-hearted, conscienceless, care-for-nobody. If 'tis good for nothing else, it should at least cure you of wanting me for a friend."

"It would, if I believed it. I do not. August," she said pleadingly, "why must you always try to make everyone think the worst of you? No, pray do not be cross. I wouldn't bother to pinch at you, if I did not care for you so much."

He caught his breath, and from under his long lashes a tense glance was slanted at her earnest face. Then he laughed and said lightly, " 'Tis unwise to care for sharp-tongued cynics like me, Smallest Rossiter. They have been known to sting."

"Like a scorpion? 'Tis said they sting when they are trodden on."

"Your enterprising scorpion stings *before* 'tis trodden on." She laughed, and he added, "As I am sure several of my—ah, lady loves would warn you."

"Oh, pish! I did not mean *that* kind of caring. Besides, I doubt you ever loved anyone, save your family."

"A man may love without giving his heart." He added deliberately, "I have had many loves."

"You mean you have had many *affaires*."

He moaned and closed his eyes. "Shock upon shock! First you upset my chaste neighbours, now you use terms no blushful maiden should even know!"

"I grew up with two brothers, have you forgot? And you might be surprised at what blushful maidens know. Can we go on now? The wind is a trifle chill."

Amused, he helped her up, and they started off again. The wind was indeed rising, and clouds were gathering to hint at rain to come. People were leaving the gardens and the nursemaid and her charge hurried along the path toward them, clearly homeward bound.

The nursemaid bobbed a curtsy. "Good morning, Miss Rossiter."

"Good morning, Bellworth. You're out early. Good morning, Susan."

The nursemaid's admiring gaze was on Falcon, and she murmured that it looked a trifle threatening so she must get Miss Susan home. The little girl's curtsy was less well balanced. She teetered, and clung to the scabbard of Falcon's sword.

It was not a steady support. Her little cart rocked. Righting it, and steadying her, he then picked up the square of blanket that had fallen, and bent to replace it saying laughingly, "Take care, young lady, else your doll will—"

He drew back with a startled cry. The occupant of the cart was not a doll but a large tabby cat which appeared less than delighted to be clad in a baby's bonnet and gown.

Falcon dropped the blanket, clapped a handkerchief to his nose and roared a sneeze.

The cat deserted the cart and fled, but finding its flight impeded paused to pedal furiously at the encumbering skirts.

The little girl wailed, "You frighted my baby!" and, encouraged by the fact that her nursemaid had run after and caught up the escapee, she dealt Falcon a strong kick on the shin.

Falcon yelped, and sneezed again.

"That will do, Susan!" said Gwendolyn sharply.

"He frighted my baby! Din't he, Belly?" shrilled the child.

Struggling to subdue a growling ten-legged feline, the nurse-maid panted that she knew as they never should've brought the dratted animal, and that Miss Susan had been told not to call her that, and the nice gentleman hadn't meant no harm.

Variously convulsed, outraged, and hilarious, Falcon's attempt to respond was lost in another sneeze.

"Yes, he did! He's a bad man!" declared Susan, drawing back her shoe.

"Kick be agaid, add I'll . . . kick you back," gasped Falcon stuffily.

"He kicked me! He kicked me!" howled Susan. "I'll tell Papa!"

"You will be quiet," said Gwendolyn sternly. "Else I shall have to tell your papa how badly you behave when Bellworth takes you for a walk!"

This terrible threat subdued the child and she ran after the nursemaid, pausing to direct black glares at the still sneezing Falcon.

"Is what I deserve," he moaned, "for bei'g ki'd."

"Well, it was kind in you to help the child, certainly," said Gwendolyn. "But if you dislike cats, you shouldn't—"

He blew his nose. "Cats have a purpose," he sighed, recovering somewhat. "They keep down hideous creatures like mice, so I cannot dislike the brutes. But they make me sneeze."

"Goodness me but they do," she said, walking slowly beside him while he dried his tears. "Well, they've gone now, and Bellworth took the cat, so you may be at ease."

He grinned at her over his handkerchief. "Do you refer to 'Belly'?"

"Poor creature." She chuckled. "I think I'd not care to have charge of Miss Susan Ditton. She's only six, but is badly spoiled already."

"How come you to know the brat?"

"She lives on the other side of Lady Mount-Durward. We meet sometimes when I take Apollo for a walk."

"Pity he didn't devour her."

"What a dreadful man you are! And how come you *not* to know your neighbours?"

His brows lifted. "Is it a requirement that one do so? I've always believed that the best thing between neighbours is a high fence."

"Then you will be gratified, sir, for the clouds have driven everyone away and we now have the gardens all to ourselves, except—" Gwendolyn paused, then, touched by sudden unease added, "Do you know these men?"

Falcon, who had been gingerly removing a wisp of cat hair from his sleeve, glanced up.

Gwendolyn heard his sudden sharp inhalation of breath, then she gave a shocked little cry as she was seized in a crushing grip and thrust behind him. Blue steel gleamed as his sword whipped into one hand and a deadly-looking dagger seemed to leap into the other.

"Run, Gwen!" he shouted, crouched and ready. "Run!"

Two men wearing loo masks, draggly wigs, and dark shabby clothing, were sprinting towards them with savage eagerness. They both held daggers and long cudgels and there could be no doubt that they knew how to use them. A third man, who seemed almost a giant to Gwendolyn, was also masked, but well dressed. He came up at a slower pace and paused beside a large beech tree.

Gwendolyn did not run. She felt paralyzed with terror, and thought distractedly, 'They are too many! Even if he can prevail 'gainst those two murderous cutthroats, that terrible giant probably has a pistol and will shoot him down!'

CHAPTER V

hey came at Falcon from both sides. The assassin to his left was tall and muscular, his features coarse and his red cheeks marked with the blue-veined mottling that spoke of a heavy drinker. He gripped his dagger in his left hand, and twirled his cudgel as though impatient to bring it home on Falcon's head. The second man was shorter, finer-boned, with a narrow face and a deeply scarred chin. He held his dagger in the right hand with the point advanced, Italian style. It was a murderous-looking weapon, curving and long-bladed; Arabian, thought Falcon inconsequently. Of the two, this was the more dangerous antagonist, for he ran lightly and gracefully on small feet, and there was a faint, hungry grin on the gash of a mouth. Two to one—fair odds save for that hulking lout by the tree, and the Smallest Rossiter who had not run as he'd told her. To his advantage was the fact that this place was too public for a long battle; they would need to be fast about their murderous business. That much his mind was able to store away before they closed.

In the first few seconds his appraisal was borne out. Red Face plunged at him, the cudgel whizzing for his head in a mighty swipe that would have crushed his skull if it had connected. He danced aside, avoiding the following slash of the dagger. His colichemarde darted; he heard Red Face howl, then had to duck under the flailing cudgel Scarred Chin swung at him. The weapon raked his shoulder and he staggered, then thrust hard with his sword, his dagger blocking the swift and deadly stab of the Arabian dagger. A rent opened in Scarred Chin's sleeve and he shouted a curse and jumped out of range, almost colliding with his cohort who came rushing in with a blood-curdling yowl. Red Face had dropped his cudgel and his left sleeve was stained crimson, but his dagger arced down strongly. Falcon countered it with his own dagger, planted a boot in the big man's stomach and shoved. Red Chin went hurtling back and down.

From the corner of his eye Falcon saw Gwendolyn running awkwardly, the big lout after her. His heart jolted and his joy in the uneven contest died abruptly. He thought 'Why doesn't she scream for help?' but then realized her cool common sense would reason that a scream might distract him. Fractional as it had been, his shift of attention was perilous and Scarred Chin's cudgel blurred at him. He restored his guard in the nick of time and protected his head, but the blow struck forcefully on his colichemarde and the sword spun from his hand. His dagger whipped up to meet Scarred Chin's and the blades rang together and locked. A pair of hard brown eyes glared at him savagely. He caught a whiff of stale sweat and garlic. It was too close now for the man to use his club. Falcon's right fist shot up and landed fairly. Scarred Chin grunted and staggered back, his nose spurting crimson.

The big man was struggling with Gwen. Rage blazed through Falcon, and he was running. He'd have wagered his entire fortune on the rogue's identity, and he shouted, "Green!" as he came up.

Rafe Green's head jerked around. Gwendolyn sank her teeth into his wrist, and he howled, shoved her aside, and bellowed, "Idiots! Kill the bastard!"

Gwendolyn screamed, " 'Ware, August! 'Ware!"

Falcon whirled. A streak of silver came at him and he gasped as pain stabbed through his left upper arm. He fell to one knee.

His face bloody, Scarred Chin wrenched his dagger free, howling a muffled but exultant, "I winged him!" and swung the weapon high for the death stroke. Straightening, Falcon brought up his own blade and struck home hard. Scarred Chin's howl became a choking gulp. He clutched his middle and retreated from the battle at a weaving stagger.

Red Face was up and attacking again, his cudgel swung high, his face a mask of rage. Falcon ran back a few steps, reversed his hold on the dagger, and threw. Red Face's eyes opened very wide. He doubled up and without a sound, fell flat.

Gwendolyn was screaming.

Terrified for her, Falcon whirled, and looked straight into the muzzle of a large horse pistol. Rafe Green's thick lips were twisted into a triumphant grimace, his finger was already pulling back the trigger. Falcon had no time to so much as duck before the shot rang out. Tensing for the impact, he felt nothing and for a split second thought Green must have missed. Then Green fired. The ball ploughed into the ground at his feet, the sagging pistol fell from his grasp and he clutched his right arm, cursing in anguish and frustration.

Falcon's gaze flew to Gwendolyn.

Her eyes were enormous. One trembling hand was over her mouth, the other held her little pocket pistol. Smoking.

He gave a whoop, and ran to her. "Bravo! You indomitable little scamp! You magnificent rascal!" He caught her up and whirled her around, laughing breathlessly.

Inevitably, the shots had attracted attention. The two old gentlemen were returning at speed. The boy with the horses was leading them into the gardens, his eyes goggling. Someone was blowing a whistle to summon the Watch.

Dazed and sick, Gwendolyn's eyes were blurring. She clung to Falcon and whispered, "Oh . . . August! Is he— D-did I . . . ?"

He glanced around. Green was beating an erratic but fast retreat towards a waiting coach. Scarred Chin was staggering after him. Red Face would not be following. "No, Smallest Rossiter. Unfortunately you failed to put a period to the poltroon."

"By Gad, sir! If ever I saw such a fight!"

"Jupiter, ma'am! You've all my admiration!"

"I say, you're hurt, sir! Allow me—"

Gwendolyn's head cleared. She gasped, "August! Oh, is it very bad? My heavens, I thought you were killed! Let me see!"

He obeyed the tugs of her little hands, and sat on a nearby bench, attempting to answer all the questions and comments, his proud gaze fixed on her anxious face. "I'm all right," he said, as one old gentleman helped him out of his coat and slit his shirt-sleeve. He peered down at the wound in his arm. It was a deep cut and had bled profusely, and Gwendolyn's eyes grew round with horror, but she appropriated his handkerchief and used it as a makeshift bandage. He said bracingly, "Don't swoon, Smallest One. It's not near as bad as it looks."

A tall dragoon left his carriage and came running. "Jolly good, Mr. Falcon!" he panted admiringly. "Nasty odds, but you were a match for the bounders! More of these da— er, curst rioters, what?"

"And a lady with him!" said one of the elderly gentlemen, indignant.

"Disgraceful!" snorted his companion. "Whatever next?"

Falcon held his breath at what came next as Gwendolyn tightened the handkerchief around his arm then scanned him anxiously.

He found a grin. "You're doing very well, ma'am!"

A softness came into her eyes. She said, "And you were magnificent."

For a frozen instant, he could not tear his gaze away. Then he shrugged and said with proper nonchalance, "But of course."

A watchman appeared, and became very important. Green's carriage had fled, but with Red Face to be taken away, and in consideration of Falcon's injury, he allowed them to leave, saying he would call at Falcon House shortly.

Gwendolyn wanted to hire a chair, but Falcon insisted that he felt perfectly able to ride.

She said quietly, "Perhaps. But I do not."

At once remorseful, he accepted the loan of the dragoon's carriage. They were ushered through the small crowd that had formed, the dragoon mounted Andante and took up the reins of Gwendolyn's mare, saying he would follow them back to Great Ormond Street. As the watchman slammed the door shut, an onlooker said clearly, "I've heard that the Mandarin can fight, but—by God, I never thought I'd see it!"

Gwendolyn cringed inwardly, but if Falcon heard, he gave no sign, leaning back against the squabs and smiling at her. He was pale, however, and she said, "You're very brave, but I expect that wound must be exceeding uncomfortable."

Her expectations were justified. In the rush and excitement of the fight he had scarcely felt it, but now he was all too aware he'd been stabbed. He told her that had it not been for her excellent aim he might not be feeling anything at all at this moment. "Who the deuce taught you how to shoot? Gideon?"

"No. Newby. He worries because of all the street violence. August, that horrid man I shot. Who—"

"Oh—*Jupiter!*" he exclaimed, sitting straighter. "I just realized! Of all things, Gwendolyn! Had you to shoot the carrion in his right arm?"

Taken aback, she stammered, "What? I— Why must you look so displeased? Had I known you preferred that I aim for his foot—" She broke off, her eyes widening with comprehension. "Good heavens! Can I believe it? You're disappointed because now you can't call him out!"

"You are quite wrong, m'dear. He has already called me out."

"Oh! You are impossible! You just admitted that you could be lying dead at this very moment, but instead of thanking God for your deliverance, you grumble because you cannot at once slay this—this . . ." She frowned. "Who is he?"

"His name is Oliver Green, though he's generally known as Rafe."

"Green . . ." she murmured thoughtfully. "Lord Hibbard Green is the man who was so horrid to Johnny and Jennifer Armitage whilst you were in Cornwall, no? My brother says he is a member of the League of Jewelled Men. Is it the same gentleman?"

"No. His son. And by no stretch of the imagination could either be named a gentleman. Lord Hibbard is most certainly with the League. Rafe may be a member. I rather doubt it."

"But surely he must be. Why else would they have followed us? Certainly, they meant your death. Unless—" She paused, her brow wrinkling. "Is this Rafe a—er, a married man?"

He turned his head and looked at her mournfully. "You have found me out, alas. Yes, our Rafe is married. To a pure and lovely angel whom I lured away to my mountaintop eyrie in the—er, the Swiss Alps. For some odd reason Rafe took a rather dim view of the affair and—"

"Wretch!" she interpolated, her eyes twinkling. "Mountain-top eyrie indeed! I wish I may see it!"

He leaned closer and sneered villainously, "That might be arranged. Though I fancy Gideon would be a marplot and cut up rough. Should you object if I was obliged to shoot him first?"

His lips were very close to her cheek. She found herself suddenly short of breath, and to hide that weakness was quick to riposte, "Do you think you would have time to fit him into your slaughter schedule?"

With a grin he eased himself back against the squabs. "You never disappoint me, Smallest Rossiter. I shall relieve your suspense. I fibbed. Dear Rafe is not wed, and I have neither made off with his bride, nor filched his mistress."

"Ah. Then he *is* a League member!"

"I suspect he is merely a dishonourable man, my innocent. He challenged me in a fit of drunken rage, but he knows himself no match for me, so likely planned to avoid a duel and throw the blame for my murder on the rioters. His esteemed sire would be delighted did he succeed in putting me out of the—"

The coachman had cut a corner too sharply and the carriage lurched. Falcon's breathless pause in mid-sentence renewed Gwendolyn's anxieties. She said contritely, "How silly I am to allow you to chatter like this. Please rest quietly. We're almost home."

"Good. I mean to play the complete hero, and be ushered in a half-swooning condition to my bed while maids fall into hysterics and Mrs. Vanechurch prays, and Chef starts preparing clear soup and gruel."

"Just as he shall," she agreed.

His arm was throbbing nastily and he felt a little fuzzy-headed, but at this his eyes narrowed. "Now see here, Mistress Gwendolyn, I'll not have you throwing Katrina into a panic, so do not really be adopting tragedy airs!"

"Oh, must I not? I had so looked forward to stealing your thunder by fainting across the threshold."

He laughed. "No, seriously, Gwen—"

"Very seriously, August, as soon as we get home you must take to your bed and we shall call your doctor."

"What rubbish! But I suppose you will enlist Tummet's support, so we'll have old Knight in, if he'll deign to come. He's blasted crusty since he found his way onto the Honours List and became *Sir* James, though—" He did not finish the sentence, but jerked forward, peering out of the window and so far forgetting himself as to wince and clutch his arm.

Gwendolyn looked at him sharply, then followed his gaze. Her heart gave a scared jump. They were turning onto Great Ormond Street now. A man and a girl, riding very close together, walked their horses around the corner from Conduit Street. Even as she watched, Katrina stretched out her hand. Morris took it and touched it to his lips.

Falcon half-whispered, "Devil take him!" He turned a flushed and furious face to Gwendolyn. "You knew! You *knew* she had slunk out to be with that thimble-wit! 'Tis why you begged me to rescue you from Lady Mount-Durward. You wanted to get me—"

"All to myself?" she interposed in desperation. "But of course. You are so diverting a companion. Happy one moment, fighting like a Roman gladiator the next, murderous the next!"

He said through his teeth, "If you do not want to see just how murderous I can be, madam, you'd best use whatever influence you have to keep my sister away from Lieutenant Dolt Morris!"

Contrary to Falcon's expectations Sir James Knight arrived at Great Ormond Street within minutes of their return. A tall, spare gentleman of middle years, with a thin face, narrow hazel eyes under bushy brows, and a fierce manner, he nodded tersely to Pearsall. "Bad this time, is it?" he barked in a harsh voice, marching towards Mrs. Vanechurch who waited at the foot of the stairs.

Pearsall answered, "I pray not, Sir James. A knife thrust in his upper arm."

Mrs. Vanechurch said fervently, "Thank heaven you are come, sir. He is in a proper rage and will not let us help him."

"Typical!" snorted the doctor. "Another duel, of course."

"They were attacked by street ruffians, as I understand it."
Sir James paused with one hand on the banister. "They?"

"Miss Rossiter was with him, sir."

"Was she, by Gad! Safe home, I trust?"

"The lady is in the small withdrawing room, Sir James."

"And should be laid down upon her bed," put in the house-keeper, wringing her plump hands nervously. "Shaking like a leaf the poor young lady was when they come home. But she is as stubborn as the young master. If you could look in on her after-wards, sir?"

Sir James nodded and stamped up the stairs, to pause, scowl-ing, as a lackey flung open the door to Falcon's suite.

The injured man was reclining on a chaise longue, fully dressed save for his coat and waistcoat, his left shirt sleeve grue-somely blotched with crimson. Katrina knelt beside him, a bloody rag in one hand and tears on her pale face, and Tummet hovered in the open door to the bedchamber, managing to look at once glum and exasperated.

". . . know perfectly well it will not do," Falcon was saying, his voice low and furious. "You do him a disservice by encouraging his advances and leave me no alternative but to—"

"You'll leave me no alternative but to have you hauled to your bed and chained there if you do not curb that abominable tem-per!" The doctor walked briskly to the side of the chaise, thrust his bag at Tummet, and assisted Katrina to her feet.

"How glad I am that you have come, Sir James," she gulped tearfully. "My brother has taken a horrid wound and will not—"

"Oh, have done, madam," snapped Falcon. "Send her away, Knight. She is beside herself."

"While you are doing all in your power to calm her, as usual," said the great doctor acidly. "The kindest thing I can do for you, my poor little lass, is to agree with your lunatic brother. I believe Miss Rossiter waits in what you people facetiously call the 'small' withdrawing room. She will likely benefit from a little comforting."

Katrina nodded and Sir James opened the door for her, then returned to Falcon. "An you expect me to tend you while you lie on that stupid chaise, you are mistaken. I wonder you allowed it, Tummet."

"Lor' almighty," protested Tummet indignantly. "You know what 'e's like when—"

"Oh, he fussed enough for two," said Falcon with a gesture of impatience. "The devil's in it that I'm surrounded by gloom merchants."

"You may be thankful that with your charming disposition you're surrounded by anyone at all! Are you able to walk to your bed, or shall I order that you be carried?"

Falcon said with a flash of his brilliant grin, "You would, damn you! No, really, James, I'm not playing the noble hero. I've a clean cut in my arm, and to please you I'll own it hurts like fury, but 'tis scarce a matter of life and death. There was no need for you to be called from sick folk who need you, so as to come and pinch at me, and then favour me with one of your stupendous bills."

"I've not yet begun to pinch at you! And a mosquito sting can be a matter of life and death." The doctor took Falcon's wrist and felt the pulse, then muttered, "Tumultuous, naturally. Added to which you are flushed, your eyes glitter more balefully than usual, and you are in a fine sweat."

"How very crude of me," drawled Falcon. But after a pause he sighed and asked quietly, "Do you really judge me a lunatic, James?"

Glancing up, Knight's narrow hazel eyes were suddenly very kind. He said in a surprisingly gentle voice, "She is a grown lady now. You must let her choose her own path, lad."

"She is a babe! A lovely, sweet-natured . . . simpleton. I only pray that, someday, the right man will come—a man worthy of her."

Knight laid down the captive wrist, and asked, "From whence will this paragon come, pray tell? Another world, perhaps?"

Falcon stared at him, then said with a wry smile, "Would you trust Katrina to choose her own mate, Solomon? Or my sire to do so?" Knight frowned, and hesitated. Falcon uttered a derisive snort, then called, "Very well, Tummet. The great man is determined to make an invalid of me. Lend me a hand to my bed. When he's done with his butchery I'll likely stand in need of it!"

Jove, but you're doing well, old lad!" James Morris eyed his companion admiringly, and adjusted his stride to match Sir Owen's slower pace. They had met in the Strand and been glad to keep each other company on this blustery afternoon. "Out trying your legs, eh?"

Furlong was cheered by the words of praise. He said, "I do think I'm making progress, and I'll never get my strength back while I lounge about in my house. It's not as if I was down at Tunbridge Wells, you know, and could take old Chaucer out for a walk every day. I feel stifled indoors, so when the rain stopped I decided to drop in on Gideon. Is that where you're bound?"

"To say truth, I don't know where I'm bound." Morris said ruefully, "Just got my weekly set-down. From Falcon."

Sir Owen glanced at him sharply, and stepped aside to allow a lady with enormous skirts to pass by. "I've no wish to pry," he said then, "but did you perhaps speak to him at last?"

"Well, he's seemed a little less—er, unforgiving of late, so I'd intended to put my hopes to the test again. As it chanced, I didn't have the opportunity. August and Miss Gwendolyn were set upon in Bloomsbury Square, of all places, and—"

"Good God! In broad daylight? The League?"

"He says not." Morris gave a brief sketch of the incident, and concluded, "By the worst possible luck, their coach turned onto Great Ormond Street at precisely the same moment Katrina and I rode up. She had just confessed she—er," he flushed, and went on shyly, "well, that she returns my affection, but she insists our situation is hopeless. I was trying to convince her 'tis not so, and— Oh, I fancy 'twas clear enough for any fool to see we are in . . . er, in love."

"Whereupon Falcon, being a proper fool, went straight into the boughs."

"Yes. Well, he was a trifle testy anyway. Had just took a knife in his arm, y'know."

"Hum. And what sayeth your fair lady?"

"That's the rub, Owen. She agrees. With him. It's the very deuce of a pickle."

Furlong's lips compressed, but he restrained his instinctive reaction and said quietly, " 'Twould seem we're both in the same barrel, Jamie."

"Oh. Are we? I'd thought, perhaps—"

"That I would have turned 'gainst Maria because she shot me down? I know everyone is of that opinion. My brother thinks me quite demented, but—" Sir Owen hesitated, then said, "Having found love at last, I find also that—that it cannot be turned on and off at will. And—she was fairly caught, don't you see? She adores that famous brother of hers. He'd signed the Agreement with the League, and—"

"Did you read it, then?"

"No, but Travis Grainger did when he carried the Agreement here from Ceylon."

"Well, I know that. But he couldn't decipher much of it."

"He couldn't read the other signatures, but he saw Barthélemy's name clear enough. Had I succeeded in delivering the Agreement to the authorities, they'd have soon identified the other signatures, which would have destroyed the League, of course. Barthélemy would have been condemned as an enemy spy, and if he was acting on his personal ambitions, without the consent of his government, 'twould have doomed him in France also. How can I blame Maria for striving to save him? My only hope must be that I'll shortly forget the lady."

Morris pursed his lips. "Aye. 'As shortly as a horse will lick his ear!' "

Sir Owen smiled wryly, and they walked on together, the distress they shared forging a deeper bond between them. When they reached Conduit Street and the magnificence of Rossiter Court, they were shown up to the apartments now occupied by Captain Gideon Rossiter and his bride of seven months. Here, they were given into the care of the captain's new butler, a thin and mournful-looking Italian, who bowed and with a grand gesture advised them he was "Travatorri! The Capitaine's excessive-new gentleman. Madame," he added sighfully, "she is in bed with the doctor." This pronouncement which set Morris reeling and restored the twinkle to Sir Owen's blue eyes, was followed by an invitation to "Come this away, for the Capitaine is entertaining for a friend, but he have say you are to be omitted."

Following him along the wide and luxuriously appointed corridor, Morris clutched Furlong's arm and gulped, "Did you hear . . . what I heard?"

Sir Owen grinned, and nodded. "Gideon has a taste for variety," he whispered.

Travatorri flung open a door and roared, "Arrived they have! A moment!" He threw up one long arm, swung to confront the new arrivals causing them to step back hurriedly, and demanded, "Your names, if you pleasure, I must denounce!"

Gideon Rossiter had risen from a chair in the spacious and sunny withdrawing room. He saw Morris' face, and intervened hurriedly, "That is quite all right, Travatorri. Come in, gentlemen!"

The butler looked stern, and closing the door behind the new arrivals, held it open a moment, watching them suspiciously.

A slim young man wearing the uniform of a naval sub-lieutenant, had stood also, and waited, his dark eyes glinting with amusement.

The door clicked shut, and Morris attempted to stifle a whoop of laughter.

Sir Owen said unsteadily, "Good day, Skye." Grinning broadly, he sank into the nearest chair. "I think I must sit down, Ross. I'm easily overwhelmed these days."

"Ye Gods!" chortled Morris, shaking hands with the lieutenant, "Where the devil d'you find 'em, Gideon? First Tummet, now this!"

Rossiter groaned and went to pour two glasses of wine. " 'Tis Naomi's doing, not mine! He is a *count*, if you will believe it! Not a louis to bless himself with, but his family was kind to my wife whilst she lived in Italy, so . . ." he shrugged helplessly.

Wiping tears from his eyes, Morris said, "Owen, shall we tell him what his 'excessive-new gentleman' said of Naomi?"

"Better not," laughed Furlong. "Ignorance is bliss, in this case."

When the bantering died down, Furlong asked, "Dare we hope you're here in your official capacity, Skye?"

The lieutenant, who was nephew and aide-de-camp to Lord Hayes of the East India Company, turned his glass in his fine-boned nervous hands, and answered, "I'm afraid not, Owen. I chanced to see the little flurry Ross got himself into just now, so I came—"

Morris interrupted sharply, "Flurry? Gad, 'tis an epidemic! Came after you again, did they Gideon?"

Rossiter sobered. "Yes—and no." He set his glass aside and leaned forward in his chair. "I'd paid an early call this morning, and decided to walk home. I turned a corner and there were four of the rogues. I snatched my sword out, but I knew from the look of 'em that 'twould be a trifle grim. Then"—he frowned—"be dashed if I can understand the business. One of them howled, 'No! It's Rossiter! Shab off!' And they ran."

"Did they now?" muttered Furlong.

Perplexed, Morris watched Rossiter in silence.

Lieutenant Skye said, "You're well known, Gideon. Undoubtedly 'twas a pack of footpads who recognized you and know something of your reputation as a swordsman."

Rossiter shook his head. "At four-to-one odds? I'm not that formidable!"

The lieutenant stood, and said with a grin, "No, but they saw me running up. And I *am* formidable." They all laughed dutifully, and he left them, saying whimsically that he must get back to his desk or be flogged at the mainmast.

The door closed behind him and they settled back into their chairs. "Nice fellow, that," observed Morris. "What did he want, Gideon?"

"Or has he decided to help us?" asked Sir Owen hopefully.

Rossiter said, "I may be fair and far off, but I think Skye and his mighty uncle are a deal more interested in our activities than they admit. Skye's a master at turning the conversation the way he wants it to go. I started by asking him for any new information on the League, and suddenly found we were discussing the Stuarts!"

Morris was gazing rather glumly at the window. His head jerked up at this, however, and he exclaimed, "The Stuarts? Jupiter! Does Whitehall believe Bonnie Prince Charlie has joined forces with the League?"

"Dashed if I know. Certainly, Skye was fishing. And I'd nothing to give him, for I know precious little of the Prince's whereabouts, save that he's somewhere in Paris and King Louis is striving to push him out of France."

Sir Owen said dryly, "He'll have his work cut out for him. Not a country in Europe will offer sanctuary to Bonnie Charlie, for fear of offending King George. Especially now that the War of the Austrian Succession is done with. Besides, Charlie's mad for his new mistress, I hear."

His green eyes very round, Morris asked, "Stuart is after King George's mistress? Why, he must be wits to let! How could he—"

"Not *George's* mistress, you gudgeon," said Rossiter, laughing. "His own. The Princesse Marie Louise de Talmont."

"Oh." Morris blinked. "I saw her once. A handsome lady, but—er, I don't mean to criticize, but—surely she must be many—er, several years his senior? And she seemed rather—ah, fierce."

"That's her reputation," agreed Furlong. "But she's also very clever and witty, 'tis said, and knows how to keep a gentleman entertained. So long as her husband looks the other way . . ." He shrugged. "Ross, there was more to that attack on you, I think?"

Rossiter said, "Would that I knew *what* more! Skye really did come running up, sword in hand, but I'd have been cold meat by the time he arrived, I promise you. I recognized a couple of the scoundrels. They were with the ugly little lot who cornered me in Westminster soon after we came home in April. D'you recall, Jamie? They thought I'd got my hands on one of those damnable little Jewelled Men, and—"

"And they came near to putting a period to you!" Morris said grimly, "I remember all too well."

Sir Owen looked puzzled. "But—if they were the Squire's men, why on earth would they have drawn back from such a splendid opportunity to get rid of you?"

"I've not the least notion." Frowning, Rossiter said, "One

thing's sure—whatever they're up to, it bodes no good for us."

Morris said thoughtfully, "It sounds as if old August was in the right of it, then. He said the men who attacked him were not—" He broke off, aghast. "Oh, Gad! I forgot! Your sister, Ross—"

"Gwendolyn?" Tensing, Rossiter demanded, "What about her?"

"Well, she was riding with Falcon an hour or so ago, when he was attacked, by—"

"*What?*" Flushed with wrath, Rossiter leapt from his chair. "And you've been *sitting* here *chatting*, without telling—"

"He's telling you now, Gideon," Sir Owen interposed hurriedly. "She's quite safe, old fellow. Likely Jamie meant to break it to you gently, but—"

"Miss Gwendolyn shot Rafe Green," said Morris, ungently.

They both stared at him, speechless with astonishment.

"Sorry," he added simply. "Forgot."

CHAPTER VI

Pray do try one of"—Mrs. Dudley Falcon ducked her head and gasped as lightning lit the long windows of the large upstairs withdrawing room—"of these sugarplums, dearest Gwendolyn," she went on, holding out the box with a plump hand. "Now, you must not hesitate, for you need something to lift your spirits after such a dreadful experience as you suffered yesterday. I vow I was never more horrified than when August told me of it! I wonder you were able to visit your family today. My sweet niece is quite prostrated with the shock."

Gwendolyn had, in fact, been visited by both her brothers the previous afternoon. Their anxieties in her behalf had been dear and touching, but she had resisted all efforts to persuade her to return home, and had pleaded, truthfully, that Katrina was extremely shaken, and needed her. She had not felt it necessary to mention that if she went back to Rossiter Court she would be forbidden to proceed with certain Plans. Nor that part of Katrina's nervous state had to do with those same Plans. After Gideon and Newby had left, so that she could rest, a Bow Street Runner had arrived to prevent her doing so. She later discovered that August had pretended to fall into a coma when the officer refused to credit his identification of Rafe Green. She had done her best to assist the earnest minion of the law, however, after which she really had been able to rest. This morning she had taken breakfast with Katrina, gone for a drive with her brother Newby, and joined her family for luncheon at Rossiter Court. Her father was in the west country on some pressing matter concerning his shipyards, but she'd spent some time with her new sister-in-law, admiring the christening gown and the robes and bonnets, several of which she herself had sewn in preparation for the arrival of the new babe. The afternoon had flown by, and she'd stayed for dinner, returning to Falcon House only half an hour since to find Mrs. Dudley in the withdrawing room with her bosom-bow, Lady Hester Mount-Durward, and a pale and forlorn-looking Katrina.

Gwendolyn selected a sugarplum while Lady Hester, large of chin, girth, and wig, and grim as always, rumbled that Katrina was missish, always had been, and always would be. "Pretty," she acknowledged, appropriating the box and helping herself to a sugared almond. She waited out a crash of thunder, then added, "But lacks gumption."

Gwendolyn saw distress in Katrina's lovely face, and interposed swiftly, "So you have been able to chat with August, Mrs. Dudley?"

"But, of course, my dear! I fairly flew to his bedside as soon as I learned of the tragedy, and—"

Her ladyship put in a scornful, "Tragedy? Piffle!"

"—and found him pale and wan, dear boy. But so kind, Gwendolyn, for he had this lovely box of sweetmeats for me, and tied with a riband, so prettily. Now why should you look astonished? August is the most generous of men, and said this delicious gift was a token of his regret for having scared me with his naughty target practice yesterday."

"Took the blame, did he?" barked Lady Hester, fixing Gwendolyn with a stern stare. "Decent. For once."

"Come now, ma'am," protested Falcon, strolling to join them, "you'll give Miss Rossiter a bad opinion of me." He bent over the dowager's hand and touched it to his lips. "Here I've been striving to convince her of what a fine fellow I am."

She gave a bark of laughter. "If you have, you rascal, 'tis the first time in living memory you've done so! And there was not the need for you to leave your bed only to say your 'good evenings' to a neighbour!"

He chuckled and sat beside her, entering the conversation lightheartedly. No one would have guessed, thought Gwendolyn, that only yesterday morning he had taken a wound. If his arm pained him, he hid it admirably, and only the shadows under his eyes told her that he was not quite up to par.

Mrs. Dudley scolded him. He should not be jauntering about, she said, when the doctor had left firm orders he was to stay abed for at least five days.

"But I have to jaunter about," he argued with a smile. "Papa remains in Sussex, and do I not stand guard over my ladies," he glanced at his sister, "there is no knowing what mischief they may get up to."

Katrina's eyes fell and she blushed faintly.

Scanning her curiously, Lady Mount-Durward's lips parted.

Gwendolyn rushed into the breach in an attempt to turn attention from her friend. "I am so glad you feel well enough to join us, Mr. Falcon. I found a book in your library this morning that I have so wanted to show you. 'Tis the account of a Jesuit priest who was allowed to visit inside China, and he writes at length of the wonders he saw there, particularly with regard to their advances in medicine I was sure you would find it interesting."

She knew that Katrina was staring at her, and that Mrs. Dudley had dropped the sugarplum she'd been about to pop into her mouth. August's eyes blazed, and the familiar tightening of his jaw told her he was angry. She thought defiantly, 'Good! You deserved a set-down for sniping at your poor sister, wretched man!'

Before he could respond, Lady Mount-Durward said heartily, "Is that so, Falcon? Lud, but I'd not suspected you was interested in China. I must tell you I've a diary kept by my late great-uncle, who was a seafaring man. He was taken by Chinese pirates and has some tales you shall read! I'd have showed it to you long since, but I'd the impression you did not care to be reminded of that rather unfortunate part of your lineage—which would be understandable enough, heaven knows. Though I have never held it 'gainst you, as so many do. I knew your grandmama, you will be aware. Not that we were friends, of course, but . . ." Undaunted by a peal of thunder, she embarked on a long and patronizing monologue and for the next five minutes nobody else was able to say a word.

Mrs. Dudley looked increasingly nervous and shot anxious glances at her nephew's set smile.

Perfectly aware that a pair of glittering eyes from time to time hurled lances of fury in her direction, Gwendolyn maintained an expression of saintly innocence and appeared to hang on Lady Mount-Durward's every word. Actually, she was mortified. August had deserved the set-down she'd dealt him, but she had never intended to expose either him or Katrina to such lengthy and barbed condescension.

When Lady Hester was briefly silenced by a particularly ear-splitting peal of thunder, Falcon stood and bowed, shutting off her obvious intention to continue. "Jupiter, ma'am," he drawled, "but you have missed your calling. Your knowledge of my family would, I feel sure, qualify you as a lecturer, and likely enthrall anyone who had an interest in the subject." He stifled a yawn, and went on outrageously, "And I might have known you would appreciate our situation, since you have suffered another—ah, embarrassment in your own family."

Lady Mount-Durward glared at him, her countenance becoming alarmingly pink. She said in a voice that had reduced many a strong man to jelly, "I think I fail to take your meaning, Falcon."

Ignoring the imploring glances of his aunt and his sister, he raised his brows and said with exaggerated innocence, "No, have I perhaps been fobbed off with silly gossip? Alas, so many of the *haut ton* have not learned the simple good manners of keeping their noses in their own pockets. I was informed, ma'am, that your grandson, Thaddeus Briley, had earned your extreme displeasure by wedding a nobody, and a Scots nobody, at that." Unmoved by my lady's gobbling incoherencies, he lifted a hand and said sleepily, "I fancy most families have a cross to bear, but heaven forfend I should stamp where angels fear to tread. I will instead beg that you hold me excused, for I vow I'm quite fatigued by all this—er, excitement. Pray do not feel you must cease to enlighten Miss Rossiter, who will enjoy to hear any more snippets of—ah, information you can give her. As for me, I bid you goodnight, ma'am . . . ladies."

Another bow and he was gone, soon to be followed by her ladyship, flushed with wrath and unappeased by Mrs. Dudley's twittering attempts to pour oil on troubled waters.

"I will tell you to your head, ma'am," she declared loudly as she stamped to the door, "that your nephew is a rudesby, and deserves all that is said of him!" Her fury intensified by the awareness that she had been a good deal less than kind to her grandson's despised bride, she turned and added waspishly, "Handsome is as handsome does, but however August Falcon may try to ignore his heritage and pose as the complete British gentleman, he will never outrun his face, ma'am! *Never!*"

Mrs. Dudley threw an anguished glance at Katrina and fluttered after her infuriated and influential friend.

Gwendolyn and Katrina, who had stood politely, looked at each other. Gwendolyn said remorsefully, "Trina, I am so sorry! I was cross because he threw that sly scold at you, but I am only a guest in your house and I should not have spoken so. My wretched tongue! Will you please forgive?"

"Of course, dearest." Katrina sighed. "You were not to know the horrid woman would pounce on it so. August and Thad, her grandson, are friends, but she has never forgiven my brother because her silly niece went into a decline over him. She knows perfectly well what his feelings are about—about our mixed blood, but I suppose she could not resist her tabby impulses."

"Perhaps, but she might not have scratched had I not given her the opening."

"You were only trying to defend me. August knows that, I am very sure, and will likely admire you for your loyalty, rather than blame you for her ladyship's unkind remarks."

Gwendolyn smiled, but before she could respond Mrs. Dudley came back into the room with agitated hands and a long and unflattering assessment of her nephew, who quite "bears off the palm" she declared, "for arrogance and a lack of consideration." Fortunately, the arrival of several of her friends lightened her mood. It was clear that the matrons were eager to gossip, and after a decent interval Katrina and Gwendolyn asked to be excused and left the ladies to enjoy the tale of August's vexatious behaviour.

Gwendolyn half expected to find the culprit lurking about on the stairs, axe in hand. There was no sign of him however, and after wishing Katrina a good night, she was only too glad to go early to her own bed.

Her abigail, a faded middle-aged French émigré named Paulette, fussed over her anxiously, recommending as she left that her "little mademoiselle enjoy the good sleep." Gwendolyn would have been pleased to do so; unfortunately, memories of yesterday's attack and of August's brilliant fight for life crowded her mind and when at last she was able to dismiss those thoughts there came others to plague her. He had been so pleased with her when she'd shot Mr. Green. She could only hope he would bear that in mind when next they met, for despite Katrina's reassurances she was very sure there would come a moment of retribution. She sighed and wished she could dismiss the recollection of the strong grip of his arms as he had swung her around, and the little blue flames that had danced in his eyes when he'd laughed down into her face . . . As she fell asleep she was bewildered to find that for no reason she could think of, she felt very tearful.

Hector Kadenworthy blinked and said mildly, "I understand your chagrin, August, but there's no call to snap my head off. Green is willing to reschedule your meeting."

Falcon jerked his whip savagely through his gloved hand and strode down the front steps towards the groom who was struggling to hold Andante. The morning was grey and there was a cold wind blowing. He glanced at the scurrying clouds and determined to be home before the rain started. "What excuse did he offer?"

"Seems to have fallen and suffered a sprained wrist. Can't expect the lout to fight with—"

"With a pistol ball in his arm?" Falcon gave a scornful bark of laughter then shouted, "Don't damage his mouth, fool!"

Kadenworthy stared at him. "What the devil's this? Green's man said—"

"Green's man lied. Dear Rafe and two bullies he scoured from the sewer did their damndest to put a period to me on Wednesday morning."

"And you shot him? Good Lord! Never say that was the incident in Bloomsbury Square? Everyone's talking of it, but there's been no clear description of the gentleman involved, and I'd heard the ruffian was shot by a lady."

"As you wish," said Falcon curtly, taking the reins and stroking the stallion's nose.

"He'll take your arm off if you're not careful," warned Kadenworthy, eyeing the big horse admiringly, but stepping back. "What d'you mean—As I wish?"

"You asked me not to say 'twas the incident in Bloomsbury Square." Falcon mounted in a lithe swing and held the black in with a sure hand. "I am all obedience."

Looking up into his set face and glittering eyes, Kadenworthy said, "You're all aflame, more like. Jove, but he's a magnificent creature. How do you call him?"

"Andante."

His lordship pursed his lips. "He don't look slow to me."

"So you know your music, do you? I call him Andante—because he's greased lightning, of course." Briefly, a grin touched Falcon's stern mouth. "Morris thinks it means the devil."

"It'll be the devil to pay with you if you took steel through your arm the day before yesterday, and ride that monster today. Appears to me he's only half broke. No, get down, August, for lord's sake! Just because Green played the coward is no reason for you to do yourself an injury."

"True. Stand clear!"

"The streets are wet, you madman! No—wait! Who was the lady? Miss Katrina?"

Falcon shouted, "A passer-by!" and was away.

Kadenworthy pulled his gaze from that thundering gallop and met the groom's troubled eyes. "That's no way to ride in the City. He'll break his neck!"

"The mood he's in today, I doubt he'd care, milord." The groom shook his head lugubriously. "He swore at Mr. Tummet something dreadful, and heaved a book at the butler. Leastways, he threw a book 'crost the hall and it nigh hit Mr. Pearsall."

"Did he, by Jove! I know he has a violent temper, but I thought he treated his people decently."

"So he does, milord. I been in his service for five years and I never seen him this put about. Mrs. Vanechurch has knowed him since he was a little shaver and I heard her tell Mr. Pearsall she's proper worried about the young master."

The object of their concern, meanwhile, was hurtling along Great Ormond Street, leaving chaos in his wake. Two chairmen leapt for their lives as they rounded a corner and came nose to nose with a great black horse and a rider with—so they later asserted—the face of a demon. A knife sharpener's barrow was almost overturned, reducing its owner to jumping up and down and screeching curses after the rapidly disappearing stallion. And two portly gentlemen riding at a sedate walk and taking up more than their share of the road uttered shouts of alarm as Andante shot between them causing their mounts to plunge and rear so that both riders were obliged to cling to the pommels or suffer the ignominy of a toss on a London street. Their shrill denunciations added to the uproar that faded behind Falcon as Andante raced on unchecked, leaving pave and cobbles behind and plunging into the open country beyond the Foundling Hospital.

It was tricky going here, for the ground was wet and uneven and the undergrowth a ragged mix of weeds and shrubs. There would be rabbit holes and mole runs very likely, and the area was said to harbour thieves and rank riders. The prospect of an encounter with a highwayman caused Falcon's lips to curve into a mirthless smile. He felt like murdering somebody; a thieving cut-throat would fit the bill nicely.

How *dared* she have subjected him to that fiasco last evening? How *dared* she—a guest in his house—egg Katrina on to defy him? For 'twas Miss Gwendolyn Rossiter, he was very sure, who was responsible for the fact that Katrina, who should have more sense, now looked with favour on that poor dupe Morris! He gritted his teeth, crouched lower in the saddle, and touched Andante's sides with the spurs so that the stallion's great muscles bunched and they all but flew across the turf. He had no one to blame but himself, of course. Against his better judgment he had allowed the chit to stay. And what did he get for his generosity? Pinched at, day and night—well, all day and evening anyway! Such joy she

took in shooting out her snide little barbs! One might think she
would tire of reminding him in her sly way of—of what he was.
How *dare* she, who knew nothing of the matter, have all but
invited that wretched dowager to unleash her venom? Betrayal is
what it was! Downright *betrayal!* From someone he had come to
trust; to feel at ease with. Of all people, he'd not expected the
Smallest Rossiter to turn on him. And after he had—

Andante stumbled and almost went down. It was all Falcon
could do to hold him together. Frightened, the stallion bucked
and whirled. Falcon's hurt arm was wrenched painfully. He knew
a fleeting moment of astonishment as his hat flew from his head.
He was falling. The breath was knocked out of him . . . .

"Pray what is meant by 'li'? . . ."

She had asked that . . . How like Fate to have turned her
enquiring mind in the direction of Confucius . . . He was once
again in the sunlit room with all the dusty books, and his tutor's
earnest voice droning on about "li," that wise philosophy that
spoke of the need to be in harmony with the universe and one's
fellow man. " 'Tis part of your heritage, Falcon, and you could do
a great deal worse than embrace it." If he did so, it appeared he
must be gentle, generous, and ever forgiving of the shortcomings
of others. (A saint, no less!) A poised, affable, cautious man of
integrity, showing respect for a properly ordered and stratified
society. And (here came the *coup de grâce!*) he must *never lose his
temper*, or show *an angry face* to the world! (Ha!) If the Smallest
Rossiter ever read that—lord above, he'd never hear the end of
it!

"Confound the blasted book!" he groaned, and wished he'd
had the sense to burn the thing, instead of merely hurling it across
the hall and then having to apologize to poor Pearsall.

"Why do you sleep in the grass?"

He opened one eye. A head, most of it lost somewhere under
his own tricorne, was hovering over him. He reached up and
removed the tricorne, revealing a mop of tangled and greasy dark
curls and a small dirty face with brown eyes that seemed too big
for the thin features.

'Famous!' he thought disgustedly. He was sprawled on his back in the mud and weeds. Of Andante there was no sign. And if this child was a gypsy, which was very probable, he'd never see the stallion again. He started to sit up, but his left arm hurt so unpleasantly that he decided to rest for a minute.

"My horse was tired," he explained, summoning a grin.

The big eyes continued to regard him solemnly. "You're beautiful."

"Er—thank you," said Falcon, hiding his revulsion.

"On the outside," qualified the child. "But you said bad words."

Falcon chuckled and hauled himself to his right elbow. "I wouldn't have, had I known you were nearby. What's your name?"

"Ling. What's yours?"

"Falcon. Is Ling your surname?"

"I dunno. It's the back half."

"What's the—er, front half?"

"Found."

"Ah." 'Poor little waif,' he thought. "Where do you live?"

"Here, mostly. When I was a child a cove on the dubbing lay found me, but Silas looks after me now. Do you hurt?"

"If I do, 'tis my own bl— er, my own fault. Where is this Silas?"

"Gone to earn our grub. I'm seven." Ling sighed. "Silas says I eat too much, even if I'm little for seven." The sad brown eyes fixed on the man's face anxiously. "D'you think I'm little?"

Falcon, who had supposed him to be about five, was aghast. "They say 'the best things are wrapped up in small packages.' " He sat up, adding a mental, 'And that's what I get for consorting with Morris!'

"Oh. Why were you so cross? Don't you got no one, neither?"

He seemed remarkably self-composed for such a small boy, and there was a rather touching wistfulness in the little face. Falcon said gently, "Yes. I am fortunate enough to have a father and a sister."

"Do they love you?"

"I—believe so."

"Oh. Is that *all* you got?"

With the impression that he'd been found wanting, Falcon

sought for additional references. "No. I—er have aunts and cousins and so forth dotted about."

"Oh." A heavy sigh. Then, "Don't you got no mama?"

"I had one, of course. She has—er, gone up to heaven." And it was odd, he thought, that this dirty, unhappy little waif should have said "Mama" instead of "Ma," or "Mum."

"Oh. I 'spect you got lots 'n lots of friends, though. A flash cove like you. So you're not never *really* alone."

Falcon was silent for a moment, then he asked, "Have you no friends, Ling? Would you like to find some?"

His hand was seized and clutched hard against the dirty cheek. It felt damp, and when that tousled little head lifted the eyes were gemmed with tears.

Ling said scratchily, "I don't mind so much about—about the friends, y'know. But—but if I could just have a mama . . . A lady to . . . take care of me, and—and love me." A muffled sob, and the boy was clinging tight to Falcon and weeping into his cravat. "I wouldn't mind if I got beat sometimes. Honest, I wouldn't. Why did she . . . go 'way? I miss her . . . very bad."

Aside from a dutiful pat or two at birthdays or christenings, it was the first time Falcon had actually been embraced by a child. He drew back instinctively, but somehow his arms went about that frail body, and he was patting the small shoulder and saying, "There, there," as if he knew the approved procedure.

Ling pulled away and dragged a muddy hand across his eyes. "A—a man shouldn't oughta cry," he gulped gruffly.

"It seems to me," said Falcon, casting an unwilling look back across the years, "that I did. Just now and then, when I was your age."

The boy sniffed, accepted the loan of a snow-white handkerchief, and blew his nose. Looking up, he said, "I 'spect they made fun of you. Account o' them funny eyes you got."

It never failed, thought Falcon. Just when you felt safe, someone slammed a claymore across your breadbasket and down you went again. He stared at the child coldly, preparing to teach him a lesson in manners.

The muddy hand shot out to stroke his cheek. "They was just jealous," said Ling kindly. "Don't you never mind. What if they are funny? They're the bluest blue I ever see. I 'spect those boys what made fun wished they'd got 'em. You're awful old, so I 'spect you've got a married wife."

Again this odd child had thrown him off-balance. Falcon began to brush grass and dirt from his coat. "No."

"Why? Won't no lady have you?"

Falcon smiled faintly and got to his feet. "Something like that."

"Oh. I was hoping, y'know, if you had a married wife but didn't have no boys, she might take me."

"What about Silas? Or is he the one who beats you?"

"Only when I been bad." The boy frowned and his ill-fitting shoe kicked at a clump of grass. "Your married wife would have to take Silas too. He'd be lonely without me, y'know." He sighed. "But you don't got one, so she won't take us. I put your horse over here," he added, slipping his hand into Falcon's. "His reins was hanging down, so I tied 'em up."

They walked toward a small copse of denuded birches. Andante was secured to a low branch, and grazing contentedly. Falcon mounted up, and the child came over and gripped his stirrup, gazing up at him with those great sad eyes. He thought 'Blast it all!' and leaned forward keeping a tight hold on the reins. "Not too close, boy. He's half wild yet."

"He's very fine. Sir, *must* you go?"

"Yes, I'm afraid—"

"Hey! Wotcher a'doing of wiv my boy? Get orf it!"

A large and shabbily dressed individual wearing a scratch wig that looked as if it hadn't seen a comb for several years was approaching at a shambling run.

'An ugly customer,' thought Falcon.

"He's not doing nothing," shouted Ling. "He just fell off his horse."

The man slowed, and came up with suspicion in every line of his red, unlovely face and craft gleaming in the hard, bloodshot eyes that in one measuring look had sized Falcon up as a flash cove, rolling in rhino. "You helped the gentleman, didya, Ling?" he asked in a wheedling tone.

"Save your breath," said Falcon contemptuously. "I'll give the boy nothing you can spend at the gin shop."

"Ow! Wotta unkind thing ter say, sir! I never touch the—"

"Where did you steal this child? And don't tell me he's your own, for he knows how to speak, which is more than I can say for you."

Silas crouched, his eyes narrowing. "What right you got callin' me a thief? You 'ristocrats is all the same! I reckon you bleed just like—" He sprang forward and almost banged his nose on the muzzle of the pistol that somehow was an inch from his face. With a shriek, he drew back, and broke into a farrago of protest.

Falcon said icily, "Will you stop that? Or shall I? Permanently."

"Please don't hurt him, sir," said Ling. "He's all I got."

Silas stopped his tirade, and pulled the boy to him not unkindly. "That's right, son. Stick up fer yer old pal."

Falcon looked at the pair thoughtfully. 'He's all I got . . .' This was the boy's life, belike, and if he interfered, he might be doing him no favour.

Silas said in a sullen growl, "I never stole the boy, mister. I took him off Tyburn Tree!"

"Good God! But he's just a child! You mean they'd—"

"Nah, nah! The cove what found him had been topped, and the little shaver was blubberin' under the gallows where he was swingin'. It were a bad night, comin' down cats and dogs, sir, and perishin' cold. So I took him, and I won't hand you no whiskers, I meant ter sell him fer a climbin' boy."

Intrigued, Falcon dismounted and tethered Andante to a branch once more. "But you didn't."

"Nah." Silas ruffled the child's thick curls. "Couldn't do it, mate. He's not a bad little 'un. But a few weeks ago a cove told me the man who'd first taken the boy had found him wanderin' about on t'other side of St. James's Park. Like the fool he was, he'd sold his duds—his clothes, sir—'cause they was flash. And after he'd got rid of everythin' that mighta helped tell who he was, it broke through his brainbox that the boy might be worth somethin' to them what had lost him. Before he could bring Found back to try and find his kinfolks, he got took and topped fer being on the dubbing lay."

"You mean the fellow who took the boy was a pick-pocket and was hanged before he could trace Ling's family, is that it?"

"Yussir."

"But you don't know his real name? Or anything about him?"

"Bin too long, I reckon. And you don't re'clect nothin', does yer, Found?"

The child shook his curls.

Falcon looked at Silas frowningly. "Walk with me, if you please. Ling, will you guard my horse? Don't come too near him, you understand?"

The boy nodded and knelt about ten feet from the stallion, fixing him with a stern, no-nonsense gaze.

When they were safely out of earshot, Falcon said, "I take it you're in Town now to try and find his family. I presume you've checked with Bow Street?"

"Lord luv'yer, no sir! They'd put Ling in one o' them homes. On the Parish, sir." He said in a hoarse whisper, "Better orf dead, he'd be."

"Then—what the deuce d'you mean to do with him?"

"Keep me ogles open, and me listeners stretched out, sir." He shrugged philosophically. "But, tellyer the truth, I ain't all that eager. We've got used to each other. It's company, y'know. Sorta like—family, Mr. Falcon. Yus, I reckernize yer now, on account of I heard so much about yer and yer—er, looks. No offence."

"Hum. Where d'you live? How do you support yourself?"

"We was livin' in the country, wiv a—er, friend. Now we're in London I can sometimes get work as a gardener. Knows how to trim trees, I do. And Found's old enough to be a link boy."

"I suppose," muttered Falcon, "there are hundreds of such children, poor creatures."

"Thousands, mate. Some born on the wrong side o' the blanket, as they say. Some born in the gutter wivout no blanket at all. Some gen-you-wine orphans. The Big Smoke's teemin' wiv 'em. Teemin'!"

"Yes. It's a brutal world, unfortunately."

"Oh, I dunno. I reckon the world's orl right. Trouble comes

· 118 ·

when coves won't put up with the hand they're dealt, and go about whinin' and wishin' fer what they can't have."

Amused, Falcon said, "But surely the desire for better things is what brings progress. Does not every man have the right to try and improve his lot?"

"Ah, but—do it? Them as I've seen, once they start "improvin'" they're never satisfied. Oh, I know a few, sir, wot's fulla ambition to "better" 'emselves. Claw and scratch every hour of the day they do. And one or two done well and made a nice bit of rhino. But seems ter me like the more they get, the less fun they have and the more miserable they is."

Falcon chuckled, then reached out. "Would you do me the favour of shaking my hand, Silas?"

The big man stared in amazement, spat on his palm, and wiped his hand on his breeches. "Lumme!" he exclaimed as they exchanged a firm grip. "Thank yer, sir, I'm sure. I— Hey!" He blinked at the coins in his palm. "Nah—it's too much, sir! I'll admit I were hopin' you might drop me a shillin' or two, but— five guineas? Lor', Mr. Falcon, I won't know how to go on!"

"Just don't spend it all in a gin parlour. Buy some shelter and food for you and the boy, and think about giving him a proper name. Good luck to you, Silas."

Riding back to Great Ormond Street at a far more circumspect pace than when he'd left it, Falcon thought about the ill-assorted pair Fate had thrown together. He could still see the wistfulness in the child's eyes when he'd shaken his hand and said his farewells. Such a solemn face for a little boy.

The philosophical Silas put him in mind of Tummet. It was remarkable that a man who had not known the benefit of college or University, who very likely couldn't even write his own name, could yet be so wise. "Trouble comes when coves won't put up with the hand they're dealt, and go about whinin' and wishin' fer what they can't have." That was precisely what he must help Katrina to see, in spite of the interference of a certain female.

The thought of Gwendolyn banished the foundling and Silas from his mind. Why he permitted the chit to so cut up his peace was past understanding. She was a thorn in his flesh; a perpetual irritant who had the power to wound him as no one had wounded him for a very long time. And who could make him laugh, and had very bravely saved his life on Wednesday morning. He found that he was smiling at Andante's ears and pulled himself up sharply. It must cease. By God, it had better cease! The Smallest Rossiter must be removed from his house and from their lives! He sighed glumly. The prospect was less than joyous. She was such a lively little thing. Falcon House would seem devilish dull without her . . .

Shocked by the jab of a spur, Andante curvetted.

Falcon quieted him and apologized. And riding on, he set his jaw grimly. She must go. This time he would not—*dare* not weaken! For Katrina's dear sake!

ou said," Gwendolyn reminded as she walked along the upstairs corridor, "that Mr. August would be back 'fly-and-spoon.' I think that would mean 'dry-and-soon' but I hadn't the chance to ask you yesterday."

Balancing several snowy cravats on one large palm, Tummet said, "No, Miss Gwen, but you didn't oughta come up the back stairs 'long o' me. Bad fer the consequence of ladies like you, it is."

"Fiddle! Now tell me, is it 'dry-and-soon'?"

"Nah, mate. You almost got it right, though. 'Fly-and-spoon' means 'spry-and-soon.' Which is what the guv—" His jaw dropped and he stared with starting eyes as Falcon strode around the corner to come face-to-face with the very lady he'd hoped to avoid. "—Ain't!" finished Tummet feebly.

'Confound it!' thought Falcon, instinctively running a hand through his rumpled hair.

"Goodness!" exclaimed Gwendolyn. "Andante threw you?"

"Either that, or I threw him! You may take your pick, ma'am."

The ice in his eyes, the heavy brows drawn into the black bar above his nose, were all too familiar harbingers of his mood. Her heart sank, but she said calmly, "Thank you. I shall retreat and consider my choices."

"As soon as I have got rid of my dirt, I'll come down and we will consider them together," he said with grim emphasis. Watching her as she nodded and limped away, he called, "Where may I expect to find you?"

She turned back and said with a mischievous dimple, "But in the book room, of course, Mr. Falcon."

"Of course," he muttered, and followed Tummet into his parlour. "Well, what the devil are you smirking about? Did you never before hear of a man going heels over arse?"

" 'Course," said Tummet, proceeding into the bedchamber and tenderly disposing of the lacy cravats. "Just never knowed *you* ter take a flyer. Brung some o' the park wiv yer, eh Guv?"

Falcon caught sight of himself in the cheval-glass, and shuddered.

"Didn't do that arm no good, did yer?" Tummet began to ease him out of his muddy coat. "Wot they call a not very protepinqshious journey?"

"By—Jupiter," said Falcon, eyeing him in awe.

"Proper jaw-breaker, ain't it?" Tummet grinned proudly. "Thought I'd never get me tongue 'round it, but I done, din't I? I'll be tossing 'em orf like you nobs 'fore you knows it!"

"God forbid! Where did you find that one? In your home away from home, I fancy."

"If you is referring to the Rose and Crown," said Tummet with a grand air, "no, Guv. A passable establishyment, but—not a word foundry, if y' take me meaning. Though a cove can pick up orl kindsa int'resting bits and pieces if— Cor! If Doc Sir Jim was to see this, 'e'd—"

"Oh, have done, man! Get some hot water and you can likely mend matters as well as that over-paid leech! And be quick, if you please! Miss Rossiter is waiting."

'Ar, but not wiv joyous antecedation,' thought Tummet. He went into the corridor and sent a lackey running for hot water and some medical supplies. "And don't let Mrs. V. see yer get 'em," he warned, "else she'll come clucking and Mr. August'll raise a proper riot!" Returning to pull off Falcon's riding boots, he said, "That there Andy Dan's a ugly brute, and—"

"Andante."

"Orl right. That, then. But I wouldn't a thought 'e could send you—"

"Well, he did. Lord, but I'm all mud! Small wonder Miss Rossiter stared! I'll wear the purple coat and lilac breeches. And— you may put down that pomatum! My hair needs to be brushed, not turned into glue!"

Tummet groaned and rolled his eyes at the ceiling. For the next quarter-hour he was busily occupied. He was watching the careful placement of a large diamond amidst the lacy cravat when Falcon asked absently, "What did you mean about picking up interesting bits and piece? Are rumours slithering about again?"

"Thick and fast, Guv." Tummet glanced at the door and lowered his voice dramatically. "Word is—'e's come back!"

"Attila the Hun, no doubt."

"Don't know 'bout 'im, mate. I meant the Young Pretender!" Gratified by Falcon's astonished stare, Tummet nodded. "Ar. Charlie Stuart's come back to put Butcher Cumberland to the test again, so—"

"You're mad! Stuart had as lief present his head to German George on a platter, as to take such a chance! You should pay no heed to such rubbishing stuff!"

Annoyed, Tummet shrugged and said loftily, "You arst! I toldya wot they're saying."

Falcon scowled at him and stood for the white satin waistcoat to be slipped on. "And by 'they' you refer to your rum touches in the Rose and Crown? Much they know of international intrigues!"

"Yus, but that's just it, Guv! They *does* know. Word goes 'round the taverns like a 'ouse on fire! Why d'you 'spose that there friend o' yourn's allus 'anging about? The stout lit'ry cove."

"Mr. Ramsey Talbot?" His attention arrested, Falcon looked up and said sharply, "*He* patronizes the Rose and Crown? Are you sure?"

"Once a week, at least, mate—whoops! Guv, I mean. And it ain't no gents club. Makes yer think, don't it?"

Falcon was thinking of it when he strolled down the stairs a few minutes later. There were any number of reasons why Ramsey Talbot might be lurking about the Rose and Crown, and certainly it would be worth making a push to learn what those reasons might be. But as for Bonnie Prince Charlie venturing onto British soil again . . . Nonsense! The Prince was brave and daring, but he was no fool, and it would be foolish in the extreme both to leave Paris, and to attempt to drum up support for another Uprising.

With an impatient shrug, he dismissed the matter from his mind, and strode with less than his customary briskness across the hall, only to pull up and stand frowning at the closed book room door, reluctant to attempt a task that should be so easy but had somehow assumed gigantic proportions.

'All you have to do, fool,' he told himself, 'is speak one brief sentence. "Madam, be so good as to leave my house!" That's simple enough, surely? Vulgar, but simple.' But this was not the first time he had nerved himself to utter those rude words, and on each occasion they stuck in his throat and he'd got no farther than "Madam" before the Smallest Rossiter had started an argument, or made him laugh—or both—and he'd wound up like a silly idiot, postponing her ouster, and with the threat to Katrina looming ever larger. He set his jaw. Well, today he would not fail! He would be coldly detached and in complete control. She would not divert him from his One Brief Sentence. He would even practice that famous "li" business and be calm and dignified, neither raising his voice nor losing his temper.

He took a deep breath, clenched his hands and lost a good deal of his "li" when he saw that a lackey hovered nearby, watching him curiously. How long had he been standing here? The man must think him properly demented which would be a prime topic of conversation in the servants' hall! He stepped forward, the lackey pounced to fling the door open, and he stalked inside.

He had half hoped she would not be here but would have either sought Katrina's protection, or, better yet, have gone home to Rossiter Court rather than face what she must know would be an unpleasant interview with him. But there she was; sitting quietly in the window seat, engrossed in a book, and managing to appear small and fragile. 'Another tome about my unhappy heritage,' he thought, and sent such a glare at the lackey that the man fairly leapt back and shut the door with a loud click.

Gwendolyn closed the book and set it aside. Folding her hands in her lap, she looked at Falcon in her candid way, and waited.

He bowed. "At least you play fair, ma'am. You could have run."

"But I could not deny you your chance to scold me," she said meekly. "I am very sorry that you fell, August. I trust you did not further injure your arm."

She had scored at once, with that subtle reminder that she had saved his life when he was attacked. And it was truth, heaven knows, for how many females would have had the gumption to— He caught himself up and dragged back his resentment, saying with one of his more impressive scowls, "Had I not been obliged to be concerned for your safety, I'd not have taken the injury."

Gwendolyn shook her head and looked reproving. It had, he knew, been a mean remark, and he improved upon it. "You are expecting that I should thank you for shooting Green so deedily." He bowed again. "Very well, be advised that I am duly thankful, Miss Rossiter."

She said gently, "You did thank me, Mr. Falcon. At the time."

Gad, but the woman was cunning! The memory of sweeping her up and whirling her about, and of how slender and light she had been in his arms rushed upon him. He bit his lip and with an effort retaliated, "It was an inadequate return for the service you rendered. I shall have to find some more tangible way to—reward you."

She caught her breath, then said, "There. Now you have properly set me down and you will feel better."

He did not feel better. He felt utterly miserable, and he had barely begun! Drifting closer to her he drawled, "Shall I, indeed? I might do so were you able to explain to me by what right you persist in interfering in what don't concern you!"

"I had no right," she admitted repentantly, "and I am truly sorry for what happened with Lady Mount-Durward. Had I known—"

"And thereby hangs a tale, for there is such a great deal of our *personal business* you do not know, ma'am. And that is—I'll not wrap it up in clean linen—is none of *your* business! But ignorance doesn't stop you, any more than delicacy. You had the unmitigated impertinence to deliberately goad that dreadful—er, to goad Lady Hester into humiliating Katrina and me last evening, and—"

"No!" Distressed, she came to her feet and stretched out a hand pleadingly. "You cannot think that, August! I was upset because you were so spiteful towards Trina, but—"

Touched on the raw, his temper flared. "Spiteful, is it? I 'faith but you take a deal upon yourself, madam! What I say to my sister is none of your bread and butter!"

"Don't be vulgar!" Bridling, she lowered her hand and her own eyes began to sparkle. "Katrina is my dear friend and to see you take advantage of her gentle and sweet nature, is—"

"If I chose to beat my sister at thirty-minute intervals, day and night, 'twould be no one's concern but Katrina's and mine!" That foolish statement recalled him to his rehearsed and long lost One Simple Sentence, and he began again, "I will ask, Madam Busybody, that you—"

"That is the most dreadful thing I ever heard!" she interrupted, her voice ringing with indignation. "Such bestial behaviour would be the concern of every decent-thinking person in England! Katrina is of age! She has every right to choose her mate! You know perfectly well that she loves Jamie—"

Already infuriated with himself, her words fanned his anger. He took a step toward her, and the blaze in his eyes caused her to draw back nervously. He said through his teeth, "*Hear* me, madam! My sister will *never* wed James Morris! I'll see him dead, first!"

Gwendolyn wet dry lips, drew herself up, and argued, "He won't fight you! He loves Trina, and he knows—"

"He'll fight! Oh, I'll own he's been hard to bring up to the mark, but I've a weapon now. If I must, I'll use it. And I promise you, ma'am. He'll fight!"

Dismayed, she said, "You must think highly of him to be willing to hang for his sake!" But suddenly, the sight of his pale strained face, that molten glare in his eyes, was more than she could bear. She touched his arm and pleaded, "Oh, August, I know you did not mean that! You have not rested as you should, and 'twas fever from your wound talking, not your true self! I know that whatever you say, in your heart you do not dislike Jamie nearly as much as you pretend, and—"

He caught her wrist in a grip that made her gasp. "You *know nothing!*" He released her so violently that she staggered and fell back onto the sofa with a little shocked cry.

"I know that—that you love Trina," she stammered. "But don't you see how you are breaking her heart? Did you know that she weeps at night? Are you too full of pride to care about her grief? August—hate me, if you must. But I beg of you—"

Hate her . . . ? Could she really think that? Better if she did think it, of course. Considerably shaken, he said tempestuously, "Have done! Have done!" So much for being cold and controlled! So much for "li"! He had loved and left some of the most beautiful and most admired ladies in the land, and always had handled the manner of their parting with tact and grace. What had become of his tact and grace now? Why was it that this slip of a girl could so swiftly ignite his wrath that everything he had meant to say was swept away and forgotten? Perhaps she was right and he was feverish. Was it fever that made it seem so vitally important that she should, to some small extent, understand? He knew only that it was so, and bowing to that awareness, he sank onto the fireside chair, hands clasped between his knees, and his dark head downbent.

"Very well," he muttered. "Since you cannot keep from prying, and because Katrina cares about you, I'll gratify your curiosity."

"No! August, please! All I ask is—"

He made a savage silencing gesture. "You've seen my grandmama's portrait. Despite her—alien features, you won't deny she was a great beauty."

"Of—of course she was. And I never thought her alien."

He said sardonically, "Then you are indeed a *rara avis*. But the important thing is that she was a remarkable human being; as warm and loving as she was beautiful, and a most accomplished lady besides. She made one mistake. She loved greatly, for— But I go too fast." He drew a steadying breath. "Natasha was living with her family in Paris when my grandfather, Sir Geoffrey Falcon, was presented to her. He was ten years her senior, a diplomatist and a very dashing fellow, who had just been knighted for a brilliant piece of work. He lost his heart to her at first sight. He was one of many. All Paris was mad for Natasha. There were wealthier and more highly placed men willing to overlook her—unfortunate lineage; fine gentlemen, eager to give her their proud old names. But she was as lost in love as Sir Geoffrey, and her parents, reluctantly I believe, gave in. She was seventeen when they married. The following year he brought her to England to have her first child."

He paused, and Gwendolyn ventured, "Please stop. There is no need for you to—"

"Be still! You pestered me into speaking of something that is too painful to ever be discussed in this house. Now you shall gain some faint notion of the harm you've done with your meddling!" He stalked to the credenza, poured a healthy measure of brandy, sampled it, then carried the glass to the hearth and stood gazing into the fire.

"My mother was born at Ashleigh," he said broodingly. "Sir Geoffrey abandoned his career, and they lived in Sussex all year round. At first, they were ideally happy, but as time went by, Natasha came to see that she dwelt in a fool's paradise. The visits of her husband's friends became less and less frequent. They were seldom invited to the homes of neighbours, and never went to Town. To give him his due, I believe Sir Geoffrey never complained, but Natasha realized at last that he was shunned; cut off from the society he always had known. Because of her. Because those sterling English *aristocrats* looked down on her and named her—" his eyes glared, and he fairly spat out "*half-breed!* Natasha! Born of the love between a princess of Russia, and a great Mandarin of China! And those narrow-souled *ladies* and *gentlemen* dared judge that exquisite little creature beyond the pale! My God!"

He returned to the window and stood there with his head thrown back and one hand thrust deep into his pocket.

Gwendolyn longed to be elsewhere, but she did not dare move, and waited, feeling trapped, and yet fascinated by his story.

"Sir Geoffrey was a fine sportsman and a bruising rider to hounds," he went on at length, "but he could enjoy neither pursuit alone. I'm very sure Natasha knew how much of his former life was denied him, and how he missed that life. She worshipped him, and she blamed herself for having brought shame on the man she loved. Eventually, she begged him to divorce her. He would have none of it, of course. A second child, a son, was born, but died in infancy, and my mother grew up an only child. Natasha adored her, but Mama hated her mixed blood and tried to conceal it." As though unable to be still, he went back to his chair and sat down before resuming: "She was pretty, and the Oriental cast of feature seems to have skipped a generation in her case. She was overjoyed when she was sent away to a select young ladies seminary.

"Grandmama was still a very lovely woman, not yet forty, when my mother married and moved into this house. For years Mama refused to go down to Sussex, but my father held Natasha in the deepest respect, and after I was born he insisted that I visit my grandparents frequently. Sir Geoffrey had become quiet and withdrawn and had not much to say to me. But Grandmama Natasha!" He smiled nostalgically, and his voice softened. "The tales she would tell me, Gwen! The store of knowledge she had about nature and history and the world around us! The wonderful pictures she would draw. You cannot guess how I looked forward to those visits."

Gwendolyn said gently, "I think I can guess. I knew you loved her greatly."

"Very greatly. A love that was fully returned, I promise you. Katrina was still in the nursery when I was packed off to Eton. I was not happy there. I think Grandmama knew, for she would write the most wonderful letters and do all she might to encourage me." He paused, then said haltingly, "Mama was ashamed of my—appearance, and couldn't endure to be near me." Gwendolyn stifled a gasp and saw his hand clench hard, but he went on, "My father was devoted to Trina and to me, but he was kept busy with the estates—we have a large property in the shires, you may know—and also he was at that time very active in politics. If I studied hard, it was to please Grandmama. I counted the days till I would come home for the holidays and lay my small triumphs before her. I was shattered the following year, when I was forbidden to go down to Sussex. Grandmama was ill, Mama told me, and unable to see anyone. Papa was kind and tried to console me, but he seldom opposed Mama. I was headstrong, and 'twas in my mind that Natasha wanted me to come." He paused and set his glass on the table, his movements slow and deliberate, but Gwendolyn saw that his hand trembled. She had guessed by now what he was going to say and, dreading the telling, clasped her own hands tightly. "I had quite a sum," he went on, "that I'd saved from my allowance, and I slipped out early one morning and took a chair to the coaching station. I was very careful, when I finally reached Ashleigh, to go in the back way, and I crept into Grandmama's suite before anyone saw me." Again, he paused briefly. "I expected to find her weak, and changed. I have never—never been so horrified. She was far more than ill." His voice shredded. "She was . . . blind. And—and quite . . . hopelessly . . . insane."

It was the last thing Gwendolyn had expected. "Oh, my heavens!" she exclaimed. "How dreadful! Poor lady! What a frightful shock for you!"

He stood jerkily, went to the credenza and refilled his glass. Tossing off the brandy he returned to the fire to stand facing Gwendolyn, and she ached with sympathy to see his eyes so haunted.

"I couldn't move," he muttered. "I just stood there, staring . . . Then she began to scream and—and rave. One of the nurses ran in and saw me. I was whisked away, as you may guess." He ducked his head. "I remember nothing more of that summer. Nothing whatsoever. I went back to Eton. I never saw Grandmama Natasha again. She—died six months later."

Her kind heart wrung, she said gently, "Oh—my dear! I am so sorry!"

"Are you?" A twisted smile was levelled at her. "I was sorry too. And bitter, because that dear and lovely lady had been taken so long before her time. And so cruelly." He gave a derisive grunt. "Little did I know! Another six months went by before I learned the truth. A schoolmate told me. Gloatingly. Horribly. I was so stunned I didn't even strike him, though afterwards . . . But that's another story. I ran away from school and came back to Town and demanded the truth. My father tried to dissemble, but I'd have none of it, and at last he gave in.

"A charming widow, it seemed, had bought an estate near Ashleigh. She had an eye for Sir Geoffrey, and complete contempt for his foreign wife. I suppose poor faithful little Natasha thought it the judgment of the gods. She decided to clear the way for her beloved—to allow him to find all the happiness his marriage had denied him. So—that pitiful heartbroken lady . . . poisoned herself!" He heard Gwendolyn's shocked exclamation, and not daring to look at her, flung around to face the fire again. After a moment, gripping the mantel with both hands, he said, "Only she was not conversant with such—procedures. She took not quite enough of the poison. And she was left more or less alive, and . . . and as I last saw her."

A hushed pause. He pulled himself together and finished, "So now you know! And can you see now, madam? Can you get just a glimpse of why for not one instant would I think of allowing Katrina to follow that ghastly path? No, by God! Sooner would I see her enter a convent! My beloved grandmama was slain by pride and bigotry. And if you imagine anything has changed in this great city since then—look about you! See how they sneer once I am safely past! Hear how they name me! How they despise—" He heard a faint sound and jerked around.

Tears glistened on Gwendolyn's lashes, and a bright path slipped down her left cheek even as she gazed at him.

Astounded, he covered the distance between them in two long strides and dropped to one knee before her. "Why, Gwen," he said tenderly, taking both her hands in his. "Have you such compassion that you can weep for a lady you never knew?"

She blinked at him and a diamond drop coursed down her right cheek. "Poor, tragic . . . little thing," she said in a very scratchy voice. "Oh, August!"

He raised her hands and pressed a kiss on each. "Thank you for that sweet sympathy, m'dear."

Gwendolyn sniffed and searched her pocket.

Sitting beside her, he offered his handkerchief, and she dried her tears and blew her nose.

With a faint smile he watched her tuck his handkerchief into her pocket. "I am so glad you told me," she said. "And I promise faithfully never to repeat a word of it. Dare I ask one question? Is—is Sir Geoffrey still living?"

"He survived Natasha by a year. Her diary was in his hands

when they found him. And to read that, I promise you, would wring tears from a stone!"

She sighed. "I can well imagine."

The room was quiet for a space. It was a comfortable quiet, the tensions between them seeming to have been swept away. Watching Gwendolyn's expressive face, Falcon could understand why Katrina had become so very fond of her. She really was a taking little thing, with such a kind heart, and so genuine an interest in those around her. Not an ounce of affectation, either. Only look how she was wrinkling that dainty little nose.

Gwendolyn said thoughtfully, "I do believe you should allow Katrina to tell Jamie."

He stood, his smile fading. "Certainly not! One does not spread word of a suicide about Town. My father has enough to bear! Besides, Morris is just the kind of gudgeon to declare with great nobility and no insight that it made no difference. Huh!"

"Well, that is true, of course." Standing also, she scanned his face with deeper understanding. A smile crept into his eyes again, but she thought he looked very tired, and she said guiltily, "I was monstrous unkind to have caused you to endure such a painful retelling, August. I wish you will believe—"

He put his fingers lightly over her lips. " 'Tis behind us. Let us say no more about it."

She nodded. "Very well. But—you really do look rather pulled. It cannot be wise for you to be up and about with that nasty wound not yet healed. I think Sir James Knight would be really vexed if he knew."

"Oh, I've no doubt of it. 'Tis best not to pay too much attention to his rantings. He's a proper doomsday doctor, you know!"

"I suppose if I say he did not get knighted by ranting to no purpose, you will say that is precisely how one gets knighted."

He laughed. "You begin to know me too well, miss!"

"Even so, I wish you would rest. At least keep at home for a few days."

He had every intention of going to the Winter Fete at Overlake Park the following day, and no intention of mentioning that fact. Walking over to open the door, he assured her he was feeling "perfectly fit," but that it was kind of her to worry for his sake.

She shook her head and left him. When she reached her bed-chamber, she sat by the window and gazed out at the rainy gardens and at the little summer-house where she and August had engaged in some lively discussions. Thinking over the tragic story he had told her, she felt tears start to her eyes again. That poor little lady—and that poor tormented boy! How terribly hurt he must have been when his school-mate so cruelly told him the truth of the matter. Whoever it was should have been soundly thrashed. She smiled musingly. Perhaps he was. August had hinted that there had been something more. He fought back, did August N. K. Falcon. The poor creature had been fighting back all his life, one way or another. 'Twas remarkable he'd not been crushed by the world. 'Faith, but there was little wonder he felt as he did.

She went to the dressing table and unlocked her jewel case. The collection revealed would have been judged pitiful by most ladies of the *ton*, but she had never thought of herself as being the type to wear expensive jewels, and although she treasured some of the lovely pieces given her by her family, she seldom wore them. She took up a gold chain and a locket surrounded by intricate filigree set with semi-precious stones. Opening the locket, she gazed wistfully at the object it contained: a carefully polished but very much used golden guinea. Sighing, she closed the locket and returned it to the case, then wandered back to the window.

It was raining steadily now. She had never disliked the rain, nor did she share her brother Newby's feelings of depression on grey days. But on this decidedly grey morning she closed her eyes and directed a small prayer to whichever angel was in charge of the weather. "Please, holy sir or madam, if 'tis at all possible, might it *not* pour tomorrow?"

Falcon leaned back in the sedan chair and closed his eyes. Jove, but he was tired. He'd intended to walk to Rossiter Court, but the rain had changed his mind. He'd been lucky to find an unoccupied chair. Deuce take the fellows, they didn't have to gallop! He leaned forward and shouted a request for less speed, then eased himself back again.

Confounded arm. The Smallest Rossiter was likely in the right of it and he should have kept to his bed today. If truth were told, he'd have rather enjoyed to stay at home. But, stupid as it may be, he could not dismiss Tummet's remarks about Bonnie Prince Charlie, and he was anxious to hear what Ross had to say in the matter.

Despite his arm and the fact that he felt rather uncomfortably warm, he knew a deep sense of relief that he'd not been obliged to send the Smallest Rossiter packing. To drag out the sad tale of Grandmama Natasha had been an ordeal, but it had been worth it to win Gwendolyn's understanding. They'd have liked each other, he thought. Although Grandmama might have been a trifle taken aback by some of Gwendolyn's starts. Indeed, many people, even today, would be shocked that a young lady should hold views on such things as politics, or the history and philosophies of other nations (such as China!). And that she would voice those views in mixed company would be judged presumptuous and unfeminine. He chuckled. An independent spirit, the Smallest Rossiter, which was the very quality he found so delightful. It was remarkable in fact that she had not argued when he'd rejected her suggestion that Katrina tell Jamie Morris about Grandmama Natasha. Nor had she protested his remark that Jamie was sure to say it would make no difference. Instead, she'd said in that funny grave little way of hers, "Well, that's true, of course," which was—

He frowned. She *had* been agreeing with him, had she not? She couldn't have meant that *Morris* would be right if he made such a silly observation?

He reviewed that part of their discussion carefully. In fact, he worried at it all the way to Rossiter Court.

CHAPTER VIII

y Capitaine he is not in the home!" Travattori viewed Falcon from his superior height, flung up his head and lowered his eyelids dramatically. "The use it is not for you to beseech me, signor. Where he is going?" He gave a greatly exaggerated shrug and spread his long bony hands.

Falcon swore under his breath. The journey from Great Ormond Street had been considerably round-about and eventful. A shouting, brawling crowd had blocked the junction of Tottenham Court Road and Oxford Street. His alarmed bearers had retreated to Drury Lane, and thence to Charing Cross Road, where they were delayed once again by a troop of dragoons thundering to quell the disturbance. Having reached his destination at last it was irksome to find that Gideon was frippering about somewhere.

He left a note with Travattori telling Gideon that he must see him urgently, and went back to his bearers, whom he had fortunately asked to wait. He directed them to convey him to the Turk's Head Coffee House. They made the journey without further incident until they reached the Strand, which was blocked by a great coach broadside across the road, its team in a great state of agitation, the coachman no less agitated, and a small crowd shouting advice to the lady who was alighting from the coach and who shouted back at them when she was not reviling her unfortunate coachman.

Falcon left his chair and walked along towards the popular coffee house. Head down against the rain, and his thoughts elsewhere, he failed to see the angry lady abandon coach and coachman and march towards him under an umbrella held over her by an anxious footman.

"Stand aside, there!" commanded a loud, harsh, and all too familiar voice.

Falcon's head jerked up, and he halted.

The Lady Clara Buttershaw was tall, angular, harsh-featured, inordinately proud, and opinionated. She was widely feared and disliked, but her wealth and her ancient lineage made her a power among the *haut ton.* She had formed a deep passion for Falcon, and while rejecting him publicly, had privately thrown herself at him and made every effort to seduce him. Far from returning her affection, he thought her an impossible woman and did all in his power to avoid her. His coldness, however, she interpreted as a justifiable sense of unworthiness; his often sardonic remarks she was convinced were uttered to conceal his love, for that he should not adore her was inconceivable. In her arrogance it had never occurred to her that he would have sufficient intelligence to be aware that she and her spinster sister, Lady Julia Yerville, were deeply involved with the League of Jewelled Men. Lady Clara's bubble had burst when Falcon and his friends had confronted her and dared to interfere in one of her schemes, contriving to rescue Zoe Grainger, who had been a virtual prisoner in Yerville Hall.

Now, meeting a pair of hard dark eyes that glared fury, and a mouth bitterly downturned, Falcon found those expressions easier to face than the cloying sweetness that had so appalled him. He swept off his tricorne and made her a magnificent bow. "*Dear Clara,*" he murmured wickedly.

She uttered a screech of wrath. "*Serpent!*" Wresting the umbrella from her startled footman's grasp, she snapped it shut and swung it aloft. "*Villain! Libertine!*"

Her intentions were all too clear. With a whoop, Falcon took to his heels and ran, the lady's most unladylike profanities and the hilarity of the onlookers following him.

Grinning, the porter at the Turk's Head Coffee House swung the door wide, "Sanctuary, sir," he murmured, with a wink. Falcon laughed breathlessly and went into the warm interior, where he was at once shown to his favourite table near the fire. The encounter with Lady Clara had lightened his spirits, which were even more improved when a fragrant mutton pie and fried potatoes were set before him. He had just picked up his knife when a familiar voice faltered, "Might I join you—for a minute, Falcon?"

He thought, 'Deuce take the fellow!' and looking up was startled to see Sir Owen Furlong swaying beside his table and white as death. "You'd best be quick about it," he said, "else you'll fall in my pie."

Sir Owen sat down and leaned back against the settle, breathing hard.

With an imperious gesture Falcon secured the attention of a waiter who hurried off and returned with brandy. Sir Owen's hand shook as he raised the glass, and not until a trace of colour had returned to the drawn face did Falcon enquire off-handedly, "Get caught in the riot, perchance?" Sir Owen looked at him as though he were invisible, and he added, "None of my affair, but if you can't deal with hooligans, you should keep a servant with you when you venture out."

Sir Owen blinked at him.

Beginning to fear that the man had suffered some kind of brainstorm, Falcon waved a hand in front of his face.

"Don't hit him!" James Morris hurried up, rain dripping from his cloak.

Irked, Falcon said, "I wasn't hitting him, you silly clod. The fellow's gone into some kind of trance."

Squeezing onto the settle beside him, Morris said, "He's had a nasty shock. Oh, *do* move over, August! You ain't *that* corpulent!"

"*Corpulent!* Of all the—"

Gideon Rossiter came in looking concerned, and Perry Cranford limped after him, waving to some acquaintances, his peg-leg thumping on the floor.

"I'm most terribly sorry," said Rossiter, nodding to Falcon and sitting beside Sir Owen. "We couldn't find a trace of her."

"Her? Who?" asked Falcon.

"You sound like an owl," said Morris. "Are you sure 'twas *her*, dear boy?"

Sir Owen said with a wan smile, "D'you think I could mistake the lady?"

"Jupiter!" exclaimed Falcon, the light dawning. "If you're jabbering about the Frenchwoman who shot you down so as to steal that accursed Agreement, I'd rather think you *should* remember what she looks like!"

Sir Owen sighed. "I'll never forget for as long as I live."

Falcon gave a disgusted snort. "Which would have been a short span had the lady had her way! You cannot think Mademoiselle Maria Barthélemy, or whatever she called herself at the time, would dare show her nose in London again? Why, we'd have her clapped up in a trice!"

"For what?" asked Cranford, dragging a chair to the end of the table. "No charges were brought 'gainst her. There were no witnesses when she shot Owen and purloined the Agreement. We had no evidence. And what judge, looking at such a beautiful creature, would believe her capable of so violent an act?"

"*He* was a witness!" Falcon jabbed his fork at Sir Owen. "And had he the wit of a wart-hog *would* have brought charges 'gainst her. Instead of which, he excuses her murderous conduct and moons over her! I wonder he don't go about wearing one of those sign-board things, reading 'Human target—penny a shot'!"

Sir Owen flushed scarlet but stared at the table in tight-lipped silence.

Rossiter frowned. "Easy said, August. But you forget, I think, that Owen is in love with the lady."

"He don't forget," said Morris. "Just don't know what it is."

"Of course I know." Falcon added with his bored smile, " 'Tis a delusion. An intense but fortunately brief disorder of the brain." He gave his attention to his lunch, ignoring the mocking chorus.

Cranford said laughingly, "Expound, oh mighty expert! We yearn to hear more of your brilliant diagnoses."

"I'd not waste my valuable time. You all are infected with the disease, poor fellows, and would benefit not one whit, even if I could restore you to a vestige of common sense. Which is doubtful."

Morris swooped to snatch his plate and pass it to Cranford.

"Hey!" cried Falcon, springing up.

Holding the plate out of Falcon's reach, Cranford said gaily, "Not another bite till you educate the ignorant!"

Falcon crouched, his eyes narrowing.

" 'Ware that panther glare, Perry," warned Morris. "He's getting ready to run you through. Whom shall we notify, dear boy?"

Falcon gave him a withering look and sat down. With a great show of resignation he said, "Very well, but make an effort to attend my discourse with proper respect."

Rossiter clapped a hand over Morris' mouth. "Say on, Macduff!"

"Then let us consider the case of a comparatively sensible young female," Falcon began, adopting a scholarly air. "For reasons known only to herself, she suddenly becomes convinced she has fallen in love. Does she accept this as one of life's more interesting little quirks and go on her way with a grateful heart? No! She instead begins to drift about sighing so often that she is surrounded by a perpetual breeze, which she augments by weeping buckets of tears while declaring in accents of utter misery how happy she is!"

With a broad grin, Cranford said, "Marplot! You'll not dampen my vision of the tender passion."

Falcon shrugged. "Which merely proves my point, for males behave no less stupidly. They lose their appetites, go about smiling vacuously, and with the least encouragement bore their acquaintances to death while endowing a usually very ordinary girl with the qualities of an ethereal goddess. You may see a perfect example of such deluded idiocy"—he stared pointedly at Morris—"stumbling about Town with glazed eyes and the expression of an expiring sheep! He is—"

He was interrupted by shouts of laughter, during which he sprang up and recovered his plate.

Morris protested that he never behaved in so foolish a way. "And for your information, Lord Haughty-Snort, there's a deal more to falling in love than that silly stuff!"

"I agree," said Falcon with a bland smile. "There is the ultimate disaster. The poor fool who with humble and genuine devotion lays his heart and soul at the feet of his beloved only to be trampled upon and rejected. Probably"—again he looked squarely at Morris—"for some cogent reason which he should have anticipated in the first place." Sobering, he said, "Seriously, I once knew a fellow who blew his brains out when the parents of his chosen lady quite sensibly married her to another man. To permit oneself to become that vulnerable must surely be the most pathetic folly!"

"But a very human folly," said Cranford.

Rossiter remarked gravely, "And to fall in love is a folly you do not mean to commit, eh, Falcon?"

"Certainly not. I have my loves, mark you, but my heart is—and will remain—both intact and my own." Morris was regarding him steadily. For some inexplicable reason, he felt his face get hot and was unable to meet that fixed stare. Intensely irritated, he snapped, "Well? Say whatever is rattling around your brainbox, Sir Numps!"

Morris said solemnly, " 'He that will not when he may, when he will he shall have nay.' "

Amid more laughter, Falcon closed his eyes and shuddered.

A waiter at last hurried to their table. "Your wishes, gentlemen?"

"You'd not dare grant 'em," growled Falcon.

Rossiter said, "Oh, ale all around will suffice. Unless—is anyone hungry?"

There being no answers in the affirmative, the waiter went off looking disappointed.

"Now let's to business," said Rossiter. "If Owen's right and Miss Barthélemy is in this country, she is probably working for the League."

"Not so!" argued Sir Owen, firing up. "Her only reason for stealing the Agreement was to protect her brother. And 'tis no use glaring at me like that, Falcon. I will *not* testify 'gainst her! She did *not* mean to kill me! Heaven knows, she warned me. I just didn't believe—" He bit his lip, and shrugged. "I moved the wrong way, unfortunately."

Rossiter was watching Falcon's expression and he interrupted quickly, "Did Miss Barthélemy speak to you, just now? Or did she perhaps not even see you?"

"I walked around the corner, and there she was. It seemed— I mean—" Still not fully recovered and easily overcome by emotion, Sir Owen's voice trembled. "I think she was as taken aback as was I. She stopped dead, and—and spoke my name. Before I could say a word, she had been whisked into a carriage and was gone."

Cranford said understandingly, "It must have been a devilish shock for you. Still, 'twould be nice to know what she's up to this time."

Morris pursed his lips. "Perhaps nothing. Who's to say she didn't come back only to make sure Owen was going on all right?"

"I am," said Falcon. "If she's back, 'tis because that darling of France, her famous brother, has her doing his bidding again. And look who's just come in! Another pariah!"

"Hi, Johnny," called Morris cheerfully. "Let you out of your chains, did they?"

The unguarded remark carried all too well. Conversation in the large room died away. Heads turned, and not a few frowns were directed at the new arrival.

"Don't restrain yourself, my good block," drawled Falcon. "Climb on the table and proclaim our felon's presence to all London."

Morris looked abashed. "Oh, Jupiter! Spoke out of turn, did I?"

"Let us say your silence would have been golden."

"Never fret, Jamie." Jonathan Armitage pulled a chair up to the other end of the table and joined the group. "I'm not ashamed of being recognized."

Someone said clearly and contemptuously, "And there brays a man with no conscience!"

There were murmurs of agreement, and other voices were raised:

"Such rogues should not be permitted to mix with decent people!"

"But he's not doing so, dear boy. He's sitting with the Mandarin!"

There was a burst of laughter.

Falcon shoved Morris off the end of the settle, and it screeched across the tiles as he pushed it back and rose to his feet.

The laughter died an abrupt death and two sneering Macaronis at the far side of the room leapt from their chairs and departed in an inglorious scramble.

Falcon put up his glass and surveyed the now silent company with slow deliberation. Smiling, he enquired, "Did the person with the overgrown tongue wish to—ah, address me?"

Several of those present would have very much liked to address him, but it was said that August Falcon was at his deadliest when he smiled, and the quiet went unbroken.

He let the quizzing glass drop to the end of its ribbon. "What a pity," he murmured and sat down again to the accompaniment of a subdued burst of conversation.

Morris grinned. "Jolly nice!"

Tall and fair, with steadfast grey eyes and a strong nose and chin, Jonathan Armitage had been one of the East India Company's most promising and valued young officers. Three years earlier, with a loving family and a fine inheritance waiting in England and a bright future ahead of him, he'd been in Suez, en route to take command of his ship. While there, he had chanced to witness a clandestine meeting between a distinguished Frenchman and two middle-aged English ladies. If someone had told him that the Frenchman was the much admired soldier, Marshal Jean-Jacques Barthélemy, or that his companions were Lady Clara Buttershaw and her spinster sister, Lady Julia Yerville, it would have meant nothing to him. But all three were deeply involved in the schemes of the League of Jewelled Men, and Armitage had become a potential threat. He'd been attacked and left for dead when his ship foundered off the coast of Cornwall, his honour fouled and his reputation destroyed. Surviving the wreck by a fluke, but with an impaired recollection of his identity or his past life, he had endured two years of brutality and despair before the love and faith of a courageous girl, and the assistance of Falcon and Morris, had helped him win back his health and self-respect. He was happily married now, and fighting to clear his name, but he was still under a cloud, not knowing from one day to the next if he would be brought up before the High Court of the Admiralty and charged with dereliction of duty, a hanging offence.

"My thanks," he now said quietly. "But I can defend myself, August."

Falcon raised his eyebrows, "Whatever gave you the impression I was defending you? Do not give yourself airs."

Armitage grinned. He admired Falcon and was undeceived by the apparent set-down, but he delayed his response while the waiter served their ale. As the man went off, he said, "I went round to your house to pay you a sick call, August. I think your pretty sister was as surprised as I to find you gone out."

Falcon glanced apprehensively at the door. "You weren't such a clunch as to bring her here?"

"Never fear, you're not about to be ordered to your bed. Your sister and Miss Rossiter went out with Mrs. Haverley."

"Mrs. . . . Haverley . . ." Falcon sampled his ale, and muttered, "I know the name, but be dashed if I can— Ah! Kadenworthy's aunt, no? You remember her, Jamie. We met her down at Epsom in June."

Morris nodded. "A dear little old soul." Watching Falcon from the corners of his eyes, he asked innocently, "Where were they off to, Johnny?"

"Do not even think of it," warned Falcon.

"Only look at him lash his tail," exclaimed Morris, injured. "Well, that's one thing you cannot interfere with, August. My thoughts are my own."

"And as such are wasted on building silly castles in the air, instead of being used for something sensible."

"Nothing wrong with having castles in the air." Morris sighed, then added with a twinkle, "Unless you step out of the door!"

Falcon experienced a little difficulty in refraining from joining in the mirth. When it faded, he enquired idly, "Speaking of castles in the air, has anyone heard the rumours about Prince Charlie?"

Cranford answered, "Lord, yes. Who hasn't? They say King Louis is wildly eager to kick him out of France, and is using the Treaty of Aix-la-Chapelle 'gainst him, now that it's finally been signed."

"And that Charles insists he's entitled to remain in Paris, under the Treaty of Fontainebleau," said Armitage.

Sir Owen nodded. "Which is now outdated, of course. One can't but feel sorry for the Prince. Did you hear that his mistress—the de Talmont, I mean—has been ordered to refuse to admit him to her house, on pain of being exiled herself if she does not?"

"He must be enraged," said Rossiter. "If he truly cares for the lady."

Morris chuckled. "Did you hear that he rented a new house, right under King Louis' nose, and has filled the place with arms? He surely means to put up a fight."

Falcon murmured, "Then none of you believe he is back in England?"

Five heads jerked to him. Five pairs of eyes stared in astonishment.

Rossiter said, "In *England?* Dear heaven! I pray not!"

"He would be wits to let!" exclaimed Cranford. "One step over the border and Louis would never let him back into France!"

"And one foot on English soil and he'd lose his head before he could lower the other," said Armitage.

Morris appropriated a piece of Falcon's loaf unopposed. "To hear the talk at the Cocoa Tree, London's full of men who'd flock to shield him. And to join him!"

"And the ignoble Stuarts would bring down more death and destruction on more hare-brained followers," snorted Falcon.

Armitage said soberly, "I wasn't here during the Rebellion, but if only half of what I heard is truth, I cannot believe any thinking man would invite such another bloodbath!"

Watching Falcon, Rossiter asked, "Where did you pick up this rumour?"

"Tummet. He says 'tis whispered at the Rose and Crown."

"Gad!" said Cranford. "Old Ramsey Talbot patronizes that scruffy tavern. I wonder . . ."

"No!" Morris said vehemently, "I hold no brief for Charles Stuart, but he's not a dunce. Without King Louis' backing he'd as well commit suicide as try for another Uprising!"

Sir Owen nodded agreement. "Men may boast Jacobite loyalty in the taverns, but when it's play or pay, they go home to their wives and families. Prince Charles *must* know his chances would be dismal."

"Speaking of which," said Cranford, "only look at us! So dismal as any Newgate newcomers! August, I believe you've been hoaxing us!"

Falcon found himself the butt of much light-hearted scolding and when Gideon appeared to be no less amused than the rest, he dismissed his own unease. Enoch Tummet was not an educated man and couldn't be blamed for being taken in by taproom statesmen. The one who should have known better than to pay heed to such fustian was August Falcon. Admitting which, if only to himself, he felt obliged to order apple pie for everyone by way of apology.

They left soon afterwards and went their separate ways. Rossiter slowed his steps to match Sir Owen's pace and asked in his kindly fashion if he would like some company on the way back to Bond Street.

Furlong thanked him, but refused, declaring that he was quite recovered from his "most pathetic folly." His lips were tight and there was an angry glint in the blue eyes. Rossiter said slowly, "You don't much like Falcon, do you?"

"No. And it has naught to do with his—forbears."

"I know that. And I know he can be blasted abrasive. But I wish you will try not to judge him too harshly. His is not an easy path."

"I don't envy him it, certainly." Sir Owen frowned, then said, "But that doesn't excuse his sarcasm, nor his hatred for Jamie, who's as good a fellow as one could meet."

They walked outside. The rain had stopped but the short grey afternoon was drawing in and already flambeaux were being lit. The porter ran into the street and whistled up a chair. Watching him, Rossiter said slowly, "You mistake it, Owen. Despite what he says, Falcon doesn't hate Morris. In fact, I believe he's quite attached to him."

"Do you, by Jove! He has a deuced odd way of showing it!"

"Yes. But that's because he is so deathly afraid of him, do you see?"

Furlong did not see, although he was too polite to argue the point. Glancing back a moment later as he was borne towards his cozy little house on Bond Street, he saw Rossiter go striding off, his cloak billowing about him. Such a good fellow was old Ross, he thought, and it was like him to look for the good side of a man. He was far and fair off about August Falcon, though. Not that Falcon was a bad man—indeed he'd have made a jolly good soldier. But that was likely all he'd be good for—fighting!

Besides being Lord Hector Kadenworthy's aunt, Millicent Haverley's mother had been second cousin to Mrs. Dudley Falcon's mama, and while in town with her nephew, Mrs. Haverley paid a courtesy call in Great Ormond Street. She was a gentle little lady with a singularly sweet face and a somewhat timid disposition, and she and Mrs. Dudley thoroughly enjoyed a scandalous exchange of family confidences and the latest *ton* gossip. Their cose was terminated when Mrs. Haverley recollected that she was promised to attend a Literary Afternoon of poetry and readings at the home of Lady Dowling. Her nephew had intended to accompany her but was detained on a matter of business. "A horse, no doubt," she said with a doting smile, and upon learning that Gwendolyn was fond of poetry, begged that all three ladies go with her, because Lady Dowling had told her to bring anyone she knew who enjoyed readings. Mrs. Dudley was engaged for an early dinner party with friends and had to decline. Katrina and Gwendolyn, however, were pleased to accept, and within the hour were comfortably ensconced in the music room of the Dowling mansion.

Lady Dowling, tall, elegant, and with a pair of kindly hazel eyes, had welcomed her unexpected guests graciously. She liked Katrina, and while hoping that none of the more conservative guests would be offended by her arrival, thought it quite possible that the presence of London's most controversial Beauty might add lustre to what had begun to seem a dull gathering.

Katrina was breathtaking in a *robe volante* of pink damask, the stomacher edged by tiny embroidered red roses, and with a little cluster of red silk roses nestled amid her glossy black curls. Gwendolyn had donned a *robe à la française* of soft blue taffeta with a dainty floral pattern and a square neckline trimmed with lace. Less in the habit of attending *ton* parties, she looked about her with interest, noting the elaborate gowns and jewels of the ladies, and amused by the stares of gentlemen who were strangers to her.

Mrs. Haverley murmured behind her fan, "I think I have never before drawn so much attention!"

"Nor I, ma'am," answered Gwendolyn merrily. "If I could believe that any of those admiring glances came my way."

Even at this early hour the room was ablaze with candlelight. The glow awoke golden gleams in Gwendolyn's light brown hair, and the colour of her gown accentuated her blue eyes. Considerably astonished by such an unassuming remark, Mrs. Haverley said, "But my dear, you must certainly know that many of them do indeed come your way!"

Touched by such kindness, Gwendolyn smiled, and never for a moment believed it to be anything more than that.

A magnificent footman rang a little bell for quiet, and Lady Dowling introduced a large young man with a red face and a careless habit of dress. He scanned his audience critically and at such length that Gwendolyn thought he had forgotten what he meant to say and she jumped when he suddenly embarked upon a thunderous and impassioned poem concerning the flight from Scotland of Prince Charles Stuart and a lady named Flora MacDonald. Gwendolyn's eyes grew ever more round as the poem progressed, and when it ended she whispered, "La, ma'am, was the Prince really so naughty?"

Mrs. Haverley, her cheeks rather pink, said that whether he was or no, she scarcely thought such lurid implications were proper with young damsels in the company.

Lady Dowling evidently agreed, because when her protégé prepared to launch into another reading, she circumvented him by announcing gaily that she was sure her guests must be exhausted after hearing of such heroic exploits, and that refreshments would be served in the adjacent saloons.

At once Katrina was surrounded by eager and admiring gentlemen clamouring to be allowed to escort her. To her surprise Gwendolyn found quite a number of gentlemen, equally admiring, who suddenly recalled that they had once met Mrs. Haverley and hurried to renew their acquaintance and beg an introduction to Miss Rossiter. At four and twenty, Gwendolyn believed herself to be far past the age to attract eligible suitors. She regarded these young gallants as pleasant new friends rather than as matrimonial prospects, and was neither shy nor coquettish with them. Her natural warmth and good-humoured view of the world won her more admiration than she would have guessed, and it was a merry group that proceeded to the refreshment room.

She was chatting with an attractive young man named Duncan Tiele when Lord Kadenworthy joined them. She had met the tall peer on several occasions, the most recent having been in April when he had seconded Falcon in a duel with Gideon. She knew that both her brother and August liked him, and Morris, several years his junior, had described him as "a good old boy even if his tongue is almost as scalding as Lord Haughty-Snort's." Kadenworthy had never shown her that side of his nature. He was unfailingly gentle with her and his rather hard brown eyes would soften whenever he spoke to her. She must, she realized, be the most contrary of females because, while she felt quite comfortable with August who never made the slightest attempt to cater to her or to curb his quick temper in her presence, she found Lord Hector's obvious sympathy to be extremely irritating, a reaction she struggled to conceal.

His lordship was on his best behaviour this afternoon. He apologized to his aunt, who obviously adored him; laughed at Duncan Tiele, who protested indignantly because Kadenworthy squeezed a chair between himself and Gwendolyn; and flirted charmingly with Katrina. When Lady Dowling came up and bore Katrina off to meet someone, he went with them, pausing only to drop a kiss on his aunt's forehead and promise to return Miss Falcon promptly.

"He is such a darling," said Mrs. Haverley as she and Gwendolyn joined several other ladies who were refreshing themselves in one of the guest suites. " 'Twas monstrous kind in him to come, for he purely detests poetry. I recall when he was just a little boy and I would read to him at bedtime, he would always say "Not pomes, Aunty Missent, *stories!*" He had a dreadful time with his pronunciation, poor little mite."

Gwendolyn adjusted her cap, and said with a smile that she'd had the same preference as a child. "Do you enjoy living in Epsom, ma'am?"

"Mimosa Lodge is a lovely estate. I cannot conceive of anyone *disliking* to live there." Mrs. Haverley sighed ruefully. "Though I do rather miss Cornwall, I'm afraid."

Preparing to leave, Gwendolyn took up her reticule and asked eagerly, "Cornwall? Is that your home, then?"

" 'Tis where I was born. The family home is near Penzance. I was widowed only two years after my marriage, so I lived there and took care of the children from the time their parents died. Hector became a wealthy orphan at the age of five, poor boy." She smiled. "Now there is a proper contradiction in terms! Are you ready, my dear?"

"Yes. But I wonder if we might stay here just for a minute? I've some friends just returned from Cornwall, and can scarce believe some of the wondrous things they've told me of it."

They moved to a cushioned window seat and sat together, watching the other ladies come and go. Mrs. Haverley was only too glad to answer Gwendolyn's questions about the county of her birth. She laughed when told of August's remark that the wind had nearly blown the hair from his head, and admitted that when the gales rushed at the wild northern coastline it was as much as a strong man could do to stand against them. It was indeed, she confirmed, a land of legend and superstitions that had been handed down through the centuries and were still firmly rooted.

Gwendolyn prompted, "Some of them are rather dreadful, I heard."

"Very dreadful. Indeed, child, I'd not dare tell you some of the cures for having been 'ill-wished' as we call it. You'd not sleep a wink!"

"Ill-wished. That means put under a curse, does it not?"

"Well—I suppose it does." Uncomfortable with that definition, Mrs. Haverley qualified, "Though most of them are comparatively mild little threats, actually." Mentally eliminating the ill-wish that was believed to result in serious illness, or the death of one's cattle, she hurried on, "Hens stop laying, or a cow ceases to give milk. Not that those are minor things for a poor family, I grant you."

"Is it true that there are—let me see now, Charmers, I think that's the name—people who can banish warts and such-like? And is there not something to do with curing a child of measles by passing it under a donkey?"

"Whooping cough, my dear, not measles. And the child must be passed under the, er—tummy of a piebald horse." Amused, Mrs. Haverley patted Gwendolyn's hand. "My goodness, but you've an interest! I didn't think Londoners knew of such things. Come along now, we must go and find Miss Falcon before my naughty nephew falls in love with her!"

Gwendolyn smiled and rose obediently, but as they went into the busy corridor she said, "It seems there was something else I heard that I thought most strange. I cannot quite recall . . . Oh, I know! 'Twas to do with feathers; a sack thrown into the sea, yes?"

"Ah," said Mrs. Haverley. "Now that is one of the ugly 'ill-wishes.' But 'tis a *bag* of feathers, or a pillow, actually. The sack thrown into the sea is called being 'put to the cliff,' and is a way, an unkind way, I'm afraid, of getting rid of some living thing that is unwanted. Kittens, perhaps; or a destructive puppy or a dog that barks continuously."

"Oh dear! But—what has that to do with feathers, ma'am?"

"Nothing, my dear. The feathers serve a very grim purpose in which, if you really mean harm to an enemy, you fill his pillow with the feathers of wild birds. Folks have changed that procedure a trifle so as to extend it to an intended victim who cannot be reached in such a way. In that case, a bag is filled with the feathers and delivered, or even tossed at him. If he takes it up, the curse is fixed upon him."

Time for Gwendolyn seemed to stand still. She could see the bright book room with the fire roaring up the chimney, and hear Enoch Tummet grumbling to Apollo . . . "Wot must 'e do but pick up that there nasty bag o' feathers . . ." She tried to speak lightly. "Any old curse, ma'am?"

"Oh, dear me no! One of the more wicked ones." Mrs. Haverley lowered her voice and said dramatically, "Whoever takes up the bag is doomed to die a slow and painful death!"

"But," gulped Gwendolyn, halting at the top of the stairs, "but that's silly. Unhappily, such an end may come to any of us in our old age, no?"

"True, but the curse is to be fulfilled by Christmas Eve of the same year it is invoked. If the unhappy victim survives till the coming of Our Lord, the curse is broken, so— Good gracious me, Miss Rossiter, you are become so pale! Oh, how naughty in me to have frightened you with those gloomy old superstitions." Mrs. Haverley crossed her fingers under a fold of her gown. "There are several different versions, but to say truth, 'tis all nonsense for the uneducated and the credible to shiver over, and not to be regarded by intelligent folk. Dismiss it from your mind, my dear."

Gwendolyn smiled and said she would follow that excellent advice. But even as she spoke she knew that it would be easier said than done.

CHAPTER IX

I t was said that Overlake Lodge lacked the magnificence of the neighboring Promontory Point, the ancestral home of the Rossiters, but it was a fine estate, nonetheless. Located not far from Canterbury, in the green and lovely garden that is the county of Kent, the house contained some thirty rooms and was set in neat grounds distinguished by a large maze, a shrubbery, and a pleached acacia walk. Beyond the wilderness area were well-kept woods and a thriving dairy farm. Some critics murmured that Overlake Lodge belonged to no recognizable architectural period, and the Duke of Marbury had described it as Early Indeterminate and Late Atrocious. Mr. Rudolph Bracksby, the present owner, had expended vast sums to bring the interior up to style, but the exterior was still a grey box, its neo-classical columns and extremely large pediment ostentatious, while the abundance of griffins and gargoyles (also added by the new owner) were referred to as an appalling vulgarity. Noble shoulders were shrugged, knowing looks exchanged, and voices lowered to murmur those deadly words "*nouveau riche*" and "Cannot really be expected to *know* . . ." and, most ominous of all, "Family? Bracksby? But, my *dear* . . . !"

On this crisp November afternoon the gates to the estate stood wide, and the drive-path was crowded. This was the day of the annual Winter Fete, a fair and sale that had been held on this same week-end for at least two hundred years, and cheerfully continued by Mr. Bracksby during the decade since he had acquired the property. All proceeds went to aid widows and orphans, and if the county judged Mr. Bracksby to teeter on the brink of social acceptability, they were willing to flock to his estate to contribute to so worthy a cause. And perhaps pick up a few bargains.

Barbecue pits had been dug in the wilderness area, and the aroma of woodsmoke and roasting meats hung enticingly on the air. A large marquee had been erected next to the maze, where trestle tables and benches had been set up. Innumerable covered stalls and tents lined the drive-path, and those whose blood was sufficiently blue to warrant personal invitations were admitted to the mansion, where, for a substantial donation, they could wander about the various tables in the corridors and the ballroom which displayed the more costly items donated for sale, or make their way into the saloons and ante rooms where various games of chance were offered. Later, they would be given plates and mugs, and could patronize the long tables in the dining room, helping themselves to juicy slices of the fruits of the barbecue pits, augmented by cold meats and cheeses, breads, pies, cakes, tarts, jellies, cider, ale, or wine. Excellent fare, of which a few guests would partake so liberally that in addition to their willing charitable contributions they would later and less willingly contribute to the coffers of their personal physicians.

The afternoon was waning when Falcon's carriage moved cautiously along the drive-path. He saw little of the good natured throng or the colourful flags and bunting that fluttered from booths and tents. The wound in his arm throbbed determinedly, and he was irked by the awareness that if it continued to be annoying he might have to pay heed to James Knight's warnings and take to his bed for a day or so. A damnable coil, for he could scarce have chosen a worse time to be laid by the heels.

On the other hand, there had been no attempt to carry out the threat contained in the poem that had been sent him. In fact, the League seemed relatively quiet at the moment. There had been the attack by Green and his bullies in Bloomsbury Square, but he was sure that had been a personal matter, not connected to the Squire's machinations. He smiled, recalling the incredible courage of a most remarkable small lady, and had to jerk his mind back to business. Gideon's agents were gathering information that slowly but surely added to an ever more damning confirmation of the existence and treasonable activities of the League. Surely, in a very little time now they would have assembled a weight of evidence that even the most bone-headed government official could not ignore.

Yet his sense of unease grew, and with it his conviction that this was the lull before the storm. Thoughts so foreign to his nature irritated him. He'd never been one to brood over imagined troubles and the premonition of disaster that haunted him was as stupid as his inability to dismiss it was infuriating.

Nor was the League of Jewelled Men his only concern. The last big storm had blown some tiles from the roof of Falcon House and resulted in leaks that had damaged the ceilings of the ballroom and several ante rooms which jutted out from the main house to form the single-storey rear wing. It was typical of Neville Falcon's light-hearted and uncomplicated nature that he should thoroughly enjoy the festivities of the Christmas season, and it was his custom to host a large party on Boxing Day. August's suggestion that this year the party be held at Ashleigh had been rejected reproachfully, but if Falcon House was to be thrown open to guests and to dancing, the rear wing must be redecorated. The roof had been repaired, but no progress could be made on the interior until paint shades, wall hangings, and draperies had been decided upon. In view of his parent's appalling mis-matches in his personal apparel, August knew that, with his sister's help, he would have to improve upon whatever was selected, but he was much too fond of 'the old gentleman' to hurt his feelings by ordering the work begun without at least giving him time to consider those selections. He'd left samples down at Ashleigh last month, and his father had promised faithfully to send them back with his selections "in a day or so." More than three weeks had passed with no word, however, and while it was very possible that Mr. Falcon was having a merry time with his latest incognita, he was a fond parent and a prolific letter-writer, and had never before allowed so much time to lapse without contacting his family.

Most troublesome of all, was the other matter; an unwelcome and unwise complication that persisted in hovering around the fringes of his mind however firmly he fought to ignore it. Sooner or later, he knew, he would have to deal with—

"Wot's knowed as a 'brown study,' is it, Guv?" Tummet was performing one of his unconventional acrobatic feats; clinging to the box seat with one hand while balancing on the rim of the wheel and leering in at the partly open carriage window.

Falcon thought a startled 'Zounds! I'd not even realized we stopped!' He said sharply, "I presume you know what you're about. Be damned if I do."

"Jest wanted to make sure you was deprived-in-hell," explained Tummet with his broad grin.

"If that translates to 'alive and well,' I am. So you may cease your impersonation of a demented ape and open the door."

Tummet winked cheerily and disappeared.

Checking the priming of his small pocket pistol, Falcon reflected that he had probably offended George Coachman beyond forgiveness by insisting that Tummet drive him today. He was well aware that his servants were exceptional and it did not please him to upset them, but his "imitation valet" knew about the League, and—just in case things should get warm—was a splendid man in a fight. When notified of their destination, Tummet's shrewd brown eyes had become rounder than usual. He'd said solemnly, "If you wants my opinion, mate—" but when such a desire was forcefully denied, he'd muttered something to the effect that "Peter-and-Paul's-orf-on-a-crawl" and gone away to collect two large horse pistols, apparently preparing for the "brawl" his rhyming slang indicated.

The door was swung open and the step let down. Alighting, Falcon saw that they had halted outside the large barn in the stable area where many other coaches were already closely positioned, poles up, the teams turned out in the big paddock or being attended to by busy grooms and stable boys.

A neat groom hurried towards them.

Tummet said softly, "Orders, Guv?"

"Try if you can get the coach and our team placed where we can break away fast—if we're obliged to. Then stay close and keep your ears and eyes open."

"Ar. No wars, please, mate—Sir Mate, I mean!"

"Insolent hedgebird. I suppose you think you've a right to eat!"

Despite the gruff words there was a twinkle in Falcon's eyes and several silver coins were pressed into the valet's hand. Tummet grinned and looked after his employer's tall figure, reflecting fondly that few gents would have considered their servants' appetites, much less offered so generous a sum.

The fragrant air rang with talk and laughter as the merry crowd pushed and jostled about the stalls and barrows edging the drive-path. Mingling with them, Falcon saw that all classes and conditions were represented here, as evidenced by the costly French wigs, scratch wigs, or powdered hair of the gentlemen, and the varying types of caps worn by the ladies. Amid the babble of talk he heard the soft speech of Kent and Sussex, the affected drawl of Bond Street beaux, well-modulated Oxford accents, the sing-song voices of Wales, the brisk clipped speech of Londoners. Two Frenchmen, evidently believing nobody here would be able to understand them, were discussing the barbarous English habit of cooking meat with smoke, and of preparing atrocious puddings of suet and dough by dropping them into boiling water.

Falcon murmured, "Alas, messieurs, you will find no *colimaçons* at this party. Unless, perhaps, you choose to search about under the weeds."

Affronted, they turned to chastise him for his impudence, but recognition was almost immediate, whereupon they flushed and hurried off.

Falcon chuckled and was about to walk on when another voice halted him.

"Buy a nosegay fer yer lidy, y'r lor'ship! Only a groat! Come on, me fine—"

The solicitation ended in a shrill yelp as he jerked around and looked down at a small, dirty face, framed by untidy dark hair. He had a fleeting impression that the sadly crossed eyes reflected not only recognition but stark shock. "What the devil," he demanded, "are *you* doing all the way down here?"

The little flower-girl cowered, pulling her forest green shawl closer about her face as if to try and hide under it. "I ain't doin' nothin' wrong, yer worship," she whimpered. "Don't 'ave me took up! Please, me fine 'andsome gent!"

He gripped her elbow. "Stop that dreadful whining, and tell me how you come to be here!"

She whined louder than ever and tried to pull free, but he jerked her closer, struck by the sense of something incongruous about the poor creature.

"I'll give yer a free bunch," she wailed. " 'Ere, mate! Not s'much as a farden it won't cost yer!"

"After the ladies again, eh?" Lord Hector Kadenworthy strolled up, swinging an amber cane and grinning broadly. " 'Pon my soul, but you've catholic tastes!" He turned to the frightened girl. "Driving a hard bargain, is he, m'dear? Best be on your way. I doubt Mr. Bracksby's keepers will allow you to do business here." He tossed her a shilling, and ignoring her ecstatic moans of gratitude, slipped a hand through Falcon's arm. "Going up to the house, August? Be dashed if I expected to find you here. Didn't think you and our Rudi were exactly—ah, bosom-bows."

"True." Walking beside him, Falcon said lightly, "But the gentleman has a sister, you see."

Kadenworthy laughed. "I might have known. The luscious Lady Pamela. I thought that jolly little *affaire* was over."

"The world is full of surprises, Kade."

"Take care she doesn't give you one, dear boy. 'Tis said she don't take kindly to being—ah, discarded."

"Now whatever gave you the impression I had done so unkind a thing?"

"Be dashed if I can recall. Gossip, I expect. As usual, it rages round you like a whirlpool."

"How fortunate that I'm a good swimmer. Speaking of gossip, I've a bone to pick with you. Why did you deem it necessary to tell Rossiter that Green had insulted my sister?"

His lordship stiffened. He said coldly, "Only think, I had not dreamed I was indulging in gossip, and had instead supposed I was defending you. Ross was irked because that hasty temper of yours had been unleashed on poor dear Rafe Green in The Madrigal. I sought to pour oil on troubled waters by pointing out your justification." He halted and offered a short, dismissing bow. "My apologies an that offends your—"

"*Mea culpa! Mea culpa!*" Falcon seized his arm and detained him with force. "No, don't go off in a huff, Kade. You must try not to look so stiff-rumped. People are sure to say you caught it from me."

Only slightly mollified, Kadenworthy grunted, but allowed himself to be drawn along again.

"Your intervention was well-meant," allowed Falcon. "As I should have guessed. But I do not like my sister's name to be bandied about the clubs. No, don't fly into the boughs again! Would *you* have taken such an insult?"

"Perhaps not," admitted Kadenworthy grudgingly. "But nor would I be so quick to accuse my friends. Ross and I spoke of the matter privately. Even did you suspect *me* of gossip, you should know better than to think he'd be a party to it. The trouble with you, August, is that you expend a sight too much charm on the ladies and a damn sight too little on the men!"

Falcon purred, "Would you suggest I reverse the procedure?"

"No!" With a reluctant laugh Kadenworthy said, "Be curst if I would! What a fellow you are!"

"I stand corrected, and will admit that you likely did me a favour. I was too dense, you see, to realize Green was speaking of Katrina in that—unspeakable way. I thought he referred to me. Had I realized at the time what he implied . . ."

Kadenworthy glanced at him obliquely and read a chilling menace in the grim set of the mouth and the narrowed eyes. "Jupiter, I do believe you'd have slain him on the spot! Justified, I own, but 'twould not have enhanced your reputation, August."

"I think that is past enhancing."

"So do I!" Kadenworthy clapped him on the back, his grin taking the sting from the words.

They had reached the steps to the square grey house and two flunkeys swung the doors wide to admit them.

Lord Hector hailed a friend and went inside, calling over his shoulder, "I'm for the card rooms. If you fancy a fling at the tables, join me, August."

Falcon waved a farewell, but instead of following, he paused atop the steps to glance back at the busy crowds on the drive-path.

It was quite possible that the little flower girl had been given a ride on some carter's waggon or a farm wain leaving the city. Tinkers and the unfortunates who lived on the "padding lay" carried their wares to the various fairs and fetes, and this was one of the last such gatherings of the autumn. There was no real reason for thinking it strange to find the girl here; nor for this ridiculous sense of familiarity. He shrugged, and strolled into the wide entrance hall.

Once divested of cloak and tricorne he was plunged into a chattering crowd as young damsels, matrons, and dowagers vied with each other in the eager search for bargains; and gentlemen, with the approach of Christmas in mind, levelled their quizzing glasses hopefully at tables piled with their neighbours' discards. Even in this crush Falcon was an immediate centre of attention. Feminine eyelashes fluttered at him over their fans, male faces became stern, and strong hands tightened their clasp on the arms of their ladies. His own eyes roved the assemblage without finding his hostess, or anyone suspected of being a member of the League. He drifted to a quiet corner beside a large potted palm and observed the gathering patiently.

"If you're looking for Lady Pamela, she's outside," said a brisk and somewhat nasal voice at his ear.

He turned and gave his hand and a smile to the colonel who had come up unnoticed. "Mariner Fotheringay, as I live and breathe! You always did move like a cat!"

"And you despise cats, as I recall." Tall and lean, with a pair of hard dark eyes, and a ruthless mouth, the army officer's lips curved into a rare smile. "How do you go on, Falcon? And how is that beautiful sister of yours? If rumour speaks true, you've finally given your approval to some lucky fellow. An Army man if—"

Falcon snapped, "Rumour lies, as usual!" He added in a calmer tone, "My sister is very well, I thank you. And I do not at all despise cats. They are admirably aloof, and they serve a very useful function in this world—getting rid of rodents, which are creatures I *very* much dislike! Is that why you're here, Mariner?"

Fotheringay blinked. "Do I look like the local rat-catcher?"

"You've caught a few in your time, no? And since they've promoted you to full colonel again, I thought perhaps—"

"Then you err, my dear fellow. I am here purely to support a worthy charity and perchance find a marvellously costly gift for a—er, lady."

"At a bargain price," said Falcon with a grin. "For shame, Mariner!"

"Can't afford shame. But I'd best get on with my search before the best things are snabbled. Glad to have seen you again." Fotheringay nodded amiably and started off, then enquired as if in afterthought, "How is your father, by the way?"

"*August!*" Lady Barrett pushed past the colonel to thrust her hand at Falcon. She was acquainted with his aunt, and demanded to know all about her "dearest friend." Well aware that the two ladies had detested each other since their come-out, he responded with polite brevity, and escaped at the first possible opportunity. Fotheringay had disappeared into the crowd of those who were surrendering to the mouth-watering smells wafting from the dining room. Reminded that he had taken only a light breakfast, Falcon offered his arm to a very fat widow who was stigmatized by the *ton* for having married a wealthy merchant. Mrs. Quimby had been resigned to going in to dine with her reluctant brother. She was delighted to accept the escort of the best-looking man in the room and accompanied him, glowing.

Falcon had not chosen idly. He liked the lady for her good-humoured indifference to snobbery and for her often salty view of the world. Moreover, she was a talker and would ramble happily on with very little encouragement, thus leaving him free to, as Tummet would have said, "keep his peepers open." When he had filled her plate, at her direction, with sufficient food for three men and a boy, he seated her at a table in a corner of the room and went off to gather his own supper. Returning, he found that he had judged correctly. Between attending to the systematic reduction of the delicacies before her, Mrs. Quimby chattered. She was "awed" by his magnificent coat of blue brocade threaded with silver, and declared that the patch would be copied everywhere. She liked to see a gentleman dress well. Her dear late husband had always been neat, if not what one might call a fashion-plate. On she went, while Falcon responded attentively but kept a careful check of comings and goings. His full attention snapped to his companion when she allowed a hovering waiter to re-fill her wineglass and said, ". . . and almost too suspicious a turn of mind, I used to think. My Edgar was always insisting the crews conspired and stole him blind."

"Crews, ma'am? Forgive, but I'd thought Mr. Quimby was in the timber trade."

"Very right. But his ruling passion in life was the sea, Mr. Falcon. A warm man was my Edgar." She waved a chicken leg at him and said with a saucy wink, "In more ways than one! Else how should I have got so fat from bearing nine sons! But not a one of 'em has the eye for business his father had."

He smiled and asked, "Do you say Mr. Quimby imported timber? I'd have thought there were plenty of trees here in Britain."

"So there are! But there's trees and trees, my dear. Edgar used to bring in a cedar from the Americas that's used to build dinghies and little boxes. There's a green tree, though I cannot tell you the name, that grows in South America and is prized for making dock pilings and fishing rods. Edgar was specially partial to a black ebony that he shipped from Africa, and a grand mahogany from the West Indies. He liked teak, as well, which he got from somewhere in India."

"But—surely none of this would be easy to steal?"

The lady took up her wineglass and frowned at the contents. "There was other cargoes. Edgar had his finger in many pies. I asked him a time or two how he supposed the crews made off with so much, and he said, "They can if they take the whole ship!" She looked up at him shrewdly. "I'd only speak of this with someone I trust, you understand. Still, you likely think me just a silly old woman!"

Falcon leaned closer. "Never that, ma'am. In fact, I've a friend who's a ship's master and would agree with every word you've said. More's the pity, he cannot prove it. If there is anything you could tell me—any smallest detail that you can recall, 'twould be more appreciated than you can know."

She hesitated. "This friend of yours. In trouble, is he?"

"In the greatest trouble, ma'am. And his head at risk."

Still hesitating, she asked, "A young man?"

"Yes. And newly married."

"Oh my! How dreadful for his poor wife." She clicked her

tongue sympathetically, and began to rummage about in her large reticule. "My eldest gets into a proper taking if I gabble about business, and not without cause, I must own, for I don't mind telling you, Mr. Falcon, they said 'twas an accident, but I believe my Edgar would be alive today had he been less outspoken. Here's my card. Your friend may call upon me this coming Thursday at two o' the clock. There's a company meeting on Thursday afternoons, and I've the house to myself. If your friend is well known, you'd best have him send in his name as Mr.—hum . . . Tide!" She twinkled at him merrily. "He's likely to remember that, eh?"

Falcon took the card, kissed the lady's hand, and told her he was deep in her debt. Mrs. Quimby blushed like a girl, declared that he was a rascal, and that if he was truly grateful he'd not mind fetching her a piece of "that very intriguing currant cake."

Soon after he performed this task her brother appeared to reclaim her, and Mrs. Quimby and Mr. Falcon parted, each pleased with the other.

Congratulating himself on having learned something of real value, Falcon wandered to the card rooms and sat at a faro table between Hector Kadenworthy and Mr. Duncan Tiele. Play was shrewd and the stakes high and excitement began to rise. Someone moved too swiftly, overturning Falcon's wineglass and he sprang up just in time to avoid being deluged.

Tiele said admiringly, "Jupiter but that was fast! I think I'd never wish to cross swords with you, Falcon!"

"Nobody *wishes* to." Kadenworthy waved to a waiter to refill Falcon's glass. "Sometimes there's no decent way to avoid it!"

"One has a choice, you see," said Lord Sommers, coming up behind Kadenworthy's chair. "Decent—or living!"

Falcon bowed grandly, and thus did not see the hand that hovered briefly over his glass. There was general laughter, and the game went on. Emerging from it the richer by two hundred guineas, Falcon allowed himself to be caught up in the bargain-hunting spirit. He purchased a charming ruby pendant for Katrina, and half an hour later was paying for a blue silken shawl with a fine knotted fringe when he sensed that he was being watched. He glanced up swiftly and from across the table met a pair of brilliant dark eyes. Before he could speak, their owner walked rapidly away. He thought 'Be damned! Skye! And in civilian dress!'

That Joel Skye and Mariner Fotheringay should both be here might be the merest coincidence. On the other hand, it might mean that at long last the Horse Guards had begun to listen to the warnings of Rossiter's Preservers!

You devil! August! Do not dare!" Despite this warning, Lady Pamela Dunscroft made no move to extricate herself from an embrace that, in this particular time and place, would have raised the eyebrows of the most broad-minded of London's social set. Tall, voluptuously curved, and very sure of her beauty, she lay on the sofa of this secluded little parlour, her head thrown back, her dark eyes rapturously half closed.

Assigning her warning the importance it warranted, Falcon went about his business, his hands and lips drawing soft little moans from her until she flung her arms about his neck and pulled him down to her own hungry mouth.

"My heavens," she panted between kisses, "how I've missed you! We should never . . . have— Oh, Lud! We should never have . . . parted."

Considerably shaken, he drew back. "I think we had best— part now, lovely one. Your brother don't admire me. If he should chance to find us—like this . . ."

"Rudi's in Bath with his bosom bow, old Underhill," she said, taking up his hand impatiently. "Here, love, you know I—" She gave a little shriek and for a while there was relative quiet, if not inactivity, in the parlour.

It was some time before Falcon could escape her clinging arms, but at length he stood and shrugged into his waistcoat. "Do you know what your difficulty is, Pam?" he murmured, smiling down at her.

"Not enough of you," she pouted, making no move to restore her gown.

Lying there, half clad, she was almost unbearably seductive, and it was all he could do to resist her. "You are too aware of how desirable you are," he said.

"And you are a marplot," she responded lazily, reaching out to him. "Why must you go? So very soon?"

"Because, you wanton witch, you've a house full of County only a door away, and if—"

"That didn't stop you just now."

"A marplot I may be, but I'm not made of stone, Pam."

She sat up, her eyes glowing. "By heaven, but you're not! August, my best beloved. Don't go! I want you . . ."

He watched her with the mocking half-smile that drove her to distraction. "For your husband, Pam?"

She tensed, her chin lifting slightly.

He chuckled. "Of course not. But that's what 'twould mean were we discovered, my dear. Is it really worth the risk?"

"I sometimes think 'twould be well worth it."

"But only sometimes. Come now. Your party has been a thousand times more delightful than I deserve, but—"

"Oh, very well."

She stood and began to order her gown. But her movements were enticing, she was all female witchery and her eyes teased him, so that in desperation he was obliged to turn away.

Coming up behind him, she slid her arms around his neck and nibbled at his ear. "I could make you love me again," she whispered.

He swung around and on the instant she was pressing against him, her lips apart, inviting.

He said huskily, " 'Twould be all too easy, I fear. Egad, but that scent you wear is enough to make any man's—" The words froze on his tongue. His head jerked up.

It had been very faint, but *now* he knew what had been so incongruous about the little flower-girl!

"Oh . . . *Jupiter!*" he snarled.

Lady Pamela drew back. He was flushed, his eyes glaring wrath. She thought he looked even more magnificent than usual, but she asked uneasily, "What is it? What did I say?"

He lifted clenched fists and shook them at the ceiling. "Of all the stupid, blind, *idiots!*" He threw on his sword-belt, snatched up his coat and shrugged into it, then stamped to the door, saying through his teeth, "I'll murder the wretched chit!"

"August!" shrilled my lady, quite unaccustomed to such cavalier treatment.

Falcon turned back and looked at her as if he'd forgotten she was there. "Oh." He marched to take up her hand and kiss it hard. "Thank you, m'dear!"

Another second and he was gone. Lady Pamela gazed after him. She knew men, and, raging, she snatched up the nearest article, which chanced to be a beautiful Sèvres vase, and hurled it to shatter against the door. *"Beast!"* she screeched. "Faithless! Fickle! Horrid *half-breed!"*

Passing the object of her wrath on the stairs, the Most Honourable Bertram Crisp, Marquis of Pencader, said brightly, "Oh, there you are, dear old pippin. Come and—" Falcon rushed past without a word, the black scowl on his face cutting off that friendly greeting. Looking after him, Crisp murmured, "Whomever you seek, the poor fellow has my most profound sympathy!"

Falcon neither saw nor heard him. The lackey who strolled with lofty condescension in response to his gesture, started, went off at the run, returned with his cloak and tricorne, and then raced to the stables.

Seething, Falcon walked to the top of the steps, his gaze raking the scene. It was past eight o'clock and full dark but the drive-path blazed with the light of a hundred flambeaux. The air was cold and spiced with the pungency of sweetmeats, hot pies, and toffeed apples, and the all pervading aromas from the barbecue pits. The crowd was larger and noisier than ever. His initial scan failing to locate the face and figure he sought, he marched down the steps and entered the throng. The flickering light illumined the faces he passed, like so many portraits, briefly and brightly painted on a dark canvas. There were more young people now; farm folk who might well have walked most of the day so as to get here in time for the country dancing that would start at nine o'clock in the marquee. Falcon searched among an endless stream of cheerful humanity: rosy-cheeked lassies, their innocent eyes bright with happiness; stalwart youths guarding their sweethearts jealously; buxom farm wives aglow with health; men with the bronzed and leathery skin that spoke of a lifetime spent in the fields; children allowed to stay up long past their bedtime, racing about squealing excitedly and unintelligibly, eluding the plunges of older brothers and sisters who attempted to capture and restrain them; venerable elders fussed over by protective sons or daughters, their eyes as bright as those of their grandchildren. All wearing their Sunday best for this so long looked-forward-to entertainment. Many of them had wrapped warm woollen shawls about their shoulders, but none walked with a limp, or wore a shawl of that particular shade of forest green. Perhaps she had already left. Falcon swung about and strode back the way he had come, shouldering his way through the crowd with an impatience that won him not a few resentful glances.

He skirted the maze and followed the drive-path towards the stables. Grooms were shouting to each other as they poled up a team. His own, one hoped. And then he saw her. She stood with her back to him, talking animatedly to a sturdy individual who was shaking his head in seemingly dismayed disagreement.

Falcon half-whispered, "Tummet! Now damn your slippery eyes!"

In half a dozen long strides he was upon them.

Catching sight of the advancing menace Tummet paled and his jaw sagged.

Falcon's scorching glare encompassed him. "Bring up the team!"

Tummet gulped and fled.

Gwendolyn spun around. Falcon stood close behind her, his expression so murderous that for an instant she was speechless.

He seized her wrist and said with a smile that chilled her blood, "You forgot to cross your eyes."

She was tempted to do so, but this was not the time for either levity or evasion. She said, "Thank heaven you are come! I was just—"

"You will not thank heaven when I've done with you," he interrupted in that hushed and fierce undertone. "If *ever* a chit needed spanking—"

"Oh, stop being so foolish and listen to me! August, I have—"

The team came prancing alongside and a stableboy ran to open the door and let down the steps.

Falcon threw him a coin. "Get in the coach," he grated, his piercing glare not shifting from Gwendolyn.

"Yes, I will, but you must—"

"Get—in—the—*coach!*" He added through his teeth, "Or would you prefer that I put you across my knee here and now?"

The stableboy stood as if rooted to the spot, his jaw hanging open.

Falcon's gaze turned on him. "Enjoying the performance, are you?"

The boy gave a gasp, and fled.

Exasperated, Gwendolyn said, "How can you *be* so stupid? If you will just—"

A molten glare was levelled at her. With a squeal she jumped up on the step and dove into the coach.

He slammed the door so hard that the team snorted and sidled in fright.

Standing with his left hand on his sword hilt, he looked up to the box. "Down!"

Tummet moaned, put up his whip, and obeyed. "Guv—it ain't what you—" He was caught in a grip of iron and pinioned against the wheel.

"You knew!" hissed Falcon, without a trace of li. "You miserable, scheming, traitorous hedgebird—you *knew!*"

"N-Not first orf I didn't. Sir. But—"

His cravat was caught and twisted mercilessly. Choking, he gasped out, "What was a cove . . . to do, mate? I—"

"You let her go out into the streets at night!" In his fury, Falcon's lips drew back from his teeth. "A sheltered, innocent—child, who couldn't know what she risked! But *you* knew! With half London ravening bloody murder, and brute beasts roaming about in packs, you let an unwed lady of Quality walk out alone like a common—*tart!* By God, if I—"

"But I din't, Mr. Falcon, sir! Crost me 'eart . . . I should'a—"

"I'll tell you what you *should* have done, Enoch Tummet! You should have—*at once*—come to me!"

Tummet tried to free himself from that cruel grip and looking into the face of murder, squawked, "Mate . . . sir . . . I—can't . . . breathe!"

"And I'll tell you something else," snarled Falcon, his grip tightening. "If you ever—*ever* let that lady put one *toe* into danger I shall, with the greatest pleasure, break your neck with my bare hands!" He shook his captive savagely. "Do you *understand* me?" he thundered.

His face purpling, Tummet made a sound vaguely resembling "Yussir."

"Ow!" cried Falcon and relaxed his grip as something hard swiped at his shoulder.

Leaning from the open window and flailing her shoe at him, Gwendolyn cried angrily, "Let him go, you savage beast! He didn't even—"

He whirled on her and she jumped back inside. "I'll deal with you in a minute," he growled. "On the box, Tummet! Though it will likely be the last time you work for me!"

Tummet had sunk to his knees and was wheezing helplessly, but at this he hove himself to his feet and struggled back onto the box like a drunken man.

Ignoring the small crowd of gaping onlookers, Falcon wrenched the door open and sprang inside.

Gwendolyn crouched in the far corner, her eyes very wide, her shoe upraised in one hand.

"Now," said Falcon through his teeth, "to attend to *you*, madam!"

C H A P T E R   X

If you think to br-brutalize me, as you did poor Tummet—" began Gwendolyn, lifting her shoe higher.

Falcon interrupted ruthlessly, "You'll likely never understand how near you came to being truly brutalized when you flaunted yourself about The Madrigal after dark. What in *Hades* did you think you would achieve by following me—"

"Following . . . *you?*" Outraged, she sputtered, "Why, you *conceited*, p-puffed-up great—great *stupid!* I wasn't following *you!*"

There could be no doubting her sincerity; resentment fairly radiated from her grubby face. Perversely his fury doubled. He growled, "*Who*, then?" and pounced to tear the shoe from her hand and seize her by the shoulders. "What tulip of the *ton* has so captivated you that—"

With a sob of wrath she clawed at his hand, and as he gave an instinctive gasp and drew back, she slapped his face so hard that a lock of hair bounced down across his forehead.

For a second he looked dazed, then it seemed to Gwendolyn that blue daggers darted at her from his narrowed eyes. He swore, soft and viciously. Instead of fear, she experienced a stab of really acute pain and closing her eyes lifted her face. "Very w-well," she said. "Prove yourself a real English gentleman, and strike me back. It's what I deserve for trying to help Gideon."

He stared down at that small upturned face, very pale between the streaks of grime. The thought of striking it made him feel sick. Frustrated and confused, he flung her from him and took out a handkerchief to dab at the scratches.

A stifled sob brought his head up. By the glow from the carriage lamps he saw tears creeping down her cheeks, but she made no attempt to wipe them away. It was as much as he could do not to pull her close and comfort her. Overcoming that weakness, he thrust the handkerchief at her, and conjured up a sneer, "Typical! A cunning but infallible woman's weapon."

Gwendolyn wiped her eyes with a corner of the handkerchief, then snatched his hand and peered at the scratches. "Oh, how dreadful," she said shakily, winding the handkerchief around the damage.

"Don't pretend to be sorry," he grunted.

"No, I won't. You deserve much worse for ruining everything!"

Despite himself, at this his jaw dropped. "If *that* don't beat the Dutch! You've more than your share of effrontery, madam! What have I ruined, pray tell? Your venture into prostitution?"

She made a sound that put him in mind of a small puppy trying its first growl. Her little nose was thrust under his chin and she said in a voice that quivered with renewed wrath, "My brother would kill you for *that* foul remark, August Falcon! And you will live to be ashamed of it, I am very sure!"

He was already ashamed of it, and he muttered, "If Ross ever discovers how I failed to protect you whilst you were under my roof—"

"He would be proud!" She threw up her hands and wailed, "I tried so *hard*! And I was so *frightened*! But I triumphed at last! I *triumphed*! And then the mighty conquering hero, August Nicolai Falcon must come galumphing into my adventure and let them get clean away! Oh, the *pity* of it! When Gideon hears *that*—"

"Hold up! What are you talking about? Who got away?"

"Maria Benevento or Barthélemy, or whoever she is! And someone called Mr. Penn!"

"*What?*" he roared. "Why the *devil* didn't you say so?" He sprang up and lowered the window to howl, "*Tummet!*"

"I *tried* to tell you, horrid wretch that you are, but—"

The carriage slowed.

"Which way did they go, Gwen?" demanded Falcon.

"Back towards Town. Tummet knows, poor dear thing. But it's too late now, thanks to—"

He said grimly, "You don't know my team!" He leaned from the window. "Miss Gwen says you know the coach and which way it was going. Try if you can follow them."

A hoarse croak answered, "I am, Guv. But they got a good lead on us."

Falcon glanced westward. "The moon's coming up. Can you see their coach?"

"No. But I'll reckernize it if we get near enough."

"Good man. Then spring 'em!"

The coach lurched. Falcon closed the window and sat down.

"All right," he said sternly. "Tell me the whole. But—first, did you see this Mr. Penn?"

"No. It was too dark and I was too far off. But I once heard Miss Barthélemy read at a party, and I recognized her voice when she called to him. She got into a coach, and a big man ran over and climbed in and they drove away. I thought it might be important so—"

"So you came to me and I behaved like the world's prize dunderhead! But even so, that don't excuse your shocking—"

"*Is* it important?" she interrupted impatiently. "Who is Mr. Penn?"

"Would that I knew. And 'tis very important indeed! We first heard of him early in September when Morris and I were in Cornwall trying to help Johnny Armitage. Jennifer, she was Miss Britewell then, overheard Lord Kenneth Morris talking high treason with a man named Penn."

Gwendolyn's lower lip sagged. Aghast, she echoed, "Lord Kenneth *Morris*? Not—not Jamie's uncle?"

He'd supposed Gideon would have told her the details, else he'd not have mentioned the matter. He thought, 'Damn! Too late now,' and said, "Not exactly. Some sort of cousin to his father, I believe. But he's the head of the Family Morris and up to his ears in the League of Jewelled Men. With luck, our mysterious Mr. Penn and Maria are going to one of their secret meetings. If we can just come close enough to find out where they rendezvous! Jove, what a piece of luck that would be!"

Caught up in his enthusiasm, she clasped her hands and said eagerly, "Oh, how grand if we could think we had helped a little."

"We?" he asked with a faint smile.

She nodded. "Katrina and me. You cannot know how—"

"*Katrina?* The devil! Do you say my sister also wanders London's streets at night disguised as—"

"You may un-knit your eyebrows, sir! Katrina wanted to help but she was afraid that—"

"Yes, of course. She is such a gentle soul."

Gwendolyn gritted her teeth and drew a deep breath. "—But she was afraid that she would be recognized. So she helped Amazon Rossiter don her disguise and arranged for a chair to come to the back door to take me up, and—"

"And must have been suffering a softening of the brain to have agreed to so outrageous and reckless an escapade! Furthermore, I did not say you are an Amazon. I merely—"

"Implied it. And if my—our—*plan* was reckless and outrageous, 'tis my impression that we are faced with a possible national disaster, which would seem to me to warrant taking a few chances." He started to respond, but she leaned to press a hand across his lips and went on fumingly, "At least be sufficiently generous to admit that I have learned something of value this afternoon. What have you accomplished since you arrived?"

He pulled her hand away but said nothing, and she peered at him suspiciously. "Why is your face so red? Did you—"

She was interrupted by a shout. Falcon started up and in that same instant the coach swerved wildly so that he was thrown to the side. A jolting rocking confusion; the shrill neighs of terrified horses; a sense of falling. He made a desperate lunge for Gwendolyn and clamped his arms about her just as a violent shock wiped everything away . . .

How is your father . . . by the way?"

Falcon blinked as those words echoed in his ears. It was dark. He couldn't see who had spoken. He seemed to be quite alone. He was stiff and uncomfortable, and his left arm hurt. Puzzled, he sat up and banged his nose on the seat of a carriage. He stared at it stupidly. It was tilting at a most peculiar angle. If it didn't straighten out, he thought, it would probably fall. Memory returned with a rush, and with it a heart-stopping terror.

He whispered, "Gwen?" And then was shouting her name frenziedly, and fighting his way to the door that hung at an angle and wide open, above him. He became aware that the coach had come to rest against the base of a great oak tree and that one of the lamps was still burning. It was a distant awareness, for the only thing that really mattered was that he find her. And that she—*please God!*—be alive. He was outside, and running about, still calling her name distractedly as he sought for any sign of a small figure . . . a forest green shawl. "Where are you?" he cried wildly. "Gwen! Answer me!"

The glow from the lamp shone on something pale in the grass. He ran to it and dropped to his knees beside that still face. She lay without any sign of life. Small, motionless, pathetically broken; and precious beyond the power of words.

His hands went out to snatch her up, then recoiled. Trembling, he felt her cheek. It was warm. Scarcely daring to touch her, he lifted one limp little hand, stroking it as he begged sobbingly, "Gwen? Oh, Gwen you *cannot* be dead! Gwen—my precious . . . Smallest Rossiter . . . My darling, my darling! For the love of God—*speak* to me!"

She murmured faintly, "What . . . do you want to . . . talk about?"

He gave a strangled cry, and pressed her hand to his cheek while the sly murmur at the edges of his mind became a shout that he could no longer ignore or refuse. It was there: powerful, unconquerable. It had claimed him at last, and he surrendered with a great surge of gladness and gratitude.

Gwendolyn murmured wonderingly, "Are these . . . tears I feel?"

"No," he said gruffly. "Yes! My dearest most cherished creature! I thought— I thought I'd . . . lost you! And— Lord! What a fool I am! Gwen—are you hurt? Can you move?"

Breathless with anxiety, he watched her tentative movements.

"I think I have . . . some bruises," she reported. "But if you will be so kind as to help me up."

If he would be so kind! With the greatest caution he slid an arm under her shoulders and lifted gently. She gave a stifled exclamation as she sat up, and he shrank in terror. "What? What? Don't move! Why will you not tell me? Where does it hurt?"

"Everywhere," she said with a breathless laugh. "I think when I was thrown from the carriage I must have landed most ungracefully. I shall be very stiff tomorrow, but—nothing worse, I believe. If you will help me, I can stand, and—"

He gave an impatient snort and helped her to her feet.

She swayed dazedly, then uttered a startled cry as she was swept up in arms of steel and cradled close against his heart. It seemed a perfectly satisfactory arrangement. She sighed and rested her head on his shoulder until he set her down with her back against a tree.

"Lie quietly and rest for a minute or two," he said gently, his fingers caressing her cheek. "I must find poor Tummet."

Mortified because she had not at once enquired for the faithful man, she exclaimed. "Oh, what a muddle-head, I am! And the horses, August!"

He begged her not to move, and went off, limping stiffly, and discovering some new bruises of his own. Tummet was extricating himself from a gorse bush and swearing with force and fluency as he picked thorns from his person. He got to his knees as Falcon came up. "Tree across the road, Guv," he said with no little apprehension. "Didn't see it in time, sorry to tellya. I 'opes as Miss Gwen—"

"She is bruised and shaken. Nothing worse, thank God." Falcon extended a helping hand. "What of you, my poor fellow?"

It was an improvement, thought Tummet, over being named a

"scheming, traitorous hedgebird." "Never mind abaht me, Guv. We gotta find the team."

By a great stroke of luck the oak against which the coach had come to rest had snapped the pole cleanly, and the horses were discovered grazing peacefully a short distance down the hill. One appeared to have suffered a sprained hock, and the other was cut about the knees but not so severely as to prevent its being ridden. The two men freed the animals from their harness, and then righted the coach. Two wheels were sprung, the windows shattered, and the side smashed in. Viewing the wreckage, Falcon could only marvel they'd not all been killed.

Tummet said wearily, "Will I go and fetch help, sir?"

"Not before I apologize for handling you so roughly. I shouldn't have allowed my temper to overmaster me. But I'll want an explanation, even so."

"I c'n see why you'd a'been put abaht, Guv. Thinking I'd bin a party to Miss Gwen's larks. Wasn't."

"We'll sort it all out later. Are you sure you're able to ride? If not, I'll go and you can stay with the lady."

Tummet insisted he was "writ-as-a-riddle," adding that it must be only a few miles back up to the London-to-Dover turnpike where he was sure to find help. He didn't look "fit as a fiddle," but Falcon's own head was none too clear, and the violent episode had done his arm no good at all. He helped Tummet mount up, then returned to the tree and sank down beside Gwendolyn.

It seemed perfectly natural for his arm to go around her, and that she should snuggle against him in so trusting a way. They were both bruised and battered, they had survived a narrow brush with death, and they were sitting all alone on a dark and chilly heath. Yet no two lovers drifting in a gondola under a summer Venetian moon could have been more blissfully content as they shared a comfortable silence.

Gwendolyn thought mistily of those wondrous words she'd never thought to hear him say, 'My darling . . . My dearest most cherished creature.' And the knowledge that she was loved as deeply as she loved, was so great a happiness that she was almost afraid to believe it.

Falcon was reliving that nightmarish moment when he'd

thought to have lost her, and the wonder of this love that had crept upon him so quietly so gradually, to spring at last, with such awesome power that in this one short hour his life was changed forever. Only it was not one short hour, of course. For some time his inner voice had been warning that his feelings towards her were changing, only he'd fought against it and denied it. He tried to think of just when, during the many occasions that the Smallest Rossiter had teased and argued with him, she had managed to take possession of his heart. He found he could not even recall their disagreements with much clarity, for tonight there seemed to be a soft haze over everything.

"Mr. Falcon?"

He hugged her closer. "Yes, my lovely rascal?"

"You're very quiet. Are you thinking better of—of what you said just now?"

"It could have been better said, if that's your point."

"Did you . . . really mean it, dear August?"

"For as long as my life shall last, my priceless Smallest Rossiter."

She shivered, and he asked anxiously, "Are you cold?"

"No."

"Yet you shivered. Here—" He twisted out of his cloak and wrapped it around her. "Better?"

"Yes, thank you. But . . ."

"But—what, beloved?"

"I should rather be kissed, if you don't mind."

If he didn't mind! There was no need to turn her face, for she had it poised and ready. "I am all consideration," she murmured.

He laughed softly, and kissed her; not as he'd kissed any other woman, but as a man kisses the lady of his choosing, the perfect one who will forever rule in his heart. She kissed him back, her lips sweet and shy, and just as he would have wished them. And they held each other close and murmured of their love and the wondrous perfection of it, as lovers always have and always will, until she sighed, "I never dreamed 'twould be the same for you as it is for me. You will think me very silly, but— May I move this? It's digging into my ribs."

He blinked at the small package she had found in the pocket

of his coat. "Oh," he said, shifting it to the other side. "A little gift for Trina. Which reminds me." He pulled out another package. "My first and most inadequate gift for you, dearest."

She opened the package and admired the shawl rapturously, then exclaimed, "Oh, I forgot! I've a gift for you, also!" She drew a small flat box from the pocket of her skirt. "I found it on a table with the most odd collection of trinkets. I vow I could have spent hours there, and a very strange old lady told me that her late husband had been used to bring fascinating things from his travels throughout the world."

He said smilingly, "That sounds like my friend Mrs. Quimby."

"Why, that is so! She told me her name and—" She stopped, and snatched the little box away suddenly. "No! Don't open it now." She slipped it into his pocket. "I'd rather you saved— August?" She reached up to touch his brow. "How warm you are! And—oh, heavens! You are so pale! You're hurt and you've not told me!"

Her anxious little hands were tugging at his coat, and he said in amusement that it was very sweet to be maudled over, but that he was perfectly fit, save that he felt rather tired. "It must be the shock," he murmured. "Of the amputation, you know."

She peered at him worriedly. "Amputation?"

"Of my heart. Who'd ever have guessed I should lose it to a street-walking baggage?"

She responded with mock indignation, but her words echoed unintelligibly. He pulled her close and kissed her again, and quietly fell asleep.

How is your father . . . by the way?"

Falcon frowned up at the ceiling. Who had said that? He seemed to remember—

"Well, now! 'Bout time you woke up, Guv!" Tummet's broad grin hovered over him and the beady brown eyes were watching him intently. "When you takes a nap, you takes a nap!"

He yawned and stretched luxuriously. He was in bed in his own room. Odd, because it had all seemed so real. He said, "D'you know, my psuedo-gentleman's-gentleman, I had the most strange dream."

"Didyer now." Tummet touched his cheek lightly, and murmured, "Hum."

"Need a shave, do I? As I said, I dreamed I damn near . . . throttled—" He stopped short, reached out and jerked his valet's neat stock aside.

"Hey!" yelped Tummet. "Now you gorn and spoilt it!"

The bruises were lurid. "The deuce!" whispered Falcon, and lay back, his mind whirling. If *that* had been no dream, then nor had the rest of it! He'd really seen Joel Skye and Mariner Fotheringay at Overlake Lodge! He'd really had that most promising conversation with Mrs. Quimby, and spent a sprightly hour with Pamela Dunscroft, and— He sprang up in bed, then clung to the mattress as the room reeled and dipped around him.

Tummet said something and tried to lie him down again.

Resisting doggedly, he gasped, "Let be! What the—devil's wrong—with me?"

"Jest what Sir James said, mate. You runned yerself inter a proper relapse, is what. Scared poor Miss Gwen 'alf to death, you done! Lucky I come back quick-like."

"Miss . . . Gwen," whispered Falcon, and sank down again, closing his eyes. "Oh, God!"

"Pretty sharp, is it, Guv? Proper inflamed Sir Jim said."

It was more than "pretty sharp." How like Fate to creep in under his guard and deal him a lifetime leveller! He muttered bitterly, "And what a ghastly mull I made of the business."

"Now, now, Guv. Don't go fretting yerself into flinders. You done good, considering yer arm were so nasty. Leastways— Wotcher doing?"

"Getting up. What would you think. Bring me some clothes!"

"Do nothing of the sort, Tummet!"

Gwen's sweet clear voice. His heart turned over. Her hands were on his shoulders, her eyes, soft and tender, were scanning his face. And somehow, he must deal with this like—like a gentleman.

She asked gently, "How do you feel, my dear?"

"I would feel better, ma'am, an you would take yourself from my bedchamber."

Shock came into those honest blue eyes. Then, she smiled. "So that's your game, is it? 'Twill avail you naught, August Nicolai K. Falcon, and so I warn you!"

'God bless your valiant soul,' he thought, and threw back the bedclothes. "The choice is yours, ma'am."

She glimpsed a nightshirt and a shapely but hairy leg. "Gwendolyn!"

Katrina hurried in, followed by Mrs. Vanechurch, who said in a near scream, "Mr. *August!*" and put her hand across Gwendolyn's eyes.

Tummet stood with his arms folded, grinning from ear to ear.

Falcon knew when he was beaten, and he lay down again. "Women!"

*

Wanted to see me?" Jonathan Armitage stuck his fair head around the edge of the door and looked cautiously at Tummet, who sat by the bed reading a newspaper aloud.

" 'S'all right, mate," said Tummet, standing. "Doc Sir Jim says 'e can 'ave visitors, so long as they don't get 'im all stirred up."

"Come on in, Johnny," growled Falcon. "And pay no heed to this varmint."

Armitage approached the bed and scanned the patient, propped against many pillows and looking, he thought, considerably wrung out.

Falcon told Tummet to fetch his coat. "The one I wore to the Fete yesterday."

"Day afore yestiday," corrected Tummet, going into the dressing room.

Shocked, Falcon exclaimed, "Good Gad! Have I lost a day, then? Is this not Sunday?"

"Monday." Armitage sat on the side of the bed. "What a fool you are, August, to go rushing about from Land's End to John o'Groats with that ugly hole in your arm. You'll accomplish nothing for us if you get yourself knocked up, you know."

"Oh, will I not?" Falcon felt in the pocket of the coat Tummet offered him, and took out a small flat box. An invisible mule kicked him in the ribs, and his hand trembled slightly as he replaced the box and felt in the other pocket. "Where the devil is that card? A lady is expecting you to visit her on Thursday afternoon, and—" He checked, noting the uneasy exchange of glances between Armitage and Tummet. "Now what are you two looking so greasy-eyed about?"

Armitage said in a very gentle voice, "I expect you've forgotten, August. You told Gideon all about it, and he sent for me at once."

Falcon stared at him. "I—did? You know that you're to send in your name—"

"As Mr. Tide. Yes, old fellow. You gave me her card. And I cannot thank you enough."

"Devil with your thanks! I just must have forgot, is all. Did I also tell you—" He glanced aside as the door opened.

Morris. Transfixed as by a sabre, Falcon thought, 'Now I know how you feel, my poor dolt. I know all too well.' He turned his face away, heard some whisperings, then the door opened again and closed softly. Morris had gone, thank heaven. But when he looked up, it was to discover that Armitage had left. Morris was sitting beside the bed, watching him.

"No," he said wearily.

"I didn't ask."

"I can feel it, winging to me on the air. Why else would you have come?"

Morris looked offended. "Fella's—er, not up to par, his fr— acquaintances come to say how-dee-do and—er, so forth."

He'd always said he didn't need or want friends, and Jamie had respected that. Poor old Jamie. If things were different . . . He said, "Give it up, Morris. You're too good a man to waste your life, and you'll never have my consent. The only hope for you is to bury me, and even then, I doubt she'd accept you."

Morris looked aghast. "You really are sick! You never said I was a good man before!"

"It must be the effect of all these well-wishers calling. Are you the last? Or is the hall thronged with lovely ladies preparing to descend upon me with tearful eyes and heaving bosoms?"

Morris pointed out solemnly, " 'A heaving bosom is often nothing more than a hope chest.' "

Unable to restrain a grin, Falcon protested, "You villain! Coming here and throwing maxims at my head when I'm a helpless invalid with nothing to throw at you in return! Begone! And keep away from my sister!"

"Now there's a grand incentive for you to hurry back to your customary pose of surly gaoler." Morris lifted a restraining hand as Falcon sat up menacingly. "No, no, you really cannot murder me yet, August. I've not given you my report."

Staring at him, Falcon echoed, "Report?"

"Yes. I trotted down there yesterday. Shouldn't have. My parent don't hold with Sunday travel. Still, all's well, so far as I could see. Though, dashed if I know what you expected me to find."

Mystified, Falcon said, "Find—where?"

"Well, that's it. If *you* knew, you should've told me, so—"

"Fiend seize you, Jamie! You're enough to try the patience of a saint! Where—have—you—been?"

"You know dashed well where I've been! Why you cod's head, 'twas you begged me to go down there, wasn't it? Said you was worried about the old gentleman, but—"

"My—*father?*"

"Well, of course! Don't you—" Morris paused, looked dismayed, and came to his feet. "Think I'll be toddling, old boy. Ain't yourself. Should've known when you said I was a good man. Fever, that's what 'tis. Beastly business."

Falcon frowned at the closing door. A fine game they were playing with him! First Johnny, now Morris. He might have forgot that he'd told Ross about Mrs. Quimby's offer, but he was blasted well sure he'd not have sent Morris down to Ashleigh to check on the old gentleman! Certainly, he would remember having done so outlandish a thing. It must be that they were trying to keep him chained to his bed so as to shut him out of some new mischief of the League's making. Or perchance Ross was uneasy about that stupid bag of feathers that had been hurled at him in Cornwall. Lord, but how could grown men be such fools?

He flung back the coverlet. Inactivity always galled him, and inactivity just now was an invitation to thought, and to think was disaster. Especially if he allowed himself to remember all the things Gwendolyn had murmured in his ear after Trina and the housekeeper had left just now. He shouted, "Tummet!"

His coat still lay across the foot of the bed. The coat of blue and silver brocade he'd worn on that magical November Midsummer's Eve. He pulled it to him, touching the sleeve lingeringly.

Tummet hurried in, and groaned.

"Never mind that," said Falcon briskly. "I've wasted too much time, lounging about in this damnable bed. I want a bath and a shave, and clean clothes."

"Now, Guv—"

"Exactly so. *Now!* Oh, and I'll wear this coat."

"*That* one? But—it wants pressing!"

"Then—*press it!*"

Katrina jumped up as Gwendolyn came into her private parlour, and ran to embrace her. "Dearest Gwen! The more I think about it, the more hopeful I become! Sit here and tell me everything. What did he say after we left? Oh, the way he *looked* at you! My darling brother has lost his heart at last! I cannot believe it!"

Smiling, Gwendolyn allowed herself to be led to the small sofa by the hearth. "There is nothing to tell. After you and Mrs. Vanechurch left, August fell asleep. Or pretended to. I didn't believe it, of course, and I gave him a thorough talking to, I promise you."

Katrina hugged herself rapturously. "But after the accident he kissed you, so he'll have to ask for your hand, which means he won't be able to refuse his consent to Jamie and me! Oh, I *never* dared hope— Now, why must you look so grave? You never think he has changed his mind? Already?"

"I think he means to be difficult, Trina. I am very sure he loves me, though why he should, when I am so—ordinary—"

Katrina wrapped her in another strong embrace and said with vehemence, "You are *not* ordinary! You are pretty and bright and kind, and always there is a smile in your eyes, and—"

"And I am crippled."

"Pho! You go with a little limp is all! Perry Cranford lost his foot and is one of the most attractive men I know! And if it comes to that, *we* are—"

Gwendolyn put a silencing finger across her lips. "You had a lovely Grandmama who was half Russian and half Chinese, which is of no concern to me whatsoever and would not, I am sure, weigh with Gideon."

Katrina said gravely, "It might weigh heavily with your other brother, and with your Papa."

That was very true. Gwendolyn felt a qualm and said with more confidence than she felt, "Oh, I'll bring them around my thumb, never fear. But—may I ask you something? I know August has fought many duels. Has he been wounded before?"

"Once. Some years ago, when he fought a German count— Von somebody. I forget the name. August said he was the finest swordsman he'd ever met, and they parted best of friends. But even then, 'twas no more than a shallow cut across his shoulder. The only other time he was hurt was when Jamie accidentally shot him last Spring, and you know about that."

"Yes. Were the symptoms the same?"

Katrina answered slowly, " 'Twas a gunshot wound, which is always more dangerous, so they say. And you know how impatient he can be. He suffered a slight relapse because, as usual, he would not obey the doctor."

"When you say 'a slight relapse,' do you mean he was delirious at all? Did he suffer . . . lapses of memory?"

"Good gracious, no! Has he done so now?"

"Well, he seemed to think today was Sunday."

"Yes, poor dear. And he quite forgot he'd sent Jamie down to Ashleigh. Still, 'tis natural enough he'd be muddle-headed, you know. And he slept most of yesterday away." Katrina said with a fond smile, "How dear it is to see you worry for him, but pray don't worry too much. Papa says August is fashioned from Toledo steel. He will be quite recovered, and rushing about in his usual fashion in no time, wait and see."

Gwendolyn smiled, and wished she could stop thinking of a foolish old superstition, and a bag of feathers.

CHAPTER XI

The large and comfortable study in Laindon House on Curzon Street was briefly silent. Then, "Dead?" Sir Mark Rossiter leaned forward in his chair, and said an aghast, "All three?"

Gregory Clement Laindon, the Earl of Bowers-Malden, shrugged his massive shoulders impatiently. "Why should that surprise you? Heaven only knows how many deaths can be laid at the door of that murderous League. They don't balk at executing their own—look at Norberly, and Burton Farrier, and now that sorry fool, Gil Fowles! Why should they hesitate to put a period to my poor fellows?"

Sir Mark leaned back again and stared at the earl, shocked by what he judged to be a hard and callous attitude.

Both in their mid-fifties, they had known each other most of their lives and their heirs were close friends, but the two men had little in common. Although the earl did not run to fat he was very tall and of muscular build, and his great booming voice and sometimes fierce manner tended to put others in awe of him. His head was often described as "leonine," his features were strong but not unpleasant, and a gleam of humour lurked in the green eyes that were so like those of his son, Horatio. Sir Mark was also tall, but he appeared slight by comparison with the earl. Still handsome, and always elegant, he had waged and was winning a desperate struggle to restore both his good name and his financial empire after having been all but ruined by the machinations of the League of Jewelled Men. He said now, "Then you don't believe that Lord Norberly's death was accidental?"

The earl drew a breath as if exercising strong restraint. "Accidental? My dear fellow, do but consider! For some odd reason Norberly delighted to climb mountains, and by all accounts was good at the game. Yet—and conveniently while walking alone—he suffered a fatal fall from a not especially precipitous Scottish hillside. We know he was a member of the League of Jewelled Men. We know he had a large hand in contriving your ruin. And that he blundered the task set him by an organization whose leader punishes failure with death! An accident? Nonsense!"

Irked by the note of condescension, Sir Mark concealed the reaction. He said gravely, "Then 'twould seem that your poor fellows must have been close to learning something of import. They were watching Fowles, I take it?"

"Yes. I make no doubt the newspapers will raise a great to-do and claim they were thieves and murdered him."

Sir Mark looked sombre. "So much violence. Does Gideon know of the ugly business?"

"You've not seen him today?"

"I returned to Town scarce an hour since. Both my sons were from home."

"Of course! Blister me if I hadn't forgot! You've been in the west country. At your shipyard, no? I trust all was well there?"

"Very well, I thank you. One good thing to come out of such a disaster is that we've now been able to improve and modernize. I've installed a new dry dock that—" He broke off and added guiltily, "Not that anything can compensate for the lives that were lost in the fire, you understand."

"No, of course not. But those tragedies can be laid to the League's account. You were no way responsible." Sir Mark gave him a grateful look, and the earl asked, "So, have you been able to put your people back to work yet?"

"We have, indeed. The sheds are all rebuilt and work has begun on two new frigates!"

"My congratulations. And today you came seeking Gideon, did you? Not here, I'm afraid. In fact, Horatio's out looking for him. If he don't find him at your house, I fancy he'll know where to search."

"I'm very sure he will. However, I actually called on you because of a letter I received from Neville Falcon."

"About his great surprise party, eh? D'you mean to go down to Ashleigh?"

"I suppose so, though 'tis a deuced awkward time of year. Shall you go?"

"Don't see how I can avoid it, my dear fellow. Neville apparently means to honour our sons for their efforts 'gainst the League. Is a nice gesture, and Lord knows, they've earned a deal more thanks than a surprise party."

"I agree, but be dashed if I see the need for all the secrecy. It seems a touch childish for us parents to creep down there and cry "Surprise!" at the young fellows when they arrive. Shall you take Lady Nola? If I know Neville, he has something outlandish in mind."

The earl laughed. "And you think Neville's 'something outlandish' will be feminine in nature, do you? One of those harem dancers, for instance? Might be so, at that, he's a frippery fellow. Well, my lady's broad-minded and would likely thoroughly enjoy it."

Sir Mark thought that most probable. A stickler for proper behaviour, he failed to see the kind heart that dwelt behind the loud voice and bluff manners of the Countess of Bowers-Malden, and found her both intimidating and more than a shade vulgar. Afraid that his reaction might be noted, he murmured evasively, "Neville wasn't always frippery, you know."

"Really?" Nobody's fool, the earl had seen that brief prim pursing of the lips and was annoyed. He glanced rather pointedly at the clock on the mantelpiece.

"As I recall," said Sir Mark, settling back in his chair with a reminiscent look, "when his wife was alive he was very much interested in the Exchange. Had a jolly good head on his shoulders. I fancy the family coffers grew, rather than diminished, under his care. At one time, I thought he'd run for Parliament . . ." Lost in the nostalgia of bygone days, he expanded on the subject at some length.

'He's going to go prosing on forever,' thought the earl, who wanted to talk with his wife before she left for a luncheon party. He took out his pocket watch and wound it ostentatiously. "I rather think that August has done well enough," he said. "Say of him what you will, he's a young fellow with no cobwebs in his brainbox! Speaking of which, I—er, fancy you've heard about his accident?"

"I've not! More trouble? Nothing serious, I trust?"

"Fortunately not, but, er—your daughter was with him at the time."

Five minutes later, Bowers-Malden was free to seek out his spouse.

Tummet alerted Gwendolyn, and when Falcon hurried down the stairs she limped from the library, book in hand, and nerved for battle.

She was wearing a morning dress of white, embroidered with bluebirds, and about her shoulders was a fine shawl of blue silk with an elaborately knotted fringe. Her eyes were a deep azure glow in her pretty face, and the many petticoats she wore in lieu of hoops swirled softly as she moved and emphasized, he thought, her dainty fragility.

His fingers tightened spasmodically on the flat box in his coat pocket. He thought, 'This is going to be hell!' and he drawled, "If I dare remark it, the shawl becomes you, Gwen."

Her smile was a caress. "I'd have felt cheated if you'd not noticed. I shall always treasure it. I suppose I am not to comment on the fact that you have not rested nearly long enough, and are being exceeding foolish."

"Your own behaviour has been far from wise." He waved away an interested footman, walked into the library beside Gwendolyn, and closed the door.

She sighed and faced him. How calm he looked. How coldly remote and quite in control of himself. "I guessed you would not give up easily," she said wryly. "Do you mean to pretend you don't remember the things you told me after the accident?"

"I'll confess my memory of the entire time is, to say the least, clouded. But it makes little difference. Whatever I said was spoken at a moment of great emotional shock, besides which I evidently was in the grip of a fever, and—"

"Oh, *do* stop being silly! I love you, and I know that you love me, but if you don't want me, I quite understand. I harbour no delusions, August. I am neither beautiful nor accomplished, and I go with a limp."

He caught his breath hissingly. Very briefly his eyes glared rage, then the thick black fringe of his lashes concealed them, and he murmured, "I'd not have put it in just those words, m'dear, but"—he shrugged—" 'tis perhaps best that we be honest with each other."

"I agree. When do you mean to begin?"

He frowned and turned away to draw a chair closer to the fire that burned brightly on the hearth. "Perhaps you should sit down."

She put aside her book and followed obediently. "I collect the inference is that I am too frail to stand for long." With a sudden dart she avoided the chair and was breast to breast with him, her hands tight on his coat. "Tell me that you don't love me," she demanded huskily.

Her little face was upturned and so inviting, her eyes full of tenderness, and he could smell the fresh but tantalizing fragrance that had betrayed her pose as a poor flower-seller. More than he had ever wanted anything in his life, he wanted to crush her to his heart and kiss those soft, rosy lips. With a really heroic effort he said, "I shall never tell you that I do."

"Foolish man! Your eyes tell me."

He pulled her hands away. "Then I must take care not to let them rest on you." He stepped back as she reached out to him once more. "Gwen, stop! Go back to your family. The longer you stay here, the harder 'twill be, for both of us."

"No!" She hurried to block his way as he turned towards the door, and seized his arm. "August—my dearest love—"

"Don't!" Anguished, he pulled free. *"Do not!"*

"I will! I must! You choose to be a noble martyr to nonsense, but don't you care that you are sacrificing my happiness, also?"

"Nonsense?" He wrenched her small gift from his pocket and thrust it at her. "Is that why you chose to present me with this box of incense? To remind me of 'nonsense'?"

She said hotly, "I sought, as I always have sought, to make you learn more of the wonders of China. To help you see that there is nothing shameful about your lineage. That there is much, in fact, to be proud of! No, do not shake your head! If you were not so blindly arrogant and stubborn—"

" 'Tis because I am far from blind that I ask you to leave." He slipped the incense back into his pocket, seized her arms and went on, low-voiced and with passionate intensity: "You had your say, now listen to me. If you truly love me, then you are incredibly stupid! You have, from the beginning, told me of my faults. God knows, you have seen my horrid temper often enough. If you now add stubbornness to the list of my failings, so be it. I never sought your love, nor the love of any lady, especially an unwed lady, who could so easily be ruined in the eyes of that merciless clan known as The Polite World! Whatever *you* or *I* might think of my forbears, do you think *they* would look upon us with less revulsion? Or—"

"Much care I for what the *ton*—"

"Of course you care!" He shook her, and said fiercely, " 'Tis the world you've known all your life. 'Tis every friend you've ever had, everyone you've ever known, every member of your family, wherever they may be scattered. You cannot *begin* to realize what it means to be looked upon with contempt, to be cut and mocked and ostracized. Have you so soon forgot what I told you of the fate of my dear grandmama? Do you suppose that the scorn shown to her would not be visited on you, if I asked for your hand and was accepted?"

"You have done considerably more than ask! You kissed me, which to any man of honour constitutes a proposal of marriage."

"Yes. I'll own that I behaved very badly at a moment when I truly believe my mind was—was scrambled."

" 'Twas not too scrambled to prevent you calling me your— your beloved, and saying that you would love me for as long as life—"

He interrupted hurriedly, "The fact that I said anything of that nature to you under *any* circumstances will be to my everlasting discredit! I am very, *very* sorry for that lapse, and beg you will forgive and *forget* it!" Unable to meet her eyes, he released her and said huskily, "Go away, Gwen! Else I must!"

"And if I do go," she said in desperation, "you will be proud, and feel you have behaved as a gentleman should, is that it? Four lives ruined: four chances for happiness shattered, only for the sake of your selfish and foolish would-be nobility! A pretty cause for pride, Mr. August Falcon!"

Stung, he riposted, "Oh, do not tittup around it, Miss Rossiter! Say the whole! August—Nicolai—Kung—Falcon! Or as your world names me, the Mandarin of Mayfair!"

She stretched out her hands to him. "August, oh my dear, 'tis your world too. You are more English than Chinese."

"To be part one thing and part another," he said bitterly, "is, *en effet*, to be neither!"

"Then go on as you are, if that is your wish. But do not throw love away! Do not break my poor heart."

Moving out of reach of those small beseeching hands, he demanded, "Can you not see that 'tis because I would move heaven and earth *not* to break it that I send you from me? Do you really think that, having rejected Katrina's many suitors, having denied her marriage with the man she thinks she loves, I would now be so irresponsible as to shrug off everything I have ever held true, and snatch my own chance for happiness? Can you *truly* believe I'd carelessly subject you to the years of misery my Grandmama suffered? Or allow Katrina to be snubbed and slighted until eventually, inevitably, despite all his fine vows of fidelity, Morris turned from her? No, by God! Selfish, bad-tempered, arrogant, and all the rest of it, I may be. But I'm not *that* base!"

He tore his gaze from her grief-stricken face and strode to wrench the door open. With harsh finality he said, "Go back to Rossiter Court, Gwen. To the world you know and where you are respected and more admired than you guess. If you do not, you will give me no choice but to take Katrina to—to India for a year or so!"

"You c-cannot," she gulped, tears beading on her lashes. "You promised m-my brother to help him fight the—the Squire and—"

His nerves in shreds, he snarled, "Be damned to my promise! And be damned to the Squire!"

The door slammed behind him.

Y'r drunk, August," observed the Marquis of Pencader, peering at Falcon owlishly.

"I am nothing of the kind! What it is, you're a fool, Bertie! Drunk or sober."

"Falcon can't be drunk," argued Lord Kadenworthy, who had been gazing drowsily into the fire in the quiet downstairs lounge of The Madrigal. "Not yet ten o'clock."

Seated next to Sir Owen Furlong, Peregrine Cranford contributed, "Now that's true. Too early. Night's not begun. There's hardly anyone here yet."

Falcon gave him a fulminating look. "Idiot. I won't speak for the rest of you, but I do not count myself a nobody, and I'm here!"

"And spoiling for a quarrel," said Sir Owen coolly. "Do not waste your scowls on me, Falcon. I'll not fight you."

"Your life's too sweet, eh?" sneered Falcon. "What happened? Did your admired would-be murderess rush to your arms once more?"

Sir Owen's jaw set. "If I hadn't promised Ross—"

Kadenworthy interjected hurriedly, "Easy, gentlemen, easy! We're all on edge tonight, because of poor Fowles."

"*Poor* Fowles?" murmured Cranford in Sir Owen's ear. "Poor traitor, more like!"

Kadenworthy stood, took up the bottle of cognac on the table beside Crisp, and went around refilling glasses, pausing beside Sir Owen to murmur, "Perchance 'twill mellow Falcon's mood."

The marquis, who had kept Falcon company since his early arrival at the club, smiled vacuously. "Wazzat 'bout a lady in Owen's arms? Who, you lucky dog? Not—not the beau'ful Benevento, eh? Heard she was—was back in Town."

"She is," said Sir Owen, his gaze fixed on Falcon's dark face.

Cranford asked, "You've seen her, Owen? Since the other day?"

Sir Owen shook his head. "Unfortunately, no. But 'tis my dearest wish."

Falcon choked over a mouthful of brandy, and laughed rather hilariously. Crisp lurched to his feet and began to pound at his back, and Falcon sprang up and shoved him away. "Let be! And you said *I* was drunk!"

Kadenworthy bent over Cranford's chair and whispered, "Thank the lord Morris is not here yet! Get him out of here, Perry, else Owen will certainly strangle him."

"Or vice versa. What the deuce ails him?"

"He's in one of his black moods. Heaven knows why, but he's out for blood tonight."

The marquis clutched at a chair-back and blinked at Falcon. "Know that look," he said, waving an accusing finger. "Ain't goin' to meet you 'gain, August. No, no, no! Wastin' y'r time, dear boy!"

Cranford said, "Oh, come on, August. Let's go and find Ross. He may be at White's. The Madrigal's dull as dust tonight."

Falcon stared at him for a frowning moment, then nodded, and they went out together.

Lord Cyril Eckington, who had eavesdropped on their conversation behind his copy of *The Spectator*, left his chair and wandered towards the stairs and the gaming rooms. Drawing level with Furlong, he remarked loudly, "I trust young Cranford's a fair marksman. Your friend the Mandarin's in an unusually foul mood tonight, even for him!"

Furlong said in his cool fashion, "Well acquainted with all his moods, are you, Eckington?"

"I wonder you didn't share a few words with him," drawled Hector Kadenworthy, his scorn apparent.

There were some smothered chuckles. Eckington offered a contemptuous mumble about "impertinent young Bucks" and went huffily on his way.

Proceeding on their own way, Cranford and Falcon had little opportunity for conversation. It was a clear night, the air carrying the chill touch of approaching winter. Despite his peg-leg, Cranford suggested they walk instead of calling up sedan chairs, secretly hoping a brisk stroll would cool Falcon's temper. They skirted a large and angry crowd milling about on Piccadilly, and reached White's to find the members agog with the news of Gilbert Fowles' murder. There were shouted demands for the Horse Guards to "do something" about the increasingly unsafe streets, and several sombre references to "revolutionaries."

Falcon shouldered his way through the lounge. He couldn't see Rossiter anywhere, and when he asked Cranford if he could spot him the reply was echoingly unintelligible.

"Speak up, blast you," he snapped. "No need to whisper!"

Cranford caught his arm and pulled him to a halt. "Falcon, are you feeling up to par? You look deuced odd!"

He felt odd. His head was on fire and the room was strangely blurred and colourless and filled with silly individuals whose mission in life seemed to be to annoy him. He shook off Cranford's hand irritably.

From somewhere in the crowd a man laughed and said with unfortunate clarity, "If the Mandarin finds old Morris playing Romeo to Miss Katrina's Juliet, he'll look a sight more than odd!"

Falcon plunged into the throng demanding furiously, "Who said that? Speak your filth to my face, you—you damned craven! Speak up, blast you!"

There was a sudden silence, those near to him drawing away uneasily.

"August!" Cranford tugged at his sleeve and panted, "What a' plague ails you, man? Come—we'd best get home!"

"Aye! Home! And fast! If Jamie Morris is lusting after—after m'sister behind my back, I'll put an end to it—and to him!"

He whirled about and shoved his way through the quieted crowd while men stared after him with varying degrees of contempt or curiosity, and Peregrine Cranford thumped along as fast as his peg-leg would carry him.

The cold outer air was pleasant on Falcon's heated face. He glanced up the street. Fog restricted visibility to about twenty yards.

Shouting for a chair, Cranford hobbled off and was lost from view.

A gleaming light coach pulled into the kennel. A footman

swung down and opened the door, and Lord Coombs alighted, drawing his cloak tighter about him.

"Borrow your coach, Coombs," growled Falcon.

It was more a demand than a request, and his lordship protested indignantly, "The deuce! Why should—"

"Emergency!" Falcon pushed him aside and shouted directions to the coachman.

The footman's jaw sagged as he looked from his astonished master to the dangerous Mr. Falcon.

Coombs said grudgingly, "Oh, very well, if 'tis an emergency. But—"

"Spring 'em, dammitall!" howled Falcon, reaching out to slam the door closed. "Spring 'em!"

Peregrine Cranford had just secured an empty chair when he saw the carriage flash past and caught a glimpse of the occupant. "Dear heaven!" he gasped, climbing into the chair. "To Falcon House on Great Ormond Street. As fast as— Hold up!" He leaned from the chair as Newby Rossiter came down the steps of the club, arm in arm with a dandified crony. "Rossiter!" shouted Cranford, gesturing frantically. "Where's your brother?"

Newby sauntered over with maddeningly slow steps and a smile on his handsome face. "Dashed if I know. Why?"

"For the love of God, find him! Tell him to come to Falcon House. Quick!"

Sobering, Newby asked, "Why? What's to do?"

"Tell him 'tis a matter of life and death! Hurry! *Please!*"

Newby stared at him, but nodded, and Cranford urged his chairmen on.

Leaning back against the deep cushions of his purloined coach, Falcon closed his eyes, enjoying the rush of icy air from the wide-open windows. Dashed fine coach had his lordship. And a fast team. He felt cooler now, and his head was less muddled. He looked out of the window. No fog here. Must have been very localized. Peculiar, that. The coach was turning onto Great Ormond Street. Already? *Jolly* fast team! They must have sprouted wings. The thought amused him, and he giggled softly and as abruptly scowled. What the devil was he grinning at? His life was in a shambles and, worse, he'd reduced another and most precious life to a shambles. Besides, 'twas foolish to have come rushing home like this. As if Jamie would call on Katrina in such a hole-and-corner fashion. Soul of honour was Jamie . . . 'gainst his nature to do anything on the sly. Why he'd allowed himself to become so angry was a puzzle. He must, he decided, be more than a little drunk. Logical enough. He'd been drinking most of the afternoon. Usually, though, he knew when he'd had as much as he could handle. And if life had taught him anything it was that liquor didn't drown one's sorrows. If anything, the sorrow became sharper. All liquor did was make a fellow feel like the very—

The coach came to a rocking halt. Somebody let down the steps. Falcon groped for his purse and thrust some coins in the footman's hand, then was striding across the flagway. He paused at the front door and leaned against the wall, drawing in deep breaths to steady himself, but when he reached for the bell it swayed foolishly from side to side. So he must be foxed, even if only slightly. It would not do. He couldn't like either Aunt Dudley or Katrina to see him over the oar. Most of all—the Smallest Rossiter must not— But she'd gone, of course. Couldn't stay here after what he'd said to her. He drew a hand across his eyes shrinking from another spiteful jab of grief. How empty the house would be without that sunny presence. Like a blasted great mausoleum! He heard a horseman approaching and pulled himself together as he turned to see who was arriving. It was not a caller, however, but a lad walking somebody's horse. He glanced idly at the animal and stood rigidly still, his breath held in check. He'd know that beautiful piece of high-strung tomfoolery anywhere!

He strolled down the steps and as the boy drew level called, "Has Lieutenant Morris been here long?"

" 'Arf an hour, milor'. Give or take. 'Ere 'e is, now, if—"

Morris was coming from the alley beside the house, his head down and his manner despondent.

Falcon gave the boy a shilling and sent him off, then held the reins himself. Waiting.

Windsong recognized her master and whinnied.

Morris looked up, gave a gasp, and recoiled. "What the devil . . . ?"

"You treacherous hound," said Falcon furiously. "Is this the way you serve me? Creeping about to meet her on the sly when I'm safely out of sight?"

Affronted, Morris answered, "I did not meet her at all, if you want to know! I just like to—to be near her for a little." He flushed and added shyly, "To look up at her windows now and then, you—"

"Like any peeping Tom," sneered Falcon.

Morris' chin came up. He said with unusual hauteur, "I think you know me better than that! And I resent—"

"What you resent is being caught at your slithery tricks! Well, you've been caught fairly, and I warn you—"

"Oh, a pox on your silly warnings! I suppose the truth is that you now find you're caught in the trap of your own making, and you don't like the feeling! Mayhap you'll learn that you're as human as any other fellow."

"I think not," said Falcon silkily. "You see, half-breeds we may be, but at least there are no traitors in my family!" He saw the colour leave Morris' honest face, and added, "Or would you deny that the head of your house is a murderous crony of the Squire and your name dishonoured and—"

"Be damned if I'll take that!" Morris' hand flashed out, the back of it striking Falcon across the mouth so that he reeled back a step.

"Found some gumption at last, have you?" he said, triumphant.

"You may send your seconds to—"

"Seconds—hell! By the time they call on me you'll be yellow as butter again!"

"Damn you, Falcon! I'll fight you any time—anywhere!"

"Then you'll fight me here—and now! Not afraid of the dark, are you?" He led the way around to the back garden and opened the side gate, turning Windsong loose to graze. Swinging off his cloak and tossing it aside, he shrugged out of his coat and waistcoat. "There's a moon, and the flambeaux from the Mount-Durward house throw plenty of light—unless panic is dimming your vision."

Morris gritted his teeth and discarded his own cloak and coat. "You're mad," he grumbled, watching Falcon tear off his shoes.

" 'Tis against the law to fight without seconds. Besides, how the devil can I fight you? You've a damn great cut in your arm—"

"And am ten times the swordsman you are with one hand tied behind my back, which should even the odds." Falcon rolled back the lace at his wrists. "Have done with your silly cowardly objections. You've hidden from this fight long enough. Tonight we'll see an end to it, once and for all!" He flexed his sword between his hands, the familiar exhilaration making his blood tingle as he looked about the quiet garden. "You've tripped across this land often enough in your dishonourable pursuit of my sister, but I want no cries of 'foul,' so I'll remind you that there's a low spot in front of the summer house that will likely be soggy. And there's fresh gravel on the walks, so have a care for your feet!"

"A moment," said Morris sternly, as Falcon faced him for the salute. "Let's have this clear, August. I've a fair notion why you're pushing this meeting, and why you're breaking your word to Gideon. I want it understood that if I win, I'll be free to pay my addresses to Katrina."

"If you *win*? For Lord's sake, don't be so stupid! *En garde!*"

Two swords swept into the salute. Two athletic young men, each of whom knew his weapon and the rules, faced each other, one stern and determined, one smilingly confident. And in the chill, moonlit garden the long-postponed duel began.

For a few minutes the blades met in brief and cautious testing, then Morris thrust in *sexte*. Parrying smoothly, and returning the thrust so quickly that Morris barely blocked in time, Falcon chuckled. "The Hungarian school, eh?" he taunted. "I might have known, Jamie. You fight like a soldier." No sooner were the words out of his mouth than he had to deflect a fast following thrust. "Aha!" he said, pleased, as his blade circled warily. "You've been taking lessons!"

"I have," admitted Morris. "I knew you'd insist on this nonsense sooner or later."

With reckless daring, Falcon allowed his blade to swing wide. "Have at me then."

On the instant, Morris lunged in *tierce*. Agile as a cat, and in the very nick of time, Falcon parried with a straight arm and a slightly lowered point, his move so fast that his sword seemed a whiplash of light as the moon caught it. He returned the thrust at once, but in that same instant the moonlight dimmed, and he was obliged to hold back slightly. He was sobered by the realization that the duel could have ended there and then. He evidently still had a touch of fever, and would have to exercise care in this uncertain light, for he had no wish to really hurt the lovesick clod.

It was destined to be his last moment of confidence. The moon must have drifted behind a cloud, and he had to narrow his eyes to see Morris' darting point. Irritated, he fought with more force but, impossibly, twice, Morris almost had him.

He neither saw nor heard the opening of the side gate and running footsteps, for the fog seemed to have got into his head and he was horribly conscious that he was not fighting well.

Coming up beside Cranford, who stood watching helplessly, Rossiter exclaimed, "Lord above, what brought this about? They both gave me their word to postpone!"

"Some silly clunch made a remark at White's that properly set Falcon off," said Cranford. "Damme, that was close!"

Horatio Glendenning, who had been with Gideon when Newby found him, said anxiously, "I've never seen August fight so recklessly. He must be mad!"

"If he found Jamie here with Katrina, he very likely is," said Rossiter grimly, then gave a gasp as Morris shouted with excitement, his blade singing down Falcon's in a near disarm.

Dismayed, Cranford said, "Falcon's playing with him—luring him on, and the poor fellow is too confident by far!"

"Oh, Lord!" groaned Glendenning. "The women are watching from upstairs! This has got to be stopped, Gideon!"

Rossiter started forward, then retreated before a wild flurry of whirling glinting blades. "I wish you will tell me how," he growled. "The pace is too fast! If I interfere I'm liable to get one of the idiots killed!"

Both duellists were short of breath now. Falcon, bewildered, felt that he was trapped in an ever thickening mist and knee deep in mud. Morris was exultant, knowing he had never in his life fought as well. He saw his opportunity as Falcon disengaged.

In that hideous fraction of a second, Rossiter thought, 'Dear God! He's going to try a counter-disengage! No, Jamie! No!'

As though the entire world had been slowed to a crawling pace, Falcon watched Morris form a parade. 'He's too close to my sword,' he thought. His face alight with excitement, Morris plunged forward only to stumble on the wet grass. It should have been so easy. All Falcon had to do was swing his sword aside and get clear. But instead, he watched stupidly as Morris failed to recover, fell heavily onto the point of his sword, and sank to his knees. And still, time was as if held in check. Falcon gazed down at that upturned, incredulous face; at the freckles that suddenly stood out in stark contrast to the deathly pallor of the skin; at the accusing, horrified green eyes and the crimson fingers clutching the blade of the sword that had plunged deep. And, as in a dream, heard the choked disbelieving, "Au-gust . . . ?"

There came shouts of rage and Rossiter ran to wrench the sword free, shove Falcon aside and kneel to ease Morris down.

Glendenning was saying, "No, m'dears! Keep back! Stay back, I beg—"

Falcon stared dully at Morris' shirt, so white a second ago, now all blood.

A terrible strangled screaming, and Katrina rushed to fall to her knees beside the man she loved. "Jamie! Oh, merciful God! No! No!"

Cranford shouted, "You there! Fetch Dr. Knight, and for Lord's sake, *hurry!*"

A footman went off at the run. Clad in a voluminous purple dressing gown, Mrs. Vanechurch passed him, bandages fluttering in her capable hands.

Rossiter, on his knees and striving desperately, glanced up and grated, "Well, madman? Are you satisfied now? *Are* you?"

"I—I never meant . . ." mumbled Falcon.

"Like *hell!*" said Cranford, bending over the stricken man. "You *said* you'd put an end to him if you found him here!"

Near hysteria with shock and grief, Katrina stared at her hands wet with Morris' blood. Her head lifted and she gazed at her brother piteously as if unable to comprehend the tragedy. Then, "*Murderer!*" she screamed. "You've *killed* him!" Springing up, she beat at August's chest with those terribly stained fists, crying shrilly, "I'll never forgive you! *Never! Never! Never!*"

He watched her numbly, making no attempt to restrain her, or to move away from her blows.

Gwendolyn ran to take the distraught girl in her arms and say comfortingly, "Do not grieve so, dearest. Jamie is young and strong. He will likely make a fine recover."

Over Katrina's shoulder, she met Rossiter's eyes. He shook his head grimly, and she had to hold back her own tears.

Katrina sank against her, weeping so hysterically that Gwendolyn dreaded she might suffer a complete collapse. Holding her close, she said, "We must help. Come, we'll go and make ready for the doctor."

Falcon caught at his sister's arm and said brokenly, "Trina—you *must* believe me! He fell! I never meant—"

Katrina's head came up to reveal reddened swollen eyes and her lovely face so twisted with grief it was almost unrecognizable. She slapped August's hand away, and said in a shrill broken voice, "Do not *dare* touch me, *liar!* I *saw* it! 'Twas cold, de-deliberate murder! You've killed that kind and—and valiant gentleman, just as you've longed to do. Are you proud, my dear brother? Are you happy that you've destroyed my every hope for happiness?"

"No! Trina, do not! I didn't—"

"You've k-killed more than the man I love. You've killed every spark of the love I had for you! For as long as I live I will loathe and—and despise y-you . . ." Her voice was suspended and she sobbed uncontrollably.

His hand fell. He met Gwendolyn's eyes and found there only a cold disgust.

She said contemptuously, "How *could* you!" and led Katrina away.

CHAPTER XII

alcon House was too modern for any Stuart monarch to have actually honoured it with his presence, but in the autumn of 1651 when young King Charles II was being hunted through England by the merciless troops of Oliver Cromwell, Elsworth Falcon had recognized and, at the risk of his own life, sheltered the exhausted monarch. Charles, not one to accept such loyalty as his due, had rewarded Elsworth with a ring taken from his own hand, and after the restoration had bestowed on him the splendid estate of Ashleigh in Sussex. The family had prospered, and when the London house was built King Charles' ring had been mounted in a glass box displayed beneath a portrait of the "Merry Monarch" that hung in the suite reserved for very important guests.

It was to this luxurious apartment that James Morris had been tenderly carried after the duel. And it was here that Falcon waited, silent and seemingly invisible to all who passed by. He had stationed himself in an alcove of the corridor outside the King Charles suite, and when the door opened could hear Gwendolyn murmuring comfort, or Katrina's soft weeping. The case clock in the lower hall announced the hour, and he was dully surprised to count eleven chimes. He'd thought it was long past midnight. The clock ticked on and he watched the quiet procession of solemn-faced footmen and tearful maids as they carried away bowls or brought up steaming copper ewers or medical supplies.

And with each one that came, he thought, 'Thank God! He's not dead yet! Stay alive, Jamie! Don't die!'

Again and again he relived the events of this disastrous night, trying to understand what had happened. He'd been feverish at its start, because of the wound in his arm; he had drunk more wine than was his habit; he had been in a quarrelsome mood because— Well, never mind that. The thing was that he'd allowed his temper to get the best of him. His wretched temper. But there was no excuse. He should never have forced Jamie into a duel when he was in such a condition. If only the moon hadn't gone out, or that drifting fog hadn't—

A hand touched his shoulder, and he shrank instinctively.

Tummet bent over him. "It's nigh two o'clock, sir. You'd oughta—"

"Don't be ridiculous! It just struck eleven! How can—" But even as he spoke, he heard the twin chimes. He hadn't slept! Hadn't closed his eyes, he would swear! Yet three hours had slipped away. He thought, 'My dear Lord! Am I quite mad?'

Tummet had said "sir." How grateful he would have been for a "mate" or "Guv." Anything but that "sir"—so formal and proper. And cold. And how different the man looked with the twinkle banished from the beady eyes, the mouth set in that stern and unfamiliar line.

He asked wearily, "How is he? Has Knight come yet?"

Tummet stared at him. "Sir Jim come at once. Stopped and spoke to you. Don't you remember?"

"If I remembered, would I have asked?" He could have bitten his tongue the moment he spoke. He had no right to use such a tone. Not he, who was such a poor excuse for a human being. He must learn humility. If Jamie died he'd have murdered one of the best men who ever lived. A man he'd come to be as fond of as—as the brother he'd never had. If Jamie died, he'd never forgive himself any more than Trina would forgive him. Or—the Smallest Rossiter. He sighed heavily. She'd be free of him. She already was free of him, for the look she'd directed at him, and those three scornful words, had spoken volumes.

He jerked away as a hand touched his brow. Tummet was

gone. Sir James Knight straightened and said brusquely, "He has no fever. What gave you that notion?"

Peregrine Cranford said rather lamely, "He was behaving in an—odd sort of way all evening. I thought perhaps . . ."

"You are too kind. He don't deserve such consideration." Knight looked at Falcon as he might regard a slug that had crawled onto his surgical knife. "Do you wish that I look at that arm, sir?"

Falcon stood and said quietly, "No. I am perfectly well, I thank you."

Sir James snorted. "Which is more than one could say for your latest victim. You'd best set Tummet to pack your portmanteau, sir. An extended stay in foreign parts is indicated."

Falcon felt sick. As from a great distance he heard himself ask, "What—what d'you mean? Are you saying—"

"I am saying, you murderous idiot," said Sir James harshly, "that you need have no more worries. The very fine young man you have seen fit to destroy in the prime of his life will never marry your sister."

Crushed with grief and remorse, Falcon bowed his head and half-whispered, "He's—gone?"

"I doubt he'll last the night out. Even if he does, he'll never walk again. Congratulations, sir! You have opened my eyes. Like a perfect fool, I never thought you really warranted what men said of you. Till now!"

Some indeterminate time later, Tummet said, "Sir?"

Falcon looked up, vaguely surprised to find that he still stood here, and that Tummet was watching him in an aghast fashion. He said dully, "Yes?"

"The lieutenant's asking for you."

Falcon cringed inwardly. He couldn't go in there and face poor Jamie. And the terrible loathing that would glare at him from Trina's dear eyes. And—Gwen . . . ! Well, he must, that's all. This, he supposed, was what was meant by one of Jamie's oft used old proverbs, 'He who calls the tune must pay the piper.' He had called the tune, God forgive him! A dance of death! And the piper must be paid. He straightened his shoulders and walked across the small parlour and into the sick room.

The bedchamber was dim, a single candlestick on one of the chests of drawers providing the only illumination. Two chairs were drawn close to the right side of the bed. Katrina was asleep in one, a blanket spread over her. She was pale, her face ravaged and dark circles under her eyes. Coming up on the other side he did not look directly at Gwendolyn, but he could feel her eyes on him. A nurse had withdrawn to the window seat, and watched, a silent faceless silhouette.

He had to force his feet to carry him closer, and the sight of the wounded man was like a blow to the heart. Jamie looked already dead. He lay on his back, arms at his sides, and his eyes shut. Save for the freckles his face was without colour, even his lips were pallid. 'He looks so young,' thought Falcon achingly, and bending over that still figure he murmured, "Jamie, Jamie! If only I could make you understand! I didn't want her—or you—to go through what—"

Morris stirred slightly. He coughed, a thin painful sound, then looked up, panting distressfully.

Dropping to one knee beside the bed, Falcon said, "Jamie—I am so *very* sorry! Please believe that had it not been for the moon disappearing so suddenly, and that damnable fog rolling in from nowhere— But I never *never* meant to—"

The hand on the coverlet, so strong just a few hours since, moved feebly. Incredibly, the pale lips were twitching into the shadow of a smile, more wounding than the vilest curses. Stricken, Falcon took that helpless hand and held it between both his own.

"Tried . . . tell 'em," Morris whispered. "Not—not y'fault. I . . . slipped."

He was gasping for breath. Gwendolyn called softly, and the nurse hurried to wipe a damp cloth across her patient's lips. "That's enough, if you please," she said, with a cold glance at Falcon.

Morris' head moved in agitation. "No! Must listen . . . Find her . . . good man, Lord—Lord Haughty-Snort. Are . . . some about, y'know. Let her have . . . chance at . . . happiness . . ."

His head tossed and he coughed again, then groaned.

The cloth the nurse held was crimson. She said sharply, "Go, sir! Go!"

Falcon stumbled to the door and, blinded by tears, groped for the handle.

Outside, Tummet saw his face. A moment, he watched the erratic stumble along the corridor. Then, "Cor!" he muttered, and guided his "guv'nor" to his own apartments.

In the days that followed it seemed to Falcon that he had been relegated to some private hell in which he could neither undo what he had done, nor endure the consequences. Begging to be allowed to help, he was politely refused. Katrina seldom left the bedside, and if she encountered him in the corridors acknowledged by neither word nor look that he existed. To see the sister he adored so utterly reject him was scarcely to be borne, and to know that he deserved such treatment plunged him into despair. When Gwendolyn passed by she turned her head away and he did not dare address her.

He was allowed to visit Morris for two minutes once a day, but with each visit the condition of the sick man appeared to have worsened, and there was no longer any attempt to smile or to speak.

Morning and evening he waited fearfully for Knight's calls, but the great doctor had little to say to him. When he pleaded to be allowed to go down to Sevenoaks and break the news to Mr. Fletcher Morris, then bring him back to London, Knight looked through him and said that Lieutenant Morris had given strict instructions that his family was not to be notified while there was the faintest hope of recovery. "If it becomes necessary for them to be sent for," he added, "his *friend*, Captain Rossiter, will go and break the news."

Crushed, Falcon retreated.

The members of Rossiter's Preservers called frequently, but Dr. Knight had decreed that in addition to the other "pests" who bothered his patient, only one each day was to be admitted, and they were not to speak, but could wave, or smile, no more.

During these visits they could not fail to see Falcon waiting in his usual corner near the sickroom door, but he was, for the most part, ignored. Gideon Rossiter looked at him tight-lipped, his eyes blazing as though he yearned to do bloody murder. Horatio Glendenning and Gordon Chandler would not look at him at all. Jonathan Armitage frowned but at least nodded as he went by, and Peregrine Cranford looked distressed and told him that the news was "all over Town," his expression warning of the kind of reception that awaited Falcon when he showed his face to the *ton*. To his astonishment, the most compassion he received was from Sir Owen Furlong.

Astounded when Furlong stopped beside his chair in the alcove and asked how Katrina went on, he told him, and thanked him humbly for deigning to talk to him.

In his calm fashion Sir Owen said, "Jamie swears 'twas an accident. That he slipped."

"He did. But—I had plenty of time to swing my sword aside."

"Yet did not."

"No." Falcon drew a hand across his brow distractedly. "That is what I cannot understand. It seemed as if I was standing aside, watching it all, but—but caught in a sea of mud and scarce able to move."

"Perry Cranford said you were not yourself all the evening. He thought you had a fever."

"Yes. So did I. But James Knight said I had no fever. So I cannot use that as an excuse."

Sir Owen looked at him thoughtfully. "How is your arm now?"

"As good as new, almost. Owen, 'tis kind in you to be so generous. Dare I ask if you've seen your—your lady?"

"I've not. But," he reached into his waistcoat pocket and took out a note which he passed to Falcon.

It read: "My brave English gentleman. Forgive me. Forgive me. I shall always love you. Maria."

Falcon stared at those words and returning the note, said, "That must be very dear to you. Perhaps, someday, when this is all over . . ."

"Yes." Sir Owen sighed. "Perhaps, someday."

On Friday, ignoring Tummet's carefully uttered warnings, Falcon left the house. Jonathan Armitage had been engaged to meet with Mrs. Quimby the previous day, and he'd hoped Johnny might stop in at Falcon House and tell him what happened. Only Rossiter had called, however, and he had marched past without "seeing" him and left as icily remote as ever.

Again ignoring Tummet's advice, he called up his new carriage. It was a racy vehicle which had attracted a good deal of attention when first he drove out in it. Lightly built, with oversize wheels for speed, it was a bright maroon red picked out in cream, the interior all cream, the rugs cream with maroon trim, and his initials painted in graceful gold script on the door panels.

"Jest in case," grumbled Tummet, "some friend o' the Squire wiv a cocked barker in 'is pocket don't reckernize the coach first time 'is peepers rest on it!" This remark eliciting no response, he enquired, "Is I going?"

"No."

"Is I allowed to know where yer going?"

"I want to have a word with Mr. Armitage. Wherever he may be."

Tummet said, "Ar," and watched the coach out of sight, heavy-hearted. Turning, he found Gwendolyn standing in the open door, also looking after the coach. He joined her and they walked across the hall together.

At the foot of the stairs, she paused and said softly, "Speaking as a friend, not a valet, Tummet—how is he? Do you think he— regrets what he has done?"

He hesitated. "I think as 'e would do it all over again, Miss Gwen. 'Cause in 'is eyes, 'e's pertecting of Miss Katrina. But I don't think 'e meant the doo-ell to turn out like it done. I think it's tore the 'eart right outta 'im."

She nodded, and said sadly, "Yet, even now, he must lie about it."

He frowned a little. "I ain't never 'eard 'im do that, Miss Gwen."

"I'd not have believed it, had I not heard it with my own ears. Twice. When he came to see poor Lieutenant Morris after they fought, he tried to excuse himself on the grounds that the moon had disappeared, and that fog had rolled in. You know as well as I that there was a bright full moon all evening, and not a trace of fog. Only yesterday, I overheard him tell Sir Owen Furlong that during the duel his feet were trapped in a sea of mud so that he was unable to move, whereas in fact the grass where they fought was very dense and though it was wet it wasn't at all muddy. Besides, you know how lightning fast he can move when he fences, there was time and to spare for him to have retired his blade when he saw Jamie slip. Had he wished—"

"Beg pardin, but 'old up a bit, Miss! Let's 'ave that agin, willya? Every single word as you can rec'lect, if you don't mind."

Puzzled, Gwendolyn repeated her remarks. When she finished, Tummet was silent, his craggy face twisted into an horrendous expression of concentration. She asked curiously, "What is it?"

He started. "Eh? Oh—just a bee in the old brainbox. Think it'd be orl right fer me to step out fer a bit, Miss? I'd like to 'ave a word wiv me real guv'nor. Well, me guv what was, as y'might say."

"My brother? Why, yes, of course. I'll speak to Mr. Pearsall. You run along."

She would have been surprised to find that Tummet took her at her word, and did, indeed, *run* along.

At least," said Hector Kadenworthy, dabbing at the back of Falcon's neck with the wet cloth the host had provided, "it wasn't rotten."

"Thanks be for small mercies." Falcon raised his head and glanced around the sparsely occupied dining room of the Turk's Head Coffee House. If anyone present had witnessed the collision of the egg with the back of his neck, there were no grins evident. Though that would be hard to verify, since every head was turned away from him. He said grimly, "I'd like to meet the coward who threw it! You run a risk by helping me, Kade."

His lordship shrugged. "I'm not likely to embrace you, I'll own.

You're a sight too hot-at-hand, as I've told you before. But I'm not such a fool as to think you deliberately set out to slaughter poor Morris. How does he go on, by the way?"

"The same. Rather—rather hovering . . . between life and death, I suppose you'd say."

Despite himself, his voice had trembled. Kadenworthy glanced at the haggard face, then said, "Our riotous populace has been busy these past few days. You'll have heard Sommers' coach was overturned in the Strand yesterday?"

"The devil! Ambrose Sommers? Why he's one of the best-liked men in Town."

"Not by some elements, apparently! Night before last, all the ground floor windows of Dowling House were smashed by rock-throwers. Our old London is not the town it was. I wonder you reached here without being set upon."

"More or less. We were surrounded by an unfriendly crowd on Ludgate Hill, but I was recognized." Falcon's smile was fleeting and did not reach his eyes. "My—er, nickname was shouted, and I was given a rousing cheer when some ruffian proclaimed I was on their side, and was helping them to—reduce the aristocratic population."

Kadenworthy was silent for an awkward moment, then said heartily, "So you're on the hunt for some luncheon, are you? You've chosen a good spot. The food here is not too awful."

"Actually, I was hoping to find Armitage. Have you seen him?"

"Not today. Did you try Rossiter's or Furlong's?"

"Both. I'll keep looking."

"Stay and take luncheon first. You look half-starved."

Falcon thanked him, but declined, saying he wasn't hungry. As he left he heard someone remark scornfully, "You've some dev-ilish odd friends, Kade! I'd have thought you liked Jamie Morris too well to hob-nob with the murderous Mandarin."

For the space of a heartbeat Falcon paused on the threshold, then he went out into the windy afternoon. He sent the porter to wave up his carriage, and directed the coachman to Henrietta Street.

Florian, the handsome gypsy youth who served Peregrine Cranford as general factotum, was politely inscrutable, his velvety dark eyes betraying no hint of the admiration that had formerly brightened them when Falcon arrived. Mr. Cranford, he said, was likely to be found at The Madrigal. A pause. "With the other gentlemen."

Falcon met his eyes steadily, and left. The point had been made. They were meeting and he was not invited.

He had never been welcomed with open arms at The Madrigal, but today, apart from the porter and the steward, who looked at him woodenly, everyone he met immediately presented their backs to him. Distant faces became stern as he was recognized, and his progression through the countless backs and the sudden silence in the downstairs lounge was one of the most harrowing experiences of his life. There was a time when he would have flown into a rage and at once challenged the first man to so deliberately cut him. Today, he could only suffer the humiliation without protest and scarcely blame them for such treatment. By calling up a waiter, who dared not ignore him, poor fellow, he discovered that Captain Rossiter and some friends were in one of the upstairs ante rooms. Climbing the stairs, his palms were wet, and he could feel perspiration trickling between his shoulder blades. Three men coming down were chatting gaily until they saw him. Faced with the choice of either going back up again, or being obliged to come close to him as they passed, they stopped dead, their dismayed expressions so ludicrous that he could not resist drawling, "You could always vault the rail, gentlemen."

Instead, single-file they slid past, their noses practically scraping against the wall as they turned their faces away.

Somebody said indignantly, "The gall of the fellow! And poor Morris on his death-bed!"

Falcon's heart contracted painfully, but he walked on keeping his head up somehow.

When he opened the ante room door, Rossiter, Furlong, Gordon Chandler, and Perry Cranford were sitting around a card table, obviously in a high state of excitement. Cranford was saying, ". . . have to listen to him! If the lady's right, the League has crews working at—"

Rossiter, who faced the door, stiffened and came to his feet. Cranford stopped talking, and heads turned.

They all stood then, staring at Falcon with paling, apprehensive faces.

Rossiter said rather hoarsely, "Is it—has Jamie—"

"No." Falcon closed the door and leaned back against it. "I—hoped you might not mind letting me know what Johnny learned from—"

Chandler said, "Do we have to take this, Ross?"

"As has been said—we need him," said Sir Owen.

Rossiter, of them all closest to Morris, said frigidly, "I believe I once made that remark. But I think England must survive without the aid of Mr. August Falcon. Who knows which of us might be the next to—annoy him?"

Never in his life had he bowed in humility; always his pride had been as a banner he flourished to the world. To plead would be the depth of degradation. But . . . Falcon drew a quivering breath and his fist clenched so tightly that the fingernails drove into his palm. He said, "Would you accept my word of honour that I had no intention to—"

"To kill the man you'd sworn to destroy?" Chandler said a harsh, "Hah!"

Rossiter said, "If such a declaration came from a less skilled fencer, I might. As it is—I believe I'm not that credulous!"

Falcon could bow no lower. He left, closing the door quietly behind him.

The return down the stairs and through the hostile gathering was nightmarish. It took all his resolution not to panic and run and by the time he was in his carriage he felt limp and had to wipe the sweat from his face. He told the coachman to go straight home, and leaned his head back against the cushions wondering if Jamie yet lived, and if Gideon would demand that Gwendolyn leave Falcon House. It would be better if she did so, he thought wearily, save that at a moment when Katrina was very badly in need of kindness and support, Mrs. Dudley was confined to her bed with a putrid sore throat. The Smallest Rossiter was such a fount of kindliness. Darling little Gwen.

As they turned onto Great Ormond Street a coach was stopping in front of Falcon House. A footman assisted a cloaked lady to alight. The wind blew her hood back, revealing red curls and a look of terror on a plump comely face. A cold hand gripped Falcon's heart. He let down the window and called, "Pull up here, Coachman!"

Katrina ran from from the mansion and embraced the new arrival.

So they'd had to call for Jamie's sister. A course he had straitly forbidden unless all hope was gone.

Falcon shrank into the corner. A shaken whisper escaped him. "God forgive me . . . !"

On the box, George Coachman shivered, and watched the afternoon skies darken.

After a while the front door at Falcon House opened again, and a footman peered out at the stationary vehicle.

"Johnson," muttered George Coachman, and waved imperatively.

The footman sprinted along the street. He slowed as he passed the horses and gestured a question.

The coachman leaned down. "What's he doing?" he hissed. "Can you see?"

Johnson slipped one elegantly shod toe onto the lower rung by the box and hung on as he leaned perilously to peer in at the window. He climbed up to sit beside George, who whispered, "Is he asleep?"

"Dunno, mate. He's all bowed over. Looks dead."

"Dead! If that ain't just like you! A regular ray of sunshine!"

"Well, whatcher going to do? Can't sit here—"

Falcon shouted, "Drive on!"

Inside the mansion the butler hurried from the stairs as a lackey was taking Falcon's cloak and tricorne. "Sir, you should know that—"

Falcon flung up one hand. "Not now, Pearsall."

"But—"

"I shall want Andante at the door in ten minutes' time."

"Very good, sir. But—"

Falcon stopped and turned his head to stare at him.

The butler gulped, bowed, and fled.

Falcon took the stairs two at a time. In the upper corridor two maids chattered solemnly, their dusters idle until they saw him and became frantically industrious. A footman, hovering about near the King Charles Suite, raced to fling open the door to his parlour. There was no sign of Tummet. Falcon stalked into the dressing room. He found a small valise neatly packed away in a deep cupboard together with several portmanteaux and a folding cot. Going into his great bedchamber he tore open drawers and assembled two clean shirts, four cravats, undergarments, a night-shirt, brushes, combs, and other essentials for a two- or three-night journey.

En route to the clothes presses, he shed his coat and waistcoat, then paused, somewhat taken aback by the grim stranger he saw reflected in the cheval-glass. He looked tired and older, and there were lines in his face that had not been there last week. He shrugged slightly. As if it mattered. Nothing really mattered now save that he do what he knew Jamie had longed to do: find some way to expose the League of Jewelled Men for the murderous trai-tors they were. Not that, even if he succeeded, it would expiate his own guilt. A gallant and very worthy life had been wiped away senselessly, and much too soon. There was no turning back the clock, no act of atonement that would make all right again. But he must do his best.

He opened the doors of the larger press. His eyes skimmed over the twenty and more coats that hung there and came to rest on one of light blue brocade threaded with silver. He took it down tenderly, wracked by memories of the love he had found at a win-try fete. To wear it would be to scourge himself. And yet, it would be as though he took a trace of his beloved lady with him on this journey that might well prove to be his last.

They had gathered in the withdrawing room on the first floor of Sir Owen Furlong's tall narrow house. The morning was cold and foggy, making travel difficult, but with the exception of Jonathan Armitage, they were all there, watching Sir Owen as he paced about restlessly.

Rossiter put down his cup of chocolate and said kindly, "But you said you only caught a glimpse of her, old fellow."

"And 'tis like pea soup out there," added Peregrine Cranford.

Gordon Chandler threw another shovel-full of coal on the fire and asked, "Did Miss Barthélemy wave this time? Or call to you?"

"Neither," said Sir Owen. "But it's not too foggy for me to have seen her clearly, even if only for an instant. She looked—she *is* ill! I am sure of it! If I could just find that damned slippery servant of hers, I'd—"

The door was flung open and Enoch Tummet came in looking worried, damp, and bedraggled.

Rossiter said, "Well?"

" 'E ain't come back, Guv. Took a valise and some clothes. Not near enough fer a gent. But what worries me is—"

"He likely went down to Sussex." Rossiter's lip curled. "His sire would stand by him, no matter what he'd done."

"Parents have their uses," said Glendenning with a faint smile. "Speaking of which, has Mr. Fletcher Morris been—told?"

"A groom was sent off," answered Tummet. "I bin wondering, Guv and gents, wot you thought abaht me concloosins drawed."

Gordon Chandler said, "I appreciate your loyalty, Tummet, but—"

"But it sounds pretty far-fetched," put in Rossiter. "Speaking for myself, in view of his reputation, I'd need to see something more substantial before—"

"But we *got* something more sunstandil—er, wot you said, Guv! Don't ferget that there bag o' feathers!"

Chandler said, "Oh, come now! This is 1748, not the Middle Ages!"

"You ask Mrs. Armitage," argued Tummet with great earnestness. "You jest ask 'er! Knows all abaht Cornwall and ill-wishes and that lot, does Mrs. Jennifer! And you know too, don'tcher melord?"

Glendenning looked embarrassed, but said, "I—er, certainly believe, along with—was it Hamlet?—that there's a good deal more in heaven and earth than we know about. And I don't mind admitting that if a bag of feathers was thrown my way I'd run like hell sooner than take it up!"

"There you are, then!" said Tummet looking at them all in triumph.

Gordon Chandler, more practically minded, said gently, "You're a dashed good fellow, but—"

Desperation driving him, Tummet held out a crumpled sheet of paper, and interrupted, "And I found this 'ere in the pocket of one of 'is coats. Jest this morning! Never said a word abaht it, 'e didn't."

Taking the paper, Rossiter smoothed it out and read slowly,

"Words of advice to the unwise Mandarin *of Mayfair:*

> *Never sleep, guard your back, and,*
> *like a craven fool—hide.*
> *Few will weep, alas, alack, but*
> *you'll not see this Yule-tide.'*

"It's signed 'S.' "

Glendenning's eyebrows lifted. "Our charming Squire. Well, well."

Rossiter glanced around the circle of intent faces. "Did anyone else get a note like this?"

Nobody had.

"Why the devil didn't the birdwit say anything of it?" muttered Sir Owen.

"I'd say that was typical," Chandler reasoned. "With his almighty pride he'd consider it something to be handled personally."

Sir Owen frowned. "Still, Tummet's notion seems to me too devious and chancy. More like a woman's scheme."

"Still, if the League did plan it all," said Glendenning, "much as I loathe the beastly lot, I have to give 'em credit, for 'twas timed to perfection. No matter what he said, Falcon must have been troubled by that wound. Perry noticed he was more than usually irritable and not himself. Add to that his hot temper and his determination not to have Jamie for a brother-in-law, and such a trick might be a pretty sure bet to succeed."

"Yussir!" interjected Tummet eagerly. "Jest wot I thinked

meself. And if it *were* schemed by a female, why if ever there was a woman wiv reason to 'old a grudge 'gainst me temp'ry guv, it's Lady Clara Buttershaw!"

There was a moment of surprised silence.

Cranford said, "But Lady Clara's not the Squire! She couldn't be! I was there when she found out that the League has allied itself with the French, and she was genuinely astounded."

"Still," said Rossiter slowly, "Tummet's right in one sense. She could very well have conjured up this ugly little trap intending August to be killed."

"Instead of which, poor Jamie was the victim," murmured Sir Owen.

"If Falcon thinks Lady Buttershaw was responsible," said Glendenning, "he'll have gone to keep an eye on Sundial Abbey, I'll warrant."

Chandler shrugged. "Much good will it do him! We've had the place watched for weeks. Nobody ever goes near it save for tradespeople and the servants, and the earl's a veritable recluse. Wherever the League meets, 'tis not at the country seat of the Earl of Yerville!"

he fog drifted among the trees like a sepulchral white veil that muffled sound as well as limiting the view. Falcon was tired and had dozed off in the saddle. He woke with a start when a low-hanging branch made contact with his head. There was no stream in sight, but dismounting to pick up his tricorne, he could hear fast-flowing water somewhere nearby.

"Fool!" he muttered, peering around. "Now you've managed to lose yourself!" Andante snorted and nuzzled the back of his neck, and Falcon rubbed the stallion's velvety nose. "Forgive me, do you? Though I've ridden you hard these three days. Very well, you shall graze for a while. I'll not mislike a rest myself."

When he'd loosened the girth and secured the stallion's reins to the end of a low-hanging branch, he sat down, settling his back against a tree. During several long sleepless nights he'd gone over and over every detail that was known of the conspiracy of the League of Jewelled Men, and had convinced himself that their meeting place had to be in Sundial Abbey, the country seat of the Yerville family. The present Earl of Yerville was a reclusive old fellow and might not be in any way involved in the conspiracy, but his two nieces, the formidable Lady Clara Buttershaw, and her sister, Lady Julia Yerville, most certainly were active members.

None of the known conspirators had ever been seen approaching the estate, by day or by night. Certain of them were known to call at Yerville Hall in Town; to visit Lord Hibbard Green's hideous Buckler Castle not far from Romsey; or even to journey to Promontory Point, which the League had seized from Sir Mark Rossiter. But never once had any of the individuals believed to be members of the founding committee ventured within a mile of Sundial Abbey. However, and Falcon thought this significant, a few days prior to his death Gilbert Fowles had been traced as far as Leatherhead; Rudolph Bracksby had been followed and lost at Guildford; and Hibbard Green's trail had ended near Farnborough. Each of those towns was located within ten miles of the Abbey. If that, in fact, had been their destination, how they'd covered the remaining distance without being seen was a mystery. But 'twas a mystery he intended to solve.

The three days since he'd left Town seemed more like three weeks, during which time he'd accomplished nothing, but he had made a solemn vow to Jamie to complete the task they'd set themselves, and though it took his lifetime, he would keep his vow. Jamie . . . God bless his valiant soul, they would probably be lying him to rest this very day. His head bowed lower. He should be at that funeral. Of all men, he should be there. They'd think him a poltroon to have stayed away. Was a poltroon worse than a murderer . . . ?

"You all right, sir?"

The youthful voice almost made him jump out of his skin. The hand over his eyes dropped and in a blur of movement he was on his feet and crouched for desperate action.

A squeak was followed by a gasped, "It's only me!"

Falcon looked into a pair of brown eyes that seemed too big for the small face. It wasn't such a thin face as he remembered, and the black curls were damp but not dirty. "Ling?" he said incredulously, restoring the pistol to his pocket. "What in the name of Zeus are you doing out here?"

"We left Edw'd and some of our stuff in the old place," said the boy, "and had to come and pack up. I thought 'twas you, when I see Danny. Who's Zeus?"

'Danny?' thought Falcon. 'Ah—Andante!' He glanced to where the stallion cropped contentedly at the lush grass. "You didn't go too near?"

"I tried to stroke him, but he looked not pleased, so I come to see if it really was you, or if he'd been prigged. Who's Zeus? I asked you afore."

"I beg your pardon. Zeus is a myth— Er, a long time ago, people believed he was the god of thunder."

"Oh. What does he do?"

"What gods usually do, I fancy. He makes out schedules for wind and lightning and such, and punishes the guilty. But never mind that, tell me what you meant by the 'old place.' Did you and Silas live near here?"

The dark head nodded vigorously. "Sometimes. In our cave. He's down there now, and I'm 'sposed to keep watch. No one never sees us though, 'specially in the fog. It's just the river you got to be careful of."

Falcon sat straighter. "Is your 'cave' anywhere near a great estate called Sundial Abbey?"

"I dunno as you could say 'near.' " The boy's brow wrinkled with concentration. "It's *there*," he elaborated. "Sort of—under it."

"Glory," murmured Falcon. "Bread cast upon the waters!"

"You can get to it that way," said the boy, misinterpreting. "But it's tricky if the river comes up high. So me and Silas and The Dancing Master we just creep in through the cut."

"The 'Dancing Master'? Jupiter! D'you mean the highwayman?"

"Yes, sir. Awful fierce he is. He said he'd scrag Silas if he ever telled about where he lives. But he don't mind us now, 'cause he likes to talk, and he says he lives a lone and lorn life."

"I, ah, expect he does. D'you think he's at home now?"

"No, sir. He went off s'morning, soon as the tree come down. He gets awful scared then. So do we."

Deciding to unscramble that remark later, Falcon said, "Then—let's go and find Silas."

I jest can't b'lieve it, sir!" Silas wrung Falcon's hand and beamed at him. "I were meanin' ter bring the boy round t'call on yer one day, so you could see how he's done better. But I never thought you'd come and see us! Not *here*! How'd you ever find us?"

"They took the tree down," said the boy. "That's how he found the path."

Silas scowled at him.

Intrigued, Falcon said quickly, "Don't worry. I'm no informer." He glanced around the 'cave' curiously. Ling had led him to a narrow path winding through woodland and a tangle of briers and overgrown shrubs. The path sloped downwards and they'd come to a fast-moving stream and followed along its banks until it veered off to the east and disappeared from sight. The path was little more than a rough defile; a gloomy place, slippery underfoot and shut in by trees and sheer banks and littered with chunks of rock. Ling had pushed through a thick curtain of vines and threaded his way among crumbling ruined walls to a massive half-open door which he'd closed after they passed through. They'd followed a glow to a wide room lit by a torch that blazed in a wall brazier. Ling's "cave." Most probably the cellar of some long-abandoned castle or priory.

Silas had turned from a rough table and run to greet them. He was a different man from the unkempt individual Falcon had met in the fields beyond the Foundling Hospital; his garments neat and new, his wig tidy, and the beery flush gone from his clean-shaven cheeks.

Andante whickered, and Silas said with a grin, "Fetch the nag this way, sir, and we'll look after him while the boy sets out some ale. I'll tell yer straight though, we daren't stay but a few minutes."

They crossed the room and came to a narrow passage wreathed with cobwebs. It was chill and damp, and Andante's hoofbeats were loud on the flagged floor and echoed from the stone walls. An outer door gave onto a small crumbling sort of lean-to that had been converted into a makeshift stable with two troughs, one half full of water.

"This is where me friend, Tom, keeps his nag," confided Silas, as Falcon unsaddled the stallion. "He wouldn't like it if he knowed you'd come here, him being always just half a leap ahead o' the Constables, y'see."

They started to rub down the horse with handfuls of straw. Falcon asked, "How did he find the place? I'd think it would stay hidden for eternity."

"I wouldn't tell none but yerself, Mr. Falcon, and I'll ask yer to keep it under yer chap-ho, as the Frenchies say."

"You've my word. Go on."

"Well, the fact is, Tom—that's not his real name—were runnin', and he fell down the cut by chance, and hid here, safe as a bird. It were a fine place fer a Gentleman o' the Road, and Tom's lived here ever since. On and orf. And now and then."

"Until they take the tree down," murmured Falcon shrewdly.

Silas glanced at him from the corners of his eyes, and went over to pour oats into the second trough, to which Andante proceeded without delay.

When they returned to the main room Ling had put out tin cups and a jug for the men, and a cup of milk for himself, and was carrying over a thick plate with some hunks of bread and cheese.

Silas grumbled that there was no time to eat. "You know we gotta be away 'fore it's full dark."

Ling said pleadingly, "It won't take a minute, and Edw'd's got to be fed, you know."

"Oh, all right," muttered Silas. "Sit y'self down, sir."

The boy grinned and ran off.

Seating himself at the table, Falcon accepted a piece of the bread and asked, "Why must you be away before dark?"

Ling galloped back to deposit a small cage on the table. "Here's my Edw'd! See?"

Falcon saw, turned perfectly white, and was across the room in one leap.

Silas howled with laughter. "Strike me pink if ever I see a cove move s'quick! It's no bigger'n my thumb! It won't bite yer, sir!"

"He's a very nice mouse," said Ling earnestly. "And I've taught him manners, ain't I, Silas?"

"Yus, you have, boy. But you'd best take him over there and shove a bit o' cheese in his box for him, if he upsets our guest."

Not until the pet had been taken to the farthest shelf did Falcon venture back to his chair.

"Lor'," exclaimed Silas, still grinning. "I'd never've thought a grand fighting man like you would be scared of—"

"Well—I'm not," lied Falcon. "That is to say, I don't like them. They—ah, they carry disease, 'tis said." He was vastly annoyed to see his hand tremble as he reached for his ale, and he asked again, "Why must you get away from here before dark?"

The big man sobered, and looked uneasily at the boy. "You bin good to us, Mr. Falcon, and I owes yer, but—"

"Yes. You do. And now I need your help. Desperately." He leaned forward. "I give you my word of honour, I'll never betray you, or your friendly rank rider. But if you care anything for England, tell me all you know about this place."

"Cor!" gasped Silas, banging a clenched fist on the table and setting the mugs jumping. "So that's the way of it! I *knowed* there was something nasty goin' on up at the Abbey!"

Seething with impatience, Falcon said, "The tree. That has something to do with the business, no?"

"I reckon it do, sir. All's quiet here most of the time, but every few weeks—more often lately—a gamekeeper, leastwise he's *dressed* like a gamekeeper, he comes and takes the tree down. You likely see it lyin' 'longside the cut?"

"I saw a fallen tree, but I don't think it had been chopped down, and—"

"It ain't, sir."

"It's in a tub, Mr. Falcon," put in the boy excitedly. "They—"

"Now you finish yer milk and go and get the rest o' your things put in the bag," said Silas, fixing him with a stern look. Ling obeyed reluctantly. Silas passed the cheese and said softly, "It don't do fer the boy to know too much, sir. Just in case."

Falcon nodded. "The tree normally blocks the path, is that it? And periodically 'tis pulled down so that riders can pass?"

"Aye, sir. Not riders, though. Most times they come by boat till the river turns off, then they walk through the cut. Arter dark, always. I dunno where from, but they're masked and go so secret-like that I guessed they was up to no good! Tom, he knows how to fight, and he's no coward, but this lot, they scare him silly. He says 'spite o' their masks, they're all flash coves, and flash coves can do murder and no questions asked. He's got it in his head that his life wouldn't be worth a bent groat if they found him here, or any of us. If that tree's down when he comes home from his—er, night's work, he goes to earth somewhere else! Quick and quiet!"

Falcon thought a triumphant, 'Excelsior!' He said, "I wonder they would take it down in the daylight."

"They never do, sir. Only once before, when it was foggy, like it is today." He drew a battered timepiece from his waistcoat pocket and held it up to the light. "Lor' a'mighty! 'Tis past four, Mr. Falcon! We gotta get outta this! You can tell me what—"

Ling ran to them, his face pale and frightened. "They're *coming!* Listen!"

Falcon sprinted to the front door. Silas rushed to take down the burning torch and stuff it into a nearby bucket of water. Groping his way through the dark towards the outer path, Falcon heard the footsteps of at least three men. He saw the gleam of a lantern bobbing along from the left, and he drew back and stood very still.

His hand was grasped and behind him Silas hissed, "Quick! If they see us, we're dead as mutton!"

Falcon pulled free. "I must find out where they go! Wait!"

Someone stumbled on the path, and swore in a growl of a voice that was unmistakeable. Falcon's heart gave a leap of excitement. Hibbard Green!

Peering through the vines he was able to make out three figures following a fourth man, a tall individual, who carried the lantern. They were all cloaked, with hoods drawn close, and masks covering their faces. The bulky individual would be Lord Green. The one behind him was almost as heavily built, while the last man was short and slight. So they *did* meet at Sundial Abbey! Or under it! Scarcely daring to believe his good fortune, Falcon decided to follow, and make sure of where they went, but then he must get out fast, for he had no desire to act the fool and risk being caught by six ruthless men who had announced their intention to murder him.

"Wait up, Squire! We can't see the lantern back here!"

Another familiar voice, and as the fifth conspirator passed within a yard of him Falcon thought, 'Rudolph Bracksby! No surprise there!'

The leader halted and said irritably, "Not so loud! D'ye want to be overheard?"

So that was the voice of the infamous Squire! Cold, deadly, authoritative. And unknown.

Hibbard Green gave a snort of derision. "By whom? The owls? I'll warrant there's not a soul for miles around save for the dod-dling earl's minions, and they're likely too boozy to—"

"We survive by leaving nothing to chance. Where's Ruby?"

"Making fast the boat. One of the oars nigh drifted off."

"Then he must find his own way. He should know it by now. Come. We waste time!"

Off they went again.

Falcon turned back and whispered urgently, "I must follow them a short—Silas? . . . Ling?" His whispered words seemed to hang on the air. Dismayed by the sense that he was com-pletely alone, he crept back to the inner room, and tried again. "Silas? . . . Dammitall, I *need* you! Never say you've gone scurrying off like a scared rabbit?"

Not a sound. Not a breath of movement. And there was not a second to lose. Swearing under his breath, he eased his sword in the scabbard and retraced his steps to the curtain of vines. The faint glow of dusk was almost gone now, the gloom in this brood-ing place making it impossible to see clearly for more than a few yards. He stood head down, straining his ears, and was able to detect soft footsteps, but the sounds were to his right, not the left. Which meant that either one of the larger group was returning, or that "Ruby" had already passed by en route to join them.

It was a desperate dilemma and his life the forfeit if he erred, but, "Nothing ventured . . . " he murmured, and gathering his cloak tightly around him moved swiftly to the right.

The air was much colder now that the sun was gone, but the fog had lifted somewhat. The footsteps were closer. His hand slipped to the hilt of his sword. If one of the bastards was coming towards him, he'd have to move fast. And then he saw something moving just ahead. Luck was with him; the traitor was following his friends, not coming back this way. Abruptly, the ground to his right fell away sharply. He could hear water again, and guessed that the river had curved once more and ran past the bottom of the slope.

A moment later he saw light emanating from what he at first

thought to be a low window, but then realized was a partly open door at the foot of a flight of steps leading down to a cellar. It must be their entrance to the abbey. He paused. In which case, thank heaven, this was as far as he need go.

He turned to retreat. A large hare hopped across the path, caught sight of him and was gone with a flurry of leaves and twigs. 'Damn!' he thought, and slipped into the trees.

Clearly suspicious, "Ruby" spun around and came back. If he shouted, or fired a shot, the game would be up.

The traitor's hand dropped towards his pocket. Falcon dared not wait. Pistol upraised, he sprang and struck hard and true. "Ruby" uttered a choking grunt and went down to lie in an unmoving and ungainly sprawl.

Falcon's eyes darted to the stone steps and the faint light from that lower doorway. There was no one in sight. Their meeting place, of course, might be some distance away. A building this old and this vast was very likely riddled with secret rooms and passages. He frowned. They would soon miss Ruby, and by the time a search party arrived and found the right room, the Squire and his cronies could have scattered and there would be small chance of surprising them again. On the other hand, he was here. He might be able to get close enough to overhear their plans, and he had been provided with the perfect disguise to enable him to bluff his way if he was caught. And he owed it to poor Jamie to at least try to do the thing properly.

He took off his cloak and flung it aside, then tore open his victim's cloak, revealing a tall trim figure clad in a habit of rich mulberry velvet. The wrong size and shape for General Underhill, whom he'd strongly suspected. Which left his second choice. He rolled the man over, removed the cloak and whipped it about his own shoulders leaving the hood hanging back. Luckily, they were much of a size. The fellow wore a full head mask, with holes cut for eyes, and the mask hanging loosely to the lips. Falcon raised the heavy head and seized the top of the mask. "Your grand unveiling, Sir Villainy," he whispered. "And if you're not Gideon's papa-in-law, I'm a—"

The light words died as he pulled off the mask.

He did not look upon the haughty, handsome features of

Simon Ordway Lutonville, Earl of Collington, and father of Naomi Lutonville Rossiter. He gazed instead at the last man he had expected to see. The last man he would have wished to see. And, painfully stricken, he whispered, "Oh, my dear God! . . . Kade!"

The shock was so great that for a moment he was motionless, gazing in miserable disbelief at Hector, Lord Kadenworthy, who had never looked upon the "half-breed" with disdain; who had seconded him in his duel with Gideon, and agreed to perform the same office in the duel with Jamie. Who had even treated him with kindness after that tragedy, when everyone else had turned their backs on him. Kade, who had once risked his life to help a Jacobite fugitive escape, although the man was not a close friend. Good old Kade, sharp-tongued and sarcastic—no more so than he himself—a sportsman to the core, a man of principle whose honour was beyond question. With his great wealth, his social position, his several estates, his obsession with horses and the new race meeting at Epsom, why on *earth* would he—

"Ruby . . . ?" the voice was a distant howl. "Close the damn door!"

Falcon abandoned pointless conjecture and regret, dragged the mask over his own head, and pulled the hood of his cloak close about his face. There was no time to bind Kadenworthy, but he dragged the limp form to the bank and prepared to roll it over, restraining himself at the last instant so as to search frenziedly through his lordship's clothing. He found the tiny jewelled figure in a waistcoat pocket; pink jade set with five glittering rubies. He slipped it into his own pocket. Murmuring, "I'm truly sorry, but you brought it on yourself, old fellow!" he shoved the unconscious man over the edge of the bank and watched that ever more rapid tumble until Kadenworthy was lost to sight. He heard the splash, and winced, but perhaps such a death was the best way out of this ghastly situation.

Springing up he raced to the crumbling stone steps and started down. Someone was coming. He threw up a hand, affecting to be dazzled by the dim light.

The hooded figure stamping towards him, snarled, "For Lord's sake what have you been about? You know the Squire don't take kindly to being kept waiting. Tonight, of all nights! Close the damned door!"

Not waiting for a response, he went back the way he had come.

Falcon, his nerves quivering with excitement, slammed the door shut but took the precaution of opening it wide again before he followed.

Just inside, a candle burned on a stone bench. It threw a very small circle of light, but he took it up gratefully as he pursued the disappearing individual he believed to be Lord Hibbard Green.

He was in a wide hall, a place of pitchy darkness and clammy cold. The cellar of the original Sundial Abbey, no doubt, of which the home of The Dancing Master was probably a part. The air was musty, the silence absolute save for Green's fading footsteps. He was obliged to run when the candlelight he followed vanished. His haste almost brought disaster; Green had turned a corner and Falcon found himself teetering at the edge of a steep flight of steps winding downward. Panting, as he regained his balance, he sprinted to catch up and almost collided with Green who had turned another corner and stopped to throw open a door.

His chance to slip away was gone. There they were; the other four hooded and masked gentlemen of treason, sitting at a table that appeared to date from the construction of the room, and staring at him.

'Treed, by the Lord Harry!' he thought, and wondered how the devil he was to get out of this.

"What a'God's name ails you?" bellowed Green.

Falcon snatched out his handkerchief and sneezed. "This curst cold," he moaned.

"You said nothing of it in the boat," said the man at the head of the table, his tone sharp with annoyance.

"Seems t'be getting worse." Falcon's gaze raked the cold bare room. It was furnished only with a massive and ancient credenza, six chairs, and the table, in the centre of which another lighted candle struck sparkles from the five jewelled miniatures, one set in front of each man. He had expected something more grand, yet in a macabre fashion it was appropriate that here, in this musty darkness, hooded and cloaked, trusting not even each other, the

League of Jewelled Men spun the webs that brought death and destruction to so many.

The short member with the topaz studded miniature before him said, "Then be good enough to turn your head from me."

Falcon grunted. This end of the table was closest to the outer door, which Green had closed but not locked. If he had to make a dash for it, this position might give him some slight advantage.

Green took his place which luckily left only one chair unoccupied. Falcon drew it farther from Topaz and sat down. Silence. Eyes glinted at him through the slots of masks. He was supposed to do something. 'Jupiter! My token!' he thought, and hurriedly retrieved it and set it up in front of him.

The silence was unbroken. Still, they all watched him.

Panicky, he thought, 'Now what?' and sneezed again, this time involuntarily, and with such force that he blew out his candle.

The man at the head of the table said dryly, "You took your time."

This must be the mighty Squire. Evidently "Ruby" had been expected to extinguish his candle upon entering the room. Relieved, he shrugged in a gesture of helplessness and apology.

The Squire said, "Our last meeting in this place, gentlemen! Our long years of waiting are almost done!"

Cheers and much shouting and back-pounding.

It occurred to Falcon that if this was their last meeting, they might decide to unmask, in which case he would have to get out very fast indeed. He could blow out the candle with another sneeze, and be through the door before—

The large man he guessed to be Rudolph Bracksby asked, "Does that mean all goes as planned at Ashleigh?"

Ashleigh? Falcon tensed and sat motionless, all thought of retreat at once abandoned.

"Better than planned, Emerald," said the Squire with a chuckle. "Sir Brian Chandler actually condescended to leave his beloved Lac Brillant and grace the gathering!"

There was a burst of laughter at this. A chill crept down Falcon's spine. What deviltry were these bastards contriving now?

He was sure he'd identified all but two of the varmints. The larger of them, with a figurine that gleamed blue in the candlelight, peered at Falcon curiously. "You fail to see the joke, Ruby?"

Falcon sighed. "So would you if you had my throat," he said thickly.

The Squire stood. "I've something that will help your throat, my friend. Tonight, we complete our map, plan our final coup, and—celebrate! Let's to business."

Emerald took up the candle and they all stood and trooped after the Squire. Trailing behind, Falcon wondered uneasily where they were off to. The end wall was of stone blocks that shone damply in the candlelight. It contained neither door nor windows, the surface broken only by a shallow arched recess enclosing what appeared to be a marble washbowl built at waist level and edged by a band of intricately carven stone.

He wondered cynically if there was to be some kind of baptismal ceremony, but his levity vanished when the Squire suddenly drew out a long-barreled pistol and held it cocked and ready. "For the last time, my friends," he murmured.

Each of the men facing him held up their figurines, Falcon hastening to join what he at first judged to be a childish ritual. Bracksby, or Emerald, gave the candle to the Squire, and stepped forward. He placed his miniature in the centre of a rose carven in the rim of the bowl, then moved back. The large unknown individual fitted a token of lapis-lazuli and sapphires into a slot beside a leaf.

Falcon's blood ran cold. So this was all done by rote and not only did he not know when his turn came, but he hadn't the faintest notion where his filched figurine belonged! He began to sweat as Hibbard Green placed his opal figure in the center of a flower. Nobody looked at Falcon. The silent minutes seemed to stretch out interminably. Was it his turn now? About to move forward, he restrained himself in the nick of time as the short member deposited his golden crystal and topaz figurine in the loop of a stem.

Falcon's nerves were tight and strained. There were only two of them left now. Himself, and the Squire, who watched him steadily. Surely, the last move would be reserved for the leader? He thought, 'Dearest Grandmama, guide me.' and stepped forward. If that trigger finger tightened, he might still have a second in which to blow out the candle and run for it.

There was no outcry.

Praise heaven, he must have guessed rightly! He bent over the bowl. Next hurdle—where to put the confounded object? There was an indentation in the very centre of the bowl. That, surely would be the Squire's place. Or would it? Might it instead be a very logical trap? There had been two tokens placed in flowers, one in a leaf, one amongst the stems, and there was the centre slot. He scanned the carvings around the rim. Ruby's place might very well be somewhere other than flowers and leaves. He thought in desperation, 'You're taking too much time, dammit!' roared a sneeze and contrived to drop his figurine in the bowl. Retrieving it, he saw another slot in the very front of the rim in the centre of what looked to be an acorn.

He had his choice. The centre slot, or the acorn, and again, his life hung on the right move. His thought of Grandmama Natasha became a prayer for help. He set his token in the slot in the middle of the bowl, and watched for the movement of that deadly trigger.

Green's brutish voice growled, "Well, stand aside do, Ruby! 'Sblood, but you're dense tonight!"

Sweating, Falcon moved back and drew his handkerchief. Another test passed. How many more?

The Squire gave his pistol to Bracksby, and held up his jewelled figurine. It was a striking piece; a deep amethyst set with four large diamonds. Bracksby trained the pistol on him as he positioned the little figure in the acorn.

Falcon heard a muted rattling, and the bowl seemed to him to move slightly. 'Be damned!' he thought. 'The little icons are keys to a blasted great lock!'

Bracksby returned the pistol to the Squire. Sapphire and Opal pushed at the wall above the bowl, and with a soft scraping sound the entire alcove swung back to reveal a pitch black chamber beyond. Falcon's nostrils wrinkled to a foetid stench so powerful that it snatched his breath away. It was evidently not unusual because nobody commented. He retrieved his miniature from the bowl as the others did, but his hope that they were not going into that stinking hole was short-lived.

The Squire said, "Are you brave tonight, Ruby?" and handed him the lighted candle. "Cheer up! We've a fine candelabrum in there now."

Hibbard Green sneered, "Go on, Sir Galahad. They've likely already gone, sooner than risk catching your cold."

He was clearly expected to lead the way. Darkness didn't unnerve him, but—who were "they"?

He walked inside. The air was disgusting and so thin that it was an effort to breathe. The flickering candlelight shone upon a silver candelabrum overturned in the centre of a table. Six fairly modern chairs were positioned around it. There was a massive chest against the left-hand wall, and two more chairs flanked a credenza on the opposite wall. He was evidently required to light the candles. He walked over to the table and reached out. Something lean and dark, with a long pointed nose and a whip of a tail darted from behind the fallen candelabrum. His heart seemed to stop. His brain screamed, 'A *rat*! My God in heaven! A *rat*!' The one thing of which he was deathly afraid! And almost he had touched it! He felt weak and nauseated, and had a stunned thought that it was a good thing he was masked, for he was sure he'd turned white. His need to escape was overpowering and he had to clench his fist until the bones ached to keep from shrieking his terror and running madly from this nightmarish place.

Somebody laughed, and a hand snatched the candle. He couldn't make out what was said, but despite the mockery it was clear that they all were revolted by this room.

The Squire tossed a rag at him. "Here, see if you've enough courage left to clear off the table."

Fighting waves of sick dizziness, Falcon made himself wipe dust and droppings from the table top. There had just been one. It was gone now. They mustn't see how his hands trembled. He'd promised poor Jamie, and to allow a childish fear to defeat him would be unforgiveable. Besides, he *must* find out what they meant about Ashleigh . . .

Now that the rest of the candles were burning he could see that the room was large and low-ceilinged and that there were no windows or any normal kind of door. Opal and Sapphire, both big men, started to push the alcove shut, but Topaz, a scented kerchief held to his nose, protested and said they could surely let some air in "this grisly dungeon" for a few minutes. The Squire nodded, and the alcove was left a few inches ajar. There was an identical bowl on the inside, which likely meant they'd have to go through the whole unlocking rigamarole again in order to leave. It became unpleasantly clear to Falcon that once the alcove was closed his chance of escape in an emergency would be nil. Common sense whispered that he should get out now, on whatever pretext, before that deadly "door" swung shut. But that was the coward's way and must not be heeded.

The Squire took a seat and pulled a folded map from his cloak pocket. They all gathered round to inspect it, and joining them Falcon thought, 'Jupiter! 'Tis practically identical to the map Ross drew up!' In place of X's the sites of the League's pilfered estates were indicated by red squares, each shaded in and connected by lines drawn to adjacent blue circles marked by initials. Military objectives, of course. He scanned the map narrowly. There were more sites than Gideon had guessed. A large one in north Devon, another some miles east of Bristol, and to the south— He caught his breath. "Ashleigh" was printed in a square connected to Portsmouth. Unlike the other squares it had not been shaded in. His thoughts flashed back to the meeting in Falcon House—it seemed years ago now—when Ross and Jamie had been set upon in the street. He could almost hear Gordon Chandler asking why Glendenning had been sent down to Bosham and pointing out that the League already had seized nearby Larchwoods. And Tio Glendenning answering that Larchwoods was a small estate and if the League armed it with a view to attacking Portsmouth, they would need a larger base. Ashleigh would give them a "larger base"! Why in the devil had he been too dim-witted to foresee and guard against that menace?

He was stunned when the Squire bent forward and with a red crayon shaded in the Ashleigh box. There was great excitement. Questions rang out and were rendered incomprehensible as they overlapped in the outpouring of enthusiam.

Smiling broadly, the Squire straightened and gestured for quiet. Bracksby was at the credenza, pouring wine. Topaz offered the first glass to the Squire, then served the others. Falcon was last, but his attempt at thanks was drowned by a roaring sneeze. Topaz fairly leapt back, and several annoyed glances came his way.

"My 'pologies," he mumbled.

"Of all the times to catch a cold," grumbled Opal.

The Squire said triumphantly, "Gentlemen— Let us drink to our final and most brilliant success!"

Falcon's toast was silent and very differently worded.

His voice eager, Bracksby asked, " 'Tis in our hands, then?"

"As good as."

'The devil it is!' thought Falcon grimly.

Opal, alias Hibbard Green, rumbled, "I cannot credit that he was so stupid as to agree to such madness. He must be desperate, indeed!"

"He will walk into our trap, I promise you," said the Squire.

"And—the others?" asked Topaz.

"Are en route. Like lambs to the slaughter."

Sapphire sounded unconvinced, "What about young Falcon?"

"With luck, the breed is off somewhere blowing his brains out, because he cut down that fool, Morris," said Green.

Falcon was seized by a scalding desire to cut down one toad named Hibbard, Lord Green. He was astonished when Topaz came up and slapped him on the back, saying admiringly, "Thanks to you, Ruby. Even if it did work in reverse."

"A most successful ploy," agreed the Squire, raising his glass. "I'll own I really didn't think 'twould work at all!"

Work in reverse? What the deuce were they talking about? Falcon managed a bow and said hoarsely, "The benefit of a devious mind."

"And a damned diabolical drug," said Green much amused. "Do not ever use any of the stuff in *my* glass, Ruby!"

A *drug*? Kade had *drugged* him? His friend . . . Kade? So that was why he'd felt so—

"A toast!" Topaz rested his hand on Falcon's shoulder and called in that strange, husky voice. "To—the devious—"

Shaken by another explosive sneeze, Falcon could not stop and had to set his glass down and drag out his handkerchief. Perhaps he really had caught a cold. 'Twould not be surprising after lurking about these damned dank ruins for hours on end!

He lowered his handkerchief, and was at once aware that something in the room had changed.

Topaz was standing close beside the Squire, who had risen to his feet, and both were staring at him. The other members were looking at each other uncertainly. The familiar sense of danger made his pulse quicken. He tensed, every muscle ready. The candle—then the door.

Topaz said shrilly, "I demand an unmasking!"

"Our Topaz believes there is a traitor among us," purred the Squire.

They all jumped up in alarm.

'Now!' thought Falcon. With a sweep of his cloak he brought darkness to the room, then sent his chair tumbling and lunged for the door.

The blackness was absolute. Shouts and howls of rage deafened him. Reckless, he collided with the wall, groped along it and found the alcove. It took all his strength to wrench it open an inch or two, but it was done and he was through and breathing cleaner air.

He raced across the outer room. His groping hand touched the table and then the door. Sprinting dangerously and desperately, he thought, 'Around the next corner . . . then wind about till you reach the stairs!' He felt the corner and turned it, then set off in what was, hopefully, the right direction.

Voices were howling fury and confusion. Someone had tumbled over a chair by the sound of it; someone else was roaring for a light; feet came stumbling in pursuit. If he could just get to the outside steps, he might have a chance, but it was so damnably dark.

He ran full tilt into a wall and, falling, flung out an arm instinctively. His fingers touched a stair! Gasping for breath, bruised but elated, he sprang to his feet. With one hand on the wall and the other gripping his pistol, he galloped up the stairs. There had been another turn here—then the wide hall, and the outside door. From the corner of his eye he detected a faint following glow. They were hot after him, and they could see! He muttered breathlessly, "We'll get there, Jamie old lad! We'll get there—yet!" He found the corner and the light behind him was blotted out briefly. The sound wasn't. Lord, how they howled! He must go by instinct now. He moved as swiftly as he dared and suddenly there was a rectangle of less dense blackness off to his left. The door! Praise heaven and Grandmama Natasha! The door! Scarcely daring to believe such luck, he ran straight for it, was through, and taking the outer steps two at a time.

The night air was cold and blessedly clean and threaded by raindrops that touched his brow like a cool caress.

From behind him came a thin nasal scream of, "There he *goes!* *Shoot,* you fool! *Stop him!*"

It was a voice he knew. A voice that took his breath away. But before his lips had time to form the name, a deeper shadow loomed before him. A mighty club slammed across his ribs driving the air from his lungs and sending him hurtling back down the steps.

Shocks; sudden fierce pain; shouts and a shrill scream; a fading wry amusement because he must have sent them all tumbling like ninepins . . .

wendolyn awoke when Apollo growled and hauled himself to his feet. She had dozed off in the fireside chair in her private parlour. A book lay at her feet and she picked it up and read the title sadly. "*Mandarin—The Elite Superbly Educated Princes of China.*" Tears stung her eyes and she quailed from the all too familiar pang of loss and disillusion.

Someone scratched on the door. A hoarse whisper was half drowned by Apollo's growls, but she heard enough to recognize her evening caller, and ordering the dog to "Lie down!" went to open the door.

The black habit did not become Enoch Tummet, making him look haggard and older. "Might I pop in, Miss? Jest fer a minute like? I know it's late and not proper, but—"

"Don't be silly. This is my parlour, not my bedchamber." She returned to her chair, waved him to the sofa, and watched him expectantly. "Well?"

He spread his hands. "Nought, miss. Nigh four days now, and not a word." He searched her face anxiously. "I don't s'pose 'e bin in touch wiv you today? No letter nor nothing?"

"No. But—in the circumstances . . ."

"Yus, Miss. I know."

"You're worrying," she said gently.

He shrugged in a helpless fashion. "Mr. August ain't a easy

gent, I know. And there's no denying 'e's fought a lotta doo-ells. But 'cept fer one time what was forced on 'im, none of the other parties was left in a bad way. Fact is, they goes 'round boasting 'cause they fought 'im! I bin wiv the guv a good few months now, and we bin through a thing or three tergether. And I feels like I knows 'im."

Gwendolyn said nothing.

Slanting a quick glance at her pensive face, he rubbed his big hands on his knees and went on pleadingly, "You know, don'tcha, Miss, that a lotta things Mr. August says is said outta pride, or 'cause 'e's down-'earted, and not wanting no one to see it. Dead set 'e always bin 'gainst Miss Katrina wedding the poor Lieutenant, I know. But—this 'ere! It's all *wrong*, Miss Gwen! I see 'em fight together when we was in Cornwall, and they fight like— like a team. If one of 'em's in a ticklish spot, t'other's right at 'is side. I tried to tell the other gents. I dunno if they paid no 'tention. Now I can't find none of 'em. And all this time going by! I don't blame you fer not finding it in yer 'eart to fergive Mr. August, arter wot 'e done. But—but I were 'oping, seeing as Cap'n Rossiter's yer brother, Miss, well, I thought if *you* was to go to the Cap'n—"

Her heart already over-burdened, Gwendolyn responded rather more sharply than she intended, "And tell him—what? That you're afraid because Mr. Falcon picked up a bag of feathers?" Tummet's rugged features reddened, and she said quickly, "Oh, I'm sorry. I'm afraid I'm rather tired."

"Ar. Well it's been 'ard on all of us. No doubt o' that."

"No. And you're so good to have faith in him in—in spite of— I didn't mean to be unkind."

"Don't you go worrying yer pretty 'eart over me, mate. I'm jest a rough sorta cove. And it's truth what you said. That there bag o'feathers is in me dreams o'nights! But if you'd seen some of what went on while we was in Cornwall! No 'counting fer it, no 'ow! Only—'tis more'n that, Miss Gwen. 'Tis the way Mr. August were took!"

Confused, Gwendolyn blinked. "Took?"

"Ar. So sudden-like, it were. No matter what people say, me guv's loyal to them as 'e takes a fancy to. And 'e'd took a fancy to the Lieutenant, I'd swear it, Miss." He scowled darkly. "That there fete! That's what done it!"

Gwendolyn said in bewilderment, "Why, we had that horrid accident, but—"

"What weren't no accident," he interpolated grimly. "I went back next day and took a look 'round. That there tree trunk was drug 'crost the road. You could see the marks on the grass still. They *knowed* we was arter 'em!"

"Good heavens! But—but even if that is so, I don't see how—" She fought away the bittersweet memory of strong arms about her; tender words, and those very dear kisses ... "Do you mean because he fainted like that?" she asked hurriedly.

"Thing is, Miss Gwen, I don't reckon 'e did no such thing. I gotta say it without pride, but I've knowed some low persons in me lifetime. *Low* persons! Some what 'ad took to the poppy. And 'ashish—and wuss!"

Gwendolyn said angrily, "Do you *dare* to imply that Mr. Falcon is in the habit of resorting to drugs?"

"No, Miss Gwen! That I do not! But I seen men as is. And I know the signs. And Mr. August 'ad 'em all! Only I were too thick 'twixt the ear 'oles to see what were right in front o' me orbs, or glims, as y'might say."

Her heart began to beat faster, and she gripped her hands tightly. "Tell me."

Encouraged, he said, "Well, Miss, you'll remember as Mr. August didn't seem to know what day 'twas arter the accident? Nat'ral enough, sez you. No, sez I. On-nat'ral! There wasn't 'ardly a bump on 'is noggin, but 'e slept the clock round like a man in one o' them commas, or whatever they call 'em! Burning 'ot, 'e were, too, but I thought 'twas all on account o' that bad arm. And—quarrelsome? Cor! Fairly panting ter go out and chop someone inter gobbets, 'e were. Talking fast and sorta wild. And *still* I never put two and two tergether! Not till I thunk back when it were too late, and recollected that 'is eyes 'ad looked strange, and 'e didn't wanta eat nothing. Strike me blue and pink stripes if I wasn't blind like a bat! But—it never come inter me 'ead, y'know."

Trying to find her way through the maze, Gwendolyn whispered, "Do you say that someone deliberately drugged Mr. August?"

Tummet nodded vehemently. "So I do b'lieve, Miss Gwen. And them as done it like as not kept at 'im, sly like, talking ugly 'bout the poor lieutenant and Miss Katrina. Egging 'im on. D'you remember 'ow 'e kept complaining arter the doo-ell 'bout the fog? There weren't no fog that night! 'Cept inside 'is 'ead, maybe!"

"And he said that he was knee deep in mud," she muttered. "I thought he was making it up! Trying to excuse what he'd done."

"If I'm right, Miss Gwen, me guv'nor was telling the honest truth—as it seemed to 'im. I knowed a sailorman once as got took with the poppy—opium, I mean. But then they give 'im other kindsa things, and 'e couldn't never get orf 'em, poor cove. And 'e told me that when 'e tried ter walk sometimes, that's what it felt like: as if 'is arms and legs wus very 'eavy, and 'e were wading through treacle! Don't y'see, Miss Gwen? It all fits! That there wicked League writ the guv a pome—a 'orrid thing it were—warning they meant to—to punish 'im."

"*Châtiment quatre!*" she whispered. Tummet looked puzzled and she said, "It means the fourth punishment. The League threatened to strike at my brother and his friends again. And—what better way than to twist August's mind? To confuse and manoeuvre him into fighting, and *losing* a duel to the death with— Oh! How horrid! How could *anyone* be so sly and wicked and *evil*?"

"And clever, Miss Gwen," he said, his face very grim. "They could've got rid of two o' their enemies with one blow, 'cause if Mr. August were killed the lieutenant would've 'ad to get outta England quick-like. 'Sides which, them slow-tops at the 'Orse Guards would be sure to say just what they *is* saying now! That Cap'n Rossiter's Preservers is nothing but a wild lotta bored young 'ristocrats trying to stir up trouble."

Gwendolyn stood and wandered about, wringing her hands. "If we're right, their plan went awry, and yet they still won! August must be distracted with remorse! There's no telling what he may do!"

"I know jest what 'e'll do, Miss. Go arter 'em! And blaming of 'isself fer the poor lieutenant, it'd be jest like 'im to charge 'em like there was a troop of 'eavy dragons follering, 'stead of being all by 'isself!"

Gwendolyn gazed at him, her eyes big and frightened in her pale face.

He said sombrely, "A grand fighting man is me guv, Miss Gwen. But St. George, 'e ain't! And the man don't live what could take on that lot single-'anded and live to tell abaht it!"

She dare not dwell on the ramifications of that remark and tried not to give way to panic. "There's no use going to my brother. He and Lord Horatio and Mr. Armitage went to Bristol because of the information Mrs. Quimby gave them. And goodness knows if we could persuade the others to believe us, even if we could find them! 'Twould mean more time lost, and four days have been wasted already! Have you any idea at all where Mr. August may be?"

He hesitated. "I know 'e was sure that the League did their meetings out at the country 'ouse of that crazy lady what were so mad fer 'im. Lady Buttershaw, I mean, and 'er sister wot creeps around dressed in white and smiles so sad all the time." He shivered. "Gives me gooseflesh, *she* do!"

"Lady Julia Yerville? Yes, they're a strange pair." Gwendolyn wrinkled her brow. "Sundial Abbey is the country seat of the earls of Yerville. It's in . . . Surrey, I think. But I heard my brother say that the estate has been watched for months, and nobody we know to be connected with the League ever goes there."

"Ar." Tummet said dolefully, "Well then, that's that, as they say. 'Oo else we got as we're sure of?"

"Mr. Rudolph Bracksby is almost certainly one of the leaders. But again, his estate has been closely watched, with never the least sign of nocturnal activities. Besides, Overlake Lodge marches with my father's country seat, and if the League has been using it as a meeting-place for several years some of our keepers or tenants, or—*some*body would surely have noticed any late-night activities by this time."

"Hum. Wot abaht that nasty baron who nigh put a period

to Cap'n Johnny Armitage in Cornwall? Now there's a gent I'd think were ripe fer secret meetings and all kindsa sticky business."

"Yes, indeed! And we have proof that Lord Hibbard Green is a member of the League. But I thought you had people keeping watch at his estate?"

"We 'ave, mate—er, Miss. And a 'orrid place it is, that there Buckler Castle, but me spies couldn't find nothing funny going on. On the other 'and . . ." He looked thoughtful. "It's old, Miss Gwen. Awful old. I wouldn't wonder if it's fair riddled with secret passages and crafty ways of going in and out. We know there's dungeons underneath, 'cause 'is lor'ship kept poor Sir Anthony Farrar dahn there a year or so ago, and treated him very unkind. Another thing we got to take inter account, is that Mr. August cannot abide neither of them Greens. Not 'is lor'ship, nor Mr. Rafe!"

They looked at each other. Gwendolyn said intensely, "It sounds the most likely place for him to have gone, doesn't it?"

"It do, Miss Gwen! But—four days is four days. Lord Green and Mr. Rafe Green, they got a score to settle wiv Mr. August. What's got me worried is—they might've settled it!"

She gave a gasp. "Oh, Tummet! We must *do* something!"

"Yus. I were thinking that p'raps if you was to go to Lord Hayes at East India—"

"I've a better plan! First thing in the morning, we will go and find him!"

He stared at her. "Lord Hayes, Miss Gwen?"

"No, you great silly! Mr. August! Now that Miss Katrina has the lieutenant's sister here to stay with her, I dare leave for a little while." Deep in thought, she pressed her folded hands to her mouth, then said, "Now—this is what I want you to do . . ."

If it was a dream, it was a very unpleasant one. Falcon had a vague sense of having been hauled about a great deal and of having failed most damnably at a vital task . . . Something icy cold splashed into his face, and he gasped and opened his eyes. And with a hideous sinking feeling knew that it was not a dream.

He was still in that ghastly, foul-smelling room, half-sitting, half-lying in a chair. Four members of the League of Jewelled Men were gathered on the other side of the table, blurry but identifiable; three seated, one standing, and all watching him, like some hellish jury. Hector, Lord Kadenworthy, sat shivering nearby, wigless, wet, and bedraggled, with Topaz dabbing a bloodied handkerchief at a cut on his head.

The Squire murmured, "Ah, that's better. But you really should make an effort to sit straight, dear August. Like a proper British hero, you know."

Falcon's side felt as if he'd been hit with an axe; and his hurt arm was throbbing again. He managed to haul himself upright, and drawled, "Anything to please you, dear Reggie."

There was a chorus of gasps. Every head jerked to the Squire.

"Never!" exclaimed Lord Green.

"The devil!" whispered Sapphire, clearly aghast.

The Squire leapt up and drove the back of his hand hard across Falcon's mouth. "Damn you!" he snarled furiously. "You always were a marplot!" He wrenched off his mask, revealing the undistinguished features of the man London considered to be a dandified weakling.

Kadenworthy, who had lifted his head, muttered an awed "By God! It really *is* Smythe!"

The room was spinning slowly about Falcon. With an odd sense of detachment he knew that the Squire was saying something, the words echoing and unintelligible. As though ordered, Bracksby stood and removed his head mask. There were a few startled exclamations. Smythe glanced at Falcon. "One shock after another, eh, poor fellow?"

"Oh, no." Falcon could taste blood but his head was clearing, and although his voice was unsteady he made an effort to speak plainly. "We know you all."

"Lying 'breed!" snarled Green.

"And good day to you, dear Hibbard," said Falcon.

At this there was stupefaction. Green lurched to his feet and tore off the hood. His fists clenching, he howled, "Pox on you, Squire! If they know us they're very likely outside at this very minute!"

On a note of hysteria Sapphire shouted, "How 'a God's name did they find this place?"

"Fools!" said Smythe in the icy and inflexible voice that seemed so incongruous coming from him. " 'Tis of *peu d'importance.*"

"The devil it is!" argued Green furiously. "I value *my* head!"

"Then use it! Were Lord Hayes, all Rossiter's patriotic idiots, and a full regiment of dragoons surrounding the abbey, they could search forever and not find this room. Is why I chose it!"

"They could find the outer room," Topaz snapped. "And I've no desire to explain my presence here—have you?"

Falcon glanced to the alcove and his heart sank. It was tight shut now.

Kadenworthy put in rather wearily, "They could prove nothing, unless Falcon was with us."

"Precisely," said the Squire. "Which he will not be, of course. Still, I'll own I've no love for this chamber, myself. Though it has served us well." He paused, and smiled at Falcon. "Very well, indeed." He held up his head mask. "We're done with these ugly things. Off with 'em, my friends, or shall we indulge poor Falcon and let him name us?"

"Oh, have done." Topaz reached up to remove the hood. "He already knows I'm a member."

In point of fact, Falcon was astonished as the small "man" with the husky voice became Lady Julia Yerville. They had known she was involved, of course, but he'd not dreamed she was on the ruling committee. Nor, it became evident, had the rest of the group.

Sapphire muttered, "A *woman?* Zounds!"

"Your predecessor, Lord Derrydene, didn't care for it, either," said Smythe. "But Lady Julia has been of great help to us."

"Not to me," said Falcon. "Your cats brought about my downfall, I think, ma'am."

Her smile was brittle. " 'Tis always the little things in life that trip us, eh, Falcon? Were I not fond of cats, you'd not have sneezed and now be—"

"Obliged to fulfil the curse," finished Smythe. "As you said, m'dear—the small things. Such as—a bag of feathers."

"Nonsense," said Falcon, trying not to think of his probable fate.

Sapphire pulled off his mask disclosing a pudgy, florid face, a small mouth and hard little brown eyes. It was not a face Falcon knew well, but memory stirred. 'Jupiter!' he thought. 'Be dashed if you ain't Geoff Delavale's scheming uncle Joseph Montgomery!'

Sapphire jeered, "Surprised you, didn't I, Mr. Mandarin?"

"Not at all," lied Falcon. "You're one of the cowardly swine who tormented poor Quentin Chandler when he fell into your greedy hands! We knew Smythe had been driven to scour the kennels for recruits!"

The Squire moved very fast to intercept the big man's infuriated lunge at Falcon. "Patience, Montgomery. He has very little time, you know. We'd not want him too battered to appreciate—everything."

Lady Julia sat down in the nearest chair. "And *we've* little time, Reginald. With the door closed the air in here grows ever more foul. The sooner we're out of it, the better."

Bracksby dragged over an extra chair, and they arranged themselves around the table again.

Bracksby asked, "May we hear the whole now, Squire?"

"You may indeed." Smythe proceeded to list their bases and the reports that had been received from the commanders. He spoke at length and with force, referring to the map frequently. Clearly, he had all the facts at his fingertips, and despite his discomfort Falcon listened intently. He very much wanted to hear what Smythe had to say, even if the chance of using his knowledge was slight.

"As I said, gentlemen, our forces already surround the last objective, awaiting only the signal to attack. The first move in the final campaign will take place tomorrow." Smythe grinned and added, "Thanks to your sire's most valued assistance, August."

Falcon's attempt at a laugh was cut off by the immediate stab of pain through his ribs, but he managed a breathless, "Rubbish! My father may not admire the king, but he'd never join a traitorous group like this!"

"Your sire," purred Smythe, "is at this very moment waiting with eager expectancy to play host to—Charles Stuart, the Young Pretender."

Falcon stared at him. Was it possible? Was that why the old gentleman had been so reluctant to come back to Town? He'd always despised the Hanoverian succession, but surely— There was laughter. He realized that he must look as dismayed as he felt. He said scornfully, "I always thought you were short of a sheet, Reggie."

"The Bonnie Prince," said Smythe, "is in England even now, under the escort of several gallant and loyal gentlemen, including his friend Henry Goring, of course, and—*your* friend, Gordon Chandler's Jacobite brother."

Quentin? 'Twould be just like that reckless madcap to risk returning to England!

Smythe chuckled. "No comment? Then allow me to advise you that there is to be a very secret party at Ashleigh on Thursday evening. Among the guests will be," he paused and listed slowly, "Sir Brian Chandler—The Earl of Bowers-Malden—Sir Mark Rossiter—Mr. Fletcher Morris—Captain Derek Furlong—Mr. Piers Cranford—" He broke off and said apologetically, "Unfortunately, we had to substitute brothers in those last two instances, Sir Owen Furlong's sire being in India, and Peregrine Cranford's parents both deceased. But, all things considered, we did fairly well, I think."

Chilled, Falcon said, "If you expect me to believe that any of those good men would support another Uprising—"

"But not for the world, my poor fellow, would I so mislead you! They were invited to a party that don't exist. Your father will be at his wit's end trying to cope with them while enemies of the Crown stay in his house. The invitations, you see, were sent by *us*, asking that the 'guests' attend a surprise party to honour Gideon Rossiter's brave little band for their efforts 'gainst the wicked League of Jewelled Men!" There was laughter at this. "How could they refuse?" he continued. "The day after tomorrow they'll troop down there. And after they're all arrived, a second troop will call—led by your friend, Colonel Mariner Fotheringay. Oh, 'tis most precisely timed, I do assure you. We've had our fellows packed like sardines into Larchwoods. Directly Fotheringay sets off to the Tower with his famous prisoners, our men make their move, and Ashleigh is ours!"

If what this Bedlamite said was truth, thought Falcon numbly, every one of those fine men would be charged with High Treason! Poor Mr. Fletcher Morris would not attend, of course, for he would by now be grieving his son. But the others would be fairly trapped. He could envision his father facing the horrors of public disgrace and execution. And as for the fate of his beloved and his dear sister . . . He thought a frantic, 'My God!—No!'

Watching his face, Smythe laughed exultantly. "But my dear Mandarin, how very pale you are become! 'Faith! I almost said—'white.' "

Green and Montgomery shouted with mirth.

Kadenworthy looked scornful.

Falcon made an effort to conceal his emotions. "I have never admired you, Smythe, but when I was a boy I'll own I sometimes wondered just what I did to arouse such animosity in you."

"You know perfectly well what you did!" Suddenly, it was as if they were alone here, reliving that undying animosity, and Smythe leaned nearer, his voice charged with loathing. "You dared to bring your Oriental eyes, your half-breed self to *my* school! And instead of behaving with respectful humility as you should have done, you had the *gall* to pretend to be an English gentleman!"

Falcon grinned. "As, for instance, to captain the cricket team?"

"The crowning insult! That they would award that honour to a *mongrel* who should never have been allowed to be enrolled, and who behaved with such filthy damned arrogance! *Gad!*" Smythe's fist slammed on the tabletop. He was flushed, his eyes glittering with the passion of the fanatic. He spat out, " 'Twas unbearable! A deliberate affront to the entire school! I vowed then that someday I'd make you pay—"

"And so you did." Falcon's lip curled. "With words and

unspeakable viciousness. For which, as I recall, I—er, paid *you!*"

"Ah, but now 'tis my turn! The last laugh, eh, Mandarin? If you but knew how I long to stay here. To watch you die by inches and laugh at your agony is my right, you cur!"

Somebody coughed in embarrassment.

Smythe realized that he was leaning across the table towards this hated enemy, and that they were all staring, and he drew back.

Lady Julia frowned uneasily.

Kadenworthy drawled, "But how vitriolic, Reginald. Did you tie cans to kittens' tails when you were a lad?"

"I did not!" Smythe said slyly, "I will admit that I once put a dead rat on the pillow of this impudent upstart." His grin widened. "He woke up, nose to nose with it."

A haze blurred Falcon's vision. He launched himself across the table so fast that his hands were on Smythe's throat before the others could restrain him. *"Filth!"* he snarled, but they had him then; and he was torn away and slammed back in the chair and, briefly, out of awareness.

After a while, he could hear Kadenworthy arguing, ". . . how the arrest of a clutch of traitorous aristocrats will do the thing."

"Of itself, it will not," answered Smythe. "But 'twill create a sensation, you'll own. And while the public is reading of that great scandal in Friday's newspapers, we strike again. On that very day, Prince Frederick and his Princess are to attend a luncheon party with Pitt, which—"

"Which will enrage the King and Queen," said Lady Julia, amused.

Smythe did not care to be interrupted. "Well, in this case, ma'am," he said rather testily, "their Majesties will not be put out, because their son and his wife will never reach the luncheon. As they leave Leicester House, four of our men, posing as officers of the King's Guard, will ride along the street and the Prince and Princess will be assassinated!"

It was all Falcon could do to lie still. Appalled, he heard the aghast exclamations. Reginald Smythe, he decided, was most definitely as mad as a mangle.

"Both of them?" Lady Julia sounded shocked.

His eyes tight-shut, Falcon could all but see Smythe's narrow shoulders lift in a shrug. " 'Twould be more effective, I do believe. Only think, my friends. 'Tis well known that the King and Queen are at daggers drawn with their son. The King both loathes and fears William Pitt, which is precisely why Prince Frederick befriends the man. When he is murdered, apparently by officers of the King's Guard, the news will sweep England that the Prince was slain at his father's orders! That, coupled with the shameful treachery uncovered at Ashleigh on the previous evening, will cause an enormous public outcry throughout the nation which our people will whip to fever pitch, I promise you."

Kadenworthy argued, "It will take weeks for the news to travel throughout the nation."

"Not so! We have couriers already carrying the word. I tell you that by Saturday the country will be in a state of disorder and anarchy! At exactly three o'clock on Saturday afternoon, a mob will storm St. James's Palace. Simultaneously, our forces attack here"—his long bony finger jabbed at the map—"and here . . . and here, and—"

"And curds and whey!" Falcon pulled his head up, and said as firmly as he could, "Is that really what your masters have told you, Reggie?"

Smythe shot a malevolent glare at him.

Green jeered, "*We* are the masters, you stupid clod! Ain't you learned that yet?"

To laugh was not easy, but he managed it. "What stuff! D'you think we don't know this plot is too big for you and your addle-pated Squire to have masterminded? D'you think we don't know about your silent partners? The great financiers and bankers who manipulate you all from behind the scenes? Or about Barthélemy and—"

Smythe had looked genuinely taken aback, and now snapped, "Silence that bastard, Hibbard!"

"A moment, Squire," said Joseph Montgomery, tugging at his lower lip uneasily. "*Barthélemy?* The French have no hand in this, fiend seize 'em! Right?"

Holding off Lord Green, who advanced on Falcon looking murderous, Kadenworthy demanded, "I'd like an explanation, Smythe."

Green bellowed, "He's making it up, you silly ass! To divide us!"

"If there's any truth to it," said Kadenworthy grimly, "consider us divided! I was not unwilling to be rid of German George and his crew. But be damned if I'll help deliver England to the French!"

"Ask her noble ladyship!" Falcon pointed to Lady Julia, who was frowningly silent. "She and her sister arranged the matter with Barthélemy in Suez, three years—"

Green snarled, "I don't believe a word of it!"

Lady Julia stood. " 'Tis perfectly true, Hibbard. And it is truth that we have other and powerful backers, who prefer to remain anonymous."

"Such as the mighty Lord Eaglund," murmured Falcon, drawing a bow at random.

Kadenworthy's brows lifted in surprise. Smythe's face was unreadable.

"But Marshal Barthélemy does not act for France," added Lady Julia, her voice rising above more consternation. "He is with us for his own ends."

Smythe said quickly, "And brings us munitions, troops, and five hundred thousand louis! A good deal of which we will divide amongst us, my friends."

It was a vast sum, and a telling stroke. Falcon saw their faces, and knew he had lost.

Kadenworthy wandered back to his chair.

His little eyes alight with avarice, Joseph Montgomery took Falcon's chin in a bruising grip. "One more word out of you, Mandarin, and you won't live to see the candle gutter!"

The candle was still burning at midnight when Falcon awoke and dragged out his watch. He had to blink to see the dial. Before they left, Smythe had given the members of his committee permission to exact whatever personal vengeance they felt due them. Falcon had been mildly surprised when Kadenworthy had not taken advantage of the offer. Lord Green, however, had made up for that lapse, until Lady Julia had protested angrily—or at least, he thought hers was the last voice he had heard.

He was lying against the wall, beside the credenza. They'd taken the chairs out but the other pieces of furniture remained; not that they'd be of much use as a refuge since the rats obviously scaled them easily enough. He peered around the room fearfully. The creatures had evidently not come after him since the committee had left. Smythe had said they wouldn't.

"So long as your candle burns, my dear fellow they won't attack." He'd added with a sly grin, "Though I fear the flame cannot last all night. Especially since 'tis always night down here. Are you still as afraid of rats as you used to be? Well, take heart. They don't really want you. They'd rather eat grain or insects. Just try not to startle them; they do bite if they're startled. But 'tis very doubtful they'll bring about your demise. You will expire, my dear fellow, from thirst or starvation—if you don't suffocate first. There is very little air in here, as you'll have noticed. Which helps to keep our meetings brief. And in case you're wondering, the only way to open the door is by the use of our tokens which we will, of course, take with us." He'd gone on to describe the last moments of the hapless prisoners who'd been left here to die in "the good old days." Some of the details so horrible that Lady Julia had demanded he stop.

Falcon had been sick with fear at that point, but rage had lent him the strength to drawl, "No, never deny him, ma'am. His circle of friends is small, but 'tis quite logical he should be intimately acquainted with rodents."

Smythe hadn't liked that, and had turned to the door, calling, "Your turn, Hibbard. Adieu, dear Mandarin. You cannot know how the contemplation of your fate lightens my spirits."

His fate . . .

Falcon strained his ears. Had that been a scampering? He sat up and huddled against the wall, shivering. How bitterly cold it was. And how crushing the silence. When the candlelight was gone and he had to face death all alone in suffocating blackness, he would surely go mad. The impulse to beat on the walls and scream for help was strong but he fought it, knowing it was useless and that he would use up too much air. The words of the Cornish curse echoed in his mind. 'A slow and painful death . . .' It would be that, all right. Unless he found a way out. There *must* be a way out! Irritated, he thought, 'Well don't just sit here trembling! Find it, you silly clod!' He dragged himself to his feet. It was too painful for him to stand straight, but he began to hobble about, poking, scratching and knocking. And two hours later, breathless and exhausted, his nails torn, and the candle much lower, he acknowledged defeat and clambered onto the credenza rather than sit on the floor.

The loathsome Hibbard, curse and confound the creature, had left him with a galloping nosebleed. It was staunched now, but Smythe had said that when the rats came—

He cut off that line of thought, but the one that succeeded it was not much better. Was it becoming harder to draw a breath? Surely not. But clearly, there was no way out.

No way out.

He was entombed in this stinking, frozen silence.

And nobody knew he had come here—or would care if they did know. Unless—might *she* care? Just a trifle, perhaps? His precious Smallest Rossiter?

He leant his head back against the cold stone blocks, aching with the longing to see her sweet face—just once more.

He must stop being so damnably selfish, thinking only of himself. He must shut the coming horror out of his mind. He thought of the men he had not wanted for friends, and who were the best friends any man could have. He thought of his beautiful sister—whose heart he had broken. And of his dear and foolish sire. All doomed, as he was doomed.

He closed his eyes wearily and wished he didn't hurt so much.

He must have dozed, because when he looked up he saw with a sickening jolt of fear that the candle was guttering.

He had not known real terror since Smythe had put the dead rat on his pillow at school. He knew it again. Paralyzing, demoralizing, stark terror.

Panicked, he got down from the credenza. He must not let the candle go out! He *must* find something to burn!

The candle flame flickered again.

Gazing at it with wide, horrified eyes, he had the first faint intimation that he was no longer alone in the room.

A soft rustling . . . and the clicking of claws . . .

CHAPTER XV

Thy had left Town before the household was stirring, and without stopping for breakfast lest someone attempt to detain them. It was a grey, chilly morning, with occasional raindrops carried on a rising northeast wind. Despite the hour, they encountered heavy traffic on London Bridge, and by the time they reached Wimbledon and stopped at a likely-looking posting-house to change horses, Gwendolyn was very hungry. So was Tummet. So was Apollo, who made his needs known so loudly that the ostler reaching for the reins of the leader leapt back with a yelp of fright. It was all Tummet could do to calm the man, but when he attempted to take Apollo "fer a nice little trot" the dog showed him such an expanse of teeth that he withdrew his generous offer.

"I quite fails ter see, Miss Gwen," he grumbled, "why we brung this 'ound of the devil along wiv us. Trouble, 'e'll be. Nought but trouble!"

Gwendolyn took up the trouble-maker's lead. "We brought him because he is Mr. August's dog and dogs are said to have especially gifted nostrils, so 'tis my hope he will find his master, even if we cannot. Do you go and order some food for us, and a bone for Apollo whilst I take him for a walk."

Tummet hesitated uneasily. Cap'n Rossiter wouldn't like him to let Miss Gwen walk about alone. And Mr. August had made it all too clear what he'd do if his "imitation valet" ever again allowed her to endanger herself. He fingered his throat reminiscently.

Reading his thoughts, Gwendolyn smiled. "Never worry, my loyal friend. Apollo would devour anyone who tried to harm me."

That was very true. And she had called him her loyal friend! 'Cor!' he thought and, beaming, went into the posting-house.

Apollo had been confined and inactive for a much longer period than he liked. There were several promising trees and shrubs requiring immediate attention, but when Gwendolyn then found a sturdy stick he was willing to play. She threw it a good distance down the hill behind the posting-house, and he went thundering in pursuit and came thundering back, grinning happily and with much flapping of ears. She confirmed his belief that he was a good dog, and he relinquished the stick and then went tearing after it again. The minutes passed, but he did not reappear. Gwendolyn waited. Perhaps he'd lost the stick. Curious, she walked a little way, calling his name, and then halted in dismay.

He had found a new game. A nun stood at the foot of the hill, trying to coax a tiny white dog back to her, while her pet flirted and Apollo pranced and leapt about and generally showed off for his new friend's benefit. The nun was evidently quite young, for her figure was slender even in the bulky habit, and she moved gracefully and was surprisingly undaunted by the big hound.

Gwendolyn limped to the rescue, apologizing as she reached for the stick. She had not brought her cane; the sloping, uneven field was her undoing and she lost her balance. She righted herself quickly, but the nun snatched up the stick, and proffered it, turning away shyly so that her face was hidden by the deep *coiffe* of her habit.

"Thank you," said Gwendolyn. "My wretched dog! But he has been in the carriage for some time and—"

"Yes," said the nun in a charming, husky voice. "I know."

She must have seen them drive up and watched that silly business with the ostler. Gwendolyn said sternly, "Apollo! *Down*, sir!"

At the top of the hill, Tummet brandished a large bone and

called, " 'Pollo! See wot I got fer you, 'orrid 'ound that you is! Look!"

That evidently struck a promising chord and the dog abandoned his new acquaintance and raced up the hill.

"Throw it in the coach!" called Gwendolyn at the top of her lungs, then thought, 'Good gracious! The Sister will think I'm a real hobbledehoy!' "If we don't"—she explained, turning—"we'll never get him away from—" She checked, and stood rigidly still. The nun was facing her squarely, and surely there had never been a nun like this. Delicate features in a pale oval of a face with great sad dark eyes and a lovely mouth that trembled on a wistful smile.

The faintly accented voice said, "Ah, you know me, I see. You are the sister of Captain Gideon Rossiter, yes?"

Gwendolyn drew a deep breath. "And you are Maria Barthélemy—or I believe you called yourself Benevento at the time when you shot Sir Owen."

The dark eyes closed very briefly. When they opened the lashes shone with tears. "*Oui.*"

"And now you are a nun." Gwendolyn's lip curled. "Is it a danger to me that I have seen you in your new disguise? Perhaps you mean to shoot me, too."

Miss Barthélemy shrank as though she had been struck. Her head bowed, and slender hands covered her face. "Do not . . . I beg you! I—apprehend how you must despise me, but—"

Gwendolyn gave a disgusted little snort and turned away.

At once the other girl caught her arm. "Please—I *implore* you! I have waited so long to—"

"If you do not let me go I will call my servant."

"I will do whatever you say. I shall down upon my knees fall, if you ask it. Only please—*please* Miss Rossiter! If you have ever loved—give me a moment. A moment only."

That she was distraught there could be no doubting, and she looked quite ready to fall on her knees.

'If you have ever loved.'

Gwendolyn suffered an anguished pang, and said in a less stern voice, "Very well. But only a minute."

Five minutes later, sitting on a bench under the deep eaves of the posting-house, Maria Barthélemy said, "I loved him so much, do you see? But my brother—all my life he has guarded and cared for me. We are so close, so—belonging. Sir Owen had that horrible Agreement that my Jean-Jacques had signed."

"To join with the League of Jewelled Men in attacking my country," said Gwendolyn.

"*Oui.* This it is truth, and I fear utter folly. My brother had won the support of some very, very wealthy Frenchmen. But he acted not as a representative of King Louis. If the agreement were made public, he would have been disgraced, ruined, guillotined. This was very bad, I know. But"—Maria spread her hands helplessly—"what am I to do?"

Gwendolyn tried to put herself in the same predicament, making a choice between August and Gideon. She shivered. " 'Twas a terrible decision. But—could you not have shot at Sir Owen's foot or—"

"I aimed at his arm." Maria sighed. "He thought, I suppose, that as a woman I could not shoot, and he—what is it you say?—he dodged. And oh, Miss Rossiter, I have been half mad with fear and repentances, wondering each moment of the day and night how he is. I could not bear it, so I went back to France to see my brother, only to find he was gone—somewhere. I left him a note, telling him that Sir Owen is my love—my life, and I came to London, to beg his forgiveness."

"But Owen said he did see you, and that you rushed away before he could talk to you."

"Yes. My servant was with me. He is very faithful, and there was a soldier beside Sir Owen, and Louis was sure Sir Owen would have me arrested as a spy, so he pushed me into the coach and we drove away. My poor Owen looked so ill—and then I was ill because this climate of yours is very horrid. I beg your pardon, but so it is. And then I waited and waited, hoping to see Zoe Grainger, who might, I think, understand, but never do I find her. I have to be very careful, for I could be arrested, you will know this."

"No, ma'am. Sir Owen refused to bring charges 'gainst you. London still knows you only as Maria Benevento."

Miss Barthélemy's ruddy lower lip dropped, and her eyes

opened very wide. She clasped her hands prayerfully, and whispered, "He did this? Ah, can it be so? My gallant *mon homme, comme il faut!*"

"Quite so," agreed Gwendolyn. "Sir Owen is a fine—"

Maria caught at her arm tempestuously. "You do not understand! *Il y va de sa vie!*"

"*All* our lives are at stake! We are even now trying to find August Falcon. If you know where they meet, I implore you—"

Horrified, Maria exclaimed, "They have him? Ah, *mon Dieu,* but they hate him! If I knew where he was I would tell you, I swear this! I have been watching Falcon House and I hear there is a terrible tragedy. And then, at last, this morning I have seen you, and we follow, *mon Petite* and me. Are you going to search for Monsieur Falcon?"

"Yes. At Buckler Castle, for—"

"No, no!" Maria shook her head. "It is not there where they meet. This I *do* know. And now I beg of you—how may I find Owen? He must be warned not to go to the party!"

Gwendolyn stared in mystification. "Party? What party? I do not understand."

"Then you must warn your brother. All of them. The party, it is not—" Her eyes had moved past Gwendolyn. A look of fear came into them and she gave a little gasp and stopped speaking.

Gwendolyn followed her gaze. Ostlers were running to change the team of an arriving coach, and a lady who had been calling to her coachman was in the act of drawing back inside the carriage. There was nothing else to be seen that might have alarmed Maria, but when Gwendolyn turned the girl was hurrying off. Following quickly, she called, "Wait! Pray do not go away, Miss Barthélemy."

"I must. I dare not— She must not see me." Maria walked on, her little dog prancing ahead happily.

Gwendolyn ran to put a detaining hand on her arm. It was shaken off. The French girl said low and urgently, "*There* is one who can help you! But be very careful. Go. Talk to her!" And she was gone, almost running in her anxiety to get away.

Gwendolyn stared after her. s*There* is one who can help

you . . . ?' Bewildered, she hurried across the yard.

The ostlers were leading off the team of the luxurious coach. As she approached, the window was lowered and a familiar voice called her name. Astonished, she said, "Mrs. Haverley!" and thought, 'Now why on earth should I "be very careful" of this gentle little soul?'

A footman swung open the door, and a neat maid alighted, curtsied to Gwendolyn, and went into the posting-house. Hector Kadenworthy's aunt said, "Get in, please do, my dear. I cannot take my face out in public at this moment. Oh, how glad I am to see someone I know! Do pray sit here beside me. I declare I am quite . . . distracted!"

To prove this declaration, she drew a damp handkerchief from her muff and dabbed at her tears. She clearly had been weeping for some time, for her eyes were red and swollen and she was trembling, her hands never still. Even at such a moment however, her breeding did not desert her and she enquired politely if Miss Rossiter was well, and if she travelled alone.

"My servant accompanies me, ma'am." By all the rules of correct behaviour Gwendolyn should now do her utmost to calm the lady and turn her thoughts from what had upset her. But Maria's warning compelled her to ignore correct behaviour, and she said, "Never mind that. Whatever has so distressed you?" She glanced up the road. "Does his lordship ride escort?"

"No." Mrs. Haverley bit her lip, and made an obvious effort to control her emotions. "How is your father? I trust—"

Gwendolyn took her hand. "My dear friend, what is wrong?"

Mrs. Haverley's face crumpled and she burst into tears. "Oh, Miss Rossiter, I—I am so fearful! I have n-never seen H-Hector like this." She emerged from her handkerchief and said jerkily. "Always, the dear boy had a—a rather quick temper and—a tendency to a sharp tongue. Though *never* with me! Never!"

"No, of course not, for he loves you dearly. But whatever has happened to throw you into such distress? Is Lord Kadenworthy ill?"

"No—and yet I think he must be. In his mind, at least. But I must not talk of—of private troubles. You will think me very silly. Now—"

"I think you need someone to talk to," said Gwendolyn, overcoming her scruples ruthlessly. " 'Tis such a coincidence that we should chance to meet here. But perhaps 'tis not. Perhaps I was meant to be here so as to—to comfort you, ma'am. And you surely know I am not one to gossip."

Mrs. Haverley tried to smother a sob, and the dam burst. She said, "I have never known him to—to drink to such excess, or to talk so wildly, and with so little—*sense!* Oh, but I am not making sense either, am I?" She drew a hand across her brow, and said in great distress, " 'Tis just that—I do not know what to *do!*"

"There, there." Her nephew had evidently come home over the oar, and what that had to do with herself was past understanding. Yet Maria had seemed so very frightened. Holding the older woman's trembling hand again, Gwendolyn said soothingly, "Men are so troublesome, are they not? Is it that Lord Hector came home last evening in a—perhaps inebriated condition?"

"No! Not then! And I don't know why, but *whenever* he goes there he returns in a black humour, so I was a little anxious and waited up for him."

"Goes—where, ma'am?"

"To an inn called The Quarter Deck. 'Tis somewhere near Guildford, I believe, though I am not sure exactly where, and at all events he doesn't stay there but hires a horse and rides off again. Which of itself seems odd. And I only know that much because the coachman is walking out with my maid, and—" She sighed, shook her head and lapsed into silence.

Gwendolyn said gently, "Ah. An affair of the heart, perhaps?"

"No, no! I know about those, and— Oh, but never mind. The thing is that last night Hector came home in the most dreadful rage. Joe Coachman told my woman that his lordship had been thrown, but it must have been into a puddle, for his clothes were all muddied and he had the most dreadful gash on his head. Perhaps that is why—" Again her voice trailed off and her eyes became remote.

"Why, then I expect you have your answer, ma'am. A blow on the head can—"

"Can cause a man to close up his house? To tell me to go back to London and start packing anything I wanted to take with me?

To walk the floor all night long, drinking that dreadful brandy and mumbling and swearing and saying the most hideous things about black holes and rats, and—and murders?"

"Good gracious! That does sound alarming. Could it, do you suppose, be a fever? Did you call his physician?"

"No, for he would have none of it, and kept saying 'twas not his health but his common-sense that had betrayed him. And he seemed not to notice that I was even there, but ranted on and on making half-finished remarks like—oh, that he should have got out long ago. In August, I think he said. And foul smells, and—"

Gwendolyn's ears had perked up. She interrupted, "Your pardon, but might he rather have been speaking of Mr. August Falcon?"

"What? Oh, no, no! And why Neville should have given his son a month for a name, I shall never understand, but he was always a rattle-brain, you know. 'Twas something that had *happened*, in some hideous place. Hector kept saying that, only with the most dreadful language! And he said that he might as well be—be *dead*! And that he had brought it on himself, and we must go away, because they—whoever *they* may be!—had lied in their teeth! And—Oh, Miss Rossiter, I do not *want* to go away, unless it could be back to my loved Cornwall! But he speaks of—of the *Americas*! Away from everything and everyone we know! And— oh dear, oh dear! I am too *old* to start all over again!" Having come to the end of which bewildering recitation, she burst into tears once more.

Gwendolyn's heart was beating very fast. She made an effort to comfort the lady, and murmured, "Never worry so, poor soul. Chances are 'twas the drink talking and by the time your nephew comes to join you— I suppose he intends to meet you in Town?"

Mrs. Haverley's head jerked up. "So he said!" she cried hysterically. But I wonder— Miss Rossiter, he was so—almost *crazed*! I dread to say it but—but I fear he—he may intend to—to do away with himself! Oh, my poor, poor Pen! Always so good and—"

Gwendolyn's heart seemed to stop. She caught Mrs. Haverley by the arm and demanded, "*What* did you call him?"

"Pen." Mrs. Haverley blinked at her wonderingly. " 'Tis a childish nickname. I told you that when he was small he could not pronounce words properly. He could never say Penzance when people asked him where he lived, and they would laugh and say 'twas not 'pen' but Penzance, and the child would become enraged and shout "Pen! Pen!" So it became a nickname. Why, some of his friends call him that to this day." She smiled nostalgically. "I remember once . . ."

Gwendolyn scarcely heard the rest of that reminiscence. Her heart was pounding, her mind racing wildly. She had seen Maria Barthélemy driving away from Overlake Lodge with a man called "Pen." He had appeared to be a very large individual, and Kadenworthy was slender, but he was tall and a many-caped cloak tended to exaggerate a man's size. August had said that Mr. Penn was a member of the League. Was it possible that 'twas not a surname, but a nickname? If that were so, then Lord Hector Kadenworthy must be a traitor, which did not seem likely. August and Gideon liked the man, and why would someone of great wealth and possessions seek to destroy the system under which he was so happily endowed? And, yet, down through history rich and influential men had rebelled against the status quo. Certainly, the coincidences were too strong to be dismissed, and she'd always suspected that Lord Kadenworthy could be ruthless. Furthermore, he had been in the great house at the fete and had probably enjoyed a glass of wine with his 'friend' August. And August's erratic behaviour had started that very night. How easy 'twould have been for a friend, trusted and above suspicion, to slip a drug into his wineglass, just as Tummet suspected.

"Miss Rossiter?" Mrs. Haverley's tearful eyes were peering at her anxiously. "Are you all right?"

"I—er, I beg pardon, ma'am. I was trying to think how to help. Is Lord Hector still in Epsom? Perhaps, were I to go down and see him—"

"How kind of you, my dear. But—he won't let you in. The knocker is already off the door."

There were advantages, thought Gwendolyn, to having a former burglar acting as one's coachman!

Falcon was awakened by another stab of pain; in his wrist this time. With a shout of mingled revulsion and terror he jerked his hand away. His voice was hoarse now and didn't seem to scare them off as much as it had at first and once again he was sickened by the horror of feeling them all around him, of knowing that if his movements startled them their sharp teeth or claws would sink into his flesh.

He was still on his knees, and had dozed off while leaning against the wall and trying to compose a prayer. He had not been much in the way of praying, but he prayed now, with all his heart. "Dearest Grandmama Natasha—I know I deserve to be punished, but *please* ask—Him, or—or one of the saints you've met, to help me find a way out! Not just for me, dearest, though I'm . . . very afraid. But if I don't get out, you know, my father and my sister, and my dearest love, will either perish by the axe, or starve! And the rest of those fine men and their families, also. And they don't deserve such a terrible fate. You know that, Grandmama!" He added a postscript to his prayer, requesting that Natasha would kindly take care of poor Jamie, who would likely not know his way about up there.

It was appalling to realize that he should have allowed his eyes to close for an instant. But he was so tired, and it was ever more hard to breathe. Green had warned him with great jollity to remain as still as possible so as to preserve his supply of air, but— the devil with that! Did they expect him to just lie down and let the rats gnaw on him while he slowly smothered? He was shamed by the memory of having come perilously close to abandoning hope before he'd found the gift from his beloved. It had made him laugh, rather hysterical laughter unfortunately, when he'd remembered how she had begged him at the Fete not to open it at that particular moment. He'd forgotten the gift and had discovered it when the candle was almost gone and he'd been searching the great pockets of his coat in a frenzy of desperation to find something to burn before all light vanished from this ghastly cell.

He'd been overjoyed to find the small flat box, and more overjoyed when he realized what it contained. Having succeeded in lighting the first stick of incense he'd found that the pungent aroma did much to drown the foul smells of his prison. And tiny as it was, the glow had heartened him and enabled him to cling to his sanity through the long nightmarish hours since the candle died. He'd stumbled about until he found the bowl on the alcove and had begun to scrape and chip away at the crumbling mortar below it, reasoning that the locking mechanism must be somewhere inside. The work had proven hard on his hands, and on his knees, and a jeering little voice whispered that even if he loosened the block it would likely only grant him a glimpse of the outer darkness. But there was the hope that if he could come at the locking device he might win to freedom! Freedom and fresh air, and a chance—please God!—to warn his father and his friends of the pit yawning at their feet, and perhaps to also prevent the murders of the Prince and Princess of Wales!

He ran his fingers along the shallow groove that was the result of his hours of scraping. He didn't seem to have accomplished very much and the prospects for success seemed faint indeed. But the Smallest Rossiter and Grandmama Natasha had given him the miracle of hope, and to that hope he would cling for so long as his strength and his lungs and his mind prevailed.

His knees were bruised and stiff and he held his ribs as he went to the credenza and bent closer to the incense box. He'd made a small hole in the top to form a makeshift holder for the sticks. The little spark was still bright, and there was an inch or so left on this one. Whatever happened, he must not let it burn out before he used it to kindle its successor. Once before he'd fallen asleep, and the rats had awoken him—providentially in time to prevent that precious spark from dying altogether. There were only two sticks left now. When they were gone . . .

He wouldn't think about that. He must get back to work. Smythe had taken his spurs and the small pocket knife he carried, which would have been invaluable. The diamond pin in his cravat had served for an hour or so, but then had snapped and he'd been unable to find it. He had despaired until he thought of his boot buckle. He'd had quite a battle to tear it off, but once in his hand it had proven a fairly efficient tool. It must have fallen when he dozed off, and he groped about anxiously.

His questing fingers touched a cold wormlike thing and he gave a shuddering cry as the long tail whipped away and the rodent scampered across his hand. He huddled against the wall, eyes closed, shaking convulsively and whispering Gwendolyn's name . . . concentrating on her laughing, mischievous little face.

And after a while, he summoned the courage to grope about again until he found the precious buckle and could fight on.

Mimosa Lodge was gloomy and hushed, the only signs of life emanating from the wainscotted study. Here, a single branch of candles shone on the gentleman seated at the desk, his quill pen scratching rapidly across a sheet of paper. The slim, well-manicured hand paused and the gentleman glanced over what he had written. "I, Hector Chauncy Jefferies, Lord Kadenworthy, being of sound mind—" He gave a derisive snort, and muttered cynically, "Extreme *un*-sound mind, if truth be told!" He read on, "—sound mind and body, do hereby declare this to be my last—"

The candles flickered. He glanced up, then leapt to his feet. "How the devil did you get in here?"

"We broke in," said Gwendolyn Rossiter coolly, limping from the open door.

His lordship scowled at her, then his crooked smile dawned. "I am flattered." He stifled a hiccup and offered a rather wobbly bow, "And here I'd fancied you did not care for me overmuch."

"Do not be flattered, my lord." He was obviously half drunk, and she prayed that condition might aid her.

Tummet drifted in from the corridor, and stood watching stoically, arms folded, but with a horse pistol in one hand.

"Aha!" Kadenworthy hiccupped again, and apologized. "So your visit is not of a—er, social nature, ma'am."

"I do not socialize with traitors."

He stiffened. The high flush vanished from his saturnine features, and he sat down abruptly. " 'Twould be interesting to know what—"

"Nor have I the time to bandy words with you, sir." Gwendolyn advanced to sit, uninvited, in a deep chair facing the desk. "We have proof that you are a member of the League of Jewelled Men. We know you are planning to leave the country." His faint bitter grin caused her to add hurriedly, "Or take what is termed the 'honourable way out.' One gathers you can stand no more of the Squire's methods, or perhaps he distrusts you, and you know what happens to his people in that event."

Kadenworthy drew a deep breath and leaned back in his chair. He looked older suddenly; bitter and drawn and defeated. " 'Pon my soul but you do know a lot, m'dear. Does it not occur to you that 'twas foolish in the extreme for you to have come here—even with the—er, fabled cockney valet standing guard?"

"No. For I knew you had turned off all your servants. I have spoken with your aunt, you see, and—"

His face contorted and he leaned forward to interrupt harshly, "You've not told her of your suspicions?"

So this conscienceless man cared for the lady at least. Gwendolyn replied, "She knows nothing. As yet."

"Which means—you may feel obliged to tell her. To do so will serve you no purpose, madam, save to break the heart of a gentle and pure-hearted woman."

"An unhappy result, which may be averted, sir, if you will tell us where to find August Falcon."

His reaction was startling. He flinched and actually shrank back in the chair. Briefly, his eyes closed. Then he appeared to recover himself and sat straighter. "You really judge me a villain! You not only believe me a traitor to my king and country, but you expect me to betray the men you judge to be my fellow-conspirators. Are there no limits to my infamy, ma'am?"

Gwendolyn considered him thoughtfully. Despite the sardonic words, his lips twitched and a little nerve pulsed beside one eye. Trying not to panic, she said, "I do not know. Are there? I had thought you a hard man, my lord. I would never have judged you capable of treason; or of the heartless murders of hundreds of innocents aboard the ships you have sunk; the fine men you have ruined, the families you have destroyed only to—"

"Have done! Have done!" He wrenched from his chair and paced to the window. After a brief silence, he slumped down on the window-seat and stared at the polished floor muttering, "I've not the heart to put up an impassioned denial. We were engaged in a war. An undeclared war, perhaps, but a war nonetheless. And in war one fights with whatever weapons come to hand. I have nothing to lose by withholding the truth; and nothing to tell you that could in any way help you to reach Falcon." He glanced up, and smiled without mirth as Tummet raised the pistol and trained it on him steadily. "Shoot, friend, and you likely do me a favour. I swear to you, Miss Rossiter, that were it the dearest wish of my heart to help Falcon, there is no possible way to do so."

Gwendolyn had pinned all her hopes on this man, and her heart convulsed. She dashed a hand across her eyes, and said, her voice trembling, "I can only beg you, sir. 'Twould be a—a blot removed from your heavenly accounting."

He watched her curiously. "By Jupiter! You care for the rascal!"

"Yes." She said with pride, "I love him."

"Poor child. I cannot help you. Even if I pointed you in the right direction, 'twould avail you nothing. It is too late, you see."

She gave a little anguished cry.

Tummet growled, "D'you say me guv'nor's dead?"

"For his sake—I hope so."

Tummet swore softly.

Gwendolyn's clenched fists pressed at her lips.

As if very weary, Kadenworthy stood, strolled back to his desk, and poured a large portion of brandy. He drank deep, then sat down, muttering, "The time is long past when anything might be done. The time was past two years ago and more, when I performed one of my—my few acts of kindness, and helped a man escape execution." He laughed loudly, and poured more brandy into the glass.

Enraged, Tummet started for him, but Gwendolyn waved him back. "I think none of us is wholly evil, sir. Perchance you fell into bad company, but—"

"*Fell* into?" His lordship laughed again, a harsh, bitter sound.

"I did not fall, dear lady. I was pushed. A fine young officer found out I'd helped Treve de Villars escape to France when half Britain's military might was after him."

Tummet, who had admired the dashing Trevelyan de Villars, started.

Gwendolyn exclaimed, "Good heavens! Do you say someone *blackmailed* you into becoming a traitor?"

"He could have ruined me," Kadenworthy muttered broodingly. "Just when I was getting the new Race Meeting organized. 'Twas my life—my passion, to see it a success. A few words only would have brought my world tumbling down. Already, that devil Fotheringay suspected me. I'd have been condemned, past doubting. I'd have lost everything. Including my head." He smiled that bitter, twisted smile. "You see what happens when a bad man does a good deed, m'dear? Disaster! I was enraged, and then the invitation to attend a meeting of the League was sent to me. I'd no love for German George. To see the Stuarts back on the throne would not have distressed me. So I decided I'd as well be hung for a wolf as a lamb." He twirled the brandy in his glass and stared at it. "For a long time I was a very minor member, but I was protected from Lambert, the swine who blackmailed me. How, I do not know. But I was grateful, you may be sure. I did what I might and eventually became a member of the Ruling Council. I'll own to suffering some qualms when I discovered the full breadth of their activities, but"—he shrugged—"it was too late to repine."

"Then—why have you left the League now? Is it because of— of what they have done to . . ." Gwendolyn's voice broke. ". . . to—August?"

"He deserved better, poor devil. I think, perhaps 'twas one of the—last straws, as they say." He scowled and said in sudden fury, "But mostly it was that they lied to all of us, damn them! Their plan is not to rid Britain of the monarchy and establish a republic! Rather, 'tis the scheme of a group of ambitious madmen on both sides of the Channel to seize power for themselves! To turn this England into a slave state benefitting only a few!"

"And among them, Marshal Jean-Jacques Barthélemy," muttered Gwendolyn numbly.

Astounded, Kadenworthy exclaimed, "Where you get your information, I do not know, ma'am. Are the authorities also aware?"

Tummet growled, "They bin told."

"And would not believe, I'll warrant! Typical of Whitehall! And the Squire has agents everywhere, of course, to stifle and twist the truth." He grunted disgustedly, then said, "You hold there is good in every man, Miss Rossiter. Perhaps he is kind to his mother—or to his horses. I believe he is a stranger to compassion otherwise. Certainly, his hatred for Falcon borders on madness and Smythe will show no mercy to—"

"Smythe!" she gasped, incredulous. "*Reginald Smythe* is the Squire?"

"Now snap me garter!" exclaimed Tummet, equally incredulous. "That shrivelled-up worm?"

"You do worms an injustice," said Kadenworthy.

Gwendolyn sprang up and ran to his side. "Then if you so despise him, tell us what we ask, and before you go, write a full confession, naming names and—"

"And breaking the heart of the only lady who ever truly loved me? Never!"

She bit her lip. "Then—only let me know where I may find August, and I swear on my immortal soul I will never tell your aunt you were involved in treason!"

Kadenworthy glanced at Tummet, who crossed his heart with the pistol muzzle and said, "Me own soul, ditto."

His lordship was silent. Then, he said slowly, "He is shut in a sealed room under Sundial—" He stopped, his head flinging up as another draught rippled the candles. "Someone has entered the house," he whispered. "Have you a carriage waiting?"

Tummet nodded. "Behind your stables, milor'."

"Then get out the window. Quickly! Quickly! If they think I've told you anything, your lives aren't worth a farthing! Go! I'll try and delay them!"

"But—" began Gwendolyn.

Tummet snatched up the brandy decanter, thrust it at Gwendolyn, grasped her elbow and ran lightly to the window.

It was full dark now, and they made their way silently across the rear lawns, seeing and hearing nothing untoward. They were breathless when they reached their carriage.

As they drove into the quiet country night, they heard the distant but distinct bark of a pistol shot.

CHAPTER XVI

I t was too dark to journey any farther on this crowded day, and Tummet found a modest little inn a mile or so west of Epsom. Fortunately, he had borrowed ample funds from Falcon's cash-box, and he was able to procure rooms for them. They had stopped en route to purchase a few overnight necessities and valises for respectability, but the proprietor clearly thought it odd for a young lady to travel escorted only by her coachman. There could be no doubt but that she was of the Quality, however, and that, together with the luxurious coach and the high-bred team, lulled his fears. Apollo presented another difficulty, but when Tummet nobly volunteered to sleep in the stables with the hound, the host relented.

Gwendolyn took a light supper in her tiny room and went early to bed. She was wracked by anxiety and expected to lie awake all night, but the feather bed was comfortable and she slept soundly until the maid brought her hot chocolate at six o'clock. She washed and dressed quickly and after a hurried breakfast they set forth once again.

The sky had lightened to a pewter grey. It had rained steadily through the night and there were deep puddles and potholes to worsen the poor state of the roads. Longing to set the team to a stretching gallop, Tummet was obliged to proceed with caution. To the distracted Gwendolyn, the miles seemed to be covered at a snail's pace, but shortly before ten o'clock they reached a pretty hamlet east of Woking, and stopped to change horses and enquire the way to Sundial Abbey. The host of the solitary inn was a taciturn individual, but he jerked a thumb to the southwest and gave them terse directions, ending with, "You can't miss it, though why you'd want to go there is beyond me. Terrible bad road. Ugly old pile. And haunted into the bargain!"

They could, and did miss it. He had neglected to tell them there was a fork in the lane, and they emerged from a copse of trees to find themselves in a field of surprised cows and under attack by a scarlet-faced farmer who roared his intention to call in the constable and charge them with unlawful trespass and with having frightened his cattle half to death. His accusations were unwarranted, Tummet became incensed and a bout of fisticuffs was only averted by Gwendolyn's offer to pay the exorbitant damages demanded by the pugnacious man. They drove back to the crossroads and in this instance the inn-keeper proved to have been right. The lane deteriorated into a track resembling an obstacle course that worsened until it was a sea of mud. After several attempts to drive around it, the coach lurched and was stuck fast. Gwendolyn could barely keep back tears of frustration and was all for striking off across the fields on foot, but Tummet pointed out that the inn-keeper's directions had not been too clear, besides which the stiffening breeze was cold. "It won't do us no manner of good, Miss Gwen, if it turns out to be ten miles 'stead of four, and you get yer feet soaked and take a chill. 'Sides, we might need the coach when we find me Guv'nor." Bowing to that sobering thought, she helped him collect brush to set under the wheels, and with the aid of a passing shepherd they were able to extricate the coach and go on.

It was half-past eleven o'clock and the lodge gates were closed when they reached Sundial Abbey. There being no sign of a keeper, Tummet climbed down from the box and opened the gates, and they proceeded boldly along a drive that wound uphill for a mile or more before the house came into view.

Sundial Abbey was undeniably very old, and it was long, massive, and surrounded by deep meadow grasses and wildly overgrown trees. On this dark day it looked mournful and neglected, but it commanded a superb view of the surrounding countryside and on a bright sunny morning and with a little more care expended on the grounds, Gwendolyn thought it could be mellow and beautiful.

A gardener, digging without much enthusiasm in a weedy flowerbed, regarded them incuriously, but they saw no other sign of servants or the occupants of the abbey.

Tummet drove around to the side, past a barn and paddock where some horses grazed. Continuing to the rear, he guided the team off the drive-path, across a weedy meadow and into one of several stands of trees. Here, he pulled up and climbed from the box to hand Gwendolyn from the coach.

"This is a queer set-to and no mistake," he said. "Not so much as a stable boy come out to see who we is. What now, Miss Gwen?"

Before she could reply, Apollo sprang from the carriage and went racing off. Her commands that he stop were ignored, but luckily she was able to catch up with him and snatch the lead while he was distracted by the charms of a gorse bush. Out of breath, she glanced back. Tummet had secured the team and was hurrying to join her.

"What in the name of all the furies is *that?*" A short, chubby-faced and over-dressed young man came through the trees and drew back in alarm as Apollo strained at the end of his lead and barked shatteringly. There was no doubt that the newcomer was well bred, but it seemed to Gwendolyn that there was a dissolute air about him.

She spoke sternly to the dog, who lay down in the wet grass and grunted in a disappointed fashion. During the drive she had rehearsed a speech for such an occasion as this and dropping a slight curtsy she said, "Good day to you, sir. My dog's name is Apollo. I am Mrs. Oakenberry. My husband and I are on our way to Aldershot, and had stopped a short distance from here to obtain directions when our little boy wandered off, and"—she pressed a handkerchief to her lips—"and—we have not been able to find him!"

"Well, he ain't here."

She opened her eyes at this rudeness, and the young man had the grace to flush, and add, "That is to say, I live here, more's the pity, and—"

"You are the Earl of Yerville?"

"Lord, no! That's my father. Only he's in the shires and the house pretty well closed up till after Christmas. Even if he wasn't, you'd not pry him from his easel, I can tell you! Fancies himself an artist, silly old—" He broke off that improper remark and said a belated, "I am Sidney Yerville. Where's your husband, ma'am? Is that his decanter?"

Tummet, who had listened with admiration to Gwendolyn's sad tale, touched his brow respectfully, and said, "Begging yer pardon, Mr. Yerville, but the master's searching 'round the hamlet. He bade me bring some wine, in case the young master's come a cropper."

"Yes, indeed," said Gwendolyn. "Some children have just told me they were playing in your woods, and that they shut my son in some cellar room or other, and he won't be able to get out! 'Pon my soul, but I am faint with terror."

Yerville said derisively, "They've been hoaxing you, ma'am. Ain't no cellar rooms under the Abbey. M'grandfather had 'em all knocked into one great wine-cellar, and I promise you if children came near the place they'd be sent packing with a flea in their ear. That wine-cellar's Papa's pride and joy. Unless . . ." He paused, frowning. "I suppose they might've got into the ruins of the original abbey. But the locals believe they're haunted and most folks won't come within a mile of 'em even in broad daylight! The path is over there," he gestured vaguely to the densely wooded area on the eastern side of the hill "if you can find it. 'Tis overgrown as any jungle."

"Have we your permission to search about?" asked Gwendolyn. "I am fairly distracted!"

"Search all you wish." He looked towards the distant roof of a cottage. "I'd help, but I've an er, appointment." He grinned, and winked at Tummet, man-to-man fashion. "If your boy's like most young 'uns, he's likely having a May game with you. I'd not wander about too long, though, ma'am. The path by the river is slippery and can be treacherous. If you've not found your son by dusk, you'd best go up to the house and rouse someone to organize a search party. The assistant chef and my man and a few of the staff are here. They're a damned lazy lot, but if you make enough fuss they'll likely bestir themselves." He waved airily, and without a backward glance hurried off.

"A fine earl he'll make," said Tummet with disgust.

"Yes, but never mind that. Lord Kadenworthy said Mr. August was locked in an underground room, and I don't doubt the ruins are just the kind of place that horrid Reggie Smythe would choose!" She started towards the trees that Sidney Yerville had indicated, only to utter a moan of frustration as Apollo tore free again and went off at his ungainly prance across the meadow. "Oh, you wretched beast!" she exclaimed. "Come back at once! Apollo! Come!"

The hound did not come, but began to sniff around some boulders, then threw himself down and rolled about ecstatically with all his legs in the air. He was too elated to notice retribution approaching in the form of Tummet who managed to creep up and grab his lead. "Come on, you perishing monster," he growled, tugging. Apollo sat up and regarded him without warmth.

Gwendolyn had made some purchases at the tavern, and she flourished a piece of cheese. "Here, boy!"

All cooperation, Apollo sprang up and caught the tossed square of his favourite delicacy. "Found something choice to roll in, didn't you," grumbled Tummet, handing the lead to Gwendolyn. "You're s'posed to be finding yer master, you silly brute! Not wallering in something that smells 'orrid!"

"He evidently does not find it horrid." Gwendolyn patted the dog, then bent lower and sniffed. "Oh!" she gasped. "Oh, Tummet! 'Tis—'tis *incense!* I gave Mr. August a small box of incense sticks at the Overlake Lodge Fete and he slipped it into his pocket. You never think . . . ?"

He thought it most unlikely, but he didn't have the heart to discourage the poor little lady, and he said, "Ain't nothing impossible, Miss Gwen."

She dropped to her knees and peered about, then gave a squeal of excitement. "See! Only look here!"

A thin wisp of smoke wound from the base of the boulder.

They stared at each other, then they both began to push and tug until the boulder rolled over. Apollo, who had watched this endeavour with great interest, started to burrow furiously at the wet earth, his powerful paws sending clods of dirt flying in all directions.

"Look! Look!" shrieked Gwendolyn.

His eyes bright with excitement, Tummet said, " 'Pears like part of a stone wall under there, Miss Gwen!"

"Mr. Yerville said the ruins were over in those woods, but they may very well extend this far!" She clutched his arm. "Oh, Tummet! Mr. August might be right beneath us! Hurry! Do hurry!"

Despite her anxiety they were obliged to go slowly when they reached the woods, for the undergrowth was dense. Apollo had refused to come with them, preferring to roll about on the grass, but he suddenly shot past below them on a narrow path half hidden by a fallen tree.

"A spanking good guide 'e is! Be lucky if we can keep up wiv 'im!" Tummet took Gwendolyn's arm and they hurried after their canine pathfinder. When they reached the stream Sidney Yerville's warning proved justified; the ground became slippery, the path sloping ever downward until they were in a narrow defile, the walls shutting out the sky. Gwendolyn's hopes lifted slightly, but she was wracked by a growing sense of dread and limped along as fast as she could, clinging tightly to Tummet's hand. The stream veered off soon, and they came among ancient ruins, the dim light making it hard to see stone slabs that had fallen to litter the path. Tummet lifted Gwendolyn over several large chunks, but the obstructions presented no challenge to Apollo, who gamboled along, tail wagging, only to suddenly plunge off to the right and disappear.

Tummet panted, "Now what, Miss Gwen? Shall we follow the 'ound or—"

"What you'll do, my cove, is put up yer mauleys, 'fore I dishes yer!"

Gwendolyn gave a startled cry as a dark figure hove up ahead. The lower part of his face was covered by a black scarf, and one fist held a frighteningly large horse pistol aimed straight at them.

Tummet slipped a protective arm around Gwendolyn, and said

indignantly, "You got yerself lost, Mr. Rank Rider. No stage-coaches dahn 'ere, and no need to frighten the lady!"

The highwayman leaned closer. "Here, I know that voice," he said, his own voice a deep rumble. "Dang me ears and innards if it ain't old Tummy!" He stuck the pistol in his belt and put out a brawny fist.

"Dancer! Cor, love a duck!" Tummet shook hands and staggered as he was clapped heartily on the back. "Wot in the world is you doing 'ere, mate? Never say this is yer ken? Whoops—forgot! Miss Rossiter, this is me old chum, Tom. Knowed in the trade as the Dancing Master."

His "old chum" discarded the makeshift mask disclosing a round, surprisingly agreeable countenance and a pair of bright hazel eyes. He bowed with a flourish. "Pleased ter meetcha, marm, I'm sure."

To be formally introduced to a famous highwayman was a new experience for Gwendolyn, but she managed to conceal her astonishment and say a polite, if rather foolish, "How do you do?"

"Fairish, marm, fairish. If you'll just wait a bit, I'll light me lamp and you can both step inside me residence." He disappeared into the black aperture that yawned behind him, there was the scrape of flint and tinder and a moment later a lantern's glow revealed a stark, mouldering chamber with what appeared to be a passage beyond. The highwayman led them inside. "Daren't wait about here," he said. "I were just leaving."

"Fer good?" asked Tummet, still holding Gwendolyn's arm.

"Aye. Some slippery spy's gorn and found me ken—that's to say, me home, marm," Tom sighed. "I bin comfortable here, this last year and more. Not that I don't have to be careful, mindyer. But it's bin safe, give or take, and sorry I am to give it up."

He led them past other passages and yawning holes that long ago had been rooms. The lantern glow glistened on muddy paw prints on the stone floor, and the Dancing Master asked chattily, "That your dog, Tummy? A big fella, ain't he? Thought he was going to come for me, but orf he went. Here we is, mates." He stopped in a large untidy chamber in which had been assembled the rudiments of life: charred logs on what had once been a great hearth; a cot and tumbled blankets; a table and chairs, shelves holding cooking implements and provisions, and a variety of covered pots and bottles, plates and mugs and a few pieces of cutlery. "Home sweet home," he announced, with pride.

"Very nice," said Tummet. "What makes you think you bin spied on, Tom?"

"I'll show you." The highwayman led them across the room and into another passageway. Suddenly they were in daylight again as they entered a lean-to with two troughs, both empty, and a fine saddle propped on a bale of hay. The planks of the rear wall hung in shreds. "Kicked it dahn, drat him," said Tom disconsolately. "A beauty though, ain't he?"

Gwendolyn heard the hiss of Tummet's indrawn breath. She was incapable of speech. Through the shattered door she saw a fine chestnut horse grazing contentedly in a small clearing. Nearby, another animal grazed. A splendid black stallion, the pale light gleaming on his glossy coat.

Her numb lips formed the word soundlessly, "Andante!"

The last incense stick had burned itself out long hours ago, and he'd had to sing to stay awake and to keep up his courage. Long-forgotten songs from childhood; hymns he'd not thought of since he'd left school, croaked out in a strange unknown voice that shook—only because he was so terribly cold. It was stupid to sing, because it hurt his ribs, but it pushed back the crushing silence a little. Lord knows how long ago he had taken the last sip of the water he'd hoarded in the cup they'd left him. He was parched with thirst and so hungry that he began to think of the rats in a different light—a sure sign, he thought, shuddering, that he was losing his mind.

One thing he'd accomplished as a result of his endless scraping—it was less painful to breathe. The air was as foul, but he had made a tiny hole when a long sliver of mortar had crumbled and he'd been able to use his pencil to poke it through to the other room. It was a mixed blessing: it meant that the wall was not so thick here, but also that he had not found the locking mechanism. He could see no alleviation of the dense blackness when he tried to peep through the hole, but he knew it went all the way through because air came in, enabling him to draw a breath. Which was pointless, probably, and would only prolong his suffering.

He had constantly to fight against giving way to terror and despair. The certain knowledge that death was near could no longer be denied, but he wanted to face it proudly, not slobbering and mindless. He was haunted by tales he'd heard of people who'd been locked in some lost room, or had perhaps been buried alive, their bones coming to light long after all search for them had been abandoned. At school he'd read of a hapless lady whose husband had offended some king or other, and who had been shut up and left with her little son to starve in darkness. When found, there was every evidence that the poor creature had gone raving mad before she'd died. A fate that probably awaited him if— He caught himself up and forced his thoughts to Gwendolyn, and her dear gravity as she'd tried to instruct him about "li" . . .

Claws scratched his cheek. He'd slipped down the wall again! He dragged himself upright, jerking a hand across his eyes and uttering the rasping sound that was the closest he could come to a shout, and the rat scampered away.

How long had he fought them off in this freezing blackness? It seemed an eternity, but he'd be dead if it was an eternity. And oh, how he yearned to live! To be able to warn Papa of the League's trap. To tell Joel Skye about the whole ugly business. To see his love and his family and his friends again. And to find Reggie Smythe! Dwelling on what he'd like to do to that miserable wart sustained him for a while, but he found that he was sagging down again. If he allowed himself to sleep, he would escape this horror for a while. Perchance he'd wake to see Grandmama Natasha smiling at him. Or would Jamie stand between them and deny him the right to see her? Probably while throwing his wretched maxims about . . . 'Be done by as you did, August Falcon!' or some such rot. And there he went again, conveniently forgetting his own guilt, and that poor Jamie would be more than justified to lecture him! How could he forget what he'd done? Squirming, he pleaded, "I'm so sorry I sent you up there. I didn't mean it, Jamie. I was tricked. Smythe really killed you—not me. You'll let me see

Grandmama, won't you, Jamie? Please, dear old fellow . . ."

He seemed to lose touch with reality for a space and when he awoke he was dead at last, because he heard Grandmama Natasha calling his name.

"August? Are you there?"

Couldn't she see him? Come to think about it, was heaven this dark? Grandmama was in heaven, no doubt of that, so why—

Ah, but there was light now. Just a tiny beam—the finger of an angel reaching out to him, probably. When it touched him, his side would stop hurting, and this hellish thirst would be quenched. Awed, he whispered, "Grandmama?"

"Guv? Answer us, for Gawd's sake!"

Falcon blinked. *Tummet?*

A rat raced across his legs and he flailed at it with a renewed surge of strength. "Get away, damn your filthy hide!"

A shriek. A joyous shout.

They'd *found* him!

Oh, my dear God!

They'd *come!*

An ear-splitting screeching sound, a rumble, a blinding light. He blinked behind a hand half-raised against the sudden glare, but he recognized the Smallest Rossiter, running to him, tears streaming down her face.

Half-sobbing, half-laughing, she cried, "August . . . my darling! How like you to . . . to swear at us when . . . we come! Oh, Tummet! He's alive! He's *alive!*"

Soft, warm arms about him; smacking kisses on his bristly cheek; hands caressing him, holding him close—blessedly, wonderfully close. Dazed, scarcely daring to believe, he clung to her and tried to speak, but his throat was choked with emotion, his teeth chattered with the cold, and he couldn't say a word. She was murmuring repeatedly that it was all right now, and not to try to talk—it was all right. He knew that Apollo was racing about madly, scattering small shapes in all directions. Tummet patted his head in clumsy but affectionate comforting while growling curses under his breath and saying in a very gruff voice that he'd like to get his hands round someone's throat. A stranger was there; a big man who hovered about with a flare in his hand, but he couldn't seem to see who it was. Everything was very blurred and fragmentary and wonderful. And he was so grateful, so unspeakably thankful . . . If he could only stop shaking . . . If he could only tell them . . .

🌼

It was really Apollo who found you." Gwendolyn had to struggle to keep her voice steady as she tended Falcon's hurts with the medical supplies that the Dancing Master kept in his "ken." The shock of finding him in that stifling ghastly room, his haggard, beard-stubbled face and terribly battered condition, but most of all the look of horror that was still not gone from his eyes, would haunt her for as long as she lived. After Tummet had given him a few swallows of the brandy the terrible convulsive shuddering had eased somewhat, but he'd seemed dazed and not quite aware until the two men had supported him back to this room. They'd sat him at the Dancing Master's table and, cautiously, they'd satisfied his craving for water, and between water and brandy and the bread and cheese he was now trying not to eat too ravenously, he was looking much better. He seemed incapable of speech, however, gazing from one to the other of them with a look of humble rapture that wrung her heart, so that she had told their story first to give him a chance to recover himself.

"We were going back out to the path," she went on, bathing a bite in his arm. "We'd hoped to find a way into the ruins farther along, but Apollo went rushing off down a pitch bla— er, a side passage. Mr. Dancer told us he'd once explored along there and that it went on and on into what he'd guessed to be some ancient dungeons."

"So we follered Apollo, on the off-chance 'e were arter that there incense he was so took with," put in Tummet eagerly. "We come up in a reg'lar maze of dungeons. 'Twould 'ave took us years to find you, Guv. But that there 'ound follered 'is nose, and soon we could smell the incense too."

Falcon thought, 'The incense you gave me, my love.' He smiled at Gwendolyn but she was blurred and again there came the fear that he would wake to find this was just another dream, so that he reached out and touched her cheek anxiously. She was really here, thank God! And good old Tummet. And there was so much he wanted to say to them. But how could he make them know what it had been like, trapped in that foul impenetrable blackness, suffocating from the lack of air, crushed by the even more dreadful silence? How explain the paralyzing alone-ness, or the fear?

Gwendolyn felt him shudder, and read something of it in his eyes. She nestled against that trembling hand and kissed it, winking away tears because of the splintered nails and lacerated fingers.

"It must have been a miracle that you had it with you," she gulped. "Apollo loved the scent and followed it to a tiny room behind the one where you . . . were."

"And there was a great rusted old lever in the wall," put in Tummet. "And the smell of that there incense strong 'round it. So Dancer and me give it a tug, and stap me if the wall didn't come open, and there you was! If ever I see such a perishing 'ole, without no doors and no light, and no air neither! And all them rats! Gawd! I'd 'ave gone orf me tibby in—" He broke off as Gwendolyn nudged him sharply.

The shock and ecstasy of rescue were merging into exhaustion now, and for Falcon the room had become smaller and smaller, the outer areas fading into a dim mistiness. His head nodded, but he fought sleep away and slumped in the chair, ecstatically breathing the cold and clean air and the heavenly smell of rain; glorying in their dear and familiar voices, and in the knowledge that they had cared enough to . . . to search for him . . .

His shirt felt odd, and he discovered he was wearing a garment several sizes too big, but clean and freshly ironed. He didn't seem to remember them doing these things for him. Confused, he knew there was something he'd meant to say; something important. He began hoarsely, "You are so good . . ."

Gwendolyn had been brushing his coat, and she put it down and knelt beside him. "Your own shirt was in rags and so dirty and Mr. Dancer very kindly loaned you one of his." She touched his side lightly. "My poor dear—what a frightful bruise! Does it hurt very badly?"

"It doesn't matter, now that— What I mean is— I don't know how—how I shall ever be able to thank you for coming to find me. I never dared hope . . . That is, I did not expect you would forgive me . . . for—for what I did to poor . . . Morris."

She held his hand and said in her gentlest voice, "Jamie told us that he slipped. And Tummet thinks—we both believe you were drugged."

"Yes, I was." He sighed. "But—that won't bring Jamie back, will it? I am still the man who—who killed him!"

She exchanged a startled glance with Tummet, and exclaimed, "But—dear one, Jamie is not dead."

The faint colour that had returned to Falcon's drawn face drained away. He stammered, "But—but I saw his sister come, and J-Jamie said his family was only to be told if— Gwen?" He searched her face frantically, then turned to Tummet. "For the love of God—do not try to spare me!"

"The lieutenant's sister come to London to shop," explained the valet, "and 'eard 'bout the doo-ell, and that's why she come calling. Mr. Morris is alive, Guv, but Doc Sir Jim says—"

"That he is going along much better than we dared to hope," interpolated Gwendolyn hurriedly.

It was too much. Overcome, Falcon bowed his head into his hands.

Gwendolyn stroked his hunched shoulder and said gently, "My poor dear. Is that why you went off all alone, without a word to any of us?"

He mumbled, "I wanted to try in—in some small way to—"

With a thunder of big paws, a flapping of ears, and some happy panting, Apollo raced into the room and hurled himself at his master.

Tummet howled; Gwendolyn gave a shocked cry as she was staggered; Falcon uttered an involuntary shout and doubled up, clutching his side. The sudden sharp pain wiped the haze from his mind. Straightening as Tummet chased the exuberant hunter outside, he gasped, "Jupiter! What am I doing? What day is this?"

"Why—'tis Thursday, my dear, but—"

"Dear Lord! What is the hour?"

Tummet came back in and tugged out a large silver pocket

watch. "Five and twenty minutes to two o'clock, Guv!"

Falcon dragged himself to his feet.

Standing also, Gwendolyn protested, "August! You must rest!"

"I must get to Ashleigh! I may already be too late! Tummet—is Andante—"

" 'E's outside, Guv, and frisky as any colt. And if yer thinking on riding 'im dahn to Sussex—"

"Nonsense!" Gwendolyn clung to Falcon's arm. "You cannot even stand up straight! Tummet, he is delirious! We must not let him kill himself!"

Falcon said, "Should you prefer that your father be executed?" He saw her become perfectly white, and went on grimly, "My sire hosts a surprise party at Ashleigh this evening. The parents or brothers of the men who have helped Gideon fight the League have been invited, which will surprise Papa, for none of them are on his guest list. The invitations are forgeries sent out by the League of Jewelled Men!"

Maria Barthélemy's pale worried face came into Gwendolyn's mind. This must be the party she had spoken of. She asked in bewilderment, "But—but why would the League trick our parents into going to a party at Ashleigh?"

"Because the guests my lamentable father *has* invited include Gordie Chandler's madcap Jacobite brother, and Prince Charles Stuart! Association with either is punishable by death. And unless I mistake it, dragoons have been informed of the business and are likely already on their way to arrest the lot of 'em!"

Gwendolyn gave a gasp of fright.

"And that," muttered Enoch Tummet, "leaves the devil to pay, and no pitch 'ot!"

Daylight was fading to dusk when the coach rattled over the old hump-backed bridge and bounced onto the ground again with a jolt that almost threw Falcon from the seat. Accustomed to the atrocious roads, he awoke and blinked drowsily at the dim-seen countryside.

His revelation of the deadly threat at Ashleigh had spurred an immediate rebellion in the Dancing Master's "establishment," during which his intention to ride post-haste for Sussex had been rejected out of hand by both a determined Smallest Rossiter and an equally determined Enoch Tummet. There were too many lives at stake, they'd argued, for their fate to be entrusted to one man, especially a man in such a weakened and exhausted condition that he would most certainly topple from the saddle before coming anywhere near his objective. Instead, Gwendolyn and Tummet would drive to Ashleigh, and Falcon could snatch a short rest before starting to London and the Horse Guards. To this plan, he in turn had said a flat and emphatic "No!" If the League had its mercenaries stationed all about the estate, and if the military was already en route, the only hope of getting through such a blockade was to approach Ashleigh by stealth. He knew every inch of the property; every hidden way onto the grounds, every curve of the river, every cove in the coastline. He alone could hope to elude the watchers and then gain access to the great house without betraying his arrival. He had also dismissed Gwendolyn's alternative plan in which Tummet would drive the coach down to Ashleigh so that Falcon could sleep en route, while she would go to the Horse Guards alone.

They'd been so intent on a swift resolution of their difficulties that they'd not noticed when the Dancing Master returned. He'd announced his presence by remarking that dang him if he'd ever heard of such wickedness, and he'd do whatever he might to help "old England." He had gone on to remark that they would be the better for another coach and horses and offered to go and "borrow" these articles from the Yerville stables. Tummet had assisted in this illicit enterprise while Falcon appropriated the highwayman's razor and shaved himself hurriedly. The two men had returned to report contemptuously that the earl's remaining servants were all "drunk as lords," and had shown very little interest in the theft of their employer's property.

The end of it was that Gwendolyn and Tummet had set off to London in the Earl of Yerville's elegant but ponderous equipage, while Falcon, his faster carriage tooled by a highwayman, had benefitted from a few hours of deep sleep.

His side was no less painful now, but he felt inestimably

refreshed and his head was clear again. He saw that they were far past Haslemere, for a fading band of gold streaked the darkening skies, and looming black and distant against it was a great fortification that could only be Arundel Castle. He called to Dancer and when the coach stopped climbed out and advised that they were dangerously close to Ashleigh and ran the risk of encountering the Squire's men at any second. The highwayman was reluctant to let him go on alone, but fearing that the coach may already have been seen, Falcon sent him off on the Brighthelmstone road while he himself slipped silently into the trees.

It was just past five o'clock, and every second increased the risk of the arrival of the military. He could only pray that the troop would wait so as to be sure that all the traitors were in the trap before they sprang it; and that somehow he would get there before them. The woods were dark and hushed and the need for haste desperate, but he resisted the impulse to run, and instead crept along. His caution was justified. All too soon he heard the murmur of voices to his left; a muffled laugh, and the snapping of twigs under booted feet. Then, from the right came a squelch, an irked exclamation, and a soft but forceful flood of French deploring the "sodden English lands."

They were all about him; but they were watchful and waiting, which meant the dragoons had not yet arrived.

He crouched at the base of a tree considering his next move, then caught his breath as a man passed within a yard of him.

It was perilously close, and he dare not fail. He pulled off his boots and Dancer's coat and shoved them cautiously under a shrub. Then, with every nerve strained and taut, he crept forward. There was only one chance, and it would tax his strength and endurance to the limit. But surely, Grandmama Natasha had spoken for him, else he'd still be dying by inches in that hellish cellar—with the rats.

A splash. A London voice snarling, "Quiet, damn yer eyes! Fotheringay's got ears like a hawk!"

So Mariner was in command of the dragoons. One wondered for how long he'd known of the plot, and if it was chance that at the fete he'd enquired, "How is your father, by the way?" And if it was also chance that the remark had so haunted him.

The hurrying voice of the river was close by. Papa had taught him to swim when he was a very small boy, and with the river bordering the estate and the Channel so close, most of the summers of his youth had been spent more in the water than on land. But he'd been in his teens then, and in perfect condition, and the days had been warm, and he'd been able to stop whenever he wished. Now he was not exactly in perfect condition, and it was a cold November night and he had a long way to go.

Here was the bank at last! He shivered as he lowered himself into the icy water. The tug of the current was hard and immediate. The rains had brought the river high.

At least, he thought, his teeth beginning to chatter again, the cold might numb his confounded side . . .

CHAPTER XVII

This is maddening!" Gwendolyn turned in her chair to look up at Tummet, who stood wooden and expressionless beside her. "We have been waiting in this stupid room for hours! Why do they not allow me to speak to the silly man?"

Actually, they had arrived twenty minutes earlier, but each moment seemed an hour to Gwendolyn. Constantly thwarted by the state of the roads, they had persevered and reached London at dusk. They'd taken one swift detour to Rossiter Court, but had found neither Newby nor Gideon at home, and Gwendolyn's heart had sunk when she'd learned that her father was "away with friends." She had sent lackeys scurrying about Town to find her brothers and desire that they join her at East India House. In her anxiety it had not occurred to her that her gown was badly creased, her shoes muddy, and her hair dishevelled. Those all-important details had been noted at first glance, however, by the succession of minor officials to whom she had been referred, and who had attempted, unsuccessfully, to dismiss her.

The important middle-aged gentleman, impressive in Company uniform, in whose office they now waited had barely concealed his disapproval. Lord Hayes, he said with a lofty smile, was not to be disturbed. Lieutenant Skye, my lord's aide-de-camp, was in conference and there was no telling when he would emerge.

Seething, Gwendolyn rose to her feet and announced, "I cannot wait about like this! 'Tis vital that I speak with Lieutenant Skye—*at once!*"

The already arched brows of the important gentleman arched higher. "Perhaps you could divulge the nature of your business?"

" 'Tis a matter of life and death!"

His amused glance flickered over Tummet and confirmed that the fellow was also creased and dishevelled, and looked more like a pugilist than a personal footman, or whatever he was supposed to be. "In that case, ma'am," he drawled, "you should rather take the matter to Bow Street."

Ever more irked, Gwendolyn said, "There is to be an assassination attempt on the Prince and Princess of Wales!"

"Is—er, that a fact? Well, well. Then I'd suggest, ma'am, that the Horse Guards would be a more suitable location to—"

"I am acquainted with Lieutenant Skye," she snarled, gritting her teeth. "And he is most anxious to hear my news. I *demand* that you announce me!"

The important gentleman was also acquainted with Lieutenant Skye, though only during business hours, and he could not envision that dashing young officer enjoying a dalliance with a lady who went about Town with muddy shoes and her hair all anyhow. He smiled politely, and returned to the important letter he was writing, which was a request for an extra day off at Christmas time. "I am sure the lieutenant will tell me if you are expected, ma'am," he murmured.

Tummet took a deep breath, stepped forward and began to sing at the top of his lungs:

> *"On a sunny morn, when we set sail*
> *And the ship not far from land,"*

"Stop that noise at once!" demanded the important gentleman, his face reddening as he sprang to his feet. "Are you gone—"

Tummet roared louder,

> *"When I did spy a fair pretty maid*
> *With a comb and a glass in 'er 'and!"*

"Be—*Quiet*!" howled the important gentleman, tearing his hair.

Tummet sang louder and, delighted, Gwendolyn joined the chorus in her clear soprano:

> *"While the raging seas did roar,*
> *And the stormy winds did blow—"*

"DESIST!" roared the important gentleman, adding to the din.

"What the *devil* . . . ?" Sub-lieutenant Joel Skye wrenched open the door of the inner office.

Beyond him, Gwendolyn saw Gideon, Tio Glendenning, and Peregrine Cranford gathered around a map table. She ran past the astonished Skye and hurled herself into her brother's arms. "Thank heaven," she cried. "Gideon, I must see you *at once*! We found out who the Squire is, and—"

"Did you, by Jove!" Lord Hayes was coming in, the important gentleman's goggling eyes shut out as he closed the door. "We must hear this, ma'am!"

They all crowded around, and Skye asked eagerly, "What of those fellows Rossiter brought in from Bristol, my lord? Is there a hope we can charge them?"

The mighty East India Company Director relaxed his lined face into a rare smile and turned to Gideon, "Thanks to you and your friends, those treacherous rogues are convinced their entire scheme is known. How you did it is beyond me, but they're falling over themselves to betray each other, hoping to win transportation rather than the gallows." He frowned suddenly. "When I think of the positions of trust they held, and so mercilessly abused—!" He squared his thin shoulders and said in a lighter tone, "Well, I suspect we've only begun to see that ugly web unfold—but unfold it will, I promise you! And we've you young fellows to thank for it!"

" 'Twas August Falcon gave us the clue we needed," said Owen Furlong.

Rossiter added, "And Captain Jonathan Armitage who followed it."

"Hum," said the Director. "Now, my dear lady, pray sit down and tell us your story."

"Well, I will," said Gwendolyn. "But you must promise me, my lord, that my brother and his friends will escort me home then, for I have also some personal news of great importance to them all."

Gideon looked at her sharply, the triumph in his lean face fading into uncertainty.

Lord Hayes nodded. "Agreed. Now—who is this mysterious Squire, and how did you unmask the wretched creature?"

"His name is Reginald Smythe," she said, and over-riding their stunned exclamations, she rushed on. "He has hundreds of men scattered throughout the southern counties. At this very moment August Falcon is risking his life to try and stop them, but if he—if he fails, they mean to stage a full-fledged revolt." She held up her hand for quiet. "It will begin at Leicester House, with the assassination of the Prince and Princess of Wales, and—"

All, then, was pandemonium.

Devilish odd, if you were to ask me!" Sir Brian Chandler stood with his back to the fire in Ashleigh's smaller withdrawing room, his aristocratic features betraying annoyance. He was tall and distinguished, rather too thin, and with a pallor that spoke of indifferent health. Intensely patriotic, he had been heart-broken two years ago when he'd discovered that his younger (and favourite) son was a Jacobite rebel, and terrified when that reckless individual had almost paid with his life for his allegiance to the Stuart Cause. Quentin Chandler was safely in France now, but Sir Brian's doctors forbade him the Channel crossing and he'd not yet seen his baby granddaughter. In fact, he seldom left Lac Brillant, his great estate near Dover, and to have journeyed almost a hundred and fifty miles over frightful roads on an invitational he'd felt it impossible to refuse had tired him. To have then been met with what he'd sensed was more shock than delight had at first astonished, and then enraged, him.

He glanced at the men assembled in the luxurious room. He was well acquainted with Sir Mark Rossiter and the Earl of Bowers-Malden, both of whom looked as annoyed as he was himself. He had not previously met Piers Cranford, a handsome young man, astonishingly like his twin, Peregrine; nor did he know Captain Derek Furlong, younger brother to Sir Owen, who had recently brought his East Indiaman into Bristol Harbour. Both were well-bred young fellows of good family and it was understandable that they should refrain from criticizing their host, a man twenty years their senior. Unfettered by such restraints Sir Brian said impatiently, "Am I the only one to have gained the impression I wasn't expected at all? Be damned if Neville's jaw didn't drop a foot when he walked into the hall as I arrived! Have I the straight of it, gentlemen? This *is* a surprise party for our sons—no?"

Derek Furlong nodded, his sun-bronzed face anxious. "And our brothers, sir. Cranford's and mine, that is."

Sitting on a deep sofa before the fire, Bowers-Malden boomed, "It appeared to me that the party was a surprise for Neville also. The butler put me in here, and when Neville came to greet me, he looked as if he couldn't believe his eyes!"

They all, it seemed, had received the same impression.

"If that's the case, by Jupiter, I'll hear it from him!" said Sir Brian angrily. "And I'll not be fobbed off by some slippery-tongued butler!" He set down his glass and marched to the door.

The corridor seemed remarkably devoid of servants. Any great house was well supplied with footmen and maids, and whatever Neville Falcon's eccentricities, this was most decidedly a great house. Increasingly astonished as he wandered past a succession of darkened, unheated rooms, Sir Brian thought, 'Be dashed if the entire place isn't deserted!' A possible explanation dawned. He scowled at a splendid candelabrum in the stair hall and advised it explosively that the scatterwitted Neville had forgot the date of the party and had installed one of his confounded lightskirts in the house! Fuming, he lit a candle, stamped up the handsome staircase, and was just about to shout a demand for his host when he heard voices. Male voices, holding a note of urgency. If this really was a hoax, Falcon would get a proper flea in his ear! He flung open the door to a large study. "Neville, I'll know what the deuce—" he began, and stopped short.

The dozen or so gentlemen in the brilliantly lit room had whipped around to face him. He was vaguely aware that a short dark man held a levelled pistol, and that one of the group was tall and with a commanding air of pride about him. His eyes were fixed on another man, however; a handsome, well set-up individual with a lean, high-cheekboned face and a pair of brilliant green eyes. Shock staggered him. He whispered, "*Quentin!*" And then strong arms were about him; a beloved and so-missed voice was saying huskily, "Papa! Oh, dear sir—you should not be here!"

Someone said harshly, "Falcon, what the devil—"

Neville Falcon stammered, "Sir—I don't know how— I mean I cannot imagine what—"

A cool voice drawled, "Are we betrayed?"

The word cut through Sir Brian's dizzying joy. He released his son and jerked around.

Quentin said helplessly, "Sir, may I present my father, Sir Brian Chandler? Papa this gentleman is—Baron Renfrew, of Paris, and—"

"The devil he is," growled Sir Brian staring at a lean, handsome face and a pair of steady hazel eyes. "He is Prince Charles Stuart! Neville, you fool! Have you dragged us all into a treasonable conspiracy?"

A plump gentleman in his middle fifties, Neville Falcon was pale and aghast, but he drew himself up and said, "I'll be frank with you, Sir Brian, I cannot guess what brings you and the others here, but you must leave at once, or—"

There was an immediate chorus of protest. Recognizing most of those present at this deadly meeting, Sir Brian was not surprised when an extremely wealthy industrialist exclaimed fiercely, "The devil they must!"

Beside him, a renowned diplomat high in the favour of King George said with matching heat, "And betray us all, and His Highness to the first dragoon they meet? I say—no, sir!"

"You are already betrayed."

The new voice brought all heads turning to the door and the

butler, who supported a bedraggled and sagging figure, soaked, mud-covered, and clearly in the last stages of exhaustion.

Neville Falcon gave a cry of dismay, "August! My God, boy— what on earth—"

"I'm sorry, sir," said the butler, much agitated, "but he was crawling across the terrace, and in such terrible condition, and when I recognized Mr. August and he demanded to see you at once— Well, sir. Life and death, he said 'twas."

Quentin Chandler ran for the brandy decanter. August was deposited gently onto a sofa and Neville sent his butler to fetch hot water and blankets.

The Prince came to look down on the battered wreck and said compassionately, "My poor fellow, are you able to explain what happened to you and how we are betrayed?"

August could barely hold his head up and was quite unable to take the glass Quentin offered. He gulped down a mouthful when his father knelt and held the brandy to his lips. "No time to explain," he panted. "Estate's surrounded. Dragoons . . . here any second." He turned a grim gaze on his hovering father. "Sir . . . what in hell you were thinking of— No, never mind that. Take your . . . friends down . . . smuggler's path . . . my boat . . . *Now!* Or, we're all . . . dead!"

Without a word Neville led the Prince and his companions from the room. Sir Brian followed, Quentin's arm across his shoulders.

Scant minutes later, the butler rushed into the room, white-faced. "Dragoons, Mr. August! Coming up the drive-path!"

*T*reason?" bellowed the Earl of Bowers-Malden, rising to his impressive height and dwarfing even the tall colonel. "Be damned to you, Fotheringay! Since when is it treasonable to attend a surprise party?"

The colonel strode across the withdrawing room followed by a lieutenant and two troopers. He said coldly, "Since a member of the party chances to be Prince Charles Edward Stuart, my lord!" His lip curled as he took in their stupefied expressions. "But, I've no doubt you will deny all knowledge of the presence of His Highness!"

"You're wits to let!" said Sir Mark Rossiter.

Piers Cranford, plagued by a premonition that there was a vengeful hand behind this business, said, "My brother was maimed at Prestonpans, Colonel. You may be very sure I'd have no part of any meeting with a Stuart! And nor, I doubt, would the rest of these gentlemen."

"I demand to know what brought you here on such a wild goose chase," said Derek Furlong.

"Some blockhead playing a prank, I'll warrant," snorted the earl.

"Like the prank Viscount Glendenning played on Major Broadbent in June?" purred Fotheringay.

Bowers-Malden's eyes became veiled. In June his heir had barely avoided being arrested and charged with high treason. He had escaped execution so narrowly that just to remember it brought sweat starting onto the earl's brow. He said, "I fancy you've as much proof of this tom-foolery as you had then!"

Fotheringay bowed slightly. "When my men are finished searching this house, my lord, we'll see how—"

Very white, his lips twitching nervously, Neville Falcon hurried into the room. Sir Mark Rossiter turned on him in a fury, but before he could speak, Falcon exclaimed, "Thank God you've come, Colonel! It's this way, if you please."

They all stared at him for a frozen moment of bewilderment, then Fotheringay allowed himself to be ushered to the door, pausing only to instruct the lieutenant that no one was to leave the house.

A sergeant, clattering down the stairs with a jingling of spurs and the stamp of glossy boots, came to attention and saluted. "No sign of anyone, sir. 'Cepting the poor gent upstairs."

It was not what Fotheringay wanted, or had expected to hear. His thin lips tightened. He barked, "The estate runs down to the river. Make damned sure all boats were seized!"

Neville's heart bounced painfully. He said, "You look in the wrong place, Colonel. This way!"

Entering the main withdrawing room with his rapid springing

stride, Fotheringay paused, frowning at the unrecognizable figure on the sofa. "What the deuce . . ." He bent above the limp form and the eyes opened and blinked at him dazedly. "My God! August? I thought you had more sense than to ally yourself with that Stuart—"

"No such thing, Mariner," muttered August. "No Stuarts. Trap. League of—of Jewelled Men."

"Rubbish! You'll not fob me off with some mud and that mystical League of yours! Come now, man, let's hear some truth for a—"

August managed to get an elbow under him and dragged himself up only to clutch his side and sink back, swearing feebly.

His father unbuttoned his shirt, and both men gasped when they saw the great blackened bruise across his ribs. "My God!" said Neville, horrified. "However did you manage to get here?"

August reached out and seized Fotheringay's hand in an icy grip. "Mariner, you *must* listen!"

"Aye, while your traitorous friends make their escape!" Fotheringay pulled away, but August clung desperately so that he was dragged from the sofa and sprawled, groaning, on the floor.

Neville rushed to take him in his arms. "For shame, Fotheringay! The boy's badly hurt! Have some compassion!"

Fotheringay liked August. He flushed darkly and bent to help lift him. "My apologies. You should have let go. Now I must—"

August gripped his swordbelt "You'll have to—to kill me first! Mariner—I *beg* you! If you've any love for—for England . . . Give me two minutes—no more . . . And you may be a general 'fore the—the year's out!"

Fotheringay could not fail to be impressed. Clearly the man was in much pain, clearly he'd been very badly handled. Frowning, he hesitated.

August was so weary he could scarcely find the words, but he fought to stay awake and gasped out, "I've proof now. Know who they all are . . . can show you where their forts are . . . throughout . . . southland. This was to've been the signal . . ."

Five minutes later it was very silent in the big room. Neville Falcon looked down at his son in awe. August, who had improvised somewhat upon the true facts, had gone his length and could only lie very still and keep his failing gaze locked on the wavering blur that was the colonel's hawk face.

Fotheringay said harshly, "So to set this seditious ball rolling, I was to ride out with your father and friends under close arrest, eh? And what of the rogues who were—er, "masquerading" as Prince Charles and his friends and supporters? How am I to arrest you if they cannot be found?"

There came the staccato cracks of a volley of distant gunfire.

Fotheringay sprinted from the room and along the corridor. When he reached the ground floor the front door burst open and a trooper ran in and reported breathlessly, "Big group of—men, sir! Dunno where they come—from! Boat slipped past in—in dark!"

"Dammitall! You fumble-fingers let them escape?"

"They—they must be on the river, sir! Mayhap we can catch—"

"By the time we get a frigate after 'em, they'll be half-way to France!" Fotheringay glared at the silent knot of gentlemen who watched from the door of the small withdrawing room. "*Sergeant!*" he shouted.

The sergeant leapt to his side. "Yessir!"

"Order the men back and into the house! Lieutenant, we will need some of those silken ropes we brought. These gentlemen are all under arrest!"

Gwendolyn awoke when she heard running footsteps on the stairs. It was still dark, and her heart began to pound wildly as she threw back the blankets and shrugged into the dressing gown she'd left lying on the foot of the bed. The door burst open, and the room brightened as Gideon came straight to her, a branch of candles in one hand.

He looked pale and haggard and she flew to embrace him, babbling, "You're back so soon! What happened? What is the hour? Did you find Papa?"

He put down the candelabrum and said gravely, " 'Tis past five o'clock. We must have passed them on the way. When we reached Ashleigh 'twas already in the hands of the Squire's men. At least a hundred of the bounders!"

Her knees seemed to melt, and she clung to him, searching his face distractedly. "And—and my father? August?"

Gently, he led her to a fireside chair and dropped to one knee beside it. "We couldn't get onto the grounds, love. A villager told us that a troop of dragoons went off with a baker's dozen fine gentlemen riding with their hands tied, and two who were allowed to travel in a carriage."

She felt faint, and said threadily, "Heaven help them! Then Colonel Fotheringay must have caught them with the Prince! Which—which means that August did not—Oh, Gideon! Are they in . . . the Tower?"

"I'm afraid they are." He pressed her hand as she gave a smothered sob, and said, "Courage, dearest! I am going there now. I thought—Well, if things look bad, I thought you might want to break the news to Katrina."

She said despairingly, "How can I when I don't know what to tell her? August . . . August may be . . . killed! And her father—"

"I know, love," he said, as her voice failed. "But you can at least warn her."

"I must come with you first. They're innocent, Gideon! And—and after all we've done! You and Johnny Armitage and the others finding out about those terrible men in Bristol, and bringing them back to London to stand trial! 'Twill prove everything you said about the cargoes being stolen and the ships scuttled—will it not?"

"Eventually, yes, dear. But—"

"And only think how much August discovered, so that I could warn Lord Hayes about the Prince and Princess of Wales, and the League's wicked plans. Surely, the Horse Guards will believe 'twas a trap? That Papa and—and the rest are not Jacobites? They *will* believe us, won't they Gideon?"

He smiled into her frightened eyes, and said reassuringly, "Of course they will, love. Come now, we must hasten. The others went straight to the Tower."

It was still dark when they hurried out to the waiting coach, but the city was already stirring. Farm waggons rumbled over the cobblestones to Covent Garden, cattle were being herded to market, servants hurried to assume their daily tasks, baker's shops sent mouth-watering aromas drifting on the chilly air, candles were brightening more and more windows, and smoke began to rise from thousands of chimney pots.

As the coach wound its way through the awakening streets, Gwendolyn was praying fervently for her father and for the man she loved. At length, she said in a very small voice, "If they really were caught with Prince Charles, will the King be merciful, do you think, Gideon? Because of—of all we've done, I mean."

He thought of the inexorable laws against high treason; of the panic that had gripped London in 'forty-five when the Jacobites had marched as far as Derby; and of the relentless slaughter of people who had done far less than conspire with the Scottish Prince. But he said quietly, "I hope he will, Gwen. We must pray that he will."

Minutes later a stern-faced Yeoman Warder conducted them across a cobbled courtyard in the mighty old Keep known as the Tower of London. Through a great frowning gate they went, and across another court. Gwendolyn's blood ran cold when she saw the dreaded Traitor's Gate and she wondered if her dear father had come here by that route, as had so many doomed aristocrats down through the centuries.

They were taken up worn steps and into a cold and gloomy building that Gideon whispered was the Beauchamp Tower. A lieutenant of dragoon guards took them in charge here, and conducted them to a door which he flung open, announcing, "Captain and Miss Rossiter, sir."

A general, Colonel Mariner Fotheringay, and four civilian gentlemen, all looking rumpled and owly-eyed, were gathered around a table, listening intently to the man seated there. A bowed figure, his dark head propped wearily on one hand, his voice halting and slurred. With a muffled sob, Gwendolyn flew to his side. "August! Oh, thank God!"

He looked up at her, joy coming into his drawn face.

Fotheringay performed some hurried introductions. Gwendolyn found that she was in the company of a distinguished cabinet minister, a renowned and powerful member of the House of

Lords, an equally renowned Member of Parliament, and a distinguished diplomatist. General Early, a stocky and fierce-looking individual wearing an ill-fitting uniform, bowed over her hand. "We owe you a great vote of thanks, ma'am. Mr. Falcon has filled in many details for us, but we are well aware that had it not been for you, he'd not have lived to do so."

Gideon demanded harshly, "What of my father, sir? I trust you realize he had nothing to do with—"

Lord Tiberville interrupted in a high-pitched irritable voice, "Your father and his friends were brought here under close arrest, Captain." A twitching smile dawned. "Just as that damnable League had hoped."

Sir Jonas Holmesby, elegant despite an untidy wig and creased coat, said, "They've enjoyed a hearty meal and are comfortably abed, ma'am. At this stage of the game we don't want our treacherous Squire to know that, however."

Gwendolyn caught her breath. "Do you say you believe us at last?"

"We do, indeed, Miss Rossiter." Henry Church, M.P., who had a reputation for belligerence, barked, "Better late than never!"

"Shall you be able to stop the revolt, General?" asked Gideon. "If Falcon's right, there's very little time."

General Early growled, "You should be aware, Rossiter, that the Army can move fast when there's need. At this moment we have despatch riders racing to every installation this curst seditious lot threatens. We'll have cavalry and dragoons ready for any attack in ample time, I promise you!"

"And what of the planned assassinations, sir?"

"Our agents will impersonate the Prince and Princess. We'll be on the alert to arrest four officers of the King's Guard—which they're not, of course—the instant they ride towards Leicester House. Our infamous Reginald Smythe will find he's shot his bolt, Captain! Thanks to you and Miss Rossiter, we—"

"And Mr. Falcon." Gwendolyn put her hand proudly on August's shoulder.

"Ar-humph," said the general gruffly. "Of course. Falcon. Quite so."

CHAPTER XVIII

ondon awoke to a brisk Friday morning of blue skies, pale sunlight and the start of a shocking series of events that was to turn the great city into a maelstrom of excitement and alarm. The newspapers carried shocking accounts of a treasonable plot and of numerous aristocratic gentlemen having been arrested in Sussex and conveyed to the Tower under heavy guard. Names were conspicuous by their absence. When rumours began to circulate that they had included Prince Charles Edward Stuart and the Earl of Bowers-Malden, angry crowds formed on the streets, and a near-riot ensued when the word spread like wildfire that there had been an assassination attempt on the Prince and Princess of Wales.

Interest shifted to Leicester House, and the *Spectator* put out a late edition that unleashed more consternation. The front page was devoted to an article by Mr. Ramsey Talbot stating that a wide-spread plot to topple the government had been foiled by a courageous group of young patriots led by Captain Gideon Rossiter, heir to Sir Mark Rossiter. Thanks to prompt and efficient action by the Horse Guards, the would-be murderers of the Prince and Princess had been seized before they could carry out their wicked scheme, and during questioning they had incriminated many fellow conspirators. Furthermore, the traitors conveyed to the Tower the previous evening had not, it appeared, been the gentlemen first suspected. Rather, those actually incarcerated included Lord Hibbard Green, Mr. Rudolph Bracksby, and Mr. Joseph Montgomery. Warrants had been issued for the arrest of others suspected of involvement in the plot, including the alleged leader, a gentleman well known about Town, (and here the *Spectator* was obliged to use initials only,) Mr. R———— S————, and two influential and highly born sisters, the Ladies J———— Y————, and C———— B————. According to Mr. Talbot's reliable sources, among those sought for questioning were the philanthropist Viscount R———— E————; Lord K———— M———— of Cornwall; and Marshal J.-J. B———— of France.

The final name was a bombshell. To dislike the House of Hanover was one thing; to have the government brought down and the nation arbitrarily handed over to the French was quite another. The House of Lords and the House of Commons met in extraordinary session. Whitehall bustled with stern-faced cabinet ministers and high-ranking military and naval officers. His Majesty was said to be preparing to address Parliament. Diplomatic envoys were despatched post-haste to Paris. Street corners, gin shops, taverns, and ordinaries were crowded; gentlemen gathered in the clubs and coffee houses; and the names of Gideon Rossiter and his Preservers were on everyone's lips. Scandalmongers had a field day. Several ladies were said to have fainted when they realized the identities of "the Ladies J———— Y———— and C———— B————," and the *ton* was thrown into a delicious frenzy speculating as to the identities of the "many others" believed to be involved in the plot.

On Saturday morning, the city was again staggered to learn that Lord Hector Kadenworthy was definitely implicated, but had disappeared; it was rumoured that his large financial holdings had been liquidated, and the proceeds had also disappeared. Mr. Reginald Smythe, now known to be the ringleader, was still at large, and when exhaustive searches of his various homes and all known haunts failed, it was theorized that he'd had an escape route ready for just such a disaster. That he'd fled without bothering to alert his lieutenants became obvious that afternoon, when large numbers of mercenaries attacked military and naval installations. To their surprise they met not feeble and undermanned defenders but alerted and well-armed opposition. Many attacks were quickly abandoned. Perhaps out of desperation determined fights were waged at Windsor, Portsmouth, and Dover, but were overborne, the survivors flying for their lives.

August Falcon awoke late Saturday afternoon. When he found he had missed all the excitement, he was infuriated and came near to shouting at Tummet for not having woken him. In the nick of time he remembered the nightmare he had so narrowly escaped. Pale sunlight was streaming in at the windows. He was stiff and his side still hurt, but he felt rather astonishingly well. It was the first day of a new lease on life. And he was a new man. He thanked Tummet once again for his loyalty and devotion, and humbly begged to be put in possession of all the facts. He was not, however, sufficient of a new man to heed Dr. Knight's demand that he stay abed and rest for a week, especially after the doctor, exasperated, told him that Morris was out of danger but would never walk again.

Gwendolyn called and requested that Tummet come down and speak to her. He presented himself with such a glum face that her heart sank.

"Whatever is it!" she demanded anxiously. "Dr. Knight told me that Mr. August's ribs are not broke, and that he is recovering nicely."

"Nicely! Ar, well I 'spect you could say that, Miss Gwen. As fer me—I dunno if I can be-a-bandit."

"Stand it?" she translated. "Stand what?"

He gave her a look of stark tragedy, and lowering his voice confided, " 'E's took to calling me 'Enoch'! Even said 'me dear fella' once when I said I was sorry fer dropping the jam in 'is shoe. Only time 'e swore, Miss, was when Doc Sir Jim was examining 'is side."

Relieved, she said, "Is that all! I fancy he is not quite himself. 'Twill likely take a little time for him to adjust to being alive and out of that—that hideous place."

" 'E says 'e's a new man, Miss. A new man, 'e says. Cor!" He went off, shaking his head as his reborn employer came into the room, fully dressed and shooting the lace at his cuffs.

Having paused to pat Tummet on the back as he passed, Falcon said, "Smallest Rossiter!" and held out both hands to her, a fond smile on his battered face but with veiled, inscrutable eyes.

"My dear," she murmured, avoiding his hands and slipping closer to caress the healing cuts around his mouth. He jerked his head away. He was not bowing forward today, probably because his ribs were tightly bandaged, and, apart from the marks the Jewelled Men had left on him, he appeared cheerful and his old poised self. But—different, somehow. She was aghast to realize that the difference consisted of a gleam of silver in the thick dark hair at his right temple. Her throat constricted at the sight of this mute testimony to his ordeal, and she struggled to hide her consternation. "Dr. Knight said—"

"The man's a professional marplot!" He led her to a chair by the fire and ignoring the one beside it, which she patted invitingly, occupied another across the hearth while remarking that the doctor had terrorized Tummet and Katrina with his gloom-mongering. "I can only be grateful that you have been so kind as to pay me a sick call."

Startled, she thought, 'A sick call? Is that what this is?' It was so smoothly said; his smile so bland and assured. There had been not a word or gesture or the slightest hint of love, and he had deliberately avoided being close to her. She sighed, but sensed that he was far less recovered than he appeared to be, and so refrained from really teasing him, beyond saying, "I have been so anxious for you, my love." His hand tightened on the chair arm when she used the term of endearment, but he made no comment, and she went on: "I expect Tummet will have told you all that has happened?"

"I hope he has. Is there any new word? Any word of that wart—Smythe, for instance?"

"Not that I'm aware. Gideon and Tio seem almost to have moved into the Horse Guards, and Johnny Armitage and Perry are at East India House. Gordie has escorted Sir Brian back to Lac Brillant—he was concerned for the old gentleman after the shock of seeing Quentin here."

He nodded frowningly.

The thought of how narrowly they had all escaped disaster made her shiver, and she said quickly, "You know that Lord Kadenworthy helped us to find you?"

"So Tummet said. But what of the shot you heard?"

"There was a paragraph in the *Spectator* saying that a robbery had evidently been attempted at Mimosa Lodge, the country seat of Lord Kadenworthy, during his lordship's absence. And that one of the thieves had been found in an expired condition on the premises."

Falcon leaned back in his chair and said a quiet, "Aha. Then Kade is safe away."

"Do you mind that very much?"

He shook his head. "I like to think he was sorry for the fate Smythe planned for me. I wonder why such a good man as Kade should have joined that loathsome crew."

She told him what Hector Kadenworthy had said of his involvement with the League. Falcon looked grave but made no comment, and after a moment she added, "I collect you know that your father has gone abroad? He was here for an hour or two. And most anxious for you."

"Yes. I wish I'd seen him. But he has always wanted to spend the winters in Italy. 'Tis—as well. Under the . . . circumstances."

She had expected him to be furious, but he looked more downcast than angry, and she said kindly, "Thanks to you, there was no proof he'd entertained the Prince, and he was not charged with—anything."

"Was he not?" His lips tightened. "I fancy your father, among others, may have some thoughts along those lines. Is that why you have left us and gone back to Rossiter Court?"

"Papa wanted me to come home. But, I think he bears you no—er, real animosity." The recollection of her father's thundering tirade against Neville Falcon caused her to add hurriedly, "Of course, as you may guess, the Earl was rather—er, put about, but—"

"Was he, indeed?" A familiar blue flame lit Falcon's eyes. "With a ramshackle hothead like Tio for a son, one might think he'd be the last to—" He closed his lips on that impassioned retort, and in a moment said with a sigh, "But who could blame him? Indeed, I think we Falcons have much to answer for."

She looked at him sharply. "And I think that is more than enough for you, sir. Shall I go away? Or should you like me to read to you, perhaps?"

He responded instinctively, "Some tome dealing with the Orient, no doubt?"

Pleased by another glimpse of the man she knew, her eyes glinted laughter. She said, "But of course. Unless you feel that you would do very well without my—disturbing presence."

He looked at her for a long, silent moment, then said with quiet intensity, "I think the only reason I—survived that—that hellish place was the thought of your 'disturbing presence,' Gwen."

Deeply moved, she ran to him, and he stood and hugged her but to her disappointment it was a very brief hug and he almost pushed her away. "Values become rather—out of focus in times of danger and upheaval," he said gravely. "But I am sure that now, more than ever, your family cannot like you to be in this house. You must go home, my dear. Where you belong. And to say truth, I've a sick call of my own to make."

She was being dismissed by this courteous stranger who looked like August Falcon, but was not. Troubled, she followed as he crossed to open the door for her. But it was early days yet, after all. She thought, 'There's no need to worry. He's afraid of facing Jamie and Katrina, so he's stiff and nervous. He'll soon realize we all have forgiven him, and in a day or two he'll be his old self again.'

When Falcon slipped quietly into Morris' bedchamber he had nerved himself to confront a skeletal and bedridden invalid. He was considerably taken aback to find his victim seated in an armchair before the fire, a blanket tucked around his legs, and Katrina sitting close by, reading the newspaper aloud. She glanced up and saw him and stopped reading.

Morris turned his head. He was thin and pale and ill-looking, but his smile was as cheerful as ever, and he said quite firmly,

"Hello, August. About time you came to call on your hapless victim."

Falcon found himself momentarily voiceless, and his eyes unaccountably dim. He fought quivering nerves, and stammered, "J-Jamie, I'd thought— I mean, I'm so glad you're not— Er, what I mean is—"

Katrina put the newspaper aside and came to him. He drew back instinctively, and she said, "I am glad also—that I did not lose my brother. For a while, I thought I had."

He reached out, then again drew back. She touched his cheek and scanning his face said gently, "My poor dear, you had a dreadful time, and were so very brave. Papa gave me a letter for you. I'll go and get it."

He caught her hand and pleaded, "Trina—have you—can you forgive me?"

"I am trying. I know you were drugged, but—" She stopped, looked at the man she loved, then said, "Jamie wants me to forgive you."

"I think," he said, low-voiced, "I shall never be able to forgive myself. But I mean to do everything in my power to make amends, Trina. I'm going to be a much better man, I hope, than I was. Only give me a chance, my dearest."

Morris said, "You can start making amends, Lord Haughty-Snort, by coming over here and answering the several hundred questions I mean to ask. Starting with—how in the devil did you find where the League met, and how did you manage to cope with all those rats when you can't stand the sight of a mouse, and who is this Tom fellow who Tummet insists is your new groom? Be dashed if he don't put me in mind of a rank rider who held me up on Hounslow Heath last year!"

Falcon clenched his hands tight. He had tried very hard not to think of Sundial Abbey, and even the name sent fingers of ice down his spine. But he must live up to his resolutions. He went to the chair Katrina had vacated, pausing to rest a hand on Morris' shoulder in a shy and brief gesture. "I'll do whatever you wish, old fellow," he said huskily. "Whenever you wish it." He sat down, and added, "And I'll put no more obstacles in the way of your happiness, I promise you."

Morris looked at him thoughtfully. "Do you mean you'll not object to me as a brother-in-law?"

"I mean exactly that."

"That's good of you, dear boy." Morris gave a wry smile, then shattered him by saying, "But you see, now—I cannot ask her."

The days that followed were full of excitements and alarms. Defying his parent's enraged demands that he and Gwendolyn have nothing more to do with "any of those damnable Falcons," Gideon was almost as frequent a visitor at Falcon House as was his sister. The other members of the Preservers also called, and between them contrived to let August know he was forgiven. He accepted their renewed friendship humbly, but when they attempted any praise of his gallantry in circumventing the League, he withdrew, so clearly shaken that they ceased to speak of it in his presence. When they gathered at The Madrigal a few days later, however, they marvelled at the change in him.

"He's a new man, all right," said Peregrine Cranford ruefully. "Be damned if I know what to say to him any more, for fear of bruising his feelings."

"He's so blasted humble," agreed Horatio Glendenning. "And the way he waits hand and foot on Jamie is pathetic. How can we blame August for a duel in which he was meant to be the victim? Or hold him responsible for his sire's silly nonsense? Had it not been for him, I shudder to think where we all might be today. He did splendidly."

"And was put through hell," said Gideon. "I think the experience has left him rather adrift. He'll soon get over this 'new man' business."

But Falcon's resolution did not waver. Day and night he was at Morris' beck and call. He made the rounds of the clubs each morning, then hurried home to relay the latest gossip. In the afternoons he lifted Morris into his invalid chair, bundled him up and took him out walking or driving in all weathers. He read to him by the hour, was enraged if the suite was not provided with fresh fruits and flowers daily, and hovered anxiously over the two brawny footmen who carried the invalid downstairs for dinner each evening. At first embarrassed by such solicitude, Morris began to enjoy it, and Katrina complained to Gwendolyn that each time she thought of something to do that would cheer her beloved, August had already done it.

"He is truly repentant," said Gwendolyn with a faint smile. "I believe Jamie is touched."

"Touched! He is becoming downright spoilt! Have you noticed how he has taken to ordering August about? He would not dream of talking to the servants in so demanding a way! No, how can you laugh? I'll warrant my brother never has a moment to spend with you!"

"Oh, no," agreed Gwendolyn. "He is making it very clear that he has no intention of ruining my life by offering for me. But you know his feelings on that subject, dearest."

"I know 'tis stuff," said Katrina with unusual vehemence. "Ruining your life, indeed! He is madly in love with you! When you are looking elsewhere his eyes fairly devour you! 'Tis so senseless, Gwen! I vow that sometimes he looks so despairing, I could weep for the silly creature! Do you mean to do nothing?"

Gwendolyn did not at once reply. Reginald Smythe was still at large, and although she told herself that the curse of the bag of feathers was superstitious nonsense, she suspected that August would continue to avoid her company at least until Christmas Eve was safely past. After that . . . "I mean to wait," she said, "until he tires of martyrdom."

Mr. Fletcher Morris had been obliged to journey into Cornwall on a family emergency when his cousin, Lord Kenneth Morris, fled the country. Returning to Town, Mr. Morris proceeded at once to Falcon House. He was enraged to discover that his son was still in residence, and demanded that he remove at once from the house of the man who had wounded him, and whose sire had almost caused he himself to be named a traitor. His heir protested. Mr. Morris flushed angrily and his voice rose. Jamie pleaded that he was too weak to be moved, and, besides, the lady he loved was here. Mr. Morris flew into a passion and left no doubt of his absolute prohibition of such a match. His son began to look pale and shaken.

August, who had remained in the window-seat, now stepped forward. "Enough," he said with a resumption of his former hauteur. "Pray forgive me for reminding you, sir, that your son is an adult with several years of military service behind him. He is fully capable of making up his own mind, and"—he raised a hand to silence the older gentleman's furious attempt to intervene—"and I cannot allow that you cause him to suffer a relapse."

"*You* cannot allow?" gobbled Mr. Morris, purple in the face. "Why, damn your eyes, *you* are the one put him in that confounded chair!"

If Falcon winced inwardly, he did not show it. "Precisely so," he agreed. "I endangered Jamie's life, wherefore I now mean to devote my own life to his care." In a sudden relaxing of his stern manner, he said with his most beguiling smile, "No, really, sir, you are as devoted to him as he is to you, and I know you have his welfare at heart. Will you not allow him to choose his own path? And permit me to do what little I may to make amends?"

Mr. Morris huffed and puffed and eventually, considerably baffled, went back to his country home and advised his wife that the heir to his worldly goods was making a fine recovery but was gone out of his mind.

The next day Jonathan Armitage was called to the Admiralty, where he was awarded a full pardon and his back pay restored to him. They celebrated at Falcon House so that Morris could participate. Apart from the invalid, who was permitted no more than a small glass of sherry, August was the only man to remain sober.

A few days later, Gwendolyn received a letter from Italy. It was from Hector Kadenworthy, who wrote that he had managed to escape England, and had persuaded his aunt to follow and accompany him to the New World. "I hear there are some very tolerable estates in the Virginia colony, and some fine horseflesh. I hope to be able to start anew and build myself a comfortable life out there. Pray believe I was most relieved to hear that Falcon got out of that pest hole. He is too good a man to have expired in so wretched a way. If all goes well, and you should ever come so far, you must both be my guests."

Gwendolyn ordered a chair called up and went at once to share this news with August. Katrina met her in the entrance hall and imparted with a twinkle that her brother was in the book room searching for a work by Martin Luther.

"My goodness!" said Gwendolyn. "He has really mended his ways. I'd never have guessed he would be interested in theology."

"Jamie wants it read to him. And I will warn you, dearest, that my brother is rather a grump today, even for a new man."

"Trina," said Gwendolyn reproachfully. "Do not tease him. The poor dear is trying so hard."

"Yes. To stay awake."

"What? Could he not sleep? Oh, I do hope he is not kept awake by remembering—"

"He was kept awake because Jamie summoned him at two o'clock in the morning, complaining that he could not sleep. I told Jamie he should let his man help, but he has come to think August is the only one he can really rely on."

"Oh," said Gwendolyn, her eyes very wide. "And was August able to help?"

"He read to Jamie until he fell asleep; at four. He is being very patient, but, oh Gwen!" Katrina giggled. "The maxims have been thick on the ground!"

They repaired to the red and gold parlour where a fire blazed up the chimney and Morris sat in a deep armchair before it, nodding drowsily. "At last!" he said, not looking round. " 'Tarry-long brings little home,' August. I'd think you would try to— Miss Gwen!" Pleased, he stretched out a hand. "How good of you to come to see me on such a beast of a day!"

She put her cold hand into his warm one. "I am delighted to see you looking so much better, Jamie."

Falcon opened the door. "I found it, but—" He checked. He looked wan, but his tired eyes lit up when he saw Gwendolyn. "Good morning, ma'am. Have you come to cheer our invalid?"

"Well, of course she has," said Morris briskly. "Ring for some hot chocolate for the poor frozen creature. And then you can read to us. You'll like this, Gwen."

"Yes, I'm very sure I shall. But I've brought a letter August will like to see, if—"

"Oh, he can read a letter at any time. Now sit down and be comfortable. Hurry up, Lord Haughty-Snort! Don't stand there like a statue! 'As good have no time, as make no good use of it!' "

It seemed to her that August's hands on the book gripped very hard, but he rang for a footman and ordered hot chocolate and cakes for them all before he took a seat close to Morris and began to read. The subject had to do with Whether Soldiers Can Also Be in a State of Grace. The condition of the pages was not good, and Falcon stumbled, striving to decipher the faded words. His efforts did not seem to be greatly appreciated, as Morris whispered to Katrina until the hot chocolate was brought in, and afterwards had to ask that August re-read a page as he'd not been attending. Falcon looked rather stern, but repeated the page, and although Morris took to whispering again, persisted doggedly. " 'The mad mob does not ask how it could be better, only that it be different. And when it then becomes worse, it must change again. Thus they get bees for flies, and at last hornets for bees.' "

Morris, who had been chuckling over something Katrina had murmured, turned and observed solemnly, "Yes, indeed. 'A lie today leads to two tomorrow.' "

"What?" Falcon stared at him. "The word was *flies* not 'lies'!"

Gwendolyn was unable to resist remarking innocently, "Perchance Jamie is referring to 'li,' August."

"The passage refers to nothing of the sort," he snapped, his eyes darting indignation at her. "And if you don't want to hear this Jamie, why—"

"Oh—li," said Morris brightly. "Trina was telling me about it. Now there's a really interesting philosophy, though I'll own I didn't expect you to mention it."

Through his teeth Falcon said, "I did not mention it! If you wish—"

"You know, Miss Gwen," Morris went on, "you are absolutely correct. Those old Chinese Pages had some jolly good—"

"Sages," corrected Falcon in a strangled voice.

Morris peered at him anxiously. "My poor fellow. I am being a selfish dolt and taking too much of your precious time, besides boring you to death. I should have known how 'twould be. Now, you go and—"

"No, no." Falcon took a deep breath, and repented. "I'm the

one being selfish. Pay me no heed. If you're ready, I'll continue with this."

"You are too good. But let's have a change, dear boy. Do pray find the book about this 'li' business Miss Gwen spoke of. I'd like to hear more of your ancestors. Some of 'em seem to have been quite bright."

Falcon's face was a frozen mask, and Gwendolyn held her breath. She was inexpressibly relieved when the door opened and the butler brought in a large covered basket.

"A gift for you, sir," he said, carrying it to the invalid.

Morris said eagerly, "Is that so? Looks like something in the food line. From whom, Pearsall?"

The butler offered a folded note.

Morris read aloud, "My dear Lieutenant Morris. This is just a little farewell present from someone to whom you were all so kind. I leave tomorrow to join my nephew in Italy and then we sail for the Americas. I was so sorry to hear of your illness, and I hope you will enjoy this small token of my esteem and that it may sometimes remind you of someone who is far away, but with you in spirit." He looked up, exclaiming, "Be dashed! 'Tis from Mrs. Millicent Haverley. I say, how jolly nice of her. Let's have it open."

Pearsall deposited the basket in his lap, and Morris lifted the lid. A small grey head shot up, and a miniature mouth emitted a piercing cry.

Katrina uttered a stifled squeak.

Gwendolyn pressed a hand to her lips.

Falcon grabbed for a handkerchief.

"Oh, what fun!" exclaimed Morris, lifting the little creature from its temporary home. "See here, August! I shall have a pet to keep me busy so that I won't have to put upon you so much! May I keep it, old fellow? You won't mind, will you Trina? 'Tis such a little thing. I'll call it—Millie. Unless 'tis a boy cat." He held out the kitten. "Do look and see, August. Is it a boy cat?"

With a roaring sneeze, August fled.

Late the next morning Sir Owen Furlong called, a radiant Maria Barthélemy on his arm. Pearsall showed them to the book room, where Gwendolyn and Katrina had their heads together over a collection of patterns for wedding gowns, and Peregrine Cranford was watching Morris and Falcon, who concentrated on a game of chess.

Sir Owen stared in astonishment at the kitten that purred on the invalid's lap. "Jove!" he exclaimed. "I wonder Apollo don't savage it!"

"Oh, Apollo don't mind Millie," said Morris. "August does, but he's being kind enough to tolerate her."

"I ab all heart." With a heavy sigh Falcon dabbed a handkerchief at his tearful eyes.

"Speaking of hearts," said Gwendolyn. "You are looking very light-hearted, Sir Owen."

He was, he told them proudly, walking on air, because Maria had consented to become his wife. It would have been hard to tell which of them was the happiest. When the congratulations were over, Falcon asked whether they planned to make their home at Sir Owen's beautiful farm near Tunbridge Wells. Furlong said quietly, "No. We cannot, you know. Derek is ready to settle down and look after the farm, and fortunately Maria's grandmama has a large estate outside Lucerne. We are invited to live there—for a few years, at least, until there is no danger of Maria being charged with spying."

Maria took his hand and pressed it to her cheek. "Because of me, my dearest Owen must abandon his lovely old house and—and everything he cares for."

"Without you," he said fervently, "I can care for nothing."

The room hushed as they all watched the two who were so deeply in love.

Falcon rose abruptly and went to add more coal to the fire, then stood looking down, apparently engrossed by the dance of the flames.

He claimed a kiss from the bride-to-be when they left, however, and took two, a privilege both Cranford and Morris were too shy to demand.

When the farewells had been said, the hands wrung, and the ladies had embraced, the happy pair departed.

Perry Cranford said with a show of indignation, "I wonder

Owen did not knock you down, you rogue! Two kisses stolen, and they're not even wed yet!"

Very aware that Gwendolyn watched him steadily, Falcon shrugged. "She is a lovely woman. And 'tis said opportunity knocks but once. *Carpe diem*, Perry!"

Cranford grinned. "Were I to go about *carpe*-ing those kinds of *diem*-s, Zoe would box my ears! I am most shocked, August! I'd understood you were turning over a new leaf!"

" ' 'Tis hard to turn tack on a narrow bridge,' " observed Morris solemnly.

Tomorrow is Christmas Eve," said Falcon irritably. "Can't they let us alone? What the devil do they want now?"

Braving the bitter cold of the winter afternoon he had taken Morris for a walk. Many people were out, for shoppers were busy. Morris had expressed a desire for some roasted chestnuts and they'd been waiting at a vendor's barrow on the corner of Queen Square when Tummet had run to them with a message from Gideon. "The Cap'n's fireboy brung it, Guv," he'd panted. "You've all bin sent fer by—by the King! Cap'n wants you to meet him at the house on Snow Hill, and you'll all go on from there tergether."

"Majesty wants to give old Gideon a medal, I'll wager," said Morris. "He jolly well deserves one!"

"Lord above," grumbled Falcon, paying for the chestnuts and putting the bag into Morris' lap. "Say you couldn't find me, Tummet."

"Certainly not," countermanded Morris. "But I wonder why Gideon wants you to meet at Snow Hill. I thought Sir Mark meant to sell the place now they've reclaimed Rossiter Court. Gideon never liked that queer old house, and he has a dreadful head for heights. You're sure about this, Tummet?"

"Cross me 'eart and 'ope to die! I gotta find Mr. Cranford. You best get on, Guv."

"I don't suppose I am included," said Morris wistfully.

Tummet said, "The Cap'n said *all* of you, mate. Which means you, too, don't it?"

"Yes, by Jove! I say, do shake a leg, Lord Haughty-Snort! Mustn't dawdle about, dear boy! ' 'Tis a lazy dog that leans its head against the wall to bark.' Best find us a jervey."

Falcon gritted his teeth and reminded himself once again that nothing he was able to do for Jamie could make up for the loss of his ability to walk.

Half an hour later, it was Morris who grumbled about his useless limbs as Falcon struggled to manoeuvre the invalid chair up the steps of the house on Snow Hill. When the shaken and sweating coachman had safely coaxed his scared team up the steep hill, he'd taken his pay and gone off grumbling about "mountain roads." Several horses were tethered to posts outside the house, but no one came to lend a hand, and Falcon's shins were well bruised by the time he had overcome the steps and was pounding on the front door.

"It's open," howled a distant voice. "Come on in!"

Falcon mumbled under his breath, and managed to negotiate the front door and the threshold. The house was dim and cold, but candlelight glowed from the family withdrawing room at the far end of the corridor. "Gideon?" he shouted.

"Here!"

He was almost to the door when the sense of danger set his nerves tingling. He muttered, "Stay here, Jamie," and leaving the invalid chair walked forward, throwing his cloak back over his left shoulder and easing his sword in the scabbard. Outside the lighted room, he paused, then sprang through the door, sword in hand.

Reginald Smythe sat on the arm of a sofa. "So good of you to come," he drawled.

Falcon crouched. "By God, but I've hoped for this!"

A movement to his right caused him to swing around. A tall slim man with a really shocking scratch wig stepped from behind the door, sword unsheathed.

"The most competent Mr. Jones," said Smythe. "And Rufus," he added with a nod to the side.

Rufus materialized from beyond an armoire chest. He was big, with long arms. Grinning, he tossed a colichemarde with deft expertise from one fist to the other. "Ready to play, me bucko?" he enquired.

Something sharp prodded at Falcon's back. In a lightning reaction he sprang clear. A youngish man with a dark, narrow face and a hungry look in his small black eyes raised his sword in salute.

"Ambrose," introduced Smythe, obligingly. "You see, gentlemen, how fast he is. Be warned."

"He'll have to be quicksilver to best all three of us," said Ambrose in a cultured voice.

"I might have known, you slimy coward, that you'd not have the courage to do your own fighting," said Falcon. And he thought, 'I walked right into this! Three of the bastards, and all looking as if they know point from grip!'

Smythe shrugged. "Do you know, dear Mandarin, I am a much finer swordsman than you may suspect. But I see no point in risking myself when I can hire skilled assassins to wear you down for me."

"Where have you been hiding since your ugly plot failed? In the sewers from whence you sprang?"

The man with the awful wig—'Jones,' thought Falcon—laughed. "Got a way with words, ain't he?" He twirled his sword easily. "I hates clever swells."

"I fancy you'll never be near to another." Falcon glanced to the door, wondering tensely if Morris was safe.

"Never fret," said Smythe. "The poor fellow you crippled won't be harmed. I'd have had you destroyed long since, save that I was consumed by curiosity. However did you manage to escape the lovely end I planned for you? Was it Kade's work?"

Falcon was thinking that if he could cut down one of these hounds he'd have a fair chance. "There was another door," he said. "Didn't guess that, did you, poor Reggie. My friends found it."

"Your friends . . ." Smythe jeered, "The cockney and the cripple! Ha!"

Falcon tensed, his narrowed eyes fixed on that detested smirk.

Ambrose, he of the hungry look, and the deadliest of them Falcon suspected, said eagerly, "Now, sir?"

"I want you to know," said Smythe, "that the curse will be fulfilled this evening, dear Mandarin. You had the unmitigated gall to interfere with my plans, but 'tis a postponement, nothing more. I own a most delightful villa outside Rome, and on the day they bury you, I shall be very comfortable there, making new plans."

"Silly block," said Falcon contemptuously.

Smythe flushed. Through his teeth he said, "*Now*, gentlemen!"

CHAPTER XIX

s Falcon had expected, the bully called Ambrose was first to attack, his dark eyes glittering with eagerness. In that first swift encounter Falcon took his measure and knew he was good at his trade, but that had this been a fair fight he could have bested him without much trouble. It was not a fair fight. He countered a thrust in *sexte*, his parry was beaten aside, and Ambrose leapt out of range as Jones of the horrid wig rushed to engage in *carte*. Falcon disengaged over the arm, kept his blade close to Jones' *forte* and thrust. Jones parried and disengaged as Falcon forced his blade a little; Falcon feinted dangerously wide, then thrust straight and hard. Jones uttered a yelp and leapt back, but before Falcon could determine how badly he was hit, the big Rufus came at him from the left and Ambrose from the right so that, parrying one blade, he had to leap away to avoid the other.

There came an indignant shout: "Hey! Three to one ain't fair!"

From the corner of his eye Falcon saw that Morris had wheeled his chair to the open doorway. Not daring to risk more than that swift glance, he shouted, "Get clear, Jamie!"

"Devil I will!" Morris watched the flash and ring of blades in deepening anxiety as the deadly minutes passed.

Falcon, who should have already fallen before such desperate odds, fought on with astonishing speed and brilliance.

Knowing it could not last, Morris saw the move he had dreaded, and leaning forward yelled, " 'Ware your back!"

Falcon whipped around to find Jones behind him, a bloody rent across his left sleeve, but his sword a darting silver gleam. With a parry and riposte that drew a cheer from Morris, Falcon whirled barely in time to deflect the thrust Rufus sent at his back. Ambrose's sword burned across his shoulder, and he swore softly.

Exultant, Smythe cried, "First blood, gentlemen! Let's see more, but remember—I want to finish him myself!"

"Come on, Falcon!" howled Morris. "Stir your stumps, you sluggard!"

Rufus laughed breathlessly, and sprang in with a lunge in *tierce*. Falcon beat aside his sword, disengaged in *tierce*, advanced his blade and as Rufus whipped his sword to counter, he dropped his point under the wrist and thrust in *seconde*. Rufus uttered a choking cry, goggled in pained astonishment at Falcon's reddened sword, and went down, to sprawl before the invalid chair.

Ambrose shouted with rage, and attacked, but, aware of his vulnerability, Falcon flung himself down, rolled under Ambrose's slashing sword, and was up again, to parry Jones' thrust. Ambrose sprang in and a splash of scarlet appeared on Falcon's left forearm.

"You filthy bastards," shouted Morris furiously. "Fight fair, damn your eyes!"

Jubilant, Smythe laughed. "This is not a fight, Morris. 'Tis an execution!" and whipping out his own sword he came to join the uneven battle.

The weapon Rufus had dropped was close by. Morris leapt from the chair, shouted, "Tally ho!" snatched up the fallen sword, and plunged into the fray.

Falcon was so astonished that his jaw and his sword dropped. It was a momentary lapse, but Smythe's blade ripped through his coat, scratching his side. With a shout he flung himself to the left, engaged Smythe's blade in *carte*, turned his wrist in *tierce*, passed his point over Smythe's arm not quitting his blade, and with a strong crossing sent the weapon spinning from his hand.

Ambrose rushed to fill the breach, and, cursing, Smythe darted to retrieve his sword. But Falcon was in his element now.

Jamie was on his feet! Jamie was at his back, his sword flying. Between them, they could best these filthy varmints!

The battle was short and sharp. Smythe fought furiously and surprisingly well. Falcon's blade was a blurring flash of light, his footwork masterly, his body lithe and agile, as his defense became attack. Ambrose was grinning no longer. Leaping out of distance, he panted, "Dragoons!" In the same instant, Morris thrust home, and Jones doubled up, the sword tumbling from his hand.

Falcon and Smythe fought on; each driven by implacable hatred, both men breathing hard now, faces relentless and steel ringing as the battle swept into the passageway and along to the stairs.

The front door burst open. Military boots stamped across the entrance hall. Running in after the dragoons with his sister beside him, Gideon grabbed Gwendolyn's hand and held her back. The troopers hesitated, but did not interrupt the fury that raged on the staircase.

Tummet rushed in and gasped, "Rouse the house! He's at it again!"

Gwendolyn clung to her brother's hand.

Advancing grimly, Falcon stumbled on the stair. Smythe lunged at once. A ringing parry, a startled shout, and Gideon wrenched Gwendolyn behind him as Smythe was again disarmed, his weapon spinning through the air.

Falcon's blade was at the throat of his lifelong enemy. Smythe cowered back until he was sprawling, both hands clutching the stair.

Falcon said softly. "You'll answer now, Reggie, for the lives you've squandered; for your treachery even to your own people; for the men you've ruined and the hearts you've broken! Do you care to beg, crawling venomous thing that you are?"

His sword bit deeper, and Smythe gulped, "You'll . . . kill me . . . anyway!"

"You let him off too easily, dear old pippin," panted Morris from the foot of the stairs.

"Aye," said Tummet. "Don't soil yer 'ands, Guv! Let 'em put the dirty—er, let 'em put Mr. Smythe to the question, 'fore they give 'im a traitor's public execution!"

"He's right," urged Rossiter. "Leave him to the tender mercies of the Tower."

White and shaking, Smythe gasped, "Strike true, you damned Mandarin!"

Falcon smiled. He had the right to avenge himself for that hideous black hole where he'd been left to face a ghastly death. And how many of Smythe's victims would cheer him on! He drew back his sword for the thrust that would rid the world of this filth.

From behind him came a faint scent of lily of the valley. Gwendolyn said gently, "Why would you wish to offer him a clean and honourable death, my love?"

For a long, hushed moment, Falcon did not move. Then, he stepped back and slipped his sword into the scabbard. "You are, as always, perfectly right, Smallest Rossiter."

Dragoons were pushing past. Smythe was hauled to his feet and marched off, his face a frozen mask of terror because he knew what lay ahead.

Looking after him, Falcon's gaze fell on Morris. It dawned on him that nobody seemed surprised to see the invalid on his feet. Frowning, confusion became comprehension. His eyes narrowed. He whispered, "You cheating . . . lying . . . villain!" and trod slowly and with infinite menace down the stairs.

Grinning broadly, Morris held up a delaying hand. "Now, August . . ."

"You never were in real danger," gritted Falcon. "That's why you didn't send for your father!"

Morris stepped back. "No, really, old fellow . . ."

"You've *always* been able to walk!"

"Er, well, not for the first week or so," said Morris, taking refuge behind Rossiter.

"That slippery James Knight was in it with you all along, wasn't he?"

Morris chuckled. "Thought you needed a lesson."

"A *lesson?*" He remembered his anguish and guilt, sleepless nights, waiting on the "invalid" hand and foot, countless indignities meekly endured, including an endless flood of maxims, and that *confounded* cat (which, foolish little creature, had taken a great liking to him). And with a howl of wrath he charged.

Morris gave a whoop and fled.

Attempting to restrain the outraged victim, Rossiter was hurled aside.

"August!" he shouted laughingly. "Don't forget you're a new man!"

Racing through the dining room and back up the stairs, Falcon raved, "He died! And a rascally invalid-impersonator is about to follow him!"

Half turning, his face alight with mischief, Morris tripped, was tackled and went down, fighting off Falcon's enraged attack. "No! Let be! I am not a well man and—and you deserved . . . every minute!"

Rossiter ran to wrench Falcon back. "Haven't you had enough today, you maniac?"

Struggling, Falcon snarled, "You *knew* he could walk, didn't you? And you let him take advantage of my good nature!"

"What good nature? No, really August, we had to do something—your saintliness was driving us all to distraction!"

"And you call yourselves my friends? Pox on friendship! Let go, damn you!"

Breathless, Morris gasped, "Rejoice! Lord Haughty-Snort is back among us!"

"Oh, rejoice, indeed," said Gwendolyn happily.

"If we do not get to St. James's quickly, we'll be rejoicing in the stocks," said Rossiter.

Falcon stared at him. "We really are summoned? I thought 'twas all part of the trick to get me here."

Gwendolyn explained, "Luckily, Tummet chanced to meet Gideon, and asked if he was on his way to Snow Hill. He never had sent you a note, and when Tummet explained, we came at once."

For the first time Falcon realized that Rossiter was in full dress uniform and that Gwendolyn wore a splendid ball gown under her cloak. Dismayed, he looked down at his own torn and bloodied garments. "Oh, Jupiter! I cannot face His Majesty in this condition!"

Gideon said, "I make no doubt the groom of the chambers, or whatever passes for one at the Court will make you presentable. Now, for the love of heaven—*hurry!*"

Tense with excitement, Gwendolyn stood beside Katrina in the great audience hall at St. James's Palace, one of a glittering throng summoned by Majesty to honour those who had won the royal favour and would today receive their reward.

The hall buzzed with chatter, and although voices were kept low, excitement was high. Rumour had spread its wings and there were whispers that in addition to the usual awards to diplomatists, civil servants, public figures and the military, there was today to be a special award, though who was to be honoured, and why, were unanswered questions. Thus, little groups formed and eddied and formed again around those "in the know," while eyes turned constantly to the wide open doors at the far end of the hall through which their majesties would pass.

There was a sudden ripple of activity among those closest to the doors and conversation ceased abruptly. A magnificent major domo entered and struck his staff of office three sharp raps on the polished floor. In a booming baritone he announced the approach of the King and Queen, and recited a long list of titles and possessions. The royal couple entered, followed by their lords- and ladies-in-waiting, and the assemblage, with whisperings of satin and taffeta and rustlings of whale-boned coat skirts, bowed low.

Gwendolyn had seen the King at several functions and thought him rather insipid looking, but Queen Caroline was a handsome woman, with a clear skin, blue eyes, and quantities of flaxen hair. She sailed past, smiling graciously, her magnificent bosom very much in view despite her robes.

When they were seated, the major domo struck his staff on the floor again, and the first honoree was escorted to the royal dais. The gentleman was stately and magnificently dressed and, having performed some deed of great value to his king and country, became a baron. The next to be honoured was an emotional

Member of Parliament who was awarded a baronetcy, and appeared to be in danger of bursting into tears. Several gentlemen were knighted, their exploits read off at great length to the accompaniment of much furtive whispering from the onlookers.

It all seemed to take a great deal of time, and Katrina leaned to Gwendolyn and whispered a nervous, "Where *are* they?"

As if in answer, the major domo struck the floor once again and read off a list of names that made Gwendolyn give a little leap and sent a ripple of excitement through the chamber. Another rap of the staff, and seven young men appeared and marched briskly along the centre of that long, crowded hall.

Gideon Rossiter and Morris were in the lead, both wearing full dress regimentals, gleaming helms under their arms. Next came Gordon Chandler, very fine in purple and silver, beside Peregrine Cranford, also clad in dress uniform, his peg-leg awakening a little stirring of sympathy from the onlookers. Bringing up the rear, three abreast, were Jonathan Armitage, splendid in the uniform of an East India Company commander; Horatio Glendenning, elegant in dark green velvet, and August Falcon, at the sight of whom an audible gasp resounded through the chamber. He wore the blue and gold uniform of a colonel in the King's Guard. A glittering helm was tucked under his left arm. His head was held high and proud as he strode past, well aware of the sensation he was creating, his face unreadable until he drew level with Gwendolyn, whereupon a quick wink was directed at her.

Several ladies resorted to their fans. Lady Dowling, standing nearby, said dazedly, "My heavens! Say what you will of him, Falcon is superb!"

In full agreement, Gwendolyn was overcome and had to press a handkerchief to her lips. Katrina murmured, "My rascally brother casts them all into the shade, but truly, Gwen, are they not magnificent?"

"They are," she gulped. "Every one!"

And so they stood before the monarchs, and heard themselves described as "seven of Britain's finest," while a royal aide read out summaries of their deeds in French, which came easier to their ears than German, and the onlookers, increasingly amazed, applauded with growing enthusiasm. The honours were bestowed. Gideon Rossiter, Horatio Glendenning, and Gordon Chandler, all heirs to titles, received medals for outstanding devotion and valour; James Morris and Peregrine Cranford were knighted, the kneeling and the tapping of the royal sword on their shoulders reducing both shy young men to a state of near collapse. Jonathan Armitage also was knighted, much to the delight of his twin sons, who were present with their aunt, the widowed Mrs. Ruth Allington, sister to Jonathan, and betrothed to Gordon Chandler. Last of all, Falcon was given an award of merit and made an honorary colonel in the King's Guard, the ceremony somewhat marred when His Majesty turned to the Queen and said in German, "We wanted to make him a baron, m'dear, but the peers said it wouldn't do. Still, the fellow looks splendid in my uniform, don't you agree?" Her Majesty, with an appreciative eye on the man she was later to describe as "a sinfully handsome rascal," agreed.

On the afternoon of Christmas Day seven members of Rossiter's Preservers and their families attended a celebration at the palatial Curzon Street residence of the Earl of Bowers-Malden. It was a merry party, made merrier when Falcon stood and made a formal announcement of the betrothal of his sister to "Sir James Morris." When the excitement died down, Gideon proposed a toast "To absent friends." August knew that everyone was thinking of Sir Owen, but his own thoughts strayed to his father, and when they all were gathered around the fire in the withdrawing room he told Gwendolyn that as soon as possible he meant to journey to Venice and make sure the "poor old fellow" was comfortably situated.

She said that was a lovely idea and added dreamily that she had always wanted to see Venice. He smiled, but did not rise to the bait. She thought that he looked rather strained. She herself felt as if a terrible shadow no longer threatened to at any instant destroy him and, thereby, her. It was stupid, of course, that she had allowed that Cornish curse to so prey on her mind, but even now she was unable to dismiss the notion that it had come horribly close to being fulfilled.

Similar thoughts were in Falcon's mind, but he made a great effort to appear light-hearted, joining in the laughter when Morris complained that Colonel Haughty-Snort now out-ranked him.

"Sorry Jamie, but that's how Fate treats us in this life. A demotion for every promotion!"

"Very true," said Katrina, "only think, Jamie, no sooner do you gain a title than you marry a commoner!"

There was more laughter. Falcon drifted farther back to stand where he could watch the group. How contented they were, chatting amiably on this Christmas afternoon, the mellow light of the fire flickering on their happy faces. They had all been so kind to him; never a word of anger that they'd been placed in such jeopardy by his father. Not that Papa had intended to involve them, of course. But this afternoon might well have been so different. His gaze drifted to Gideon and Jamie, and the rest of the Preservers, these fine young men and their valiant ladies, who truly were his friends, and who had come to mean so much more to him than he would have believed possible. He was quite aware that underneath the gaiety and good-fellowship they were seething because he had not been awarded a title, and because the King's remarks had been overheard and widely circulated. He shrugged mentally. He had no desire for a title and he'd been given the best possible reward: his family, his love and his friends were safe. And he was alive!

A need to be out under the sky and alone overwhelmed him. He slipped quietly into the corridor, and five minutes later was walking briskly along the flagway. The pale winter sun was low in the west and sinking towards a flying wrack of clouds. It was very cold; an occasional wind gust sent his cloak billowing and carried on its wings the smell of snow to mingle with the aroma of roasted fowl and mulled wine and Christmas pudding. He passed windows aglow with candlelight, where people gathered together about the table or around the hearth. In one house a lady in a scarlet gown played Christmas carols on a spinet, her family and guests singing merrily; in another, children squealed to the excitements of Blind Man's Bluff.

Quite a number of people had ventured out for a little exercise after their holiday feast. He was of course recognized, and since all London knew he had won the Royal praise, gentlemen raised their tricornes politely, and ladies offered shy smiles. And the instant they had passed he heard the whispered questions and comments, so that he strode along faster.

And ever as he walked, he thought of her. The fine-boned face that was so far above mere prettiness, the candid blue eyes, the high forehead and generous mouth. Her merry sense of humour, and the quick mind that had so bravely adapted to her affliction and faced the future with courage and resolution. He could recall so clearly the first time he'd met her, when she had called at Falcon House in April to ask that he not use pistols in his duel with her brother. Incredibly, he had judged her dull and ordinary then; until she'd given him some splendid set-downs. Countless of their verbal battles came to mind. Her sudden appearance at the really ridiculous duel with Gideon, during which he'd slipped in the mud and her little boot had stamped down on his sword as she demanded they stop fighting. She'd bent his favourite colichemarde, and when he'd attempted to retrieve it, had whacked him on the head with her riding crop. He chuckled to himself, causing passers-by to stare at him curiously. Hurrying on, he conjured up a picture of her sitting on the steps of the summer house with a pretty pink gown billowing about her, while she brushed Apollo—and infuriated his owner by discussing China and his dear Grandmama. Was that when he'd begun to love her?

Somewhere a clock struck four. He glanced up, and found that he was sitting on a bench in Bloomsbury Square gardens. He drew his cloak closer against the rising wind, and leaned back, his eyes remote, experiencing again the rush of emotion that had so nearly overcome him just now in Laindon House. It was as well that he was alone because he couldn't seem to subdue that emotion, and he was horrified to find his eyes blurred and his throat tight. He was so inexpressibly grateful that he'd not died with only the rats for company in the blackness and despair of Sundial Abbey's dungeons. If the Smallest Rossiter had not come, with faithful Tummet— But she had come. And praise God, he had *not* murdered

Jamie! And—well, he was seven kinds of a fool to be sitting here in the cold when he might be in a warm cozy room with his friends. Dear old Gideon and his lovely wife who soon would make him a father; Jamie and Katrina; Tio and his beautiful gypsy fiancée who had clearly enslaved his formidable parent; Perry and his brave little Zoe; Gordon, so soon to wed Ruth; Johnny and Jennifer. Each man with his love, and all so radiantly happy.

Each man with his love . . . Shaken by a deep ache of longing, he put a hand over his eyes. He had no right to grieve. He had been given so very much. 'Especially,' he thought in embarrassment as he heard people walking on the path behind him, 'that there is a hedge between us so that they do not see my stupidity!'

Abruptly, the cold didn't feel quite so cold. He separated his fingers and peeped through, although he knew. His heart contracted. He groaned, "Go away!"

Gwendolyn groped about in her cloak pocket and passed him a handkerchief. "How silly you are to feel ashamed. 'Tis not surprising you would be moved, now that it is all over at last. You feel things so very intensely."

"What I feel . . . ," he gulped, "is a perfect . . . blockhead!" His hand shook, and he had to resort to the handkerchief again. "Oh—egad! I'm—I'm sorry!"

"So am I." She sighed. "It *is* all over. Isn't it?"

He blew his nose, and nodded.

"And you do not mean to offer for me."

"No."

"Never?"

"Never."

"Yet you gave your permission to Jamie." Her voice quavered a little. "Perhaps you think he loves Katrina more than—than you love me."

A pause. "Perhaps I do."

"Liar!" She reached up and jerked his face around, and surprised such a desolation in his tearful eyes that she cried, "Oh, my dearest! Do you think I don't know? You love me with all your great brave heart!"

He said hoarsely, "Too much to make you endure what we

endure! The sniggers, the knowledge that we are tolerated only because we have wealth; the fear that any children we might have would be as scornfully despised! No! And *no!* I will *never* ask you to share that degradation!"

Tears stung her own eyes. He was so determined. So sure he was right. She took his hand and said, " 'Tis only degradation because you fight it so proudly! August, don't you see? If you would but smile when they call you the Mandarin; if you would only take some pride instead in your—your beloved Grandmama's people, the mockery would fade, and I do believe 'twould die away."

"Wishful thinking, m'dear. Do you imagine that because I may have rendered some small service, they have forgiven me for—for existing? Not so! Nothing has changed, Smallest Rossiter. To the rest of the world this has been no more than a momentary excite-ment—something they can chatter about and exclaim over for a little while. But the *ton* remains the same. The prejudices as deep and unyielding." She was very still and silent. It hurt him to see her look so small and so crushed, and he said in his gentlest voice, "Come now, 'tis getting dark, we must go—"

"No!" To his horror, she sank to her knees beside the bench, still holding his hand tightly. "A lady is not allowed to do this," she said tremulously. "But I am going to—"

"My dear God!" he cried, looking about wildly. "Get up! What will people think? Gwen, for pity's sake—"

"I love you, August Falcon," she said loud and clear. "I beg that you will do me the honour of becoming my husband."

And it had happened! The only way he could claim his love. The one unthinkable course he had never dared hope she would follow. With a choking sob, he pulled her to the bench and into his arms, and muttered brokenly, "My darling . . . Smallest Rossiter. My only love! My own!" He crushed her against him and kissed her long and hard and with all his heart. Then, he put her from him, and peered at her through the deepening dusk. "Now you are weeping too—why? You've won—you shameless hussy!"

Gasping for breath, she said through happy tears, " 'Tis

because I—love you so terribly much . . . and I have waited so long and . . . and been so very frightened."

He said adoringly, "My very dearest girl, can you possibly love me that well? Be very careful—I'll still let you draw back. I am all you despise, remember? I'm cynical, and harsh, and—and arrogant."

"Yes."

"And I have a—dreadful disposition and far too much pride."

"Yes."

"Wretched girl! Must you agree so readily?"

"There is no pleasing you, Colonel. I'd fancied you wanted a conformable wife."

He laughed shakily. "Gwen, Gwen! You know what they will say. That you had to settle for a half-breed. My darling one—are you *very* sure?"

Two dark figures hove up through the dusk. Cyril Crenshore peered, then, somewhat the worse for holiday cheer, called gaily, "Hi there, Mandarin!" And then halted, frozen, as his friend clutched his arm and gasped a horrified, "Cyril!"

Falcon waved easily, "Merry Christmas, old fellow!"

"Praise the Lord!" whispered Crenshore.

"Come away quickly!" hissed his friend. "He must be as far over the oar as you are!"

Falcon stood and bowed and offered his arm. "Are you ready to go back and break the news, my love?"

She clung to him happily. "I have been ready for—"

From beyond the hedge came an elderly and autocratic male voice. ". . . said he saw them together, somewhere hereabouts, and that Falcon, the wicked rake, was *kissing* the gel!"

"Disgusting!" sniffed a female voice. "I'd have thought the Rossiter chit could have done better than that half-breed!"

"The same might be said for him, my dear. Whatever else, he's a dashed fine figure of a man, and Miss Rossiter is far from being a Toast! Still, one wonders what Sir Mark will have to say . . ."

The voices faded.

On the far side of the hedge, two hands clung tighter, and the sounds of muffled laughter rose and mingled, bringing a special brilliance to the cold and frosty Christmas night. Very close together they walked back towards family and friends. They said little, for there was no need for words. But looking up at the dark heavens and at the stars that twinkled so far above, August Nicolai Kung Falcon was quite sure that somewhere in that majestic immensity, Grandmama Natasha was smiling.